The sexy men of Cindy Gerard's *New York* _____ _____
Black Ops, Inc. novels will seduce you. . . .

Show No Mercy

"I'm not asleep this time," Gabe said.

"I noticed." Jenna slowly moved her hips against him.

He closed his eyes on a groan. "This is really enough for you?"

Sex. He was asking if sex was enough for her.

"If that's all there is . . . then it has to be enough."

"A fantastic novel by one of the best authors in the business."
—Romantic Junkies

Take No Prisoners

"Sam, what's going on?" Abbie asked.

He flashed a badge. "FBI," he said. "Just relax. No one's here to hurt you."

"I don't understand any of this. You're FBI?"

"Go get dressed, Abbie. We are not going to have this conversation until you do."

"Is that what we had before? In my bed? Was that . . . conversation, Sam? Or was that an investigation? You didn't have to make love to me. Nail screws would have been just as effective."

"A terrific love story."
—Library Journal

*A finalist for the Romance Writers of America's
RITA Award for best romantic suspense novel*

These titles are also available as eBooks.

SHOW NO MERCY

—

TAKE NO PRISONERS

CINDY GERARD

POCKET BOOKS

NEW YORK   LONDON   TORONTO   SYDNEY

Pocket Books
A Division of Simon & Schuster, Inc.
1230 Avenue of the Americas
New York, NY 10020

This Pocket Books trade paperback edition August 2009

POCKET and colophon are registered trademarks of
Simon & Schuster, Inc.

For information about special discounts for bulk purchases,
please contact Simon & Schuster Special Sales at 1-866-506-1949
or business@simonandschuster.com.

The Simon & Schuster Speakers Bureau can bring authors to your
live event. For more information or to book an event contact
the Simon & Schuster Speakers Bureau at 1-866-248-3049
or visit our website at www.simonspeakers.com.

Manufactured in the United States of America

10 9 8 7 6 5 4 3 2 1

ISBN 978-1-4391-6586-7

This book is dedicated to the men and women of the United States military, both active and retired. There are no words to adequately express my gratitude and respect for the sacrifices you and your families have made and for the losses many of you have endured to protect and defend our nation and our way of life.

SHOW NO MERCY

The only thing necessary for the triumph of evil is for good men to do nothing.

—EDMUND BURKE (1729–1797)

Acknowledgments

Many thanks to the usual suspects who graciously share expertise, support, and enthusiasm so generously. Maria, Donna, Joe, Glenna, Susan, Leanne, you know how much I appreciate you. Special thanks to my buddy, Carol Bryant, for her brilliant suggestion that led me to the link I needed to pull the *boys* together.

To Maggie Crawford, editor extraordinaire, thank you for your brilliant edit, for loving this book, and for inviting me into the Pocket Books family.

PROLOGUE

*Outskirts of Freetown,
Sierra Leone, West Africa
1999*

Tracer rounds zipped across the murky darkness, lighting up the night sky in brilliant slashes of red, yellow and green. It made Gabe Jones think of Fourth of July fireworks. Or of bad special effects in a B-grade horror movie.

He hunkered down as a high-arcing mortar added flash and smoke and snap crackling *boom booms* to the surrealistic tableau that had become all too real, and happened all too often lately. Behind him, trees trembled from shrapnel and AK hits. Gun oil, sweat, and the scent of blood and death melded with the pungent decay of jungle rot. And the swelter factor inched up another couple of degrees when he thought about the fallout if a 60mm mortar landed in his lap. *Now there was a surefire way to cap off a perfectly shitty day.*

Fourth of July, horror movies, and jungle rot. A screwed-up combo, Gabe thought as he scanned the dripping, dirt-streaked faces of the men hunkered down around him in shallow, hastily dug Ranger graves. But then, it was a screwed-up war. Correction: It was a screwed-up "conflict." Must keep the P.C. vernacular squared away. Wouldn't want any nation, sovereign or otherwise, to get the idea that the U.S. of A. was over here waging war—even though the rat bastard Foday Sankoh, leader of the Revolutionary United

Front, and his murdering RUF militia needed to be ousted out of power.

So, no. No U.S.-sanctioned acts of war here. *Uncle Sam intervening for the greater good? Hell, no.* If anyone asked, Task Force Mercy didn't even exist, which, theoretically, made the small mixed unit of Spec Ops forces taking fire from the RUF little more than ghosts.

Fitting, Gabe thought, because before this night was over, it might also be true. Any one of them could die in this hell-hot armpit of the world where the value of a life didn't measure up to a polished chunk of carbon that ended up on the ring finger of some society maven's hand. Where mercy was as foreign a concept to the locals as peace and a full belly.

He wiped away the sweat dripping down his face with his forearm as another round of mortars set off a series of strobe-like flashes. The blasts illuminated the familiar faces of the rest of the men where they were pinned down after running across an unexpected RUF patrol.

The team was *supposed* to be on the assault. There weren't *supposed* to be any militia within a mile of their current position, yet they were getting pummeled by a squad of RUF with a shitload of firepower. Which meant that someone had royally fucked up. Someone sitting on his ass back in command central, well out of harm's way, making calls based on infrared satellite imagery, passing along bogus intelligence.

Someone who was not Spec Ops but who the big brass insisted needed to run the show. Someone who did not grasp the concept that the personnel of Task Force Mercy needed to operate with the surgical precision of a scalpel, not the ball-busting slam of a sledgehammer.

Someone, Gabe thought, covering his head as dirt and debris from a close hit rained down on him, who obviously knew jack shit or the unit would never have been caught with their pants down in the first place.

The unmistakable clatter of an M-60 belt-fed machine gun joined the fray as he scanned the faces around him. Even though they were covered with cammo face paint and grime he could ID them to a man.

Not two meters to Gabe's right, Master Sergeant Sam Lang, Delta, lay on his belly with his M-24 sniper rifle at the ready. His face revealed exactly nothing, but Gabe still knew what Lang was thinking. Same thing Gabe was: *Let's get this sideshow on the road.*

Lang was the quiet man. Lived by the Teddy Roosevelt school of soldiering: He walked softly and carried a big-ass stick. Under fire, he was stone cold and mechanical. A machine. And like every man in the unit, Gabe would trust Lang on a journey to hell and back. Which was exactly where they were going before this night was over.

Bellied down next to Lang, practically connected to his hip, was Lang's spotter, Johnny Duane Reed. A flash and swagger Force Recon marine, the cowboy had come to the unit PO'd about being pulled from his Recon team. But like the good marine he was, he'd sucked it up—even though he was still as full of himself and as cocky as a yearling stallion in a pasture full of mares.

Gabe's gaze shifted to Mendoza, Army Airborne Ranger; Colter, U.S. Navy SEAL; Tompkins, also Delta, and half a dozen others. Individually, they were all specialists in their fields whether it was explosives, sniper skills, demolition, language, logistics, radio/com, medic, or recon. In Gabe's case it was the knife. His cold steel Arc-Angel Butterfly never left his side unless someone was going to die.

Collectively, they were a force beyond reckoning. A cross-military compilation of over-achieving Spec Ops warriors from every branch of the service along with two spooks, the CIA operatives, Savage and Green.

They were the elite of the elite. Their intense training coupled with their missions the last three years had broken down the inherent rivalry between branches of the service and made them as tight as the sights on Lang's sniper rifle. They weren't just teammates. Not anymore. Not after all they'd been through.

He glanced at Bryan "Babyface" Tompkins. As if Bry had read his mind, he met Gabe's eyes then shook his head as if to say, *Fucked again*, before Bry broke into his infamous baby-face grin and they all went back to the business of staying alive.

No, Gabe thought, cutting his gaze back toward the source of the machine gun fire. They weren't just teammates. They were brothers. In spirit. In deed. In truth.

Except for one minor issue: Task Force Mercy did not exist. Not on paper. Not in any file, dossier, or Intel report on any desk, disc, or hard drive in the Pentagon.

Outside of the president's inner circle and the joint chiefs of staff, TFM was a nonentity. Inside, it was strictly need to know. The man who conferred directly with the commander-in-chief on their covert operations was Gabe's commanding officer, Captain Nathan Louis Black, U.S. Marine Corps.

Gabe sought out his CO in the dark, listened through his headset for the command they were all waiting for. Black was a veteran of more conflicts than the Saudis had oil wells. His dress blues sported more decorations than a Christmas tree. He was a fighting man's man; a leader who led from the front and without hesitation. To a man, the task force would crawl, bleed, and die for him.

It was more than an issue of command. It was an issue of trust, loyalty, even affection for Black from these often renegade fighting men who a top-level opponent of the task force had once referred to as Black's Obnoxious Idiots.

It was supposed to have pissed them off. *Not so much.* The intended slur had actually cemented the final bond that turned them from teammates to brothers. Black's Obnoxious Idiots had referred to themselves as the BOIs— pronounced *boys*—ever since.

An AK round whizzed low over Gabe's head, smashed into a tree. He ducked as a branch cracked and fell to the ground. *Sucker was getting closer.*

They were in deep kimshee if they didn't take out that big gun tossing those mortars around like water balloons.

From the middle of their ranks, Gabe spotted Black an instant before his voice rattled into Gabe's headset.

"Hold . . . hold . . ."

A precursor, finally, to the order they'd been waiting for. Soon, it would be time to dispense with this pesky pocket of resistance.

Time to earn their pay.

On Gabe's left, Mendoza crossed himself, then pressed his gold crucifix to his lips before tucking it back beneath the breastplate of his Kevlar vest.

Gabe rose to a crouch, shouldering his M-16. "Say one for me, Choirboy," he whispered.

"Not enough Hail Mary's in the world to save your ass, Lieutenant Jones.

Sir," Mendoza added with a quick grin, his teeth shiny white in the darkness. "Even St. Jude has written you off, *mi hermano*."

St. Jude. Patron Saint of Lost Causes. Given Gabe up as lost. *Ain't that just the way*, Gabe thought as adrenaline pumped through his blood like a rocket.

Black's calm "Go," finally sounded through Gabe's headset.

The team shot over the rise following Black into the fire, drawing their cue from Black's cool, quiet command.

Time, like reality, faded to black, red and the brilliant starburst white of muzzle flashes and automatic weapons fire as Gabe ran, rolled, and belly-crawled, returning fire with his M-16 as they advanced toward the RUF stronghold.

Peripherally aware of the position of every TFM team member, he advanced, shutting out the screams, blocking out the gore of the stunned RUF who dropped like flies through their steady, relentless attack.

Dodging and ducking, Gabe emptied his magazine. He'd just hunkered behind a tree, dropped down on one knee and was in the process of replacing a thirty-round clip when he heard Reed's war whoop.

He glanced toward a berm spewing smoke. Lang had taken out the mortar crew that had been giving them shit. Then Sam went to work on the machine gunner. Direct hit. The gunner's finger stuck on the trigger, spraying glowing tracers into the air. Before his crewmate could take over, Gabe sighted, fired off three short bursts and tagged him, too.

With their big guns out of commission, the rest of the resistance quickly unraveled.

"Hold fire!" Although Black had to be as revved on adrenaline as the rest of them, his voice was calm through the headset. "Mendoza. Tompkins. Sitrep."

Protocol dictated what the team already knew. The RUF patrol had been annihilated. Those who hadn't run like hell were dead or dying. Yet the team remained on guard, searching for holdouts as Mendoza crept cautiously toward the base of what had once been the RUF assault to give a report on the situation.

"Clear." Mendoza's account was short and sweet.

"Tompkins?" Black called the Delta Force sergeant's name.

No response.

Faces streaked with cammo paint and sweat, the team swept the area for Tompkins.

Gabe was the first to spot him.

"Doc!" He sprinted to the downed soldier's side. "Doc!" he yelled again as he fell to his knees. He dropped his M-16 and pressed the heels of his hands to a gaping hole in Tompkins's inner thigh.

Gabe's hands were slick with blood as their medic, Luke Colter, aka Doc Holliday, dropped to his knees at Bry's hip. The medic swore under his breath as he deftly and quickly applied a tourniquet. Behind them, several lights flashed on so Colter could see to work.

"Hold this. Tight!" Face grim, Colter turned the tourniquet over to Gabe then tore into his field kit. "And keep pressure on that wound site."

"C . . . cold." Tompkins's lips were blue, his teeth chattering as his eyes fluttered open.

"It's Africa, you candy ass," Gabe pointed out gruffly as he literally felt Bry's life draining through his fingers.

He sensed, rather than felt the presence of the rest of the team gathering round as Colter started an IV for a blood expander, handed the hanging unit to Mendoza to hold, then went back to work to stop the bleeding.

He packed the wound with dressings. Applied direct pressure on the artery.

"H . . . how bad?" Bry's voice was barely a whisper.

All eyes shifted to Colter. Sweat poured down his face as he worked at staunching the blood flow.

"Femoral artery," he said, with a shake of his head.

Bad, Gabe thought. The blood told the tale. Tompkins had to have been down a good three minutes before they had gotten to him. It only took three to five minutes to bleed out from a wound this massive.

"Itty bitty scratch, baby boy," Colter said, with all of the cheer that his facial expression lacked. "You'll be lucky if you have a scar big enough to justify a Purple Heart."

"T . . . tell . . . my mom . . ."

"Fuck that!" Reed's voice was angry as he knelt behind Bryan's shoulders, made a pillow with his hands, and gently cradled Tompkins's head. "You got something to tell her? You tell her yourself." Tears ran down Reed's cheeks as he glared down at his brother. "You tell her, damnit!" he shouted when Bry's eyes closed and his head lolled to the side.

Colter leaned back on his haunches. Wiped the back of a bloody hand over his jaw.

Gabe met his eyes.

Colter shook his head.

"God dammit!" Reed pounded his fists against his thighs.

Lang laid a hand on his shoulder. Quieted him. Quieted them all as they stood, or knelt and stared.

Dead.

Their brother was dead.

Gabe clenched his jaw and swallowed back the surge of emotion that would do no one any good.

Bryan Tompkins with his baby face, earnest eyes, and God-and-country valor, had been one of the best damn men and stand-up soldiers Gabe had ever served with. And he'd just bled out from a shrapnel wound that had left a hole big enough to shove his fist through.

And for what?

"For what?" Gabe roared, closing his eyes. "For what?"

It wasn't the first time he'd asked himself that question.

He rose slowly, adrenaline long gone, shock setting in, grief overriding it all. Then he walked into the thick of the jungle.

Where he bawled in the dark like a baby.

Richmond, Virginia
One month later

A life-size oil portrait of Staff Sergeant Bryan Tompkins in full dress blues hung over the white marble mantel of a fireplace Gabe could have stood up in. A fifteen-foot coved ceiling towered over the paneled great room that easily measured twenty by thirty feet.

Despite the grandeur of the architecture and the classy way it was decorated, the room exuded warmth and personality, comfort and informality. It was a family room in the truest sense of the word. A family lived here. Loved here.

Now they mourned here.

Who knew? Gabe thought as he stood at parade rest, still surprised at the wealth Tompkins had come from. And who knew that Tompkins's old man was none other than Robert Tompkins, trusted friend and counsel to the president of the United States, which also made him one of an elite few who knew about Task Force Mercy.

Tompkins, you sly dog. Gabe mentally saluted the soldier who had fooled them all into believing that just a good ole boy of humble origins now lay in the hallowed ground of Arlington Cemetery.

"Some digs," Reed said out of the side of his mouth as Gabe and Lang and a dozen other members of the unit stood in the Tompkins family room following an hour-long memorial service that celebrated the life and the valor of their fallen brother.

"Makes you wonder," Reed went on, loud enough for only Gabe and Sam to hear, as Ann and Robert Tompkins, Bryan's parents, walked around the room greeting each member of the team, trying to make everyone feel comfortable when their hearts had to be breaking.

"Yep, makes you wonder," Reed continued when neither Gabe nor Sam rose to the bait. "Why'd he do it? Why'd he become a grunt? I mean, Tompkins seemed like a regular guy. But, Christ on a crutch, look at this place. He was rich, man. He could have been anything he wanted to be, done anything he wanted to do. Why the military when he had all this?"

Gabe knew enough about Johnny Duane Reed's background to understand his bafflement. While Reed was vocal about everything else, his own life was pretty much off limits so Gabe didn't have all the details. Still, he'd pieced together enough to know that Reed had had it rough as a kid. Rough had led to trouble and trouble had led to a choice of a stint in stir or the marines. So no, Reed wouldn't understand what would make a man who apparently had everything volunteer for the dirty jobs.

Gabe did. Gabe understood in spades. He'd come from the same kind of money as Bry but he'd known the moment he'd met Ann and Robert Tompkins that money was where the similarities ended.

The Tompkinses were real parents. Loving, giving, proud, and accepting of their son and his choices. Gabe's parents had been . . . gone. That pretty well summed it up.

A shrink would most likely say that Gabe had joined the army to get Senator Clayton and Judge Miriam Jones's attention. Truth was, he'd done it mostly to piss them off since that's about the only reaction he ever got from them anyway, when they bothered to react at all.

He glanced at the young woman who had not left Mrs. Tompkins's side since the team had arrived. The pretty brunette with the intelligent brown eyes was Bryan's little sister. The "kid," Bry had called her when he talked about how smart she was, how pretty she was, and how damn glad he was that none of their motley crew would ever come within a one-night-stand's distance of her.

Twenty-one wasn't exactly little and a man sure didn't think "kid" when he laid eyes on Stephanie Tompkins, but if the look on Reed's face was any indication, Bryan had been right to be wary of the team.

"Twelve," Reed said, zeroing in on Stephanie. "Scale of one to ten, Bry's little sis is a definite twelve."

Yeah. She was a looker. Like her parents she was also grieving, which kept Reed and a good many more of the team at a respectful distance.

"You would be Gabriel." Ann Tompkins approached Gabe with a smile, her slim, delicate hands extended.

"My condolences, ma'am." Gabe covered her small, cool hands with his big mitts. He felt clumsy and self-conscious. This much grace made him uncomfortable. This much warmth made him humble. And Stephanie Tompkins's sad brown eyes made him feel things he rarely let himself feel.

"Bry talked about you often when he had a chance to call home. He called you the Archangel," Ann went on.

Robert Tompkins walked up behind his wife and daughter, put his arms around their shoulders. "He said you were the single most dedicated warrior on the team."

Gabe was embarrassed now.

Ann smiled with affection. "He also said you'd react just like that if anyone ever paid you a compliment."

Gabe swallowed around the thick lump in his throat. "He was a good man. A good soldier."

It was the highest tribute Gabe knew to give. It was also totally and completely inadequate.

Stephanie acknowledged his sympathy with a nod. Ann squeezed his hands one more time before she and Stephanie, with Robert shoring them up, moved on to Reed, who for all of his usual bravado, had nothing to say. Thank God, or he probably *would* have put a move on Bryan's sister.

The Tompkinses spoke with the rest of the team members who were there and after conferring softly with the team's CO, they turned back to the room.

"Gentlemen." Robert Tompkins smiled valiantly. "Bry would have been pleased beyond measure that so many of you managed to assemble here. He loved you like brothers. All of you." His voice broke and he stopped, looked away for a moment to compose himself. "Through his letters and phone calls, we grew to know and love you all, too."

"He wouldn't want any of you to mourn today." Ann's brown eyes filled with tears. "He'd want you to celebrate the bond you all have, the life you all live."

"So, no more long faces, okay?" Robert spread his arms wide, managing a smile. "There's food. There's beer." His smile widened. "I know you guys love your beer."

Reluctant grins made appearances around the room.

"Through the double doors is a game room. Check it out. I think you'll find enough toys to keep you busy for the better part of the day. Go. Relax for a while. Enjoy. You need a break so take it."

Two hours later, the BOIs were being boys over the pool table, the video arcade, and the poker table where Gabe was down fifty bucks to Luke "Doc Holliday" Colter and actually letting down enough to enjoy himself.

When it was time to leave, Gabe was as reluctant to go as he'd been apprehensive about coming. So was the rest of the team.

The Tompkinses, however, weren't finished with them yet.

"Remember, you're Bry's brothers," Robert reminded them as they assembled near their rented cars to make the return trip to the airport. "That makes you our sons. And as our sons, we want you to think of this as your home now."

Ann's smile was as brave as her husband's. "Consider us a second family. We want you to come home, boys, anytime. When you need to recharge. When you need a soft place to land. Whenever you need to . . . just come home."

Home. Family. It should have sounded like sappy sentiment—something Gabe had never had time for. Yet as he climbed into the backseat and their car pulled away those two words rang in his ears. Rolled around in his head, settled in his chest. Felt oddly comfortable there.

He stared out the window at the passing traffic. Wondered if the other BOIs had felt as strong a connection to the Tompkinses as he had.

Maybe he was just tired. Maybe he was just dog, dead tired of fighting other people's fights, of burying his brothers. Still—the idea of home, of family. It was more than mildly compelling. What a surprise.

The second surprise came at the airport when they learned their flight back to HQ was going to be delayed another hour and Black said, "Fuck it. Let's hit the bar."

All eyes locked on Nathan Black. No one among them had ever seen him drink. That didn't stop them from following as he led the way to the closest watering hole. The bar was empty, still Black snagged a couple of tables in a back corner and ordered a double scotch, straight up.

Gabe was suds deep in his draw before Black spoke again.

"I was going to wait and brief you when we got back to D.C., but now seems like as good a time as any," he said, his voice low so he wouldn't be overheard by anyone passing by.

Their next mission. Gabe figured Black was going to tell them they were wheels up in less than twenty-four and off to some third-world hellhole to do what needed to be done to whomever it needed to be done to.

For what?

As it had for over a month, the question echoed in Gabe's mind as he remembered Bryan Tompkins bleeding out. He understood that next time it could be him.

"I'm getting out."

Black's statement echoed like a rifle shot. It was met by fog-thick silence. No one blurted out a nervous *you're joking*. They all knew that Nathan Black didn't joke.

They waited. Like they waited before a mission. Hearts in their throats. Adrenaline pumping.

Black stared steadily at his scotch. "Three years ago when they tagged me for the job, I jumped at the chance to lead Task Force Mercy. I applauded the president's foresight and commitment to the mission statement and the needs of the team. I have celebrated our victories. Mourned each loss."

He lifted his head, encompassed them with a sweeping gaze. "And I've been honored and proud to command each and every one of you."

"Then why?" Reed dared to pose the question they had all swallowed with their shock.

Black's dark eyes were hooded, his expression weary and grim. "Pick a reason. Bureaucratic B.S. Armchair warriors in the Pentagon. Bad calls that get good men killed."

All thoughts momentarily returned to Bryan.

"How about the new administration that'll be taking over soon and is already making noises about making TFM go away, yet still take care of the bad guys?" Black tacked on with a disgusted shake of his head.

"Bottom line, there are factors at work wanting to integrate us back under the Spec Ops umbrella. And the intel fuck-up at Sierra Leone—well. It proved another point. We've become dispensable."

"Like Bry was dispensable," Reed added bitterly.

Black dragged a hand over his face. Nodded. "I'm timed out the end of next month. I won't be reupping."

Which meant if Task Force Mercy stayed intact, they'd have a new CO.

Quick, shared glances told the story. They didn't want a new CO.

"So," Black began again, "a funny thing is about to happen on my way home from the war." He met their eyes. "I'm going private, boys. I'm starting up my own firm."

"Private?" Mendoza asked. "Private how?"

For the first time, a small smile tipped one corner of Black's mouth. "Private as in Uncle has expressed interest in paying my asking fee to do the same work I'm doing now."

"But without any culpability on the part of the U.S. government," Sam concluded with pinpoint accuracy.

"See how swell that worked out?" Equal measures of sarcasm and cynicism colored Black's voice. "Task Force Mercy fades away, but Black Ops, Inc. will be there to take up the slack when the fire gets too hot."

"This is bullshit," Gabe spat, thinking about all the team had accomplished.

"This," Black said soberly, "is politics. But if I can keep doing what I do, get paid through the nose for it, and do it my way?" He lifted a shoulder. "Then hell, I'm there."

He cut a hard gaze around the table. "I'm open for recruits. Any takers?"

1

"Okay, problem child. Back you go," Jenna McMillan murmured when a white-faced calf made a break from the herd. Then she hung on and let the sturdy bay she was riding have his head.

A week ago, on the first day of the cattle drive when they'd started moving her dad's herd down the mountain, Jenna had learned that the gelding didn't need her help. The horse knew exactly what he was doing and like he always did, he cut that little doggie off at the pass.

Not so long ago, Jenna had known what she was doing, too. *Now, not so much*, she thought.

Dewey Gleason rode up beside her and flashed her one of his contagious grins.

"What are you smiling at you old trail dog?" She tried to sound put out with her dad's long time foreman, but she couldn't stall her own grin.

"You, baby girl. I'm just smiling at you."

Dewey was one of those born on a ranch, work-on-a-ranch, die-on-a-ranch cowboys. The genuine article. He'd been with her dad for close to thirty years now. Dewey sat a saddle like a train sat a rail. Jenna strongly suspected that her rusty horsemanship was the source of his amusement.

"So I make you laugh, do I?" she asked. "You and the boys weren't laughing last night when I cleaned you all out at the poker table." Cleaned out to the sum total of eleven dollars and twenty-three cents from the lot of them. *Big spenders all*, she thought, remembering Dewey counting his pocket change and deciding whether to call.

"I ain't laughin', Jenna Rose. Just thinkin'."

"Now there's a scary notion."

"I was thinking," he went on, "that before you went off to see the world and write your news stories you were a real cowgirl," he said, but not unkindly.

"Tell me about it," she agreed, shifting in the saddle to relieve the trail-weary ache in her butt.

Yeah, once she'd been a real cowgirl. Now she was just playing at it. Playing and passing time as she rode along with the real drovers. Still, her pride was wounded.

"Do I really look that green?"

Dewey shifted leather reins from one gnarled hand to the other. "You'll always look good to me, Jenna Rose," he said, then true to form when he realized he was waxing a little sentimental, Dewey blushed to his ear tips.

"You're still an old softy, Dewey Gleason."

Jenna would always have a soft spot for him. He'd taught her to ride. Taught her to rope. Taught her that the measure of a man wasn't determined by education or how much money he had.

Yup, Dewey was the real deal. She loved that about him.

Like the gentleman he was, when another stray tried to run, Dewey tipped his fingers to the brim of his old stained Stetson before kneeing his mount and giving chase.

Her gelding decided to follow. The bay lunged and did a little crow-hop, almost unseating her.

Almost.

See, Dewey, she thought, dredging up a small kernel of satisfaction, *I still sit pretty tight in the saddle.*

"Don't be lookin' too smug there, Missy."

There was a hint of amusement in her dad's warning as his voice drifted through the fall chill and the dust two hundred odd head of Angus stirred as they ambled down the snaking trail from the high plains and summer grazing to the south pasture where they would spend the coming winter.

"That little bay's got spunk." He reined in his buckskin to keep pace beside her. "He'll dump you yet if you don't watch him."

Because he wanted her to smile, Jenna grinned at her dad and gave him a thumbs-up sign.

Unlike Dewey, who looked like a piece of scarred, worn leather, her dad was still a handsome man despite the deep creases etched around his eyes from sun and time and smiles. But like Dewey, her dad had reason to be concerned about her riding. She *was* rusty, and they all knew that she'd been dumped from the back of a horse more than once. X-rays would show a hairline crack in her left forearm to commemorate one of those falls.

Long time ago, she reflected, buttoning the top button of her shearling jacket and turtling deeper into the wooly collar to ward off the cold.

Not so long ago, she'd been dumped again, she mused as she and her dad rode in companionable silence. Well, not so much dumped as dismissed. In her book, that amounted to pretty much the same thing.

Gabriel Jones had despised her at first sight, on general principle and because he was a narrow-minded, heartless alpha dog. She'd walked away from him and Argentina nine months ago. She hadn't been able to get him out of her stupid head since.

It royally ticked her off.

So did her reaction to the note Hank Emerson, her editor at *Newsday*, had sent by overnight mail two days ago. Guilt. Hank had managed to make her feel guilty. He wanted her back on the job.

> *I need you down there, Jenna. You're the only one who can do this story. Maxim asked for you. Said he wouldn't trust it to anyone but you. Besides, you know the territory.*

Yeah. Jenna knew the territory, all right. That's why the thought of going back to Argentina scared her.

And yet, the story enticed her.

Hank was right, Emilio Maxim was big news. There was a story there.

Maybe a big story. It was a story she could nail if she could just dredge up the guts to go back and face a contingent of demons.

"How long are you going to distance yourself from the hard news with those little fluff pieces you've been turning in, Jen?" Hank had asked yesterday when he'd followed up his note with a phone call. "I don't want the plight of the caribou in Alaska from you. I don't want to know what you know about the disappearing honey bees, for chrissake.

"I want a Jenna McMillan story. Something with teeth. Something with fire."

He'd softened his tone then and Jenna could almost see him raking his fingers through his gray hair. "Jenna. What the hell happened to you down there?"

What happened in Argentina was something Jenna had never shared with anyone. That wasn't going to change. Hank would never know. Neither would her parents.

How could she tell them that when she'd been in Buenos Aires searching for a man by the name of Edward Walker, she'd been abducted, blindfolded, and driven to a dust and adobe village in the middle of nowhere then locked in a six-by-six-foot, vermin-infested cell without food or water for days?

How could she confess that just when she'd thought she was going to rot there, she'd been hauled away again by rifle-toting thugs who had thrown her in the back of a battered pick-up and taken her to a camp full of their warthog kind?

She shivered. The bastards had had all kinds of vile acts in mind for her before she'd finally been rescued.

By Gabriel Jones.

Then the real nightmare had begun.

But don't cry for me, Argentina, she thought sourly.

She'd been doing enough crying on her own, thank you very much. All of that boo-hooing and poor-meing had turned her into a cowardly, spineless wimp.

That knowledge stuck in her craw like glue because the old Jenna McMillan didn't quit. Didn't cower. Didn't back down. Her mom was fond of saying that Jenna had been all of two years old when her dad had set her on the back of a horse and she'd been galloping full speed at life ever since.

If she fell off—and she'd fallen off plenty in both her career and her personal life—she always climbed back in the saddle.

Where was that woman? she thought grimly. *And when is the old Jenna McMillan going to report for duty?*

She forced a bright smile when she realized her dad was watching her with a puzzled frown. "So, how ya doing?" she asked before he could ask her.

She already knew the answer. He was getting older, that's how he was doing. So was her mom. Jenna worried about them. The difficult Wyoming winters and hard work had taken a toll. A lot of years had passed while she'd been off to college as a nursing major before switching gears. A stint as a volunteer for the campus newspaper had led her into journalism and an unending chase to capture stories around the world.

Haven't chased too many stories lately, though, have you, hotshot?

No, *not so many,* she thought with a defeated breath. Hank was right. She'd checked out. Bailed out. And now she was hiding out.

"I'm doing fine, Jenny. I was about to ask the same of you."

She shot him a wide grin. "Me? I'm great."

She breathed deep of the crisp mountain air, looked skyward, watch a jet trail heading south dissecting the pristine perfection of a vast blue sky. Once she'd have been itching to be on that plane—on *any* plane—following the next big story. Chasing the next big lead.

She wasn't chasing anything but dust now, much to Hank's dismay. She'd been his go-to guy for several years, covering assignments in every political and war-torn hotspot on the globe—Mogadishu, Beirut, Gaza, Kabul, Baghdad, to name a few. Many of those stories had been for Hank. She'd thrived on the action and adventure. Even relished the very real threat of danger.

Until Argentina.

Argentina had gotten to her. Argentina had debunked the myth of "fearless Jenna McMillan."

The standard joke among her colleagues was a take-off on an old breakfast cereal commercial: "Let's get Jenna to try it. She'll try anything once."

Well, she wasn't fearless now. She was gutless. After Argentina, she'd turned down stories baby reporters would wet their pants over.

What the hell happened to you down there? And when are you going to get over it?

Yeah, that was the question, all right. And that's why last week she'd thrown a few things in a bag, locked up her D.C. apartment, and come home. To get over it.

Only no Houdini type had shown up to make the boogie man magically disappear. Which meant that she was the only one who could make it happen.

"Jen?"

The brim of her dad's brown Resistol shadowed his face from the autumn sun but didn't hide the concern in his eyes. Even before he spoke again in that slow, thoughtful way he had, she knew he had her number.

"If you're so great, what are you doing here, sweetie?"

She'd never been able to lie to him. She felt weary suddenly. And guilty again for lying now.

"I'm resting, Dad. Just resting." She hedged because she couldn't tell him that she'd lost her nerve. About a lot of things.

"Hold that thought." Her father veered off to reunite a mother and her calf.

Jenna rode on. The sound of shuffling hoofs, lowing cattle, and crooning drovers, the scent of cow dung and autumn faded into the background and damn if thoughts of Gabriel *Archangel* Jones didn't rise out of the dust to complicate things even more. Just like thoughts of him had been complicating her life since she'd left him.

Gabriel Jones. They called him the Archangel, but she'd figured out early on that there was nothing angelic about that man. Or the about the Arc-Angel Butterfly knife perpetually strapped to his side or to his leg or wherever he could get to it when he needed it.

Jenna was tall. Five-nine. Gabe was taller. Possibly six-five. A very big man. He probably weighed a good two-twenty, two twenty-five pounds, and he had the skills to use his size to lethal advantage. She'd seen him in action, and she had no doubt that he knew how to deliver a fatal blow to virtually every vulnerable area on the human body, both in theory and in practice.

The man was dangerous. Times ten. The truth was, Jenna didn't really know much about him other than he knew how to operate damn near every kind of weapon in any army's arsenal, knew how to stage an assault that made mincemeat out of the bad guys, and that he could piss her off with a look.

Oh, yeah—and that he could kiss like no man had ever kissed her.

Not that she'd admitted it to him. You didn't give Gabe Jones any advantage. He'd use it to cut you off at the knees.

Weak knees, she thought grimly and ducked low over the pommel to avoid an over-hanging aspen branch. God, he was something.

He wasn't only a big man, he was a hard man: hard, brittle eyes, hard, deep scowl. He was also darkly attractive and perilously intense.

Even before she'd met him, she'd heard rumblings about the Archangel on the streets of Buenos Aires. Some reports had said he was dead, killed in Colombia in a raid on a drug cartel stronghold gone bad. Some said he was a ghost. An angel come back to avenge those who had dared cross him. No doubt he found it amusing and to his benefit that he was somewhat of a legend on the Patagonia and the back streets of the city.

She'd seen how men stepped aside when Jones walked within striking distance. At the airport, before she'd left for the States, she'd seen how women responded to him. They'd watched him with sexy cat eyes, clearly wondering what it would take to tame this man with the darkly alluring aura of the devil.

Jenna could have told them. One long piercing glare from his hard, dark gaze, and she'd understood: No woman was going to tame the Archangel.

Not that he'd have trouble finding willing bed partners. He attracted interested looks the same way he attracted danger. Make no mistake, though, and she'd thought about this a lot: Gabriel Jones would not make love to a woman. He'd have sex. Sweaty and rough. Raw and primal.

Another shiver ran down her spine that had nothing to do with the chill mountain air and everything to do with an image of Jones, naked, needy, and demanding, in her bed.

It made her think about the last time she'd seen him. The Argentinian sun had glinted off the sheen of his thick dark hair; his broad shoulders had cast a long, imposing shadow across the tarmac at Ezeiza, the Buenos Aires International Airport. He hadn't had much to say. His lips had been compressed in thought, his jaw unyielding, while a look fathoms dark, coal-mine deep, masked any emotions that might be seen in his eyes.

Yeah. A very hard man. Not to mention mysterious and cynical. Maybe in another lifetime, she'd thought then, she might have wanted to get to know him and find out what he hid behind that warrior's face that gave away nothing.

Her dad, astride his buckskin, ambled back to her side and picked up on their lapsed conversation. "You know that old sayin', Jen? The one that goes, 'you can't go home again'?"

She looked at him sharply, distancing herself from the vivid memories of Jones.

"Well, the thing is," he went on when she didn't respond, "there's more than a grain of truth to it. At least you can't go home to the 'home' you knew as a young'un."

"Home is home," she said, feeling defensive suddenly as the herd meandered down the ravine. "The sky's still blue. The mountains are still high. You're still my dad."

"And you said good-bye to all of it a long time ago."

Yeah. Because she'd had things to do. Worlds to conquer.

"You know you're always welcome here, darlin'. Your mom hasn't stopped smiling since you showed up. Well, except at night. After you turn in, she looks at me with those worried eyes of hers and tells me to talk to you. To find out what's eatin' you."

They were too perceptive, her mom and dad. She felt bad that they worried about her.

"Me, I figure you're hiding out," he went on in that wise, gentle way he had. "From what, I don't know. And that's your business."

Way too perceptive.

"But I do know one thing," he added in his steady, reassuring tone. "Whatever's working on you, you aren't going to find the answer here. And you aren't going to fix it by running away from it. The thing about you, girl, is that no matter how many times you got thrown off a horse, you always climbed back in the saddle. It's not in your nature to deal with a setback any other way."

Moments passed to the creak of saddle leather and cattle sounds. And in those moments, Jenna thought of her friend, Amy Walker, and the horrors Amy had endured at the hands of Abu Sayyaf terrorists in the jungles of the Philippines. What Amy had endured would have broken most women. Yet Amy, at great risk and at great cost, had confronted an even bigger threat and come out stronger for it.

Amy hadn't hidden out.

Like Jenna was hiding.

"What if that's changed?" She fixed her gaze on the distant horizon. She couldn't look at her dad and let him see the uncertainty in her eyes. "What if I've lost my nerve?"

"There's no shame in that," he said after mulling over her confession. "We all get tested in this old life. The shame comes from not trying to find it again. I say that only because I know you. You aren't going to like yourself much until you square yourself away, and that's not going to happen playin' cowpoke around here."

But I want to play cowpoke, the pouty little girl in her whined. She wanted to stay right here, pretend the rest of the world didn't exist, and pray for some obscure sense of safety to kick in. She wanted to recapture the security of her childhood that had cushioned all the hard blows and cocooned her from life's ugly truths.

She wanted to forget about the nightmare she'd discovered in Argentina. Stop seeing the flames as the MC6 compound had exploded. Stop smelling the stench of burning flesh and the scent of blood from the bodies that had fallen around them.

And she wanted to quit thinking about Gabriel Jones.

But guess what? So far, none of that had happened, had it? The truth was, somewhere in the back of her mind, she'd known it wasn't going to. Not hiding out here. She just hadn't wanted to acknowledge that her comfort zone wasn't all that comfy anymore.

Her dad was right. She had to find her nerve again, and Hank was offering her the opportunity to do it. Which meant—God, she hated to admit it— that she had to suck it up and get herself back to Argentina.

Something her dad already knew. Something she'd known but just hadn't wanted to admit.

"How'd you get so smart, Daddy?"

Her father chuckled and resettled his hat. "I married a smart woman. Stands to reason that some of it would rub off after all these years."

2

Jenna could have heard Hank's whoop of triumph even if they hadn't been connected by phone when she called him the next morning and said she'd take the assignment.

"Hot damn! My girl's back in the saddle!"

She couldn't help but grin. Hank Emerson was one of the most shrewd, insightful, and respected news editors in the business. He was also one of the most irreverent. "Let's remember your blood pressure issue, okay, Hank?"

"Screw the blood pressure. I love you. I want you to have my baby."

Jenna laughed. Hank was sixty-four and for the past forty years had been married to one of the most amazing women Jenna had ever met. "Lil might have something to say about that."

"We won't tell her. Welcome back, babe, I've missed you. Not to cut this joyride short, but we need to move at warp speed if you're going to nail this sucker down. Did you look at the info Maxim sent on the intel stick?"

Along with the overnight letter, Hank had included a memory stick Maxim's people had sent as prep info for their potential interview.

"Yeah. I reviewed it." The memory stick included a PowerPoint presentation overview of Maxim's company, Ventures, Inc., painting a picture of entrepreneurial excellence. "Quite the propaganda tool."

"Yeah, Maxim's pretty taken with himself and his accomplishments," Hank agreed. "Guess he wanted you to be, too."

"So that I'd write a nice, friendly piece on him and his empire, no doubt."

"Yeah. So you'd do that. Now what did you find out on your own?"

Hank knew her well. She'd been up until the wee hours this morning, researching Maxim on the web. "Emilio Maxim. Ventures, Inc. Big fat cat investor out of Boston."

"And formerly of Argentina," Hank added. "Made his billions playing the futures markets in livestock."

"Yeah, but for all of his squeaky-clean, might-want-to-run-for-public-office-someday appearances, my gut tells me something might be a little off here. I have a hunch the man is as dirty as a hog in a mud wallow."

"See, that's why I want you back. You and your gut are rarely wrong. And did I ever mention that I love it when you talk animal husbandry?"

"So now Maxim's making a move to get back into the Argentina cattle market," she went on, used to Hank's sidebars. "His meeting this week with the National Congress in Buenos Aires is about cutting a deal that will give him a majority slice of the market."

"That's where the story comes in," Hank put in. "A local isolationist group, Argentina Alliance, is on to Maxim. They figure a deal with him will rape an economy that's already fragile and they don't want him anywhere near their economic structure or the capitol. They're bound to stage some kind of protest when he meets with the congress."

"And if the Alliance runs true to form, there could be violence and uprisings and trouble, oh my," Jenna speculated.

"Exactly. Sounds like you've got a handle on this. You need to kindly get yourself down to Buenos Aires in forty-eight hours or less. And by the way, when Maxim's people called they asked specifically for you. Said he'd *only* talk to you, as a matter of fact, but his time is limited. If you want the interview you need to meet up with him at the National Congress when he goes to make his pitch to the senate. Seems there's some government reg that would kill the deal, and he wants to make his case in person for the congress to override it. If there's going to be trouble with the Alliance, my bet is it's going to happen there."

Despite a lingering trepidation, the old exhilaration stirred inside her. "I need to book a flight."

"Already booked it."

Of course he had. Hank had more faith in her than she had in herself.

"Also booked a hotel room. They wanted an address so Maxim would know where to contact you in case you had trouble connecting."

"Mighty accommodating of him," she mused aloud. "Wonder why he's so hot to give the interview? And why me specifically?"

"Darlin', that's called looking a gift horse in the mouth. However, if I were a betting man, I'd say it's *you* he's got the hots for."

"One of these days, you're going to cross a line, Hank, and someone is going to sue you for sexual harassment." Because Jenna loved him, they both knew the most she'd give him for his sexist remarks was a dirty look.

"Yeah, and maybe one of these days you'll realize your status. Jesus, Jenna. You constantly underestimate the power of your byline. You are a highly regarded, experienced journalist who has a rep for covering international affairs fairly and accurately. Why would the man *not* want one of the best in the business covering this story?"

"Wow." She was taken aback by her editor's uncharacteristically serious tone and his effusive praise.

He quickly shifted back to true form. "And what the hell. If giving Maxim a little smile gets him talking and makes him happy, who are we to disappoint?"

She laughed. He giveth and he taketh away. "That's what I love about you." And she did love the wily old fox. "You'd sell *my* soul for a story."

"Well, now I'm wounded."

"Sure you are. Just give met the details so I can get moving."

"Move with care, kiddo. Understood?"

What she understood was that Hank was giving her one last shot at backing out. He knew how difficult this trip would be for her.

"I will. And Hank. Thanks for the push."

"Anytime. Anytime."

After he gave her the flight and hotel details they said their good-byes. Jenna headed up to her old bedroom to throw some clothes and personal items into a carry-on along with her laptop. A good measure of guilt followed her as she thought about the last time she'd gone after a story in Argentina.

She'd let Hank down. He'd blow a gasket if he knew what had really happened. She'd told him there'd been no story. That it had proven to be a wild goose chase.

He hadn't bought it, of course. He wasn't stupid. Still he'd let it alone, even though she knew he had to have read the wire service reports coming out of Argentina about the death toll from an explosion that had destroyed an *estancia*—a cattle ranch—near El Bolsón in the lake district of the Patagonia.

There'd been an explosion, all right. The *estancia*, however, had been a front, not a true ranch. Inside the heavily guarded grounds was a house of horrors. MC6, a third-generation neo-Nazi stronghold run by Erich Adler and Edward Walker, had been practicing non-consensual mind control and conducting unspeakable experiments on human beings, including drug experimentation, shock therapy, and psychological deprivation.

Just thinking of MC6 and Adler made Jenna's blood run cold. She'd been in the thick of taking the compound, Adler, and Walker down. She and Gabe Jones, with a little help from their friends, had blown it to kingdom come.

The story would have rocked the world and sent Hank into orbit, but she'd killed it because of Gabe. The questions the story would have generated would have led to Gabe and his men. Jenna didn't know who they worked for or what all they were up to, but it didn't take a rocket scientist to figure out that breaking the story would expose their part in it. That kind of exposure would breed a lot of questions, jeopardize all kinds of missions, and most likely place them in danger.

Was she proud that she'd had a hand in bringing MC6 down? Damn straight. Had she wanted to tell the world about it? Absolutely. For once, she'd contributed to a major event, instead of merely reporting on it. But in the end, exposing the heinous atrocities committed there would have served no essential purpose and caused more pain for the families of the victims.

And then there was the issue of not wanting to revisit the horror.

She sucked in a bracing breath to steady her fleet of butterflies. Adler and Walker were dead. MC6 was gone. There was nothing left to fear in Argentina.

Except maybe Gabe Jones.

Tough. Regardless of how nervous she was about returning, she owed Hank a great story. She was going to give him one this time and get on with her life and her career in the process.

She glanced around her room to make certain she hadn't forgotten anything and spotted Nugget on her dresser. Her mom never threw anything away, bless her. The little stuffed toy had always been her lucky puppy.

Nugget had tagged along for every important event in Jenna's life. The little tan and white dog had been packed in her suitcase for summer camp and tucked in her briefcase on her first job interview and numerous trips in between.

"Maybe you're just what I need to get me through this trip, too, buddy."

She hesitated for a moment then thought, *why not*? It was childish, even foolish, but it felt right.

"Come on, Nugget. Consider yourself officially out of retirement."

Just like I am officially out of my mind, she thought, but she still made room for him in her carry-on and headed downstairs.

"Oh, sweetie. You're leaving?"

Her mother met her at the bottom of the stairs, wiping her hands on a dishtowel. Jenna had known it would be hard for her mom to see her go.

"It's time," she said, hating that her mom had the same worried look in her soft brown eyes as when Jenna had announced she'd changed her major mid-semester her second year at Wyoming State from nursing to journalism.

"Work?"

"Yeah, Mom. I'm going back to work."

Her mother nodded and hugged Jenna good-bye. "We just want you to be happy, Jenna. We just want you to be safe."

Safe. Jenna watched the Wyoming countryside roll by as her dad drove her to Jackson Hole where she'd catch the first leg of her flight to Buenos Aires. To some, the word *safe* would seem strangely out of context considering that she'd herded strays on horseback from the time she was five years old. She'd tangled with brutish bulls and the occasional mountain lion, and survived wicked winter snowstorms that left the family stranded for weeks at a time in dangerous sub-zero temps.

But to her parents ranching wasn't dangerous. It was simply a way of life. The only way of life generations of McMillans had known. To them the ranch *was* safe. But the thought of their little girl heading off to parts unknown, covering earthquakes, floods, political coups in third world countries, and the Gulf Wars, terrified them.

Well, yeah. It terrified Jenna, too, sometimes, but until MC6, it had also exhilarated her. She needed to get that feeling back.

Starting right now.

And what the hell, she thought, feeling that old self-confidence kick in, as long as she was returning to Argentina, maybe she *would* look up Gabe Jones, instead of just think about it.

Yeah, she thought, her heart rate accelerating. Maybe she'd just do that. It was time to be a big girl. Past time to confront him and tell him to his face that she thought he was an arrogant, rat-bastard creep.

What she couldn't tell him, what she had no intention of telling him, was that she hadn't been able to stop thinking about him since she'd left Argentina. Of all the "issues" she'd been dealing with the past nine months, that was the one that plagued her most of all.

She and her dad chatted about mundane things—the weather, the price of cattle, the hay crop—until the old brakes on his truck squealed as he pulled up at the departure's terminal.

"You sure about this?"

She shaded her eyes with a hand, squinted up at him as he walked her to the door of the terminal. "It'll be fine."

"Promise you'll take care of yourself down there."

She hugged him hard. "I promise. Take care of Mom, okay? And take care of you."

She shot him a huge grin as he climbed back in the truck and drove away. A grin that quickly faded as she headed resolutely toward her gate.

3

The FUBAR factor had set in an hour ago, and it didn't show any signs of letting up. Neither did the sun. It glinted off the windows of passing cars and beat down with relentless fury on the sizzling sidewalk.

The cement was hot on his ass where Gabe Jones slumped against a tall post sporting a trio of streetlights perched atop ornately scrolled brass arms. Tense as a cat on the hunt, Gabe nonetheless sat with his long legs sprawled in front of him, sweating in the Kevlar vest he wore beneath his poncho, working hard to carry off a drunken slouch. The faded green wool draped loosely over his shoulders stank like wet dog. It fell across his lap, hiding his Les Baer 1911—A1 .45.

His bruised and scuffed leather boots concealed his Butterfly—four inches of razor-edge carbon steel folded into Titanium billet handles. The 4.3 ounces of deadly metal felt as natural as skin against his ankle. Just like his untraceable credit card, Gabe never left home without it.

Fortunately, looking inconspicuous among the *turistas* and locals—the *porteños*—who filled the sidewalks and streets surrounding the *Congreso de la Nación Argentina* building wasn't as tough as it should be. Despite his size, Gabe had pulled it off. Hiding in plain sight was a skill he'd mastered years ago in the military. No one took much notice of the juicer sleeping off a bender. Not in Buenos Aires. Not at nine in the morning in a twenty-four-hour city where the night ended sometime around four a.m. for many people.

Of course the beggar's cup by his hip and a really rank trail of tobacco spittle pooling at his feet went a long way toward fending off even the marginally curious.

"Anything?" he asked into his chest where a commo mike was tucked in the folds of wool.

"*Nada.*" Sam Lang's gravelly voice registered through Gabe's headset, followed by Johnny Reed's frustrated "No banditos, no bureaucrats, no fat cat American client. What the hell's the holdup?"

FUBAR, Gabe thought again. *Fucked-up beyond all recognition.* This op was unraveling faster than worn tread on a bald tire. Lang and Reed were positioned twenty yards ahead of him in a small, sheltered bus stop in front of the National Congress building. They felt it, too. He heard it in both of their voices.

The rest of the Black Ops, Inc. team—they'd kept the intials BOI—tagged for this protection gig should have been here an hour ago with Emilio Maxim, the head honcho from Ventures, Inc., Reed's "fat cat," in tow.

Based on a transmission Gabe had received earlier from Wyatt "Papa Bear" Savage, however, there'd been a backlog on runway three at Ezeiza after Maxim's private Challenger jet had landed. It had held up the armored car and the detail transporting Maxim by about an hour.

FUBAR.

"In. Out. Shuffle back to Buffalo," Black had said yesterday at the final briefing on their latest executive protection gig. Famous last words.

"Maxim isn't exactly a popular man in Argentina," Nathan Black had informed them via a video conference call. From his off-site base of operations, Black briefed the BOI team responsible for Maxim's safety while the team studied a carefully crafted security plan for Maxim's arrival.

"Because he's attempting to cash in on the Argentinean cattle market," Gabe had concluded after reviewing basic background info into Maxim's file.

"Got it in one." Black's voice hadn't changed much over the years. It was still strong, deep, intense.

"And it looks like his company, Ventures, Inc., is planning to screw them ten ways from Sunday," Reed had added with a grunt, his handsome face breaking into a grin despite his distaste for Maxim. "It's a wonder they even let the bastard into the country."

Nate Black, his hard life and forty-plus years showing these days in the gray peppering his close-clipped brown hair and in the cautious way he rose after sitting in one position for too long, had scratched his head before grinning into the camera. "Yep. Just another damn ugly American."

"Why are we protecting this guy again?" Reed had asked, voicing what most of them had been thinking.

"Because it's those damn ugly Americans that keep us in business," Nate had said.

"Sure it is." Gabe had stopped thumbing through the game plan. He challenged his employer with a look. It wasn't too difficult to figure out there was a lot more here than met the eye. A scumbag like Maxim wasn't their usual type of client. "Want to try again?"

Nate had grown sober. "Okay. Here's the deal. Emilio Maxim's a big player, right? Has his own security team. So red flags popped up when his people contacted me about contracting with BOI to provide protection for Maxim's Buenos Aires trip. I figure, what does he need us for? So on a hunch, I made a couple of calls to my contacts in the State Department. Found out Maxim has been linked with Rashman Hudin."

At that point, Gabe's eyes had lifted to the video camera. "This bastard's tied to Hudin?"

Nate had nodded, understanding in his eyes. Just as the rest of the BOI team had understood. They all knew who Rashman Hudin was and why his name made Gabe tense.

"You'll all remember that Gabe recovered a set of documents from Erich Adler's body after his chopper went down on the MC6 op," Nate had reminded them.

Yeah. They remembered. The documents had outlined an international plot to wreak havoc between Western democracies and Jihadists — more fuel added to an already blazing fire.

The papers had also revealed that Erich Adler had merely been a regional head and that MC6's primary headquarters were based in the Philippines and Malaysia.

Malaysia, where Rashman Hudin just happened to be.

While the documents hadn't named names, since Hudin was on a government watch list, it was pretty easy to put two and two together and come up with a whopping ten. The conclusion then was that Hudin was most likely a key player in MC6, quite possibly at or near the top of the organization in the Malaysian headquarters.

And Emilio Maxim was linked to this bastard.

"So we're not guarding so much as watching dogging Maxim," Lang had surmised.

"Special request from Uncle," Nate had confirmed.

It made sense. Those same documents they'd recovered from Adler's body also had detailed information on heroin and cocaine trafficking, and referenced facilities where MC6 brokered the bulk of weaponry that found its way into the hands of jihadist groups all over the Middle East. The papers outlined MC6's ultimate long-term goal of resurrecting a new Nazi regime from the ashes of war between democracy and jihadists.

"So," Sam had added. "Maxim is connected to Hudin. And Hudin was connected to Adler. Quite the triumvirate."

At least it had been until Adler was killed.

Nate had nodded. "Agreed. Maxim's connection to Hudin is just a bit too interesting. So, that's where we come in."

Yeah, Gabe thought, dragging himself back to the present where he'd grown damn weary of waiting for Maxim to show. That's where they always came in.

Black and his Obnoxious Idiots may no longer be military or CIA, but they still worked with Uncle. And they were still a team. Still brothers. Still Black's boys. Warriors without an official war. Adrenaline junkies all. A misfit crew with no clue how to perform in a suit-and-tie world and no desire to learn.

Hell, the truth was, at least in Gabe's case, he'd been living on the edge for so long that a nine-to-five and a white picket fence scared him more than an AK pointed dead center at his heart.

But damn, he thought, as the Argentinean sun continued its ruthless burn and the poncho baked him like a sauna, it was times like these that made him question his choices.

Gabe scanned the ornate Italianate building situated at the end of *Avenida de Mayo* where the Argentine Senate and Chamber of Deputies were currently in session.

The thirty-odd yards of real estate between Gabe and the *Plaza de los Dos Congresos* was filled with tourists and protestors. A contingent of twenty or so protestors—none of whom walked or talked like the deadly Argentina Alliance—had gathered in force with signs and sensible shoes to voice their opinion about the government's proposed collaboration with the man Gabe and the team were here to protect. Which they would—provided the SOB ever showed up.

Yep. Some days Gabe questioned his choices. On the worst ones, he wished he were back in the military or even the CIA instead of doing contract work. Work that even the military or the CIA wouldn't or couldn't touch for fear of creating an international incident.

Today, however, was all about working with the boys. About living through the moment because his future was about as promising as a pipe dream and because he sure as hell couldn't relive his past. Too many regrets there. Too many dead bodies. Too many ghosts.

Angelina.

Her memory hit him like a mortar round.

Angelina.

Screaming in pain. Dying in agony while he'd been forced to watch Erich Adler and his clew of Nazi worms torture her.

All because she had helped Gabe.

He'd almost died that day, too. For over a year, only his quest for revenge had kept him alive and functioning. He had lived only to kill Erich Adler.

But even that impetus had been taken from him. While Gabe led the raid that had destroyed the MC6 compound and Adler's stronghold, someone else had taken down Adler's escape chopper. Someone else had been responsible for Adler's crash and burn as the bird had fallen out of the sky.

Someone else had avenged Angelina's death.

He dragged himself away from the guilt and the ache that gnawed at his gut with dull teeth. Cursed not only himself but a vindictive God when another woman came to mind. A woman who somehow managed to breathe life into that part of him he thought he'd buried with Angelina.

Jenna McMillan. *Sonofabitch*.

He did not want to think about her. She was a hothead and a smartass, more shrew than charmer, more irritant than balm.

Nothing like Angelina.

Nothing like any other woman he'd ever met. Brassy, ballsy, even brilliant, he conceded grudgingly. Classic. Regal. Beautiful. The first time he'd seen her, her poor mouth had been bruised and swollen, but even then, her lips had made a tempting statement—until she'd opened them. Closed and silent, they'd spoken volumes about what they could do to a man on a hot night and cool sheets.

At times, and totally out of character, she'd managed to appear vulnerable, something Gabe hadn't expected but had been intrigued by because he suspected she would never admit to any weakness.

Regardless, she was definitely not a woman he wanted to meet up with again.

Except . . . and Jesus this was hard to admit, especially since she hated his guts . . . it was Jenna McMillan's face he saw at night now, not Angelina's.

"Papa Bear, five o'clock."

Sam's voice rasped in Gabe's earpiece and jerked him back to the present. He watched the street for a black Mercedes. The vehicle should be in his sights soon, flanked both front and rear by two more BOI protection vehicles.

"'Bout damn time," Reed sputtered.

"Roger that," Gabe agreed and waited for the parade to appear.

Since Maxim was a high-risk client, the front vehicle, a brown van, would be the ambush breaker, but the trailer, a nondescript gray sedan, would be loaded with a BOI heavy weapons team.

"Got him." Gabe let his team know he'd spotted and recognized the unmarked, unobtrusive Mercedes as the BOI armored car transporting Maxim cruised into sight on *Avenida de Mayo.*

He flipped a switch, opening up radio contact with the new arrivals. "Y'all get lost?" he groused, laying on the twang for the detail leader's sake.

"Aw, *y'all* been missin' me." Wyatt "Papa Bear" Savage's slow, southern drawl came over the wire. "Makes me feel as warm and fuzzy as a ripe Georgia peach."

Gabe grunted. "You want ripe, try spending a few hours in this heat."

Squinting against the sun, he looked left then right as the Mercedes, with Savage at the wheel, moved closer to the front of the long, slowly sloping steps that led to the Congress building.

"What heat, Angel boy?" Light static crackled through the connection. "Nice and cool in here, bro."

Gabe grunted. "Guess that means you buy the mint juleps when this is over."

"So, whatcha'll got?" Savage asked.

"Nothing yet. It's all quiet on the western front." Which, Gabe knew, could be an illusion as slick as a magician sawing a woman in half.

The dark, tinted windows of the Mercedes did the job, preventing anyone from seeing inside, but Gabe knew Maxim would be in the backseat. Even though they'd been tagged to pick up whatever info they could on Maxim, it was still up to Gabe, Lang, and Reed to protect him on the off chance the rumors of an assassination plot targeting Maxim panned out.

Gabe roused himself with the slow, uncoordinated movements of a man accustomed to sleeping off a drunk in a public place. He rose to his feet, wobbled, and sank back against the light post as if he needed it for support while he scanned the area for snipers or anything else that might look amiss. So far, so good. Which meant exactly jack.

The trio of BOI cars slowed to a crawl then cruised to a stop in front of the *Plaza de los Dos Congresos.* The Congress building was broad and sprawling, with wide steps that rose at a low angle to the arched entrance doors. Gabe automatically searched for anything out of place.

That's when he saw her.

A wave of dizziness hit him like a triple shot of Wild Turkey.

He blinked. Did a double take.

"What the fuck?" he muttered clear of the mike.

He squinted hard into the sun. Wondered if he was having a heat stroke. "No way in hell."

His gaze swung from the woman who had just cleared the Congress building's wide arching doors back to Papa Bear, a big, brawny man who moved with the stealth of a cat as he shoved open the Mercedes's driver's side door and stepped out into the simmering heat.

Gabe chanced another glance at the woman.

It could not fucking be.

Papa Bear rounded the front of the armored vehicle and after checking all quadrants, opened the rear passenger door.

But god damn, it was.

Jenna McMillan had scooted out the main doors of the *Congreso de la Nación,* that all-American-girl-with-an-attitude-and-a-mission look on her face.

For a split second all he could see was her—killer face, killer body, long legs bare beneath a softly swaying print skirt, riotous red hair tumbling down her back.

The screech of tires on hot concrete jerked his head around.

A beat-up black van roared out of nowhere. It careened onto the plaza from a side street and plowed into the knot of demonstrators just as Maxim ducked out of the Mercedes.

"Threat, right!" Gabe shouted on the fly.

He'd already jerked the bulky poncho over his head and tossed it aside on the run when a masked man toting an AK-47 flew out of the van and started blasting away in every damn direction.

"Shit!" he swore when he felt a round zip right by his head.

Reed and Lang were on top of it. They each carried HK 9mm MP-5 submachine guns. Like a lot of former Spec Ops boys, both Reed and Lang preferred them to pistols. They were simple to use, their collapsible stocks made them easy to conceal, their size effortless to access, not to mention that in the right hands they could drill single rounds into a target the size of a man's head from fifty yards.

Both men whipped the HKs out from under their ponchos and opened fire, taking out the shooter almost instantly with no collateral damage. The van roared away with Reed and Lang still pumping lead as Papa Bear and the inside team shoved a shell-shocked Maxim back into the Mercedes.

Gabe sensed something was off. Something told him the shooter was just a diversion—and then a second car shot onto the plaza and sailed past him, driving right up the steps toward the *Congreso*'s main entrance.

Just before the car slammed into the main entry doors, Gabe caught a glimpse inside. The backseat was full of wires. He swore under his breath as he saw that the vehicle was also sitting low on the back end. When the driver ran the hell clear after jumping from the car, Gabe's worst suspicions were confirmed.

"Bomb!" he yelled, vaulting past Lang and Reed who had each dropped to one knee and were sighting down their weapons near the front and rear of the armored Mercedes.

"Get Maxim the hell out of here!" Gabe shouted on his way by.

Peripherally aware of the sound of slamming car doors and screeching tires as the BOI cars shot away from the building, Gabe bounded up the cracked cement steps toward Jenna, where she stood in shocked bewilderment watching the catastrophe unfold.

He'd almost reached her when the car bomb detonated. He launched himself, wrapped his arms around her, and dove for low and horizontal. They were in mid-air when he felt the impact of the explosion, smelled the acrid and unmistakable scent of C-4, burning tires, and gasoline.

The concussion of sound and fury and Jenna's terrified scream all faded into background noise as a consuming, searing fire ripped through his calf and his head hit the cement.

Pain exploded behind his eyes.

He saw black.

Then red.

Then nothing.

4

Jenna landed on the burning hot concrete steps with a bone-jarring thud. One minute she'd been looking for Maxim, who was late, and the next, bullets were flying, a car was racing up the steps, and a swearing, stinking drunk came out of nowhere and tackled her. Right about then the world had exploded.

Now, two seconds or two minutes later—she had no idea which—all she could do was lie there, gasping for her lost breath, crushed beneath the weight of a vile-smelling stranger.

"Get. Off. Me!" She pushed out each word like a curse when she marshaled enough breath control to speak. But he was dead weight. She couldn't budge him as all around her, fire and ash and smoke spewed into the air to the sound of screams and chaos and the blaze of the burning car.

Bomb, she realized when her mind finally engaged. She'd witnessed enough of them to know. More than enough to know that she'd never, ever get used to them. In that same moment she actually wished she had listened to her mother when she'd begged her to stay in nursing. Wished to God she was anywhere but here.

Under . . . this . . . stinking . . . man. While her story was getting away.

Anger as much as panic had her pushing, shoving, clawing, and screaming at him again to get off of her.

Nothing happened.

Then everything happened.

He flew up and away as if he had wings. She saw two very big, very bad-looking men who had hoisted him up, she realized, watching their backs as they struggled with the bum's dead weight and raced down the steps to haul him away.

Before she could breathe another man grabbed her arm from behind and jerked her to her feet.

"What . . . wait!" she yelled, snagging her purse from the step beside her. It not only held her BlackBerry but a vial of pepper spray she'd picked up after arriving.

If she could get to it.

"Wait!"

He wasn't listening. He hauled her down the steps, a blur of speed and inertia. They'd already reached the bottom before she had the presence of mind to put on the skids.

He jerked her tight against him, still behind her so she couldn't see his face. She didn't know who he was or where he was taking her, but none of this spelled *rescue* to her.

She had to make something happen. Fast.

She went limp and he relaxed his guard. Quick as a cat, she jerked her arm free, caught him by surprise, and vaulted down the sidewalk in the other direction.

Gathering the folds of her gauzy skirt, she ran like hell, until the heel on her left shoe snapped. She stumbled, righted herself and, swearing at her bad luck, kicked off her other shoe, all the while digging into her bag for the pepper spray. A bruising hand snagged her arm sending the spray flying; another wrapped around her waist and hauled her off her feet.

With the chaotic melee going on around her, she knew no one would hear her scream. So she saved her energy and lit into him like a wildcat.

She kicked. She clawed. She swung her purse at him. Finally she threw her head back and butted his.

He roared in pain.

"Gawd dammit, Jenna! Hold the hell still!"

That stopped her short. He knew her name.

And she knew that voice.

Winded, heart hammering, she struggled to look behind her and finally saw her abductor.

"Reed?"

My God. It was Johnny Duane Reed! Relief almost buckled her knees.

"So help me, if you broke my nose—"

She clutched his arm like a lifeline. "What . . . thank you, God . . . are you doing here?"

"Saving your sweet ass." His words were choppy; blood ran from his nose as they raced toward an idling gray Suburban. "And this is the thanks I get."

Reed didn't give her time to ask any more questions. He shoved her headfirst into the backseat and piled in after her. The vehicle shot from idle to warp speed before the door even shut behind them.

She finally righted herself, dragged the hair out of her eyes, and stared at Reed.

The last time she'd seen him was also the last time she'd seen Sam Lang. It had been dawn. She'd been numb with exhaustion, like the rest of them — Dallas Garrett, Amy Walker, and Gabe Jones. They'd been covered with the grime and the pall of battle following the MC6 operation.

"What"—she paused to catch her breath—"just happened?"

"Don't talk to me."

Reed gingerly touched his swollen nose with one hand, cursed under his breath.

She dug into her bag, felt past her BlackBerry and her wallet, and finally found a packet of tissues. When she held them across the seat, he grabbed them and pressed a huge wad to his nose to stall the bleeding.

The car careened around a corner and sent Jenna crashing into the far door, banging her shoulder. She bit back a yelp of pain and straightened herself again. For the first time, she noticed a man lying facedown in a pile in the cargo area behind the rear seat where she and Johnny were sitting.

A stinky, unconscious man. The same man who had tackled her on the steps when the bomb went off.

She jerked her arm away from the backseat. "What's he doing here?"

Johnny stuffed tissue into each nostril. "Breathing. I hope."

She checked. Frowned. "He . . . he's also bleeding." A deep crimson stain seeped from the leg of his torn pants.

"Yeah, he does that sometimes." Satisfied his nose was plugged, Johnny glanced into the cargo bay behind him. "Suppose we'd better do something about it."

"We?" She made a sound that pretty much told him what she thought of that idea. "I'm not touching him. That bum attacked me."

"No," Johnny said, affecting the patience of a man whose stockpile was beyond depleted. "That *bum* saved your ass."

"I thought *you* saved my ass. Look. Never mind." She tried to tame her hair with shaking hands. "I'm sorry about your nose, okay? But you could have told me who you were."

"I was a little busy with that ass-saving thing."

Okay. He had a point.

A *bomb*.

Jesus.

In a fleeting moment of terror, Jenna longed for the "safety" of Wyoming and home—hell, give her a one-ton renegade bull and an aspen twig to beat him off with.

She sucked in a deep breath. Then another. She was actually surprised when she realized she wasn't as terrified as she was excited. *Excited.* Like she used to get excited when she landed in the middle of a volatile and dangerous situation.

I'm back, she thought in triumph. She was back on her game.

"Okay. Straight skinny. What were you guys doing at the Congress?"

"Get down," Johnny ordered as a sharp *thuwnk* had her eyes snapping wide open.

Someone was shooting at them.

"Get down," he ordered again, flattening his hand on the top of her head this time and pushing her face into the seat.

The car picked up speed and shot around a corner, hurling her sideways. She grabbed for a door handle and the back of the driver's seat to keep from tumbling to the floor. When the car straightened, she gingerly raised her head—just as another man looked over his shoulder at her from the shotgun seat.

She blinked. Blinked again. She'd been so busy trying to keep from bouncing around she hadn't even looked toward the front. "Sam?"

"Jenna." Sam Lang acknowledged her in that soft, calm voice she remembered from a time nine months ago that she knew she would never, ever forget.

She peered around the headrest so she could get a look at the driver. Didn't know him, but recognized him as being cut from the same cloth as Reed and Lang.

"What is this? A badass convention?"

She should have known. Where Reed went, so went Sam. And where they went Gabe couldn't be far behind.

"What," she continued, as a building sense of doom at that prospect eroded what modicum of calm she'd gathered, "are you guys doing here?"

"Little busy right now." Sam had already turned his attention back toward the window and was sighting through the scope of an automatic rifle. She flinched, slouched lower in the seat, and covered her ears when he fired off several rounds behind them.

Ears ringing, she glanced at Johnny, and bit back a string of questions when she saw he was busily reloading a pistol.

Deep breath. Another. She wasn't going to get any information out of either of them. Not now, at any rate. For now all she knew was that she'd landed in the middle of a dicey situation. Hell. Seeing Johnny Duane Reed and Sam Lang was more than disconcerting. It made her think of El Bolsón and MC6.

It made her think of Jones. And it made her question, as she had a hundred times since she'd left Wyoming, what she'd do if she ran into him again.

It wasn't like he gave a rip about her. All he cared about—well, there it was, wasn't it? She didn't know *what* Gabriel Jones cared about. Didn't know what made him laugh. What made him cry. What made him weak. She only knew what pissed him off: her.

She worried a hand over the folds of her skirt, forced herself to lean back against the seat, realizing only then that her elbows burned. Her shoulders ached. So did her hip where she was probably sporting a bruise the size of Texas. That got her all PO'd again at the lump behind her in the cargo bay.

God, he stank. She needed air. She found the lever for the electric window and lowered it a fraction. Fresh air rushed in, hot, sweet, welcome.

From the front seat, someone raised the window, locked it.

She rolled her eyes, bypassing the idea of questioning Johnny again. It would be a waste of time. If he was going to talk, he'd have talked by now. She could draw conclusions until the cows came home, but the fact was only one thing made sense. They were here for the same reason she was. Emilio Maxim.

Why? That was the bigger question. She'd get it out of them. Eventually. Maybe when they weren't running and the bullets weren't flying.

Without fighting it, she slid straight into another memory of Gabe — because the truth was, it was easier to think about him than about the bullets bouncing off the car.

The first time she'd seen Gabriel Jones he'd emerged from the ruins of a firefight that had killed the barbarians holding her hostage. Only the glowing remains of the camp had lit the dark night. She'd been scared out of her freaking mind and thought he was one of the bad guys. Her heart stopped now as it had then as the vision of Jones backlit by the remains of the burning terrorist camp, larger than life, automatic rifle in hand, reformed in her mind.

If she'd had a gun, she'd have shot him. That's how scared she'd been. Killed him dead. As it was, an iron frying pan had been her only weapon. Jones had laughed at her when she'd warned him not to come any closer.

What are you going to do, soufflé me?

She'd never forgiven him for that.

Okay, fine. So it had been funny. What she'd never forgive him for was making her break down in front of him and bawl like a baby when she realized she'd been rescued.

In the days that followed, while she'd formed a grudging admiration for the way he handled himself in the face of the nest of barbaric snakes that comprised MC6, Jones had rubbed her every way but the right one. What little she'd learned of him since then should have had her running scared, not back down here, semi-hoping she might run into him again.

The man in the cargo bay groaned.

Johnny twisted fully in the seat to look at him. His face went hard. "Shit," he muttered, scrambling to turn around then reach over the backseat to get to him.

"He's bleeding out." Johnny's Texas drawl wasn't so slow suddenly as he tried unsuccessfully to rip open the man's pant leg.

"Damn it!" He reached up under the cuff of the guy's pants and pulled out a knife.

Jenna's heart stopped, her attention riveted on the knife. She sat up straight in the seat as the blood drained from her head and left her dizzy.

She recognized that knife.

It was a Butterfly. A cold steel Arc-Angel Butterfly.

The odds of that same knife belonging to any man but Gabriel Jones fell roughly in the slim to none category.

"Oh my God!" Jenna scrambled to her knees and leaned over the seatback to help Johnny expose the bleeding wound.

"Not God, darlin'." Johnny grunted as he worked to slice through the pant leg then parted the material that was matted with sticky deep crimson blood to expose a huge, gaping wound. "It's just Jones. But I'm sure he'd be pleased as punch to think you placed him in such high rank deity-wise."

He may be kidding around—that's what Johnny did—but his face was dead serious as he searched the backseat then reached for the hem of Jenna's skirt and started to slice off a long length.

"What can I do?" She helped him with the fabric, not caring that the skirt had cost a small fortune in a designer shop in Paris last year.

Johnny's attention never left Gabe's leg. Blood poured from the hole in thick, pumping spurts. He quickly fashioned a tourniquet with approximately forty dollars' worth of hand-painted silk. "Hold this tight."

With shaking hands, Jenna gripped the ends of the cloth while Johnny folded another length of her skirt then pressed it to the wound.

"Is he really bleeding out?" She couldn't hide the concern in her voice.

Johnny took his time replying, and for several long, tense moments as the car shot around another corner, Jenna was afraid of his answer.

"Nah," he said finally and shot her a trademark Johnny Duane Reed grin. "I just wanted to see your reaction."

Only stark relief kept her from doing much more than glaring at him.

His grin widened. "You can let up on that tension a bit now, darlin'. We don't want to *stop* the blood flow, just slow it down a bit 'til we can get him to the doc.

"There you go. Just a little bit more," he said in encouragement. "That's the ticket. Now tie it off, okay? You're doing fine."

She was *not* doing fine. Her hands were soaked with Gabe's blood. They were still shaking when she finally breathed her first full breath that wasn't fractured with fear.

Johnny lifted the makeshift pressure bandage. Blood seeped slowly from the wound now, no longer pumping, no longer pouring out like life.

Gabe groaned and stirred.

"Easy going there, big guy." Johnny dropped a hand on Gabe's shoulder to settle him. "Lie still or all my handiwork will go to waste and you'll start bleeding all over my nice bandage again."

"Fuck your . . . bandage." Gabe sucked in a sharp breath. "How bad . . . is it?"

"For you? Just a scratch. For us mere mortals, it ain't great. Sucker's gotta hurt like hell."

Another groan as Gabe shifted again, tried to push himself upright. "Jenna." Sapped of energy, he slumped back down, his face pressed into the floor. "Where's . . . Jenna?"

"I'm here," she said quickly, stunned that he'd asked about her, that he apparently cared what had happened to her. "I'm fine."

His head reared up.

He met her eyes. Stared. Swore.

"Sonofabitch. It *was* you. What are you doing here?"

The venom in his tone stung like a hard slap. It took everything in her power not to flinch.

"At the moment?" She gathered herself and smiled sweetly. "Wishing I'd let you bleed a little longer. And I'll bill you for that tourniquet, thank you very much."

Silence, tense and taut, stretched out until Johnny broke into a huge grin.

"Well, hot damn," he crowed, his voice brimming with laughter. "D'ya hear that, Sam? Just like old times."

"Screw you, Reed," Gabe grumbled, then with a muttered oath, passed out cold again.

5

Old times, my ass.

Gabe stared at the Spanish tile floor, doing his damnedest to keep the room from spinning as Reed's words came back to him and echoed in his mind along with the ringing in his ears.

He'd come to a few minutes ago. Disoriented. Disabled. Entrenched in pain. Pissed. He'd been fighting ever since to get a slippery grip on time, place, and level of threat.

Familiar voices, calm and reassuring, told him the threat was zip. The sound of Spanish guitar bleeding through the walls from the front of the building, the smell of booze, tobacco, and antiseptic told him he was in the back room of the Thirsty Dog, the cantina that fronted for what could loosely be called BOI's Buenos Aires base of operations. At times like now it also doubled as a first-aid station.

Safe and secure, he was tempted to drift back toward the dark again. He fought it, vaguely aware of a soft, soothing hand on his bare shoulder, urging him to stay down.

Concentrate.

Okay. He was in the cantina. Good. Fine. The *where* was in the bag. The *time* part was still giving him trouble. He'd get a handle on that later. Right now he had bigger problems. His head felt as if someone were laying into him with a ball peen hammer, and even that was no competition for the pain that ripped through his leg.

Clenching his jaw to stall a roar when the knife dug deeper, he gripped the metal bars of the table legs until his knuckles turned white.

"Hang on, Angel boy. I'm almost home."

Doc Holliday. Capable hands. Working on his leg. Speaking softly, voice full of concern. Which meant Gabe had trouble.

Another jagged, searing pain burned through his calf.

"Jesus Christ, Holliday," he ground out between clenched teeth. "They take away your scalpel and give you a rusty saw?"

"Well, well." A low, slow chuckle that sounded very much like relief accompanied Holliday's words. "Look who's back among the living—at least marginally."

Holliday wasn't really a doctor. And his name wasn't really Holliday. Luke Colter had been a medic with Task Force Mercy and before that, a veteran of SEAL team four. The tall, rangy Montanan also had a rep as a Wild West–type gunslinger with a passion for five-card stud.

Reed had dubbed him Doc Holliday after Colter's baptism by fire. On his first day with the team, Colter had patched up half a dozen TFM members then proceeded to clean them out at the poker table that night with a candy-eating grin and no remorse.

Like most men in the unit back then, Gabe had lost more money than he'd like to admit during Holliday's weekly poker sessions. Also, like most men in the unit, Doc had followed Nathan Black to the private sector and into BOI.

Gabe owed Doc a dozen times over for patching him up. But *Gawd damn*, Gabe thought as sweat poured off his brow and dripped on the tile floor beneath him, the man showed no mercy. "Enjoying your work, Holliday?"

"Always a pleasure, Jones. If you didn't have such a thing against painkillers, you'd be in Lala Land and missing all the fun right now. So hold the hell still. I'm just about done here."

Again, those soft, cool hands soothed just as the pain almost took him under.

"Got ya, you sneaky sonofabitch," Holliday crowed, then dropped the piece of shrapnel he'd dug out of Gabe's calf into a bowl.

Gabe breathed past the pain, registered the clunk of heavy metal against stainless steel. For the first time since he'd come to, he remembered why he had shrapnel in his leg in the first place.

Jenna McMillan.

What the hell was she doing in Buenos Aires? More to the point, what was she doing at *Congreso de la Nación Argentina* at the exact moment a bomb went off?

While Doc applied a pressure dressing to his calf, bits and pieces of the race from the bombsite flashed through his mind. The speeding car, the bitchin' pain, coming to and seeing Jenna's face above him as she leaned over the backseat.

"Hurry it up, will ya?" He glanced over his shoulder at Doc. "I've gotta get out of here."

Get out of here and find her, he thought with grim determination. Had to make sure she was okay.

Then he was going to wring her long, lovely neck.

"Sorry, Gabriel." A soft voice he recognized all too well had him stiffening with resistance. "But you aren't going anywhere."

Juliana Flores moved into his line of sight then, her soft hands still caressing his shoulder comfortingly. She smiled at him through brown eyes rimmed with both apology and affection as she squatted down to his eye level.

She should hate him. Because of him, her daughter was dead. Yet Juliana had demonstrated over and over again that she did not blame him for Angelina's death. Did not despise him for not being able to save her husband, Armando. Did not look at him with anything but affection and compassion and trust.

None of which he deserved.

"You shouldn't be here," he croaked.

Juliana shouldn't be anywhere near BOI Headquarters, or him, that's for damn sure. It was too dangerous for her. He started to push himself up.

Again, those strong but gentle hands held him down, and with far too little pressure. He was as weak as a damn baby.

"I was careful. No one saw me come here. Now lie still, Gabriel. We're not finished, darling boy. Luke took good care of you, but you need surgery on that leg."

He started to shake his head. Stopped short when it felt as if he'd rammed it into the Liberty Bell.

"Not to mention you've got a concussion," Juliana added while Doc washed up in the background. "I need to get some X-rays."

Great. Like he needed something else to slow him down.

"The day a headache gets me down is the day I pack it in," he grumbled even though the nausea forced him to lie still.

"We all know you're tough, *darling boy.*" Holliday poured on the crap, obviously getting a charge out of Gabe's incapacitated state and the idea that this slip of a woman could boss him around. "But if you want to run with the big dogs again you need to let Dr. Flores work on that leg."

"You already worked on the leg, you hack."

"Love you, too." Holliday bent down to Gabe's level and shot him a broad, amused smile.

Gabe flipped him the bird.

As odd as it seemed given their constant trash talk, Gabe knew that in his own way, Holliday was concerned about him. The bond from their Task Force Mercy days was still there all these years later. Yeah. Doc cared. That didn't mean Gabe had to be happy about lying here at Holliday's mercy.

"I need to do some work in there, Gabriel." Juliana's soothing voice cut through the pain. "The muscle—it's damaged. If I don't repair it now, you won't be happy with the way it heals."

His theme for the day. He wasn't happy about anything. But because he trusted Juliana's judgment without question, he relented. "Do what you have to do. Just do *not* put me . . . out."

Too late. A woozy, cobwebby haze seeped into his brain.

Fuck. IV, he thought just before his lights went out again.

Buenos Aires
Later that night

He lived for the night. This night, in particular, would bring cause for celebration because today, he had finally set his plan in motion.

A stubby candle burned on the blocky wooden table that sat beside his chair where he waited, completely still. He stared at the lizard slithering laboriously into the middle of the cold stone floor, and felt a grim modicum of kinship. They both survived in the dark. For both him and the reptile, however, things were about to change.

Finally, his carefully laid plans were under way. He'd reached outside his network of petty thieves, reached beyond his army of lawless misfits that he now led. Rapists, murderers, deviant dregs of humanity had all sworn allegiance to him out of terror and because of their backward superstitions. They actually believed he was El Diablo.

Let them believe. He did nothing to dispel their pathetic fears. He propagated them like a gardener, tended to them like a crop of poisonous weeds. He used them, abused them, made them his minions to do as he bid. Because of their skills, he had gradually amassed the funds he'd needed to proceed.

He smiled in the dark, pleased with his choice of pawns. Now he was anxious for news.

Time crawled as he waited. Crawled like the lizard that lay dying in the middle of the floor.

A timid knock sounded on the door.

Anticipation jacked up his heartbeat.

It would be his man, Ramón, bringing word of the events at the *Congreso de la Nación*. Finally, the waiting was over.

"Enter," he commanded without moving from his chair.

The door creaked open. A flat, pock-marked face appeared in the gloom; Ramón's stocky body inched inside.

"You have news?"

"*Sí*, El Diablo."

"Closer," he demanded when his lieutenant hesitated inside the door. "Report."

"It was as you arranged," Ramón said in careful English. El Diablo insisted that his subordinates converse with him in English, not Spanish.

"So you have him."

Ramón shifted nervously from one foot to the other, licked cracked, thick lips. "There was an unexpected development."

A cloying silence descended. "Explain."

Ramón's gaze darted from the floor and the dead lizard to the ceiling. "Our gunman arrived and opened fire. He was shot down before he could accomplish his mission. Then the bomb went off."

"Bomb?" He shot to his feet; pain ripped through his flesh at the sudden movement. "I ordered no bomb!"

"No, no, El Diablo, no! We set no bomb! Someone else. Enemies of Maxim perhaps?" Ramón ventured, near panic as he scrambled toward the door.

Yes. He forced himself to calm down. Most likely enemies of Maxim. Enemies he had paid off to back away so nothing would interfere with his plans.

"The fools did not honor our bargain. They will die for this," he promised in a chillingly quiet voice.

He turned back to Ramón and slowly approached the man. "Where is he now?"

The terrified look on Ramón's face said it all.

"You allowed him to get away?" He reached for Ramón's throat, intending to squeeze the life out of him for letting his quarry escape.

Ramón clutched at his neck as he crumpled to his knees, gasping for breath. "Have . . . mercy. We . . . are searching at this moment. Please. Please have mercy. I . . . I . . . have been your faithful servant."

"Find him!" he ordered, shoving Ramón away. "And find him soon."

He studied Ramón's face, read both the fear and the concern there. He knew Ramón thought he was insane.

"Find him by morning," he went on, his voice deceptively calm. "You have been with me a long time, Ramón. I would hate to lose you. Fail me, however, and you will suffer the consequences.

"Now go."

He shoved the terrified man out the door, then stood panting from the exertion and the unrelenting pain his physical actions had caused. Slowly, he collected himself. Slower still, he shuffled to the narrow cot and eased his ravaged body down.

Partial relief lay in the syringe on the table by the bed. The temptation to use it was great. His thirst for redemption, however, was greater. He had to stay clear headed.

He opened the wire cage on the floor. Ignored the biting teeth of the nest of Basilisk lizards as he reached inside and withdrew a large male.

"Things will change for us both," he murmured and offered the starving creature a poisoned cricket.

A reptilian tongue snaked out greedily, swallowed the morsel in one gulp.

El Diablo set the lizard on the stone floor, lay back on the mattress. Then he waited, with detached interest, watching as the poison slowly took control.

The lizard's death would be merciless, agonizing, and as final as the death of his enemies.

Bahia Blanca, Argentina
Twelve hours later

"What, exactly, is your relationship with Gabe?"

Few things shocked Juliana Flores at this point in her life, but Jenna McMillan's question did just that.

Juliana glanced up from her wine, her surprise apparently evident because Jenna turned a brilliant shade of red.

"Oh, God." Jenna averted her gaze to her lap, shook her head. "I can't believe I just asked you that."

Now this *was interesting*, Juliana thought. She leaned forward, lifted the open bottle of pinot grigio, and refilled the younger woman's glass.

She looked exhausted. Juliana could relate. She was tired, too, although glad to be home again.

Home. Her refuge. The azure South Atlantic, a restless shade of green today, pounded fifty feet below the jagged cliff upon which her villa nestled.

Fragrant flowers and shrubs bordered a lush carpet of green grass framing a huge covered portico leading into a house that seemed almost cavernous now that Armando was gone.

Everything—from the European design and Gothic arches to the gabled windows and Louis XIV furnishings—reminded her of him. Gracious, eloquent, timelessly classic.

Gone.

She couldn't think of Armando now. Instead, she thought of Gabe. She was relieved that he was resting comfortably after his surgery an hour or so ago. Juliana had insisted that he be transported back to Villa Flores in Bahia Blanca aboard the Angelina Foundation helicopter where she would have access to her state-of-the-art surgical room and her discreet, capable team who had helped her and Armando operate, no questions asked, on hundreds of patients in the past several years.

As always, thinking of Armando brought the familiar ache of loss. She had other issues to attend to at the moment so she forced a smile for her guest's sake.

"I've insulted you," Jenna said, apology in her voice, apparently assuming as much from Juliana's prolonged silence.

She probably should be offended, but Juliana found herself smiling. "No. Not insulted. You've . . . intrigued me. Your question about my relationship with Gabriel; there was a ring of challenge to it. Is that what I heard? Are you staking a claim to him, then?" If Jenna could be blunt, then so could she.

To her credit, the beautiful redhead didn't feign shock or denial or even surprise. Instead, she lifted her wine and drank deeply before her green eyes met Juliana's gaze straight on.

"Far from it." She made a self-deprecating sound. "Okay, maybe. A little one. Although for the life of me, I don't know why. In the first place, it's none of my business. In the second, it's clear that he hates me."

Because she looked so miserable, Juliana's heart opened a little. "*Hate* is a very strong word."

Jenna grunted. "Don't I know it."

Juliana watched the younger woman's face, more interested by the moment. She'd known it would happen someday. She'd known that Gabriel would find another woman to complete his life.

Gabriel had loved her daughter, but he couldn't mourn Angelina forever. For that matter neither could she, although Juliana suspected she always would.

So what then, did she think of the possibility of Gabriel and Jenna McMillan? She honestly didn't know.

Juliana liked the woman. She admired her intelligence, her . . . *spunk*, she believed was the American word for it. She had liked her upon meeting her all those months ago under some very difficult circumstances. In fact, she'd liked both Jenna and her American friends, Amy Walker and Dallas Garrett.

But Jenna and Gabriel? It was an interesting match to ponder. Because she cared deeply for Gabriel, it was also an important one.

"So you're certain he hates you and yet, here you are," Juliana said after a long moment, "back in Argentina. Back with Gabriel."

Jenna smiled, a bit sadly, Juliana thought.

"I'm back in Argentina on a story," she said. "Running into Gabe again was pure coincidence. Ending up here, at Bahia Blanca again . . . not exactly part of my game plan."

No, Juliana thought, certain that the younger woman had not expected to end up here. The boys, however, hadn't given her any choice. They'd sequestered Jenna at BOI HQ while Luke had done triage on Gabriel. Then they'd hustled her onto the chopper with Gabe and turned her over to Juliana.

Juliana wasn't certain why Johnny Reed had insisted Jenna be transported here to Bahia Blanca. He'd said it was to get her out of their hair.

Maybe the real reason was that Johnny had deduced the same thing that Juliana was beginning to believe. Jenna McMillan, it seemed, had feelings for Gabriel. To what extent, Juliana didn't know. She got a strong sense that Jenna didn't know either.

She found it very interesting.

The silence stretched out, and Juliana suspected they were both thinking back in time. It was hard to believe that the better part of a year had passed since Gabriel, piloting a dilapidated twin-engine Piper, had landed on her private airstrip with two women and a wounded man aboard.

The man had been Dallas Garrett. The women had been Amy Walker and Jenna, and the four of them, along with Sam Lang and Johnny Reed, who had traveled back to Buenos Aires on their own, had just destroyed the MC6 compound near El Bolsón. From what Gabriel had told her the operation had been brutal, bloody, and dangerous.

It had also been necessary.

Just like the death of Erich Adler, the operations mastermind and the same monster who had killed her daughter, had been necessary.

"How are your friends?" Juliana asked abruptly, needing to divert her thoughts from Angelina's horrible death.

"Amy and Dallas? Good. They're good," Jenna replied. "At least they were the last time I heard from them."

Juliana had learned that Amy Walker had had her own reasons for bringing down MC6. Gabriel had told her that Edward Walker, Amy's grandfather and the second in command at MC6, had practiced ghastly experiments on Amy's mother when she was a child.

Juliana remembered Amy as a small woman with a huge, brave heart. She remembered Dallas Garrett as a man who loved Amy with a fierceness he had not been able to conceal.

Jenna was Amy's friend. She was also a journalist, who at her own peril, had used her investigative skills and contacts to find Edward Walker for Amy.

"You risked a lot for your friend," Juliana said thoughtfully.

"And you risk a lot for Gabe."

Ah. So we're back to that. Juliana nodded. "Which prompted your original question about the nature of my relationship with him, which I still haven't answered."

Possibly because she smiled, Jenna smiled, too. "Yeah. That one."

"I love Gabriel," Juliana admitted after a lengthy silence. "As a son."

More than relief flooded the younger woman's face.

"You thought something more?"

"You're an incredible woman. A beautiful woman. I . . . I watched him with you. He's . . . different around you. Softer. More open. More . . . I don't know. Approachable, maybe? Human."

She was astute, Juliana gave her that. She liked that about her. "He would have been my son-in-law," she said, anticipating Jenna's next question.

The stunned look on Jenna's face said it all. She hadn't expected to hear that. The flash of pain in Jenna's eyes caused a resurgence of Juliana's own pain.

"My daughter has been gone almost two years now. She was helping Gabriel when Erich Adler captured her. He tortured her. And then he killed her."

6

Oh. My. God.

Jenna struggled to process Juliana's words.

Angelina, of the Angelina Foundation painted on the side of the pricey chopper, was Juliana Flores's daughter. Angelina was the woman Gabe had loved.

Jenna felt heartsick for all of them, especially Gabe. It explained his anger. Explained why he kept so much of himself bottled up inside.

No wonder Jenna felt such contempt from him. The woman he had loved was dead, killed by Erich Adler, and Jenna had almost fouled up his operation to take Adler out.

The fact that in the end she'd actually helped meant little. It was an accident that she'd been in on the raid the day Adler had been killed while trying to escape the MC6 compound. Just as it had been an accident that Jenna had ended up in the middle of a bombing today with Gabe. Another accident that she'd ended up back here, at Juliana Flores's Bahia Blanca estate.

How ironic. The prospect of blowing the lid off a story about Maxim had gotten her back down here. Finding Gabe had been a secondary mission. Now Maxim was temporarily out of the picture, and she'd probably blown her chance of pinning him down again by allowing Johnny to bully her into going to Bahia Blanca, insisting that Juliana would need her help with Gabe.

So far, not so much. Juliana had everything under control.

Jenna stared at the beautiful woman who had lost so much. Wondered how she had lost her husband. Wondered how she survived the losses of both the man she loved and her daughter. The first time she'd seen her, Jenna remembered thinking there was such drama in Juliana's face. Beneath it all, though, she'd seen pain. Now Jenna understood why.

She felt small and petty drinking Juliana's wine, eating her food, and tonight, sleeping in one of her guest bedrooms.

She was a stranger in Angelina's home, where there was nothing left of her but portraits. Jenna couldn't stop herself from looking at the oil above the fireplace. A wave of sadness swamped her. Angelina had looked exactly like her beautiful mother, with her long, wavy hair the color of roasted chestnuts; honey-gold complexion; wide, expressive mouth; and intelligent brown eyes.

She closed her eyes, felt a swirl of nausea. She'd just admitted to a woman who was still grieving that she had feelings for the man her daughter had loved. She had dared to question her about her relationship with him.

Yet it was all Jenna could do to keep herself from asking a thousand more questions.

God. She was lower than road tar.

"I am so, so sorry, Dr. Flores." The words sounded inadequate at best, too little too late at worst.

Juliana merely smiled, a forced, sad smile that said so much about her suffering. "We are all sorry. And you couldn't have known."

"Adler . . ." Jenna had to ask this one question, but it was difficult and she stumbled. "Your daughter . . . what happen—"

Juliana cut her off. "There is only one thing of importance to say about him. He can't hurt anyone anymore."

Bahia Blanca
The next morning

Gabe assessed his surroundings through closed eyes, heavy and gritty with sleep. Drug induced, he concluded, breathing deeply to clear his head.

The room smelled clean, he realized, attempting to ID the scent. Not sterile. Lavender, maybe. He shifted a shoulder, turned his head, and sank into luxury. Down pillows. Expensive linens.

Finally, he opened his eyes to soft, slanting sunlight that shone through tall narrow windows, then glanced off gleaming hardwood floors in flickering prisms of blue, yellow, and green.

It was morning. But of what day?

He lifted his arm to check his watch. Gone. Then he slid his hand down beneath the sheet to discover that his clothes were also gone.

He might have been alarmed, except he recognized the style and the opulence of his quarters.

He was lying in a huge bed in the middle of an equally large bedroom. Tall plastered walls had been painted a cool shade of blue. Pricey artwork hung everywhere, adorned dressers, bookcases. Ornate, expensive furniture—the woman loved her dead kings—filled the room. Sheer panels billowed softly in an ocean-scented breeze that eased in through floor-to-ceiling windows.

An oasis. Juliana's oasis. Yeah, he recognized her touch. He may have even slept in this bed once before.

The question was, why was he here now?

The bigger question, why was there a long, leggy, and very mouthy redhead sound asleep in a chair beside the bed? And the mother of all questions: Why would a woman who had hated his guts on first sight and from all indications hadn't changed her opinion in the nine months since she'd left Argentina be keeping vigil at his side?

He stared at Jenna McMillan's sleeping face, at the generous, ripe mouth that could fool an unsuspecting man into thinking that only sweetness and light and uncensored sex could possibly slip between those lush, sensual lips. Thick auburn lashes brushed her cheeks and covered eyes the color of forest moss. Eyes, he reminded himself, that could shoot daggers at a moment's notice and slice a man's ego to the quick.

The woman was a pest, a nuisance, and the worst kind of trouble. So why was he fighting to convince himself he wasn't glad to see her? *Drugs*, he concluded. Juliana had doused him with some heavy-duty painkillers.

That didn't answer the most obvious question. What *was* Jenna doing here?

He lay his head back down on the pillow, stared at the ceiling, and tapped his memory for answers.

They flooded in like the sunlight deluging the room.

The stakeout.

The machine gunner.

Jenna on the steps of the Congress building.

The car bomb.

Slowly, the rest of the details filed together into a progressive line. He'd come to in Doc's makeshift ER in back of the cantina. Juliana had been there. Had told him he needed surgery on his leg.

His leg. Shit. Oh, shit. His leg.

A nauseating panic boiled up in his gut. He braced himself, then jerked the sheet aside. Forced himself to look down.

It was still there.

Sweet Jesus God, his leg was still there. It was wrapped from knee to ankle in thick, sterile dressing, but it was there. Relief made him light-headed.

The soft rustle of fabric made him realize he had an audience. And he was lying there bare-ass naked.

"I . . . um . . . you're . . . oh, gosh . . . awake."

He turned his head, said nothing. Only watched as Jenna stiffly straightened in the chair and made several valiant attempts to keep her gaze above his lap level.

Tried and failed.

And damn if his dick didn't react to those huge, hungry eyes licking across his body and to the brilliant shade of red flooding her cheeks.

"So it would seem," he said, his voice gravel rough with knee-jerk carnal need. A need that pissed him off. And apparently, left the woman with the most wicked mouth south of the equator, speechless.

More for his benefit than hers, he reached for the sheet and tugged it across his lap. Then he watched her face as a breath she must have been holding for the better part of a minute eased out.

"How long have I been out of it?"

She made a big production of stretching and yawning in a failed attempt to look casual. "Since yesterday."

A day. He'd lost a day.

"How are you feeling?" Her voice lacked its usual bravado as she dragged a handful of long, unruly red hair away from her eyes and tucked it behind her ear.

Like I've been broad-sided by a two-by-four. Both his head and his leg throbbed like a bitch. But he wasn't going there. He had plenty of questions of his own, and he wanted plenty of answers.

He lifted his hand to his itchy jaw. Thick stubble. He hated stubble.

"I . . . um . . . my dad. He broke his leg once."

He turned his head, stared into uncertainty. *Where was she going with this?*

"He had to spend some time in . . . bed."

Jesus, was she blushing?

"His beard . . . well. I remember how it drove him crazy," she went on, looking at the wall, looking out the window, at the floor, anywhere but at him. "I used to give him shaves. I guess I could . . . give you one. If you'd want me to, that is."

If he hadn't already been flat on his back, her offer would have slammed him there even though she sounded about as anxious to perform the personal task as she would be to walk into a pool of quicksand.

Yet she *had* offered. Interesting.

Because she'd felt obligated? Wanted to make *him* feel obligated? Or was it the old inherent nurturing gene kicking in? He hadn't thought she had one.

Or maybe she's just being nice, Jones.

Yeah, that was going to happen.

He was about to say no, thank you, don't bother, but something stopped him. Maybe it was the obvious reluctance on her face. Maybe it was the fact that he hated living with stubble.

Maybe he just felt mean and nasty and pissed that he was so weak and he wanted to make her squirm a little more.

"Yeah. Sure. Knock yourself out," he said finally then watched her face as surprise registered, followed by suspicion, followed by determination to soldier on.

When she stood, he closed his eyes, drifted on the aftermath of sedation and gnawing pain to the sound of water running in the adjoining bathroom.

He didn't have it in him to flinch when a hot, wet cloth caressed his face and roused him. Without opening his eyes, he let a breath of tension ease out. Damn. It felt good. As she eased a hip onto the edge of the mattress then pulled a bedside stand close, he realized she smelled good. Musky and sweet. Like a woman. Like sex.

He measured his breaths, forced himself not to open his eyes, knowing that the combo of tactile and visual sensations would shoot him toward terrain studded with landmines.

Deep breaths, dumb ass.

You're in control here.

Damn right he was. For all of a nanosecond.

When she removed the cloth and carefully spread shaving gel over his lower face and throat, all of his erogenous zones stood up and took note.

Her hands were surprisingly steady. Her touch acutely soft and sensual.

It's a shave, he told himself. *Just a damn shave.*

When she leaned over him to gain better access and touched the razor to his jaw, her breast brushed his bare chest and his traitorous dick stirred to life beneath the sheet.

He fought to swallow a groan. Fought and failed.

She pulled back like she'd been stung. "What? Did I nick you?"

If only. Nothing like a little blood loss to bring a man to his senses.

He made a major tactical error then. He opened his eyes. Met hers. Reacted with his he-man gene when distress furrowed her brow, darkening her irises to sea green as her gaze flicked from his eyes to his face and back again.

"No." His voice was thick with arousal. He cleared his throat. "No. I'm fine. It's all . . . fine."

Just fuckin' fine.

Even more than the dull throbbing pain in his calf and the pounding in his head, he felt a keen, pulsing awareness of her hip pressing against him, of her woman's heat melding with his. Felt a raw, urgent need to pull all that soft, yielding warmth against him and satisfy the ache in his groin.

He folded his hands over his lap to hide the tenting action going on underneath the sheets. *Sonofabitch.* He did not want to react to this woman on any level other than indifference. Yet here he was. Raised to full mast, ready to set sail in a sea of wet, steamy sex.

It was all wrong. He didn't want to react to anyone or anything. It was how he ran his life. It was how he stayed alive. Yet somehow from the first moment he'd seen Jenna McMillan, she'd managed to test every self-defense mechanism he'd ever erected.

Suddenly he was tired. So tired, he let down his guard. When she paused to rinse the razor, he met her eyes again. In them, he saw the last thing he needed to see.

A responding physical pull.

An answering chemical heat.

The same combustible attraction that he damn well didn't want to acknowledge, let alone give in to.

And, damn it, that wasn't all. Underlying all the animal magnetism, he sensed something that thickened this messy stew of sensations.

She cared about him. At least she thought she did. *When in the hell had that happened?*

And when had what she cared about started to matter to him?

She went back to work with the razor, and suddenly the answer was painfully obvious: He'd started to care the moment he'd first set eyes on her, embattled from her abduction, scared out of her mind, poised to defend herself with a damn iron frying pan.

Jesus, she'd been something.

She *was* something. Something special. Too special for the likes of him, which was why he'd intended to quit caring the day he'd let her walk out of his life at the Ezeiza airport nine months ago.

Yeah, he'd let her go when he'd known he could have made her stay. That should have been his first clue. The woman meant more to him than a quick lay and a quicker good-bye.

Now here she was again. It pissed him off to react so strongly to her.

Made him mean because mean was the only way he knew how to react to all this need.

"What are you doing here?" he growled, weary of wrestling with feelings he was never going to act on anyway.

His gruff question startled her. Her cheeks turned that amazing shade of red again. Though he was certain she wasn't aware of it, she'd bitten her lower lip between her teeth. Nervous. He was making her nervous.

Join the club, sweetheart.

Very slowly, she let her lip slide out, all plump and perfect and pink.

And poison, he reminded himself. She had a mouth as lethal as belladonna, and a helluva lot of nerve to show up down here again and fuck with his head.

"Here? As in here, here? I'm giving you a shave."

He shot her a stone cold glare to tell her just how cute he thought she wasn't. "That's not what I asked you."

Her eyes were wide and evasive. "You mean, what am I doing in Argentina?"

"That would be the money question, yeah."

She seemed to consider as she rinsed the razor again then slid it expertly from cheek to jaw. "I'm on vacation."

And he was the queen of England.

She was hiding something. Big surprise. The obvious questions were what and why?

"On vacation. Is that a fact?"

"It is, yeah."

Her body language gave her away—the slight flare of her nostrils, the sudden crease between her brow. He wasn't letting up on her.

"So . . . your *vacation* just happened to land you at the Congress building at the very same time a bomb went off."

She looked away as she rinsed the razor. "Some coincidence, huh?"

He gave her his best hard-ass look. "Just so you know, I don't believe in the tooth fairy, the Easter bunny, or coincidence." God, he was tired. "Wanna try again?"

That brought on a world-class scowl. "You know what? I don't think I like your tone."

He barked out a laugh then wished he hadn't when pain lashed through his head. He reached up, touched his temple and discovered a knot the size of a hen's egg. "News Flash: *I* don't think I give a shit. Now what were you really doing there?"

"That would fall into the 'none of your business' category." Belligerence times ten.

He snagged the towel from her hand when she started to pat his jaw dry.

"I've got a hole in my calf the size of your explanation." He swiped the towel over his face. "You'll understand if I think that makes it my business."

"Tell you what." She busied herself gathering the shaving paraphernalia. "Why don't you tell me what *you* were doing there?"

He glared at her.

"Yeah. That's what I thought." She rose and headed for the bathroom. "What's good for the goose doesn't cut it for the gander."

Swearing, he swung his legs over the side of the bed, dragging the sheet across his lap as he did—and the room went red, white, and blue stars as he sat up straight.

Warm hands gripped his shoulders and eased him back down on the pillow before he could take a header onto the white cypress floor.

"You've also got a concussion, so just settle down and try to lie still."

Fuck.

He closed his eyes. Breathed deep and swallowed back slick, rolling nausea.

"Need a bowl?"

He sucked in two more breaths. "No. I'm okay."

"Yeah, and I'm that tooth fairy you don't believe in."

She made to move away again. He latched on to her wrist, held tight with all the puny strength left in him. "We're not . . . finished," he mumbled and knew he was about to slip under again.

"Yeah, I figured that, too." A softness in her voice almost sounded like affection. "For now, you need to sleep, okay? Just sleep."

She didn't have to tell him twice. The soothing sound of her voice, the softness of her fingers gently prying his off her wrist, and the residual pain medication sluicing around in his bloodstream all took a toll.

He drifted off to the caress of her hand across his forehead, the feel of cool sheets beneath him, and a reverently whispered, "Holy, holy cow," as the top sheet was quickly lifted then settled back down over his lower body.

7

"Holy, holy cow," Jenna murmured as she let the sheet drift back down over Gabe's lap. The man was hung like one of her daddy's prize bulls.

"Yeah, and he bellows and snorts like one, too," she reminded herself, easing back down on the chair.

She watched him sleep.

Just watched him and thought about that bare, tough, scarred body.

Lord, was he buff. But the scars. You could have played connect the dots with all the warrior wounds—some old and white, some pinker, newer.

Like the bump on his head. And the biggest problem, his leg.

What had she been thinking when she'd offered to shave him? Where had that even come from? Earning her keep, maybe. Juliana had done so much for her, it was a small chore to even the score.

Maybe she thought she could get some information out of him about what he'd been doing at the Congress.

Or maybe she'd just wanted to get close to him, she finally admitted.

She dragged a hand through her hair. Shaving him had been a really, really bad idea. Too intimate. Too much touching. Too much thinking about touching him all over.

Ho-kay. It was time to back out of there because now she had a vividly detailed game in mind where she used her mouth to connect those dots that scarred him. Where she stopped to linger, from time to time, on that part of him that had made such a huge impression on her.

A *huge* impression. So what had she expected? He was a big man. Stood to reason.

It also stood to reason that she should feel guilty about taking one final peek at the goods while he was helplessly falling asleep, but she didn't. Not even an iota of guilt reared its ugly head. Why should it? He'd reacted to her first, hadn't he? Caught her off guard.

But then, everything about this man and this situation threw her off her stride. That's part of the reason why she'd lied to him about why she was back in Argentina. She didn't want to give him any more advantage over her than he already had.

The other part of the equation was that she didn't believe in coincidence any more than he did. There was a reason Gabe and the boys had been at the Congress the same time Maxim had arrived. Those guys looked for trouble the way hawks looked for prey. Their presence on the scene could mean that her story might be as big as or even bigger than either she or Hank had anticipated.

Sam and Johnny and any number of other road warrior types couldn't wait to isolate her in a room by herself when they'd finally driven the embattled Suburban into an underground parking garage then hustled her and Gabe into the back of a cantina in the barrio in Buenos Aires.

Cantina my bruised butt, she thought. It was a base of operations of some kind. They'd gone to great lengths to make sure she hadn't seen anything, heard anything, or done anything they didn't want her to see, hear, or do. She'd also lost her purse somewhere along the way—most likely their doing, too.

She had a lot of questions about that place and about the men who populated it. Men like Gabe who played deadly games for a living and sometimes died for their efforts.

Like Gabe had almost died yesterday. That thought still gave her goose bumps.

So, okay. Part of the reason she'd ended up here was to make sure he came through the surgery all right. That's not what Reed thought. He thought she'd let him railroad her into coming to Bahia Blanca.

Fat chance. If she hadn't wanted to get on that chopper, she wouldn't have gotten on it, no matter how many big men with bigger guns informed her it was her only choice.

The way she figured it, Maxim had been long gone by then anyway. Since she'd lost her BlackBerry along with her purse, that left Gabe as her best chance of finding out what was going down.

Then there was the ulterior motive—she'd wanted to see him again. She still wasn't sure why.

"Still sleeping?"

She jumped, startled when Juliana's voice knocked her out of her rambling, sleep-deprived thoughts.

"He woke up once," she said, glancing over her shoulder as Juliana joined her by the bed. "For a while. Long enough to bitch about me being here."

"Then he was lucid."

"Oh yeah." And aroused.

Juliana took in the scene, couldn't help but see that Gabe was freshly shaven. If she reached any conclusions, she kept them to herself.

"You haven't slept, have you?" she asked after checking Gabe's respiration and pulse.

"I slept. Well, a little," Jenna confessed when Juliana frowned. She hadn't used the guest room the good doctor had given her. She'd been too wired after their little talk to lie down. Even the wine hadn't settled her.

So she'd come here instead. Sat in the chair beside Gabe's bed, studied that hard, beautiful face, the swelling and bruising slowly creeping over his temple toward his eye, and she'd eventually fallen asleep in the chair.

And we all knew what kind of trouble she'd gotten herself into then.

"Will he be all right?" Seeing him like this truly unsettled her. Even scarred and bandaged and asleep, Gabriel Jones was larger than life. There was a vulnerability to him now, though—physically at least—that was difficult to witness.

"If he gives himself time to heal, yes. He'll be fine."

"But you doubt he'll give himself that time," Jenna concluded, based on the concern creasing Juliana's forehead.

The doctor lifted a shoulder. "He's always been a terrible patient."

Jenna thought of the scar on his chest. The thick jagged line on his thigh. "You've patched him up before."

Juliana laid the back of her hand on his brow. "Too many times, I'm afraid."

The sheet had slid down to his waist, outlined his hips, molded to the thickness and the length of his strong thighs. The skin above the sheet was deeply tanned, evidence of hours spent in the tropical Argentinian sun. His shoulders were angular and broad, his chest wide and lightly dusted with dark hair. Thick veins pressed against the skin of his forearms and over the bulky muscles of his biceps.

Not only hung like a bull, built like one, too, Jenna thought, then realized Juliana was watching her. She shook her head, lifted a shoulder as if to say, *guilty*.

"Lotta man," she said. What point would there be in denying that she appreciated what she saw?

Juliana nodded. "Indeed."

"Who is he?" Jenna asked after several silent moments had passed. "Who the hell is Gabriel Jones?"

Juliana seemed to consider answering, but in the end, shook her head. "I think that's something he needs to tell you."

Jenna nodded. She'd figured as much. She even appreciated Juliana's loyalty to Gabe.

The truth was, she felt a little relieved when Juliana left the room. As much as Gabe Jones fascinated her, there was a part of her that was frightened by him, too. Or maybe frightened *for* him would be more accurate. Maybe it was better to fumble around in the dark. Maybe she couldn't handle the kind of secrets he kept.

The man lived on the wire. Men like him always did. Men like him always had a fight to fight, a war to win, a burden to bear. They didn't make for good relationship material.

Gabe Jones types were always being hunted by other men who wanted them dead. Someone had almost killed him less than twenty-four hours ago. Twenty-four hours from now, someone might try to kill him again.

Yeah, Gabe Jones's world was comprised of bullets and bad guys, sleeping with one eye open and guns—or in Gabe's case his Butterfly—under his pillows. No doubt, he'd completely lost touch with the concept of baseball, mom, and apple pie.

Men like Gabe—operatives of whatever kind—had been undercover so long and deep that the lines between good and evil had blurred, bled, and washed away like blood on a rain-soaked street.

Jenna didn't need to know details to understand that Gabe and his kind were loose cannons, rogues who played by their own rules and damn the consequences, skirting around the dark fringes of international law. They were shadow warriors who played dangerous games. Instead of betting on sports or horse races, they bet on their lives. And not for one minute did Jenna believe that Jones wasn't just a *bad* risk, he was the biggest single risk she had ever thought about taking.

And the real kicker? He could give a rip that she was even here.

It was late afternoon by the time Gabe woke up again. He was alone this time. No Juliana. No Jenna. Which was fine with him. One would mother him to death; the other would smother him with a pillow if she got the chance.

At least she would if she knew what was good for her.

Weakness slogged through his blood like hot tar. The drag on his strength pissed him off.

"Enough of this shit."

More cautiously than on his earlier attempt, he sat up. When his head stopped spinning, he eased his legs over the side of the bed. When the room righted itself one more time he decided to chance standing. He couldn't lie around forever.

"Fuck me," he ground out between clenched teeth when he tested his bandaged leg and felt the burn clean to the bone.

Mad as hell, he sat back down, ignored the throbbing in his head, and worked on a plan of action.

If he asked for crutches, Juliana would just smile and say, "Maybe tomorrow. We'll see."

Been here. Done this.

He dragged a hand over his hair, stopped to explore the bump on his head. Winced, cursed again. Then his stomach growled.

Food. That was his problem; he needed protein. Something to shore him up. There on the nightstand by the bed was a tray filled with fruit, cheese, and crackers.

"Ask and ye shall receive."

Juliana thought of everything. Everything except the fact that every minute he spent in her home was a minute that might place her in danger.

People who spent any time around him tended to end up casualties. He wouldn't take that chance with Juliana.

He took a cautious bite of cheese, then a long swallow of the milk she'd set in a silver ice bucket. He knew how messed up he really was when he was glad it was milk, not beer. When both stayed down, he dug into the rest of it.

Then ignoring the knife-like pain in leg, he jerked the sheet off the bed, knotted it around his hips, and started searching the room for his clothes.

He was getting out of here. Bad things tended to happen to good people if he hung around too long.

"Going somewhere?"

Jenna.

He hadn't heard her open the door. Which meant he was in worse shape than he'd thought.

"That's the plan."

He didn't bother looking over his shoulder as he limped over to a bureau and opened the top drawer. Jackpot. Clean pants, shirts, skivvies.

He dropped the sheet. Let her look. He didn't have time for games.

Not bothering with the shorts, he snagged a clean pair of cammo cargo pants off the top of the stack.

"You're insane."

"And you're staring," he said, putting as much smugness into his voice as he could manage. Then he sat his bare ass down on the closest chair before he fell over.

"Yeah, I tend to do that when I see something really incredible."

He grunted and worked his bad leg into the pants. "Not the most original come-on I've ever heard."

"Get over yourself. I was referring to your incredible stupidity."

"Sure you were."

He swore through gritted teeth after an unsuccessful attempt to breach the other pant leg. "Help me get into these."

"And why would I would want to do that?"

He heaved out a serrated breath, far too aware of the sweat breaking out on his brow, more than torqued at the light-headedness that came and went. All the while trying to distance himself from the memory of her hands on his face when she'd shaved him.

He was *not* going back there. That's why he kept goading her. It was just better all the way around if she was pissed at him.

"You would want to do that because every minute we spend here puts Juliana in danger."

That got her attention. It also shut her up. For all of ten seconds.

"It doesn't change the fact that you're in no condition to travel."

"That's why you're going to help me."

He'd thought it through. If he'd had any options at all, he'd have used them, but he'd come up empty. He had to take her with him. Jenna McMillan attracted trouble the way honey attracted flies. He couldn't risk leaving her with Juliana and exposing her to the potential danger, too.

Not that Jenna would willingly stay put. She'd find her own transport back to Buenos Aires with or without him, and since he was about ninety percent certain she wasn't safe on her own, that left one solution. She went with him. As soon as they got back to the city, he was putting her on a plane for the States, where she'd be out of the middle of whatever was happening with Emilio Maxim.

End of *that* story.

"Surely another day, maybe two—"

"Not another hour," he said, cutting her off. "Not another minute more than necessary. Help me find my phone. It's gotta be in here somewhere."

She stood where she was in the doorway, her expression a cross between rebellion and concern.

"Help me find my phone," he repeated more forcefully, sweating like a boxer in the tenth round as he finally managed to get into his own damn pants. "We're leaving. It's not up for a vote."

She didn't flounce, exactly, but she didn't exactly march to his drumbeat, either. To her credit, however, she did understand. He was determined to go.

So, reluctantly, she searched, and finally found his phone, along with his watch and his Butterfly tucked in the night table beside his bed.

He pretended that his hand wasn't shaking as he strapped the watch on his wrist and the knife on his hip, and flipped open the untraceable cell phone. "Find me some crutches," he ordered after dialing Sam Lang's cell.

She cut him a lethal "you're not the boss of me" glare before she flounced—yeah, she did flounce this time—out the door.

8

Sam picked up on the second ring. "Yo."

"Come up with anything on the shooter or the car bomb?" Gabe asked, not bothering with small talk, which was the way both he and Sam liked it.

"Still shaking the bushes. It all points to the Alliance staging an attack on Maxim, but we'll know more soon."

"Shooters and a bomb. Reeks of overkill to me."

"One could have been a diversion."

"Yeah, that's what I've been thinking. But something isn't ringing true."

"So where does Jenna McMillan fit into all of this?"

Gabe grunted. "According to her, she doesn't."

"And according to you?"

"According to my *gut*, she's in the thick of it. But she's not talking."

"So what happens next?"

"Depends. Where's Maxim?"

"For the time being, Nate sicced Savage and Green on him. They've got him under lock and key at the Alvear Palace Hotel. Played the protection card, fulfilling the contract, whatever BS they could come up with to keep him under wraps. He's enjoying playing the part of the irate client while the Senate committee arranges for another time to meet with him at a less public venue."

"Which is what we suggested in the first place."

"Customer's always right," Sam said in his usual deadpan delivery. "Or in this case maybe the customer had ulterior motives?"

Gabe had been playing with that notion, too. Maxim was a target, yet he insisted on a public showing at the Congress. "Too many red flags popping up. Dig a little deeper into his connection with Husin."

"Already on it. So . . . how's the leg?"

"Leg's fine. I need you to come and get me."

"Doc Flores give you your walking papers?" Sam asked.

"Just come and get me."

Sam hesitated. "Where?" he said, finally.

Gabe rattled off the coordinates for a rendezvous point a few miles away from Juliana's villa. It was one they'd used for a meet on past ops.

"Just you?"

Would that it were. "There'll be two."

"Roger that," Sam said, no more questions asked. "See you in three."

Gabe disconnected, drew a bracing breath to steady himself, cursed the light-headedness again, then dialed a second number.

"We on a secure line?" he asked when a second man answered.

"Always. Problem?"

"Not sure. Keep a little closer watch on Juliana for a few days, okay?" Gabe didn't have to explain how he'd ended up at Bahia Blanca. The man knew. Just like he knew when Gabe had arrived and the condition he was in.

"When are you leaving?"

"Now."

Gabe disconnected.

He grabbed a black T-shirt and limped back to the bed where he waited for the storm.

Five minutes later, he heard the click of the latch, felt the breeze when the bedroom door swung open wide. When he looked up, Juliana stood in the doorway, fists propped on her hips. Jenna stood by her side.

One looked like a nun about to deliver the gospel. The other looked as smug and self-righteous as a judge.

Hell, just give him a firing squad.

"You are so predictable." He smirked at Jenna. He'd known she would go straight to Juliana and tattle like a third grader.

She crossed her arms over her breasts, triumphant. "Better predictable than stupid."

Which she clearly thought he was. He switched his attention to Juliana. "Okay. Let's hear from you, too, and get this over with."

"Get the ridiculous notion that you are leaving out of your head, Gabriel. As your doctor, I forbid it."

"Duly noted. Did you bring crutches?"

Juliana pursed her lips and gave him a "you are hopeless" look.

"This is unnecessary and unwise," she pleaded in one final attempt to stop him, yet the look on her face told him she'd resigned herself to the idea that he was leaving.

"Unwise, maybe. Unnecessary? Hardly. You know I can't be found here."

"And why, exactly, is that?" Jenna piped up. She followed a worried Juliana into the room, the requested crutches in hand.

Gabe met Juliana's eyes. They exchanged a closed look.

"Let's just say we don't want to tarnish Juliana's image," he said, unwilling to share more.

"By being seen with you?" Jenna concluded.

"By being seen with *you*," he said because he knew it would get a rise out of her.

"Oh, gosh. Was that a joke?" Jenna shoved the crutches at his chest. "I'd laugh, really I would, if it was even remotely funny."

He stood, still pissed that he was so unsteady, and slipped a crutch under each armpit. Then he headed toward the door.

"Pretty familiar with those," Jenna said, her statement leading.

He stumped his way toward the main hall. "Comes with the territory." He paused long enough to glance over his shoulder and see her still standing there defiantly. "Most riki-tic, Lois. We're on a tight schedule."

"I'm not Lois Lane and you are neither Superman nor Clark Kent," she fired back. "It's crazy for you to go anywhere in this condition, and if you had the sense God gave a rock, you'd stay put."

Gabe stopped in his tracks. "Did you just compare me to a rock?"

She snorted. "I have the utmost respect for rocks. They're hard, they're heavy. They make good paperweights."

He heaved a weary breath. "Here we go. I'll tell you one thing. I have not missed that mouth. And I don't have the energy to deal with your attitude. Is there even a remote chance that we can put it in cold storage for the duration?"

She leveled him a look.

No. He hadn't thought so.

He turned to Juliana, his expression softening. "Thank you. Again."

Juliana's eyes misted over as she went to him. "You shouldn't be up yet with that concussion. And you must be so careful of your leg, Gabriel. The risk of infection is still great. You must not do anything to tear the stitches." She tucked a bottle of what he suspected were antibiotics in his pocket. She knew he would never willingly take painkillers.

"I'll be fine. The leg will be fine." Balancing on one crutch, he drew her against him in an awkward, one-arm hug.

She clung to him, moisture from her eyes dampening his shoulder.

"I'll be fine," he repeated, kissed the top of her head, and gently set her away.

"Go with God, Gabriel. Always go with God."

She always told him that even though she knew that he and God weren't exactly on speaking terms.

Then she did the damnedest thing. Juliana turned to Jenna and hugged her as well.

"Take care of him," she said softly but with those four small words, said so much more.

Gabe felt a knot clog his throat. Felt a wave of longing and sadness and utter misery wash over him—along with a shocking and profound realization. The last person Juliana had trusted to take care of him had been Angelina. He couldn't imagine why, but it seemed that Juliana had just passed the torch to Jenna.

The constants in Argentina were many, Jenna had discovered. The country was big. It was beautiful. This time of year, in this particular place, it was hot, even this late in the day.

Wearing a tan sleeveless cargo shirt and knee pants that Juliana had loaned her along with a pair of sandals, Jenna had reached the delicately dewy stage over an hour ago. Outdistancing her with a concussion and on crutches, no less, Gabe had finally slowed his pace.

"I spotted several cars in the garage," she'd pointed out when they'd first set out on foot, over the river and through the woods where she was fairly certain Grandma's house was not on the itinerary.

"It's better this way."

Better for who? she'd wondered then figured it out. *Better for Juliana.* He didn't want anyone to trace them to her, which precluded using one of her vehicles on the off chance they'd be spotted.

When they'd broken out of the woods they'd reached a narrow dirt road. Gabe had checked his watch—a complex contraption that Jenna suspected not only told time but calculated quantum physics *and* held the answers to global warming. Then he'd glanced at a sky so clear and blue it was blinding before he started stumping north.

Jenna was certain they'd walked a couple of miles before he veered off the road and headed for the shade of a jacaranda tree, its branches heavy with thousands of stunning ultraviolet blooms. He leaned against the finely scaled brown bark of the thick tree trunk.

"What?" Jenna dragged the back of her hand over her sweat- and dust-streaked brow as a slow shower of lavender-blue flowers fluttered to the ground at her feet. "Surely we're not stopping. I haven't collapsed yet—though you look like you could any second—and we've only been in the heat for, oh, gee"—she checked her own watch, a plain, serviceable watch that told the time and nothing but the time—"an eternity."

In truth, it had only been a couple of hours since they'd left Juliana's villa via a carefully camouflaged rear exit opening into a glade of trees that had eventually led them to this little-traveled road. And Jenna was more concerned about Jones than she was grumpy about the dust and the heat and the blister on her little toe.

His color wasn't good. Except for the bruising on his forehead that was quickly turning shades of red, blue, and purple, his face was pale. Though he'd done his damnedest to cover them, she'd seen more than one grimace of pain tighten his mouth.

Damn fool man.

He remained standing as she plopped down on the summer brittle grass and fallen blossoms beside his feet, peeled off her left sandal, and brushed sand from her sore pinky toe. The air smelled of dust and honey and bitterness at the same time.

"So tell me." She squinted up at him. "Have you always had a death wish or is this a recent development?"

He grunted by way of answering and offered her the small canteen of water Juliana had insisted they could not leave without.

Because Jenna knew he wouldn't drink before she did, she lifted it to her mouth, savored the warm liquid as it dried her parched throat. Only then did he drink.

Because of what Juliana had told her about Gabe and Angelina, Jenna kept her grumbling to a minimum.

Dead. The woman he had loved was dead.

The sun sank a little lower on the western horizon. Best guess, it would be dark in an hour, probably less.

Gabe inched down to sit beside her, his actions stiff and weary, yet he uttered no complaint as he coupled the crutches and laid them next to him on the grass.

Then he just sat, absently kneading the thigh of his bandaged leg. She didn't think he was even aware he was doing it. His eyes were closed, his expression an impenetrable mask covering his emotions and his pain. He was intentionally placing distance between them with his silence.

"So . . . now what?" She picked up one of the many violet blossoms scattered on the ground around them. When she held it to her nose, she realized where both the honey and bittersweet scents were coming from.

"Now we wait."

To help cool herself off, Jenna twisted her hair into a knot. Digging a hair clip out of a breast pocket—also compliments of Juliana since all of Jenna's things were in a hotel room back in Buenos Aires—she pinned the mass of hair on top of her head. Then, because there were so many and because they were there, she tucked a flower above her ear.

"Now we wait for what?" She used a tissue to wipe the dampness from her brow and the back of her neck before unbuttoning the top two buttons on her shirt and reaching inside to swipe at the perspiration trickling between her breasts.

When Gabe didn't immediately respond, she glanced over at him. He was staring at her like he'd never seen her before. Or like he wanted to see a whole lot more of her.

Like he'd looked at her in the bedroom when she'd shaved him.

Only then did she realize the provocative picture she made: her hair up off her neck, curls tumbling around her face; her shirt unbuttoned; a flower above her right ear.

Swallowing hard, she withdrew her hand from inside her shirt and self-consciously redid the buttons. Just as self-consciously, she reached for the flower, removed it, and tossed it to the ground.

"Our ride," he said, leaning forward to pick up her discarded flower. He studied it solemnly then twirled it between his fingers. "We wait for our ride." His voice was gruff.

Fatigue, Jenna told herself. The gruffness was just fatigue and pain. He was hurting.

So why did her heart decide to do a little tap dance? And why did a shock of awareness shoot from her breast to her belly as she watched those strong, rough fingers handle the delicate bloom?

Because she wondered what it would feel like to have him handle *her* that way. And because there was more to his look than anger. It was sexual, and it was strong.

Interesting since he's made it pretty clear that he hates my guts. Or does he just hate the idea of being attracted to me? she wondered, thinking of Angelina.

By Jenna's calculations it had been almost two years since Angelina had died. Enough time for him to have grieved, right?

Yeah, well, who was she to say how much time was enough, especially when Gabe blamed himself for Angelina's death.

A light breeze lifted the wispy hair curling around her face, cooling the perspiration beading her skin. She turned her face up to the sky. The jacaranda provided a skimpy amount of shade, doing little to protect them from the sun as the flowers continued to drift down around them.

Try as she might to just let things alone, she knew she couldn't. She wanted to ask him a million questions, and none of them had anything to do with her reporter gene. This was personal. So personal she didn't even know where to begin for fear that he'd cut her off before she got started.

Time dragged on as she sat there wondering how to begin. Dusk became a real possibility.

And Jenna was suddenly weary of her cowardice.

Who is Gabe Jones? She'd asked that of Juliana, who had told her she needed to ask him. She wasn't going to get a better shot at it than this. No bad guys to distract him. No bullets to dodge. No buddies to intervene.

Big gulp. Deep breath. Dive in.

But first things first.

"I don't suppose you'd be willing to fill me in on who you suspect was behind the bombing."

He cut her a "get real" look.

"Didn't think so."

She waited for all of a heartbeat.

"So, tell me something else then. How did you end up down here? I mean . . . what's a nice Anglo-Saxon boy like you doing in a place like this?"

At first she thought he was going to ignore her. After a long moment, he turned his head to look at her, his dark eyes unreadable. Slanting sunlight bounced through the rustling jacaranda leaves, flickered along his jaw, dappled the tan skin at his throat. And her heart did a little more dancing. A tango this time.

"Wondered how long it would take for you to dig out your reporter's hat." More resignation than anger colored his words.

She'd expected resistance. He had a right to be wary. She made her living as a journalist. But this had nothing to do with any story.

"This is off the record. Person to person, okay? Who are you? What *are* you doing down here? And why is Juliana in danger just being around you?"

9

Again, Gabe remained silent. Again, Jenna watched the play of fading sunlight on his skin and thought, holy, holy God, even with the bruise on his temple and his rapidly developing black eye, what a beautiful, imposing, infuriating man he was.

"Seems to me," he said slowly, "that *I* still have a question hanging fire. You haven't leveled with me about why you're here."

He was calling her bluff. And this was not the hill to die on, especially since he was actually talking.

"Fair enough," she agreed. "You were right. I'm not here on vacation."

"Gosh, really?"

She chose to ignore his sarcasm. "I'm here on assignment."

He rolled his eyes. "Let me guess. On Emilio Maxim."

"Yeah. On Maxim. What's the big deal?" she returned defensively.

"The big deal is you barely survived a bombing because of Maxim." He narrowed his eyes. "Most reasonable people would consider that a very big deal."

"Well, I consider it a really big story."

He shook his head. "You're not seriously thinking of taking him on."

It wasn't a question. It was a warning. "He's news."

"In Argentina he's not exactly a popular guy."

"The bomb kind of clued me in on that. Ready to share your thoughts on that front yet?"

"You need to back away from this one, Jenna."

"Yeah, that's going to happen. As soon as I get back to Buenos Aires I'm working up a story on the bombing and firing it off to my editor. You could make it a lot easier for me by telling me what you know."

He shook his head. "You need to back away."

Stalemate.

Fine. He wanted to play hardball? So could she. "Like I needed to back away from Edward Walker?"

He didn't say anything. He didn't have to. Jenna knew he was thinking the same thing she was. Together with Dallas and Amy, they'd destroyed Edward Walker's and Erich Adler's house of horrors, ending a world of suffering. They'd foiled an Aryan plot to turn the jihadists against the democracies of the world—as if they needed another excuse.

Gabe had wanted her to back away then, too. Because she hadn't, the world was a better place.

"Look. Maxim is news, okay?" she said. "The bombing at the Congress is news. Exactly the kind of news I was sent down here to cover."

She wasn't backing away now. It had taken too much soul-searching and self-examination to get here. She needed this story for herself more than anything else.

He must have seen the determination in her eyes. Either that, or he decided now wasn't the time to argue about it. "So Maxim's the *only* reason you're here?"

Something about his tone made her wonder: Was it possible he hoped she'd come here looking for him?

Okay, that would fall under "delusional."

And it *would be* purely delusional to believe or even hope that he might actually be glad to see her.

So, no. Ditch that little fantasy. Wasn't going to happen.

In the meantime, he was still waiting for an answer. What the hell. She had nothing to lose by tossing out another bone for him to thicken the stew. "I was also thinking of doing a piece on Juliana."

She hadn't come down here with anything but Maxim and, yeah, Gabe in mind, but the more she learned about Juliana, the more intrigued she was by her.

His eyes sharpened like the blade of his Butterfly. Whoa. Clearly *that* idea didn't set well.

"She's an amazing woman," Jenna said defensively. "A piece on Juliana would make a great human interest story. Her free clinic. The Angelina Foundation."

His muscles visibly tightened when she mentioned Angelina's name. He averted his attention to the small bloom he still held in his big hand. The contrasts were stunning. The fragile, beautiful flower; his rough, hard hands.

Jenna thought of the portrait of Angelina at the villa. Like her mother, she'd been a striking, exotic woman.

A fragile, beautiful flower.

"Juliana told me about her," Jenna ventured softly, going for broke this time. "About Angelina and how she died."

He didn't flinch, exactly. But he did stiffen, closing himself off. And in that moment, Jenna was hit with a blistering moment of clarity. It had taken nine months and this exact moment but it finally came together.

"Your mission to take out MC6," she speculated aloud, as her thoughts gelled like epoxy. "I thought then that you were working on behalf of the government, or for a private agency."

His jaw clenched. His eyes grew hollow and dark.

"Either way, it was personal, too, wasn't it? You'd been going after Adler on your own. You were on a revenge quest."

He didn't have to confirm her speculation. She knew now why he was so upset with her interference.

"I'm sorry that I almost messed things up. I am truly, truly sorry."

If silence had been a ship it would have been a freighter; a monster that displaced an ocean of water like the quiet displaced the air around them. And regardless of the "back off" signs she read in his eyes, she couldn't stop herself.

"Do you . . . do you want to talk about it? About her?"

His breathing was fathoms deep, his jaw granite hard as he stared into the distance.

Jenna thought then that she might have gone too far. Her question had cut too deep. She figured that whatever hope she'd had that he might open up to her had faded like the daylight dissolving into a lavender-gray dusk.

Disheartened, she sat in the sweltering heat and hazy light for what seemed like an eternity. Finally she reached for her sandal. Took her time putting it on. Many minutes passed before he shifted, looked away from the distant horizon to her face.

"The name is Jones. Gabriel Paul Jones. Named after my grandfather on my mother's side I'm told."

Jenna blinked at him. So, she guessed that was a no, he didn't want to talk about Angelina. Didn't want to talk about her so badly that he was willing to talk about himself.

Who the hell are you? What are you doing down here?

He was answering her original questions. Okay. As trade-offs went, this was more than acceptable. She held her breath and waited, afraid that if she said anything, she'd break the spell and he'd realize he was giving her what she wanted.

"And a nice Anglo-Saxon boy like me is down here saving the world from bad people," he continued, then apparently felt compelled to point out, "for a lot of money. A *lot* of money," he restated for emphasis. "So don't get any notions in your head that I'm doing it for the greater good."

Oh, no, she thought. We wouldn't want anyone to think there might be a heart lurking beneath all that mean. *Give me a break.*

And, well, damn and bingo! He'd just told her something else without actually telling her. She'd been right. "A lot of money" implied private contractor, not government. Of course he wasn't going to just come out and announce it. Just like he wasn't going to announce what he'd been doing at the National Congress the day of the bombing.

You need to back away from this one.

Gabe kept coming back to that just like all roads seemed to be leading back to Emilio Maxim. Most of what had happened after she'd stepped out of the Congress building looking for Maxim was a blur. But ever since the bombing, she'd been trying to puzzle it all out in her mind. Gabe sure wasn't going to fill in any blanks for her.

A thought kept goading her. Maybe Gabe and the boys had been responsible for setting the bomb. Honestly, though, that didn't compute. It was too public a place. Too great a chance for collateral damage.

Then there was also the issue of motive. What reason would they have to kill Maxim? Plus, if Gabe had wanted Maxim gone, he'd be gone. There wouldn't have been a botched bomb attempt. There wouldn't have been a public takedown, either. It would have been fast and quiet and done.

That left another more plausible possibility. Gabe and the boys could have been providing protection for Maxim. It was an interesting option to contemplate, and could explain the "lot of money" part.

"You didn't used to make a lot of money," she said, knowing it would be pointless to quiz him again about Maxim. "Not in the military. Not even in the CIA."

Yeah, she'd done some digging during the past several months. Other than the basics and what her friends Dallas and Amy Garrett had surmised, however, Jenna had pretty much come up with zip on Jones. She knew that he'd been army once. Spec Ops. Then CIA. That was the end of the info train.

With so many dead ends and locked doors, she'd started to think maybe he was still CIA. The "lot of money" part said otherwise.

If he *was* doing private contract work it explained a lot. He was probably running covert ops for someone with big dollars who played for big stakes. It explained why he had access to an arsenal and the ability to mobilize on short notice when they'd moved in on the MC6 compound, and why it appeared he didn't play by any recognized set of rules. Just like his buddies Sam Lang and Johnny Duane Reed didn't play by any rules.

Bad boys all. To the bone bad. Especially Jones. They'd be up for those kinds of jobs. Private jobs. Government contract jobs. Jobs even the U.S. military wouldn't touch.

It would also explain why she'd pretty much come up empty in the background department. They didn't call them Shadow Warriors for nothing. These guys worked off the grid. Way off.s

"So you *have* been checking me out." There was no rancor, not even a hint of surprise in his tone, just weary acceptance.

"You didn't honestly think that I wouldn't. Don't worry. It's not like I found much of anything."

"Ship at sail leaves no trail."

"Yeah, and neither do men who don't want to be found."

He grunted, and for about a nanosecond there he almost smiled. Almost. Sometimes, almost was enough.

"To address your comment about the military, yeah," he went on, surprising her again with his openness, "once upon a time it wasn't about money. It was about democracy, God and country. So sue me."

She was dumbfounded by his tone. "You feel the need to apologize for that?"

He lifted a shoulder, tossed the wilting flower onto the grass at his feet. "I was young. Stupid. I believed all the patriotic bullshit."

"But not anymore?" He couldn't miss the challenge in her voice. She didn't believe for one minute that he wasn't still a patriot, and she let him know it. Didn't believe that in a showdown between good and evil he would be on any side but good.

The fact that she had nothing but her gut instincts to go on didn't sway her. The role he played of the rat bastard mercenary didn't cut it, either. No man who had laid his life on the line as many times as a Spec Ops soldier forgot what had brought him to the dance.

He diverted his gaze to some distant spot in the thickening darkness again. Jenna wondered what he saw there, then figured she knew when the next words came out of his mouth.

"You bury enough brothers and mothers' sons and eventually you realize what it's really about. It's about greed and stupidity. It's about loss. It's about the expendable doing the shit jobs for the power mongers."

He was angry, jaded. He had every right to be. She could imagine the horrors he must have seen. The maimed and torn bodies, the blood, the lifeless eyes. She'd been in the trenches; not as a warrior but covering her share of wars. So yeah, she understood. But she didn't buy for a moment that he was as coldly calculating as he wanted her to think.

"Speaking of mother's sons," she said gently, "yours must worry about you."

Not exactly subtle. It was effective, however, because it made him smile. Not a pretty smile. Not even an amused smile. More of a cynical, world-weary one. And even before he spoke, it was his smile that made her sad.

"Not so much. No."

She searched his profile, understanding that the wounds on his body weren't his only ones. Some of the deeper scars didn't show.

She should let him alone now, but she couldn't stop herself from prodding. Not now that he was sharing something she suspected he rarely shared—a little piece of himself.

"What about your father? He must be proud of your military service."

No reaction but that cheerless, sardonic smile that seemed frozen on his face.

"What about you?" he asked abruptly, turning the attention away from himself as surely as if he'd slammed a door. "No, wait. Let me guess. Loving parents. Birthday parties. Holiday gatherings around the tree, stockings hung by the chimney with care. How close am I?"

She considered using his tactic and steering the conversation back to him but dismissed it. She figured she'd pushed him as far as he was willing to be pushed.

And while she felt his loss for all he'd apparently never had and didn't want to talk about, she refused to feel guilty about having grown up in a loving home.

"A regular Kodak moment–type of family, yeah."

He eyed her, not unkindly for a change. "Midwest, I'm guessing."

Resigned to the new course of their conversation, she drew her knees to her chest, linked her arms around them, and breathed in the welcome cool air of the coming night. "Small town, Wyoming. A cattle ranch, actually."

One corner of his mouth turned up in the closest thing she'd seen to a real smile. It was devastating—and she had the bumpy heartbeat to prove it.

"So you're what, like, a cowgirl?"

She laughed. "Thought I wanted to be once upon a time."

His eyes narrowed in speculation. "Bet you looked real cute in a little cowgirl outfit."

She felt too much warmth over the notion that he thought she might have been cute. That he'd even ventured to imagine what she'd looked like as a child—and yes, she did have a cowgirl outfit.

"Cute enough to be on the Christmas card when I was ten," she said, laughing at the memory.

It was hard to tell in the fading light, but she could have sworn his expression held a trace of whimsy. Could have knocked her over with a feather to see that degree of softness in his eyes.

"Must have been nice. To be a Christmas card."

Yeah. It had been nice. It implied parental love and pride, the whole ball of wax. Which is what her family had always given her. Which, apparently, his hadn't given him.

"Don't you sometimes wish you had a family? A nice wife, two point five kids, a dog, and your own Christmas card with a picture of the whole shebang?"

He grunted. "Yeah. That's not gonna happen."

You're going to make certain of it, aren't you, tough guy? You're going to make certain that you're never again going to hold yourself open to that kind of love. That way you can avoid the possibility of that kind of loss.

It made her angry at him and for him at the same time. Maybe even a little angry on her own account because it cut her out of the picture, too.

How stupid was that?

Face it, Jenna. Even if Gabriel Paul Jones decided he wanted to go civilian, even if he decided he wanted to do it with her—both colossal ifs—what made her think she was capable of handling the baggage he'd surely bring along for the trip? What made her think she even wanted to?

Get a grip, McMillan. She was tired, she was a little worried; she'd been through a bombing, for Pete's sake. So, yeah, she had a right to indulge in a little addled thinking. Now it was time to get grounded. It was one thing to come down here and find him. One thing to fantasize about taming the wounded beast. But for real? Was she seriously thinking she wanted a future with this man? This man who had not yet shown any true emotion toward her but acrimony?

She turned her head, lowered her face into the cradle of her arms, and answered each question with a resigned yes, yes, and yes.

Oh, God. She was in a world of trouble.

Jenna lifted her head after a long moment, still struggling to deal with the truth of her feelings. "So . . . you're going to, what? Spend the rest of your days dodging bullets and chasing bad guys?"

"For a lot of money," he reminded her.

Now *that* pissed her off. No one should place such little value on his own life. "Hard to spend it if you're dead."

He pushed out a grunt. "There is that."

Damn him and his cavalier attitude. "You really don't want more?"

He breathed deep. "Not anymore."

Not since Angelina died. Unspoken but oh, so clear.

He'd stopped wanting then.

Jenna had never loved that deeply. Never lost that much. She'd always been the one to walk away from a relationship, which made it all that much more difficult to figure out why she wasn't walking now. Hell, she should be running and screaming bloody murder at the top of her lungs every step of the way.

Not smart enough to do either, she pressed. "Don't you ever feel the need for something more?"

She didn't think he was even aware that he'd moved his hand to his Butterfly, touched his fingers to the hilt. "I've got all I need. As to wanting . . . what's the point?"

Okay. Now she was *royally* ticked. The point, she wanted to tell him, was that there was more, so much more. His life and his dreams hadn't ended when Angelina died. If he'd just once look past his grief and anger, he might even find something or someone to share that Christmas card with. Who knows. Maybe that someone was right under his freaking nose.

She didn't tell him that. For one thing, was she crazy? Just because they'd exchanged one semi-personal conversation didn't mean she knew the man. How could she presume to know what was good for him?

For another, he scared her.

Not physically. For all of his big-bad-wolf huffing and puffing, she knew he'd never hurt her physically. What scared her were all the things she knew and all the things she didn't know that had brought him to this place where his own life had come to mean so little to him.

She'd never felt this way about a man before. She didn't know what emotion to attach to the storm of feelings he raised in her. He made her angry, he made her sad, he made her frustrated. And confused. He rattled her, damn it. She *never* got rattled over a man.

But what really terrified her was that he made her think of him. Always. In all ways. She wanted in his bed. She wanted in his head. She . . . wanted.

That was the bottom line. She *wanted*. He'd made her want. Made her achy with it.

And he didn't want anything from her but to be left alone.

Tears stung her eyes, for all he wouldn't give. For all he couldn't give.

"Get a grip," she muttered under her breath.

A small silver speck popped onto the horizon moments later and slowly revealed itself as a twin-engine Cessna lining up for a landing on the dirt road they'd walked to get here.

Their ride.

In silence, she stood, brushed off her butt, then got the surprise of her life when Gabriel Paul Jones took the hand she offered and he let her help him to his feet.

"About Juliana."

Of course, Juliana. She was the one person who could penetrate the stone wall guarding his emotions and make this hard, hard man go all soft-eyed and easy edges.

"No story, okay?" He picked up his crutches, leaned on them heavily. "If you have any regard for her at all—and you should have a boatload—just forget about writing a story."

He didn't wait for her to respond. Instead, he squinted into what was now a pearl-black sky and watched the lights on the little plane as it landed, then taxied to a stop. He bent down, plucked another blossom from the ground.

Her heart picked up an extra beat when he turned to her, lifted his hand, and tucked the flower above her ear.

His palm was warm as it lingered on her cheek, a light caress as he searched her eyes for the longest moment. She waited for him to say something, to do something, like kiss her. For an instant ripe with anticipation and longing, she thought he would.

In the end, he dropped his hand, turned, and limped slowly, and she suspected painfully, toward the plane.

Jenna quietly followed, wishing she had the guts to call him out. Call him a coward. Call him a fraud. Call him everything but a son of God for turning her head and her heart and her life inside out then dumping her upside down.

Instead, she cursed herself, desperately afraid that she might be falling for a man who kept more secrets than a priest in a confessional.

10

When Sam shoved open the cockpit door, Jenna just shook her head.

"We've got to stop meeting like this," she shouted over the roar of the twin engines.

Gabe found it interesting that Sam grinned like he was glad to see her before he turned to him.

"I'd ask how it's going," Sam said as he stowed the crutches Gabe handed him, "but I think I've got a pretty good idea. Hate to break this to you, man, but you look like shit."

Gabe grunted and hiked himself painfully up into the passenger seat. "Works out fine, because that was the look I was going for." Feeling surly, he waved away Sam's offer to help and maneuvered his bad leg inside by himself.

"How's he doing?" Sam asked Jenna after she'd squeezed herself into a rear seat and Sam had settled back behind the controls.

"*He's* doing just fine," Gabe preempted with a growl. "And *he's* right here so you can ask him."

"As you can see, he's got *snit* down to a fine art," Jenna informed Sam, ignoring Gabe's glower.

Sam grinned. "You gonna get all *snitty* on me too, Angel boy?"

"Up yours, Lang. Just get this bird in the air and get us the hell out of here. You can brief me when we get back."

He was anxious to know what they'd found out on the Maxim situation but no way in hell did he want Jenna in the loop. Give her an inch and she'd take a mile down a road that would lead her straight into more trouble.

"Buckle up," Sam said. "Gonna be a long ride."

Yeah, Gabe thought. *A long damn ride.*

Sitting beside Lang in the cockpit where there was no room to stretch out his gimpy leg, Gabe gritted his teeth and toughed out a cramp. When it finally passed, he wiped a shaking hand over his face. *Shaking.*

Shit. Disgusted with himself for letting the pain get such a grip on him, he glared into the ink-black sky and tallied up his shortcomings as they flew toward Buenos Aires.

He was getting soft. In the head, mostly.

Whine, whine, whine. Worse, he'd revealed way too much of himself to the redhead settled in behind him. Bits and pieces of the conversation he'd let Jenna drag him into spun through his mind.

"Speaking of mother's sons, yours must worry about you."

"Not so much. No."

Let's just light up the candles on the cake and throw a pity party, shall we? And what the hell was that stunt with the flower about?

He shifted in the seat, uncomfortable with the truth. It had been about how pretty she'd looked; how vulnerable she'd seemed in that moment with the setting sun streaking the sky with lavender and gray. It had been about the questions in her eyes as she'd watched him, wondering—as he'd wondered—if he was going to kiss her.

He was damn glad for the darkness in the cockpit. Glad that the pinpoint-sized red and green lights on the instrument panel didn't provide enough illumination to show the strain on his face and how pansy-ass weak he was. Or the profound and unexpected regret he felt because he *hadn't* kissed her.

Kissed her hard.

Kissed her deep.

Kissed her until they'd both been gasping for breath and wild to take things to the next level.

Jesus. He was too old to be thinking about playing naked games with a woman who, for all of her tough talk and bristly façade, would expect him to stick around in the morning. Yeah, she talked the talk, played the aloof card every chance she got, but a woman like her would want the whole "shebang," as she'd put it.

He didn't have any kind of Christmas card moments in him. Not at this late date. He'd been in too deep for too damn long. He'd mixed it up with the type of lowlife psychos who, say, planted bombs in cars without regard for innocent human life.

Then there was the bottom line. People around him tended to die. Horribly.

He closed his eyes, a roiling nausea gripping him as the sound of Angelina's screams drowned out the whine of the Cessna's twin engines.

She'd begged them to stop as the bastards had cut her. Prayed to the God who had forsaken her as they'd burned her.

While he had watched, tied spread eagle to a tree. Half out of his mind with fever, his voice raw from screaming at them to take him instead. Take him . . .

The Cessna hit an air pocket, bounced through the currents, and brought him back to the moment. Cold clammy sweat trickled down his spine.

No. No Christmas card moments for him.

For too long now, stone cold anger and a thirst for bad guy blood had fueled him. He'd lost too many friends, too much faith, and for the most part, he'd lost the ability to see life through anything but glasses made foggy with the film of gunpowder and red mist to ever think he could have a "normal" life. Or a noble thought.

Little Miss Reporter was nuts if she thought he still had it in him to dredge up the gung ho, God-and-country schmuck he'd been at eighteen.

No-fucking-way.

Just like there was no way he had the time or the inclination to try to figure out why Lois Lane turned him on like a strobe light. Or why he'd let her pull all that touchy-feely information about his parents out of him.

Behind him, she stirred in the dark. He didn't look back. Didn't want to see those green eyes or that red hair and her beautiful weary face. Didn't want to think about why, any other time, her kind of uninvited interest would turn him mean. Just like interference in his personal business would just plain piss him off.

Jenna McMillan was, hands down, the most interfering and infuriating woman he'd ever met. He didn't want to care about her. Hell, he didn't even like her.

And the bomb at the Congress could have blasted her to kingdom come.

Christ. He didn't want to think about what would have happened to her if he hadn't been there to shove her out of the way.

And she wanted to do a story on Emilio Maxim? A man linked to Rashman Hudin? No fuckin' way was he going to let that happen.

"Hey. You okay?"

Sam's voice was thoughtful and only loud enough for Gabe to hear.

He nodded, aware that Sam was watching him. Aware also that he might have groaned, not from pain but from an image of Jenna broken and battered and covered with her own blood.

"I'm fine," he said and closed his eyes when the slight movement of his head sent drums beating against his skull.

Soft, he thought again. It was nothing to him if Jenna was stupid enough to get herself caught in the crossfire. If he told himself that often enough, maybe he'd start to believe it. If he put his mind to it, *maybe* he'd come up with a good plan to get her the hell out of Argentina so he could get back to—how had she put it? Dodging bullets and chasing bad guys.

He didn't know why he was even thinking about her ridiculous scenario. In the first place, he no longer knew how to treat a *nice* woman. In the second place, no *nice* woman would be stupid enough to come within shouting distance of him. Not if she had a self-preservation bone in her body. Not if she didn't want to end up dead.

Like Angelina was dead. Like Juliana could end up dead if he didn't make certain to distance himself from her as much as possible. Like Jenna could end up dead if he didn't send her packing and get her off Maxim's trail.

As soon as they landed, he'd put her on a plane for the States. How was that for a plan? Short. Simple. Effective.

Tonight, he affirmed, blaming the sinking sensation assaulting his gut on another air pocket. He'd send her out of harm's way tonight. She'd be out of his hair, which is what he wanted anyway, and out of his head, where she was able to go with a little too much ease.

And she'd stay out of his bed, which, despite the fact that she was as irritating as poison ivy, is where he'd end up taking her to scratch another kind of itch.

Bahia Blanca, Villa Flores
Same night, 11:10 P.M.

Juliana was asleep. Then she was awake.

Wide awake.

Heart pounding.

Adrenaline pumping.

Breath caught so tightly in her chest it burned.

She lay statue still for several long, eerily silent moments. Listening. Her pupils adjusting to the pitch black surrounding her in the darkest part of the night. Listening and hearing nothing but the sound of her heart beating in her ears as it pumped like a piston beneath her breasts.

A dream, she decided and slowly released her breath. It was only a dream that had awakened her and left her feeling vulnerable.

Very slowly, her heart regained its normal rhythm. as she lay there.

Missing Armando.

Missing Angelina.

She closed her eyes. Pinched back tears. Still, one slipped out, slid warm down her temple and trickled into her hair.

It was times like these that she missed Armando the most. Missed waking to the warmth of his body to comfort her, his strong capable arms to surround her, his breath warm against her face as he whispered that everything was all right and for her to go back to sleep.

And it was times like these that she wondered about her true strength as a human being. She thought of all the other widows awake in the night. She wondered how they had the strength to go on.

Only when she woke like this, her heart breaking for Armando, mourning the loss of her child, did she question her reason for living.

"But this too shall pass," she whispered to no one. Because no one was there.

Experience had taught her; with the dawn of another day, she could rise and she could start all over again. In the light, she had purpose. In the light, she didn't feel so alone.

She reached for the lamp by her bed, turned it on. Defused light softly flooded the room, banishing the darkness, but not the silence. Not the absolute and profound absence of another heart beating steady and strong beside hers. Not the deep, even breaths of a man well pleased with his life's work.

She glanced at the bedside clock. Almost two a.m. There was a lot of night ahead. Yet she knew she wouldn't go back to sleep. She never did when she woke like this.

The book on her nightstand held little interest for her but rather than make her way down to the library for another, she propped her pillows behind her back, picked up the book, and opened it.

A splinter of a sound sent her heart rate soaring again. She jerked her head toward her closed bedroom door.

Downstairs?

In the hall?

A chair leg scraping over tile?

She listened for more.

Nothing.

Maybe it was the wind. Maybe she'd left a window open downstairs and it was only the rustle of curtains against shutters that disturbed her. Maybe it was just that she was edgy now that the servants had all gone home for the night and that Gabriel was gone now, too. He and Jenna had slipped out of the villa unseen earlier. Worry for him had made her edgy, perhaps. Had her hearing noises that weren't really noises in the dark.

She forced deep breaths to steady herself. Thought about her work outside the clinic. She was used to visitors arriving at all hours of the night.

She was used to stealth; she was used to subterfuge. Over the years she and Armando had employed both to keep their underground railroad running. They'd transported hundreds of hollow-eyed, sick, and abused children out of harm's way. Their extended network had stolen them from the flesh peddlers and the porn lords and delivered them to safety.

Some had been sent only as far as Brazil. Others to the States. Still others as far as Europe where they might have a chance at a life that wasn't infected with the insidious profiteering from their innocence.

The free clinic and saving the children had been Armando's passion. After his death, after Angelina's death, she'd made it hers. Her child had died trying to help the children. Juliana continued to live by carrying on their work.

With Gabe's help, she had continued their covert operation—covert because it had been common knowledge for years that the flesh mongers paid off certain government officials to turn a blind eye.

Despicable. And so the need for late-night visitors.

Was it possible she'd forgotten a delivery? She stared across the room, searching her memory. No. She was sure she hadn't. And she'd received no advance call on her secure cell phone alerting her to a "package." Heard no secret knock at the protected rear entrance to her villa.

No. She was certain. She was not expecting a delivery of the fragile, human kind until next week. In fact, it had been a month since the last rescue. A month since she'd smiled reassuringly into the tragic brown eyes of a twelve-year-old boy who had looked at her with wary trust as she'd treated open wounds on his wrists and bruises on his back, all the while promising him that no one would ever hurt him again.

A thud from downstairs sent her flying out of bed.

She didn't try to talk herself out of it this time.

Someone was in the house.

Someone had breached her security system.

She reached for the slacks she'd tossed on the bench at the foot of the bed. Somehow managed to fumble her cell phone out of the pocket.

With trembling fingers, she punched in the number Gabe had insisted she commit to memory and told her to call if she ever felt threatened.

"Just call this number," he'd told her months ago. "He'll know it's you. He'll know what to do."

Clutching the phone close to her ear, she scurried back to her bedside table. Turned off the light. Moved on silent feet to her closet and the safe room hidden behind a fake wall.

"Yes," a male voice answered on the second ring.

She had no idea who was on the other end of the line. She only knew that Gabe trusted him. Clutching the phone tighter, she pushed aside her clothes and felt in the dark for the barely detectable seam in the partition.

"There's someone in my house," she whispered with strained urgency.

Less than a heartbeat of silence passed. "Are you in a safe place?"

She wedged her fingers into the seam, slid open the pocket door. Only after she'd squeezed inside the tight, dark opening and closed the panel behind her did she answer. "Y . . . yes. I think so."

"Don't move. I'll be there in five minutes."

And then she was alone again.

In the dark.

In the silence.

In the night.

With help five minutes away.

It might as well have been an eternity.

11

"Tonight? Are you crazy?" Jenna shook her head at Gabe. "I'm not flying anywhere. And I'm sure not going home."

Just as soon as she got hold of her laptop, which she'd left in her hotel room, she was going to fire off the bombing story to Hank.

He'd be over the moon, once he was convinced she was fine. Well, almost fine. Exhaustion and physical stress had done a number on her. Her adrenaline reserves had let down long ago. So had her deodorant. She had no idea what was keeping Gabe on his feet.

In the past thirty-six hours they'd survived a bombing and made a round trip from Buenos Aires to Bahia Blanca with very little sleep. Her muscles had launched into full bitch mode.

Gabe looked like hell—in a raw, twelve-hour-stubble, determined-alpha-male-on-a-mission way.

Damn him.

Jaw set, eyes hooded, he stood beside her in the elevator heading up to her hotel room. The room she hadn't seen for almost two days. A hot bath and a change of clothes would go a long way toward making her feel human again. Then she'd get to work on that story.

If Jones had his way, though, they'd grab her stuff and head for the airport in the car waiting outside with Sam at the wheel and it would be *"Hasta la vista,* baby."

Well she wasn't Linda Hamilton and he wasn't the "Governator."

Okay. Let's add food and sleep to the hot bath and clean clothes. She needed nourishment, rehydration, rest, and then maybe her mind wouldn't wander back to the nineties and *Terminator* movies that she hadn't liked then and liked even less now.

If she didn't stay focused, she'd end up in another time zone tonight, and she wasn't ready to leave this one. Besides her story, she had unfinished business with Gabriel Jones. Something about possibly falling for an enigma. A mystery man whose life expectancy, because of his chosen profession, was most likely on par with that of a day lily.

God. Wouldn't he love being compared to a flower? A giddy laugh bubbled out. The glare he shot her said it all. Jones didn't do giddy. As a rule, neither did she.

She needed food. Fast. To help get her head back on straight if nothing else.

The elevator stopped on the seventh floor. The doors slid open with a rattle and a whoosh.

"Okay," she said, stepping out into the dimly lit hallway, "I know we've already had this conversation, but it was so much fun the first time, let's do it again."

"Let's not."

"No, really. I insist. You say, 'I'm putting you on a plane back to the States.' Then I say, 'Are you crazy? I'm not leaving.' I think that brings us up to speed."

He cut her a bored look as he shouldered by her on his crutches and headed toward her room.

"Well, I never said it was a long conversation or even all that sparkling," she said to his back. "I just said it was fun. So why do I sense that you aren't enjoying yourself?"

"This is not a joke."

No. It wasn't. Just like seeing him this way wasn't funny. Knowing he gave a rat's rear leg about the prospect of her leaving him wasn't funny, either.

"Look," she said, trying another tack as she caught up with him, "thanks for walking me to my door. Sam's waiting for you in the car, and he's gotta be bushed, too, so you can both go on your merry way."

"For the last time, you need to back away from Maxim and get out of Argentina."

"Okay. Let's get something straight. In the first place, you don't tell me what to do. In the second place, I came here to do a job and I will do it. And in the third place, it's not like *I'm* being threatened here or anything. I mean, that bomb wasn't meant for me. You're not talking, but I think it's pretty safe to assume that Maxim was the target."

"Yeah, and you're just itching to get caught in the crossfire if someone goes after him again, aren't you? Damn it, Jenna. You're being stupid about this."

She stopped. Turned on him. "No, I'm being professional. I walked away from a story because of you the last time I was here. I'm not walking away from this one."

He reeled slightly. Fatigue could have been the cause, but she knew the moment she saw his face that fatigue had nothing to do with his reaction.

In that same moment she knew something else. This battle-hardened warrior, this professional soldier wasn't as immune to death and destruction as he'd like everyone to think. He struggled with the same images she did. He saw the same charred bodies, the same bloodied corpses.

He felt the same kind of horror. The only difference was she could afford the luxury of regret. He couldn't, and there was nothing she could say to make him know she understood.

Key in hand, she eased around him toward the door to her room.

"Wait!" His voice was sharp as he grabbed her wrist and kept her from inserting the key in the lock. "Let me check it first."

"Oh, for God's sake. You know what?" She was tired. Of everything. Of him thinking he could tell her what to do, of him making it clear that he didn't want or need anyone—specifically her—in his life. "You've lived too long on the 'dark side,' " she said, putting a lot of theatrical woo-woo in the last two words. "I'm tired, I'm hungry, and all I want to do is eat, shower, write my story, and go to bed."

She jerked her hand away from his, shoved the key in the lock and pushed the door open—and came face to face with three gunmen.

Before she could react, Gabe hit her from the side, tackling her to the ground as the blast of a gun echoed into the hallway.

She waited for the pain, visualized her own blood, then realized that nothing hurt. Nothing but her hip where she'd landed on the floor with Gabe on top of her—again.

She struggled to get up.

"Stay down!" he ordered. "And roll! Get the hell away from the door!" he choked out through a hacking cough.

"Wha—" *Oh God.*

A horrible odor hit her olfactory senses then and she realized why he was choking. She gagged on a mouthful of air. Her eyes started burning. Her gut convulsed into dry heaves.

Gabe gagged, too, as he half-dragged, half-pushed her back toward the elevator, where the air was blessedly fresh.

Jenna lay face down on the floor, her stomach convulsing, sucking air in huge, gulping breaths. Tears ran from her burning eyes. Her throat felt raw. Hundreds of pin-sized dots—brilliant red in a sea of black—assaulted her pupils.

She squinted toward the sound of Gabe's tortured breathing, barely able to make him out through the tears. He'd rolled to his side facing her door, using his body as a shield between her and whatever or whoever might still be in that room. He'd wedged the hilt of his Butterfly firmly between his teeth and he'd drawn a pistol she hadn't even been aware he'd been carrying. The barrel was trained on her open hotel room door.

"Cell phone," he gritted around the knife. "Pocket."

With her eyes pinched shut against the lingering burn and streaming tears, Jenna attacked his pants, searching pockets, and finally found the one with his cell phone.

Later, she'd think about the lean hips and flat gut and all that male heat she'd encountered. Right now, she was shaking too badly to even be embarrassed that she might have grabbed something that definitely wasn't his phone.

"Punch one," he ordered.

She did.

"Lang." Sam answered on the first ring.

She could take it from here. "Men with guns. In my room."

A split second of silence. "Anyone hurt?"

"I . . . I don't know. I don't think so."

"On my way up." He disconnected.

She closed the phone, lowered her head to rest against Gabe's back, right between his shoulder blades. Right where he was solid and strong and his deep breaths were proof that he was alive and that he planned to keep them both that way.

Finally she drew a breath that didn't feel like it dragged over razor blades. She braved peeking over his shoulder. A buckshot pattern, roughly the size of a softball, had shattered the top of the door.

"Where are they? And not that I'm complaining, but why aren't they still shooting at us?"

"Because they're probably long gone. Are you hurt?" Gabe asked with enough urgency that she realized he must have felt her shiver in delayed reaction to the hole in the door.

"No. No, I'm okay. What about you? Are you hurt?"

"Only if you count the fact that you damn near ripped off my plumbing groping around for my phone."

She made a sound of exasperation. "Now? You pick *now* to become a comedian?"

"It's all about timing," he whispered back.

She actually smiled. It was either that or cry.

But she almost cried too when she looked down and saw his leg. He was bleeding again.

Bahia Blanca, Villa Flores
11:17 P.M.

From her dark, cramped hidey-hole, Juliana heard footsteps on the wooden floor of her bedroom.

She hadn't thought it possible for her heart to beat any harder or faster. She thought surely that whoever was out there could hear the *slam*, *slam*, *slam* of it through the closet door.

She didn't know how long she'd been hiding. Five minutes? Five hours? Time passed like sludge, thick with the weight of her fear.

A million scenarios had crossed her mind as she'd hidden there. Once, she'd been certain she'd smelled smoke and had seen herself dying in a fiery inferno.

She'd wished, one hundred times over, that she'd listened to Gabe when he'd begged her to keep a gun by her bed. She hated guns. Now she hated her stupidity for refusing to learn how to shoot one.

The faint creak of hinges alerted her to the closet door being opened.

She stopped breathing.

"Juliana."

Almost passed out at the sound of her name.

So close.

Right outside the secret door.

Oh God.

"Juliana, it's David. David Gavin. It's safe. You can come out now."

Fear was a powerful thing. It could suspend time, garble words, delay reactions.

David Gavin?

Safe. He'd said safe. She rooted through that improbable possibility, not fully processing that it was David Gavin standing outside her closet door.

David was a tall, lean expatriate American who, for the most part, kept to himself in his small villa at the edge of the city, except for the one day a week he volunteered to help at her free clinic.

Now he was here? In her house? In her bedroom? Telling her it was safe?

"Juliana? It's all right. It's my phone number Gabe gave you."

Gabe had given her David Gavin's number?

Questions, questions. Her mind reeled with them. None of this computed. But then he repeated the emergency number digit for digit, confirming that he spoke the truth.

A small slice of relief wedged its way into the darkness, and confusion just as a small sliver of light now slipped under the hidden door. Very slowly, Juliana slid the door back an inch and saw the hulking frame of a man standing there. He'd turned on a light, and yes, she could see it was David Gavin.

But not the way she'd ever seen him.

When she thought of the man who worked efficiently and with concentrated purpose on the financial ledgers at the clinic, she thought of him as he appeared there: quiet, unassuming, unremarkable with his short black hair that was slightly gray at the temples, and unthreatening, with his wire-rimmed glasses and soft- spoken ways. When he spoke at all.

This man—*this man*—was a force. There was no other word for it. His stance was battle ready, his bearing that of a soldier. She'd known Gavin was tall, but he'd never seemed imposing. He was imposing now. His eyes—she hadn't realized before that they were blue—were granite hard. His expression, usually passive and mild, was intense, fierce even.

As he helped her slide the pocket door all the way open and gripped her hand to help her out, she felt the roughness of calluses against her fingers that dispelled any notion that the biggest thing he ever pushed was paper and the heaviest thing he ever lifted were pencils.

"Are you okay?"

His voice sounded rusty from lack of use and she realized then why she hadn't recognized it when he'd answered her call. He rarely spoke at the clinic. In fact, he moved around like a shadow, silent and unobtrusive—like a man who didn't want to make any waves or draw any attention.

Well, he had her attention now. So did the gun he held in his right hand. It was big and black, and he gripped it with the familiarity of a man accustomed to wielding heavy-duty firepower.

"Juliana?" he repeated. "It's okay now. You're safe. Do you understand?"

Only then, as his blue eyes pierced hers with concern, did she realize she'd been so busy processing and assessing this stunning new version of David Gavin that she hadn't answered him.

"I . . . yes." She found her voice at about the same time she realized she was still clinging to his strong, rough hand.

His very capable hand.

"Yes. I'm . . . I'm okay. Thank you," she added belatedly, still suspended somewhere between shock and a latent fear that wouldn't let go.

Feeling self-conscious suddenly with the contact, she drew her hand away. Smoothed it over her hair. Clasped it tight against her when she realized she was shaking. "Thank you for coming."

With a firm but gentle grip on her elbow, he drew her out into her bedroom. The light further illuminated his transition from what she'd always thought of as the shy, quiet, accountant type to a rugged and formidable protector.

"Was there . . . did you find anyone in the house?"

He hesitated a moment then shook his head. "No one was in the house when I got here, but they had been."

"But my security system—"

"Had been disabled."

"A burglar?" she suggested, at a loss.

His eyes became hooded. "Possibly."

"You don't really think so, do you?" she speculated, getting the distinct feeling he'd agreed just to mollify her.

He hesitated, then shook his head. "No. I don't think so. You'll have to check, see if anything's missing."

Yes, she would check. Tomorrow. Right now, she was too busy studying this man. Really studying this man she was accustomed to seeing in loose, long-sleeved white dress shirts and roomy, pleated pants.

Tonight he wore a short-sleeved black T-shirt and well-worn jeans. A T-shirt that showcased the honed muscles of his biceps and forearms. Jeans that hugged a lean waist and surprisingly muscular thighs.

Even more than the physical changes, Juliana was aware of an indefinable energy about him. She couldn't put her finger on it. Then it came to her.

He made her think of Gabe. Older, yes. Less brooding, true. But he possessed that same fierce intensity, that impression of absolute control, of total command of the situation, both physically and tactically.

"I'm beginning to think that you, Mr. Gavin, fall into the more-than-meets-the-eye category."

He smiled, looking hesitant and somewhat somber.

He had a dimple in his left cheek. *What an odd and frivolous thing to notice*, Juliana thought, especially considering she'd just spent the last several minutes frightened out of her mind.

"Are you steady?" he asked, regarding her with an expression that waffled somewhere between concern and evasion.

"That depends." She drew a bracing breath. "Are you really an accountant?"

The dimple appeared again, slowly and reluctantly. "When I need to be, yes."

Cryptic. She wasn't going to let him get away with it. Not while he was standing there holding that gun.

"And when you need to be something else, what else can you be?"

He considered, finally shrugged. "How about we go downstairs and you put on a pot of coffee? I'll bore you with all the possibilities."

There were a lot of reasons why she shouldn't go downstairs with this man, starting with his gun and possibly ending with her sudden, acute awareness that she was wearing only a long sheer nightgown. She felt vulnerable again, but not frightened.

He sensed her sudden discomfort, glanced around the room, and spotted her robe.

"You'll want to put this on." He handed it to her. "I'll meet you downstairs."

Then he left. Like a gentleman. Only the look she'd seen in his eyes just before he turned and walked away was far from genteel.

It had stunned her, that look.

So had her reaction to it.

She clutched the robe to her breast, stared at the empty space where he had been. For the first time since Armando's death, she felt a slight stirring of arousal.

She was horrified. Mystified.

Her nerves were raw, she thought, attempting to justify her reaction. She'd been afraid for her life. Of course she reacted to him. Quite possibly, he'd saved her just now.

And quite possibly, she thought, as she listened to his footsteps descend the stairs, this new version of David Gavin had shocked her into remembering that it was Armando who had died two years ago, not her.

Sobered by that thought and the weight of guilt that accompanied it, she walked to her closet and pulled a pair of slacks and a sweater off the rack.

If she took a little more time than necessary combing her hair, if she toyed with the idea of applying lipstick before discarding it, it didn't mean a thing other than that she felt the need to be pulled together before she faced David Gavin again.

And that little shiver of apprehension that accosted her as she descended the stairs to meet him? It was a residual reaction to the break-in.

He'd said he'd bore her with all the possibilities of what he could be but *bored* was a word that applied to the David Gavin she'd known—or thought she'd known—before tonight. Try as she might to dismiss it, she was overwhelmed by the notion that this man would never bore her again.

12

"CS? What's CS?" Jenna asked as Reed, having just delivered his opinion on what type of gas had burned their eyes, walked back over to Sam who was carefully bagging an empty shotgun shell casing he'd found on the floor.

Gabe sat on the edge of the bed pulling his bloody pant leg back down over his calf, while Sam and Johnny and Doc finished up their sweep of the room.

Traffic sounds rose from the street below into the room where the windows had been thrown open wide to clear the air. The thugs with the shotguns had used those same windows to make their escape.

Johnny and Doc—who had yammered on about how Gabe would be lucky if he didn't lose his damn leg the entire time he'd fixed butterflies across several broken stitches—had arrived within fifteen minutes of Sam. They'd made record time considering the distance from the Cantina to the hotel. Gabe had determined long before they'd stepped into the room that whoever had been waiting for Jenna was long gone.

"Stands for 0-chlorobenzalmalononitrile," Gabe said, answering Jenna's question. "It's a form of tear gas. Reed found an empty canister and traces of a white solid powder. We'll run it through the lab, but most likely they'll tell us it was mixed with a dispersal agent, like methylene chloride."

"Is it toxic?"

He understood why she would think so. CS made you want to gag, cry, and dive for a different area code. Jenna had taken a full hit from the blast. Her eyes were still red and teary—hell, his were, too. CS still wasn't as bad as Red Pill. He'd seen a guy get hit with it once and puke up the nickel he'd eaten when he was five. "No. More potent but less toxic than, say, a CN agent."

He glared at the shotgun blast pattern in the door. If he hadn't heard someone in the room, if he'd been a nanosecond later, Jenna wouldn't be sitting here looking like a lost little lamb. She'd be on the way to a hospital with half of her face blown off.

Goddamn concussion. It had stolen his edge. He'd been asleep on this one. Hell, he shouldn't have let Jenna within a mile of the hotel. Should have gone with his gut and sent a couple of the boys to pick up her stuff and have it shipped to the States for her. There was no reason in the world for her to have returned to the room other than the fact that she'd dug in her heels.

Damn stubborn woman.

All they'd really needed was her passport anyway. The fact that it was missing—the rinky-dink room safe where Jenna had stowed both the passport and her extra money hadn't been much of a challenge for whoever had staged this—begged all kinds of questions.

Without a passport, she was stuck in Argentina at least until she could get to the Consulate's office at the U.S. embassy and get a duplicate. That wasn't going to happen in the next two days because it was the weekend and all government offices were shut down until Monday.

They could forge one for her at BOI HQ, but that would take time, too, especially if she decided not to cooperate.

"Why didn't you have your passport on you, anyway?"

"I was mugged once in Brussels. Had my pocket picked in Rome," she said wearily. "Lost it both times. Each time I spent the better part of a day at the U.S. embassy waiting on paperwork. Missed two flights and two hot stories because of it. Since then, I don't risk carrying it anymore than I have to. So much for that plan."

"Other than your passport, have you come up with anything else that's missing?" he asked as Reed and Lang continued working the room, still searching for something that might tip them off as to who was responsible.

Trance-like, she stared bleakly at the wreckage around her, shook her head. The hotel room had been thoroughly trashed. Her clothes were all over the floor. "Why'd they leave the cash?"

She was referring to the stash of currency she'd left in the safe. Gabe had been wondering the same thing, and had drawn the only logical conclusion.

"Because this wasn't a robbery."

"Then what was it?"

He was quiet for too long. "I don't know."

She turned on him, fire in her eyes. "Well, why the hell don't you? You're the big bad boogie man basher!"

She caught herself, realized how out of control she was and shook her head. "I'm sorry. I didn't mean to take this out on you."

She was angry and afraid and feeling vulnerable. He got it. Now he was going to make it worse and dump a heavy dose of reality into the mix.

"This is what I do know. This wasn't a random break-in. Thieves hit then run. These guys had been camped out here." Cigarette butts ground into the carpet and fast food wrappers scattered around the room told the tale. "They were waiting for you. The only reason you're not dead or abducted is because we got lucky and they got a case of cold feet when I fired back."

She stared blankly at the open windows. Then he went in for the kill.

"Whether you like it or not, you'd better start thinking of yourself as a target," he said pointedly, because someone had to get it through her head she was exactly that.

She heaved a breath heavy with the beginnings of acceptance. "What can I say? Sometimes, because of my inquisitive nature, I get a negative reaction from people."

Always with the jokes. He'd finally figured it out. She used them as a self-defense mechanism when she felt vulnerable.

Because she looked the part, too, he softened his tone. "A door slammed in your face is a negative reaction. Shotguns and tear gas—that's taking it a hundred steps further."

She compressed her lips, looking as forlorn as a kid who'd just learned the brutal truth about Santa Claus. "So. I've got a problem."

Gabe shook his head grimly. "A teenager with acne has a problem. What you've got is an enemy. Don't ever confuse one with the other."

He nodded toward her crushed laptop. "Maybe it's as simple as Maxim doesn't want you writing a story about him."

She shook her head. "Wrong tree. The story was his idea. He asked for me specifically."

That got his radar fired up. "Maxim asked you to do a story?"

She nodded. "Well, not him specifically. Someone on his staff contacted my editor at *Newsday*. Said Maxim would only talk to me, and if I wanted an interview I was to meet up with him in Buenos Aires."

Gabe held up a hand when she would have continued. "So Maxim asked for the interview *and* asked for you specifically? That didn't seem strange to you?"

"Not really, no."

Yet Gabe could see that she was now giving the possibility some thought. "In some circles, I'm sort of a big damn deal. I even sleep in a T-shirt that says so."

God. She never quit with the wisecracks. He was more convinced than ever that Maxim might be behind this.

First there was the Maxim-Hudin connection. Add in the Hudin-MC6 connection and it started smelling of terrorist soup. Big stretch, but worth thinking about.

His cell rang. He dug it out of his pocket, flipped it open, and checked the number.

This couldn't be good.

"Jones," he answered and listened with growing anger as the man known as David Gavin in Bahia Blanca told him that security at Juliana's villa had been breached.

"Is she okay?" Relieved when the answer was yes, he filled the other man in on the episode in Buenos Aires. "Yeah, I'm thinking the same thing," he said when Hudin's name came up.

He disconnected, rose stiffly from the bed.

The hour they'd bribed out of the hotel security guard was about up. The guard would be calling this in soon, and Gabe didn't want to be anywhere near this part of the city when the local *policía* showed up to investigate or they'd be detained until dawn.

"If you want anything, get it now," he said to Jenna. She rose wearily and walked to the far side of the room to search through her ruined things.

When she was out of earshot, he motioned for Sam, Johnny, and Doc to come closer.

"That was Nate. Someone broke into Juliana's villa," he said quietly so Jenna couldn't hear him.

"You think it's connected to this?"

"Can't rule it out." He scrubbed a hand over his jaw, thinking, as he watched Jenna sift through the rubble for some clothes that hadn't been damaged. "Neither can we rule out Maxim as the source, or that Hudin might fit into the mix somewhere. This business of Maxim asking for Jenna—don't know about you, but I smell a rat the size of a walrus."

"Yeah. Reeks of a set-up. We need to dig a little deeper into Maxim's connection with Hudin," Sam agreed.

Gabe nodded. "When we get back to HQ get Mendoza on it. I've got a real bad feeling about this."

And his bad feelings rarely came to any good. MC6 was a big player in the terrorist world. If Hudin had a vendetta going against Jenna for her part in taking down the Argentina operation—and that's the only tie he could make at the moment—there wasn't a place on earth she could hide from him.

For that matter, neither could Gabe. Given the fact that he had also been at the bomb site because of the Maxim protection detail, he couldn't rule out the possibility that he was a target, too.

Until they came up with something concrete, though, he didn't want Jenna to know about the Maxim-Hudin link or about what happened at Juliana's. Jenna was close to the edge now. That little bit of info could push her right over.

And speaking of edges, he was about to step out on one.

He couldn't send Jenna packing now. Wasn't letting her out of his sight until he nailed this down.

"Let's saddle up and move out," he said, wanting to get Jenna out of the line of fire until they figured out what they were up against.

Determined not to let the defeated set of her shoulders affect him, he watched as she stuffed a pair of jeans and a T-shirt into a plastic bag along with a few toiletries and a flash drive she recovered from her computer.

A little stuffed dog lay on its side on the floor. She stared at it for a long time, then bent over and, looking every bit like a little girl seeking comfort in the form of something soft and fuzzy, she put it in her bag, too.

When she caught him watching her, he pulled a scowl.

She lifted her chin, some of that old defiance surfacing. "So sue me. I'm a girl."

He turned toward the door because damn it, if he didn't, he was going to go soft. He was going to walk over there, tuck her tangled hair behind her ears, pull her into his arms, and hold her until she forgot about boogey men with bombs and shotguns out to do her harm.

"Looks like you get your wish."

"My wish?"

"You're not going anywhere until we figure this out. Let's go," he said, fighting to keep his distance.

Up until the break-in, he'd been dealing with the possibility that Jenna *might* find herself in trouble. It had gone way beyond *might*.

Someone was after her, and if they had found her here, they'd find her in the States. That meant Gabe had to find them first.

Which also meant he was stuck with her.

And nothing—abso-fucking-lutely *nothing*—good could possibly come of that.

Nate sipped a cup of strong hot coffee, leaned back against the kitchen counter, and watched Juliana pace, as she tried to process what he'd just told her.

She was a mover. He'd noticed that the first day he'd arrived at the clinic on the pretext of volunteering. Some people reacted to shock and fear with silence, stillness. Juliana wasn't one of them.

She moved the way she worked. Fluidly. Effortlessly. With an abundance of effervescent energy. And she looked like she always looked.

Beautiful. Vibrant. Full of purpose.

Nate had fallen in love with her the moment he'd set eyes on her almost two years ago.

Love at first sight.

He still had trouble dealing with that tired old cliché. Unrequited love — there was another weary but accurate truism.

Not that he'd ever act on it. Not that she'd ever want him to. She had no idea how he felt about her. He'd see to it that she never would for a number of reasons, the primary one being that she was still in love with her dead husband. Ironically, Armando's death was the reason he'd ended up in Bahia Blanca in the first place.

"You're telling me that you're Nathan Black, not David Gavin."

"I am, yes." He was glad it was finally out in the open. "Juliana, would you mind sitting down? I feel like I'm watching a tennis match."

"And I feel like the ball."

Yeah. Nate imagined that she did, at least emotionally. He was responsible for bouncing her around. First he was Gavin, now he was Black. First he was an accountant, now he was — well, he was what he was. The head of Black Ops., Inc. Gabe's employer.

He poured another cup of coffee, carried it to a thick, butcher block–type table, and sat down. He hoped she'd follow his lead.

She was wired as tight as a sweating charge of dynamite, set to go off at a cross-eyed look. He felt bad about that. He felt bad about a lot of things. Deceiving her was at the top of the list.

"So all this time," she continued, still on the move, "when you were at the clinic. That wasn't about volunteering."

"It was, actually. At least in part."

She finally sat down, her eyes earnest as they met his across the table. "Talk about the other part."

"I think you already know about the other part."

She looked away, brows furrowed. He could see her mind working. Knew the moment she put it all together.

"You've been watching me. Since . . . since Armando and Angelina . . ."

He nodded when she let her voice trail off, apparently unable to say it. "Yes. Since then. Because Gabe asked me to. He knew you wouldn't agree to it."

And Gabe couldn't do it. Not then. He'd spent several weeks recovering from his injuries, and several more dealing with Angelina's death and his self-perceived failure to save her.

"All this time?" She shook her head, still in denial. "How could I not have known? How could I not have suspected?"

"You didn't know because I didn't want you to know. You didn't suspect because I gave you no reason to."

She appeared more perplexed than angry.

"But your business. How could you be away from it for so long? Why would you choose to?"

He wasn't about to tell her that his intention had been to stay only long enough to assure Gabe that she was safe.

But that was before he'd met Juliana Flores. That was before he'd realized that if protector was the only role he could play in her life, then he'd be satisfied with that much.

"I can run the company from anywhere, Juliana. Plus I found that I like Bahia Blanca. So I stayed."

Where he could be close to her.

He watched her process this information, indulging himself in the pleasure of just looking at her. It was something he rarely allowed himself to do. Her hair was long, wavy, the color of roasted chestnuts. Her full breasts and round hips screamed sex appeal. But it was her face that drew the eye and held it. Her complexion was the color of honey, her eyes wide and intelligent.

The whole package was a work of art. Subtle. Mature. Breathtaking.

When he realized she was staring back, he looked away, cleared his throat. "I've . . ." He hesitated then began again. "Besides running the business from here, I've helped make a few rescues possible, if it's any consolation."

Her eyes narrowed then brightened with comprehension. "My children? You've helped with my children?"

He nodded. "I have the connections. It would be criminal not to take advantage of them. You know me as the Captain, by the way."

No doubt there were many unidentified contacts that she dealt with on a regular basis. He'd shocked her again by identifying himself as one.

"A few? My God. The Captain has made over a dozen rescues happen. You made them happen."

He lifted a shoulder, discounting the gratitude in her voice.

She was still studying him as if she'd never seen him before. Finally, she shook her head. "I don't even know what to say. Thank you. For everything. Especially for coming tonight."

This was the part he'd dreaded telling her. "Yeah, about tonight. Your intruder tracked in dirt. The trail from room to room suggests he'd been systematically searching for something. Or someone."

"Gabe? You think he was after Gabe? Or . . . or Jenna?"

"The only way to find out is to ask him."

"Too bad he's probably in the next province by now."

Nate scratched his head. "Actually, no. He's here. Just hanging around outside." From a tree, as it were. About two feet off the ground. Trussed upside down like a Christmas goose, his mouth taped shut and the fear of God and many of his angels riding heavy on the soles of his feet.

It took her a moment to react. "You told me he was gone."

"No," he said with a small smile, "I told you that I didn't find anyone in the house. I caught up with him outside. He should be coming around soon if he hasn't already."

"Coming around?"

"He may have hit his head on something."

"Does he need the services of a physician?" she asked wryly.

He shook his head. "I'm thinking no, but it's probably time to check on him. Maybe he'll be in a mood to talk."

"I'll come with you."

"No," he said firmly. He didn't want her witnessing this. "Let's just leave it between us guys."

She wanted to object. The healer in her couldn't help but want to intervene. In the end, she gave him a clipped nod. "Please, don't be too long."

13

Buenos Aires
12:45 A.M.

On the hunt for her stories over the years Jenna had been squeezed into many small places with many big men. Places like Abrams tanks, armored Humvees, and Black Hawk choppers to name a few. Men like tank crews, chopper crews, and Recon Marines. Men who were veterans of fire fights, dicey night missions, and running-like-your-tail-was-on-fire retreats. They'd been fighting men, battle hardened, adrenaline charged, and war wary.

But as they drove away from the hotel, she'd never felt as much super-charged testosterone as in this car with Jones, Reed, Lang, and the man they'd introduced to her as Luke Colter but whom everyone called Doc Holliday. Sam drove. Johnny rode shotgun. And Gabe and Doc flanked her in the backseat like a pair of life-size bookends. Hard as bronze. Silent as monks.

It was a fun ride.

The real fun began after they arrived at their destination, parked in an underground garage, then filed up dank, dark steps to the cantina. It was same underground garage and the same back door and the same cantina they'd brought her to after the bombing at the Congress building.

Yeah, and this was a cantina the same way she was a Sumo wrestler.

"Oh, no, I'm not." She dug in her heels like the pissed-off woman she was when they showed her to the "quiet" room, as she liked to refer to it.

Jenna was far too familiar with the 10-by-10 windowless room and its pea-green walls. It was the same room she'd spent three long hours in the day before yesterday. God, was it just the day before yesterday that this crazy ride had begun?

In a daze, she glanced around. A wooden table and two chairs dominated the room. That and silence.

In her previous stay at Hotel Hell, she'd counted the cracks on the ceiling; she'd counted backward from one thousand. She'd counted the number of times heavy footsteps had strode past the door before Johnny Reed had finally sprung her then hustled her into the Angelina Foundation chopper that had whisked her and Gabe off to Bahia Blanca with Juliana.

"I am not going back in that room. Look. I've figured out that you use this place as your headquarters. You don't want me discovering any trade secrets. I get it. But I'm in the thick of this, as you pointed out."

Reed and Lang carried in the material they'd collected in the hotel room as she and Gabe stood in a darkened hallway, her pleading, him glowering.

"I have a vested interest in finding out what's going on, Gabe. I might even be able to help."

When he remained unflinching she dragged a hand through her hair. "For Pete's sake, if I wanted to blow your cover, I could have done it months ago, don't you think?"

"Woman's got a point," Doc Holliday put in as he walked by, following Reed and Lang.

Gabe shot the medic a look and held his ground. "You're tired. You can rest here. We'll bring in a cot."

"You're the one who needs a cot," she shot back. "Look at you."

His eyes were red-rimmed and bloodshot. Except for the bruising on his forehead, his color was just this side of pale. Weariness and pain radiated off him like radio waves. Then there was his leg.

"Why aren't you using your crutches?" she demanded as Gabe shifted his weight to his good leg.

"Another good point, Angel boy," Doc said as he squeezed around them again, heading back to the car for more gear.

Gabe blew out a disgusted breath. "That's right, Holliday, encourage her."

Doc stopped in his tracks, his grin fading. "Okay, here's the deal, Jones. You need to pull your head out of your ass and use it to think about what's happening here. You are not in the middle of the jungle where failure to 'carry the hell on' is going to compromise a mission. You are, however, compromising yourself and will be absolutely no good to anyone, including the lady," he said with a nod toward Jenna, "if you don't follow some sound medical advice.

"So stop acting like a Rambo action figure, get your ass out of here, get your body horizontal, and give it a god damn rest. Eight hours from now, get same said ass back in here when you'll be of some good to us, to Ms. McMillan, and to the integrity of this operation."

Silence dropped into the hallway like a bomb as the two men faced off. Jenna got the distinct feeling that men rarely dared to talk to Gabe in that tone and live to tell about it.

To his credit, Holliday didn't back down. Gabe probably outweighed him by a good thirty pounds and out-meaned him times ten, but Doc stood his ground.

He lifted his chin, challenging Gabe to take a swing at him.

Gabe clenched his jaw, slowly nodded. "Guess you told me."

Jenna let out a breath, only then realizing she'd been holding it.

"Damn straight, I did." Holliday's grin, when it reappeared, was mixed heavily with relief. "So, Angel boy, *sir*, where would you like me to take you two kids for a little R&R?"

Leadership required skills.

Great leadership mandated absolute power.

But ultimate control over those destined to follow demanded one essential element: fear.

Fear was an art form that El Diablo had perfected long ago and ruthlessly employed.

Before him two men sat naked and shivering, although the abandoned building in a part of the city where only the stupid or the foolish entered after dark was thick with damp, musty heat. As he had demanded, Ramón had bound the men to battered wooden chairs, then strapped their hands to a scarred, butcher block table in front of them. Their mouths were also bound.

He had invited three of his lieutenants to attend the festivities. He watched them now, sensed as well as saw their own fear. They would be his witnesses. They would be his voice and spread the word among the ranks that failure held grizzly consequences.

His army of men had grown to over fifty strong. No, not a supreme force, but that would all change in time. Through Ramón, he had reconnected with the old guard in Buenos Aires, who had subsequently threatened, bribed, and bought new recruits into the ranks.

His strength might not be as vast as it once was, but his network was wide. His control, however, was in jeopardy because of these men.

Ramón, standing at his side, would extract the punishment. Light from a kerosene lamp glinted off the newly sharpened blade of a woodsman's axe.

But there were points to be made first.

He walked directly to his two disappointing soldiers. Flickering light cast ghostly shadows on the dark adobe walls. He held himself under strict control. No one would see his disapproval and disappointment. No one would notice his seething rage. No one would bear witness to the pain that screamed through his disfigured body with every move he made, every breath he drew.

They would, however, fully appreciate his wrath.

Ricardo was perhaps twenty, twenty-two at most. His eyes were hollow and sunken, the eyes of an addict. The other man—Juan, he believed—was a bit older and supposedly more experienced.

Both had begged until their throats were raw, their pitiful, cowardly cries an assault on his ears. He'd finally ordered Ramón to gag them.

"Were my instructions not clear?" he asked.

Tears ran down Juan's face and into the gag knotted tightly over his mouth. He nodded.

"It was a straightforward task, was it not?"

It was true that the tracking device he'd arranged to be delivered to the reporter had failed, but still . . . that was no excuse.

These men may have failed. He would not. He would have his proof to show the hierarchy that he still deserved a place in the organization.

Patience. He had merely to maintain patience. He had waited and planned for too long to allow ineptitude to ruin things now.

He would find them again. If they were here, in Buenos Aires, he would find them.

This was but a minor delay because the two fools before him had not accomplished their mission. They would soon realize exactly what fear was and who was the master of terror.

"Ramón."

"Sir."

"Demonstrate to these men the penalty of failure."

He moved back and out of the way to watch Ramón work.

Even so, his shirt was splattered with the blood of those who had let him down and the vomit of those who would report the cost of that disappointment to the rest of the ranks.

When the last wheezing breath gurgled from Ricardo's body, El Diablo glared at his three lieutenants.

"I trust this demonstration will compel you to get me results."

14

Buenos Aires
1:05 A.M.

The R&R that Doc had suggested came in the form of a safe house. Jenna had been to safe houses before, had met in secret with protected witnesses in highly volatile federal cases on more than one occasion.

This particular model wasn't exactly standard fare. It wasn't the Ritz, but it wasn't the No Tell Motel, either. What it was, she saw as she took it in through bleary eyes, was a large, mostly empty room in what appeared from the outside to be an abandoned warehouse.

Before she and Gabe had left the cantina, they'd taken quick showers and changed clothes. After Gabe had a short, secretive huddle with Raphael Mendoza, Holliday had driven them no more than ten minutes from their headquarters to this area of the city where he'd dropped them off.

It could have been a hundred miles away given the change of scenery. Here, instead of smelling of stale beer and wine, the streets stank of machine oil and dust. Instead of the colorful stucco walls of the cantina, broken windows outnumbered the ones that were intact in row after row of connected two- to four-story brick and steel buildings.

She suspected that come daylight, the area would be hopping with trucks transporting whatever was stored in the dozens of structures in various states of disrepair surrounding the building she and Gabe had just entered.

The slam of the heavy metal door echoed through the warehouse as Gabe closed it behind them. Then they entered an elevator with a galvanized metal grate door that hummed eerily in the heavy silence of the night as it delivered them to the third floor.

Gabe, carrying a duffle that she'd heard him refer to as his "go bag," was also silent as he let them inside a large, cavernous room. He threw a dead bolt behind them then set what she assumed was a keypad alarm on the wall just inside the door.

She tossed her own bag onto one of two folding chairs that flanked a rickety card table. The guys had magnanimously given her back her purse, which now contained the sum total of her possessions. Notably absent was her BlackBerry. Even if she wanted to contact Hank and file a story, they'd made sure she couldn't, which told her they wanted to keep what was happening under wraps. At the moment, she didn't have it in her to wonder why.

God, she was weary. As weary as this room. By the light of a single dim bulb hanging from a bare wire in the center of the twenty-by-twenty or so space, she made a quick assessment of their new digs.

The floor was concrete. The walls cement block. The ceiling was corrugated tin and metal rafters. None of them had ever seen a paintbrush. The only window was high and square and intact only because of the mesh wire reinforcing the glass panes. Hanging twenty feet above it was a rickety-looking metal ladder the purpose of which she could only speculate. Fire escape? Escape route?

She didn't want to dwell on either possibility.

A battered mini fridge hummed in one corner; next to it, a two-burner hot plate sat on a scarred kitchen cabinet unit that looked like a reject from a fixer-upper. An industrial-size double sink was mounted beside the cabinet. Two wooden walls had been framed up in the opposite corner. On one wall a door hung open. Inside she spotted a lavatory with toilet and shower.

In the other corner of the room, hulking like an elephant, was a bed. A large bed, also the only bed.

She cut her gaze to Gabe.

To find him staring in the general direction of said bed.

She cleared her throat, self-conscious suddenly.

"She goes with me," he'd told the others when the question of what to do with her had come up. "Until we get to the bottom of this, I'm not letting her out of my sight." And that had been the end of that discussion.

She'd been as shocked then as she was now, now that it was obvious he'd known about the accommodations when he'd picked this particular hideout.

She tried not to read any more into his insistence that she stay with him than she did into the sleeping arrangements. If she were to speculate on either one, she'd end up thinking that he wanted her with him because he cared about her, not merely because he felt responsible for her. Or that he'd had something more strenuous than sleep in mind when he'd brought her here.

Yeah, and that was her own fatigue working. Fatigue and, she'd admit it, concern. Oh, hell, make that fear. She hadn't wanted to believe it, but it looked like Gabe was right. Someone was after her. Nothing says, *"I'm out to get ya!"* like a bomb or a blast from a shotgun.

"There should be food in the fridge if you're hungry," Gabe said.

"Am I hungry?" she contemplated aloud and dragged her gaze away from the bed when she realized she was staring at it again. "I was. The truth is, I lost my appetite somewhere between the bang and the tear gas."

"You need to eat."

"Said the pot to the kettle."

Because she knew they both needed nourishment, and because she couldn't just stand there and try not to look at that bed any longer, she checked out the refrigerator.

"A loaf of bread, peanut butter and jelly, and a six pack," she told him after inspecting the fare.

"Five star all the way, that's our motto." He dropped down into one of the folding chairs, planted his elbow on the table, and cradled his head in his hand. "Should be knives and forks and plates in that drawer.

Jenna was tired of seeing him so tired and in so much pain so she found the plastic cutlery and paper plates and busied herself making their "dinner."

"How's your head?" she asked, dropping a pair of heavily loaded PBJ's in front of him.

"How many bottles of beer are you holding?"

She glanced from him to her hands and back to him again. "Two."

"Then my head's fine."

She plopped down in the chair across from him. "Don't you ever get tired of playing the Invincible Man?"

He snagged the church key she'd tossed on the table and opened their beers. "Don't you ever get tired of asking questions?"

"Yeah, I do. Especially when all I ever get for my efforts are answers in the form of questions."

He grunted then dug into his sandwich. She did the same. They were halfway through them and their beer before he asked the question she'd been dreading.

"So—since you don't like my theory that Maxim is behind any of this, have you come up with anything?"

"Afraid not." She'd been wracking her brain, trying to come up with a reason someone would want her dead. And she wasn't burying her head in the sand any longer. Someone had nasty plans for her.

"I mean, sure, I've exposed some major secrets in the course of my career. I've even been instrumental in putting people in prison. But for someone to follow me down here? It doesn't make any sense."

"Unless it's Maxim."

She stared at her almost empty beer, worried her thumbnail up and down the label until it started to peel off the sweating glass bottle. "I told you why that doesn't compute."

"Because he asked for you. I know."

His look made her shiver. She'd come down here because she'd known she had to face some old ghosts, and here a new set of demons had come screaming out of the dark.

Slouched back in his chair, his eyes hard, Gabe finished off his beer. "Okay. Let's say you're right. I'm wrong. Any other stories you've worked recently? Anyone you've pissed off?"

She pushed out a humorless laugh. "Well, I can't see anyone from the caribou nation putting out a hit on me. Cute critters—not too smart, though. Then there was the piece on the honeybees. I hear the queen can be a real bitch."

Once again, he didn't appreciate her sarcasm. He must have heard the frustration in her voice, though, and the fear.

"We'll figure it out." Equal parts fatigue and conviction colored his tone as his gaze met hers. "We'll figure it out," he repeated.

She wanted to believe him. Knew without question that he'd move heaven and earth to find and contain the threat, if for no other reason than to get rid of her. But first he had to sleep.

"You take the bed," she said, rising.

"I plan to." He stopped her with a hand on her wrist when she would have gathered the plates and bottles from the table. "You can share, if you promise not to molest me while I'm sleeping."

"You wish," she groused as he hobbled over to his go bag, unzipped it, and pulled out some mean-looking weapons.

She recognized the rifle as an M-16—it was just like the one he'd carried during the raid on the MC6 compound. The other was a pistol. She recognized it, too. She knew enough about handguns to know that her daddy carried one just like it when he was on the hunt for a mountain lion threatening his herd. It was a Les Baer 1911–A1. And it was as lethal as the Butterfly strapped to Gabe's side.

He checked the magazines for each weapon then took them with him to the bed, but not before he reached for the string on the light and turned it off.

Light from outside—a street or security lamp, she guessed—slanted in through the high window, casting just enough illumination for her to make out his features in the dark.

"*Your* side." He nodded to the left side of the bed before he hobbled around to the right and sat on the edge of the mattress with his back to her. "*My* side. Any questions?"

"Well, it's pretty complex, but I think I got it."

He grunted then lay the rifle and the handgun on the floor beside the bed and tucked his Butterfly under his pillow. After shucking his boots, he dropped to his back like a log. He was asleep before she had a chance to remind him that, by the way, she was the reporter here and if there were any questions to be asked, she'd do the asking.

Waking him now to make that clear would be like waking the dead, and the heaviness in her limbs reminded her that she hadn't had any more sleep than he had. So she followed his lead. She sat down on the bed, toed off her sandals, and lay down beside him, her muscles screaming from the toll the past several hours had taken.

A few minutes later, she got up. She dug around in her bag, found what she was looking for, and brought the little stuffed dog back to bed with her.

Childish, yeah. She didn't care. He was soft and cuddly—unlike Jones— and she had a need for soft and cuddly right now. She'd like to meet the woman who could breeze through a shotgun blast and not need something to hold on to. Even if it was just an old stuffed pup.

Then she just lay there, listening to a silence humming through the cavernous room that was as loud as any traffic noise. Listening to the sound of Gabe's deep even breaths. Listening to her own heartbeat. Thinking about all that weaponry. Praying to God that Gabe wouldn't need to use it.

She rolled to her side, facing him, folded her hands and Nugget beneath her cheek like a mini pillow, and watched him in the dark. Watched the steady rise and fall of his chest, the slight flutter of his eyelids that told her his mind was still working even as his body had shut down in sleep.

She was close enough that if she reached out, just a few inches, she could rest her hand on his chest and feel the power and the surge of his beating heart. Close enough that if he turned his head toward hers, the warmth of his breath would feather across her face.

She wondered what he'd do if she told him she was afraid. If she told him that once, just this once, she needed a strong shoulder to lean on, a pair of strong arms to hold her together because she felt close to falling apart.

She swallowed hard, then caught her breath when he opened his eyes, turned his head on the pillow toward her. He searched her face in the dark.

"Come here," he whispered.

When she hesitated, he reached for her. "The dog can come, too."

Oh, God. He'd gone and made her smile. "Just when I had you pegged for an incurable hardass, you go and blow the image."

"Even the mighty have to fall sometime."

Tension that felt like traction bars eased out in one deep, grateful breath as he drew her to his side. She snuggled against the long, strong heat of him.

"Thank you," she whispered, closing her eyes and finally giving in to sleep.

When Gabe woke up again an hour later, he didn't have to wonder what had roused him.

Make that *aroused* him.

A long, lean body, radiating heat and playing with fire, was molded against his left side.

Pliant warmth.

Limber grace.

As combustible as C-4.

He shivered as a soft, wandering hand burrowed under his T-shirt. Lazy but very active fingers feathered across his chest, lingered at his nipple where a tapered nail teased like the lick of a hot, wet tongue, and he damn near bucked right off the bed.

But lower, where it really counted, a thick, surging need pounded through his blood like fire as the delicious weight of a nicely toned thigh lay across his lap. Rhythmically moving. Back and forth . . . back and forth . . . *Jesus, God* . . . back . . . and . . . forth . . . over his dick. His rock-hard, wildly pulsing dick.

If he worked at it long enough, thought about it hard enough, he could convince himself he was dreaming, just like she was—and she had to be dreaming because, well, hell. She had to be dreaming, that's all.

He could go with the incredible flow and tell himself and her afterward that he wasn't responsible for what happened. That neither of them were.

Fatigue, stress, circumstances—what the hell, throw in a full moon—had all teamed together to undermine their defenses and screw up their common sense.

Yeah. That's what he could tell her.

But damn it, he should wake her instead. Wake her before—oh, damn, her hand there, *right there*, felt amazing—before they both forgot that what was about to happen was the last thing she needed, the last thing he wanted, and the absolute only thing he could think about.

Other than her hair. The riotous heavy weight of it draping across his arm. The amazing vibrant silk of it sifting through his fingers as he threaded them through the strands at her temple and turned her mouth up to meet his.

Seeking her warmth like a heat-seeking missile.

Craving her taste like a junkie too long without a fix.

He was almost gone—far, far gone—when he touched his lips to hers and she took him the rest of the way down. She responded to his kiss with a soft sigh that tasted of sleep and desire and the honeyed sweetness of a willing woman.

And all he could think of was more. All he wanted was more as he deepened the kiss, finessed his tongue inside her mouth, and savored the flavor of arousal and submission and the thready anticipation of a woman who damn well knew what she was doing.

Knew it in spades, he realized.

His entire body stiffened.

Fuck.

She wasn't sleeping. She was *seducing.*

That little bit of insight finally brought him to his senses.

"God damn it, Jenna," he growled, frustrated and pissed and hot and damn it, she'd sucked him in.

A sleepy yawn. A stretchy sigh. A slow blink of thick lashes as she opened her eyes to look at him. "Humm?"

"Don't play games. You weren't asleep."

"Yeah, well, actually, I was. And then . . . then I wasn't."

As a defense, it was riddled with holes.

He scowled down at her. "So . . . what? You just decided to see if you could turn me on like a damn wind-up toy? Have a little fun making me sweat?"

Now *she* looked mad. "I didn't *decide* anything. I *was* asleep. And when I woke up, well . . . I was already . . . you know."

"Playing," he supplied.

"Involved," she amended. "And I was under the impression that you were more than a little *involved* yourself."

The proof of that was pressing against her belly, hard and huge and so not on board with the protest his brain was trying to lodge.

"So," she whispered, her expression hovering between defiance, disappointment, and dare, "is this the part where I'm supposed to apologize?"

He searched those wide, probing eyes, trying like hell to come up with a list of reasons he needed to haul ass out of this bed and hit a very cold shower.

And came up empty.

Fuck it. There'd be time for apologies in the morning.

"This is the part"—he fisted his hands in her hair and rolled her to her back—"where you're going to be sorry you ever started this."

"This is the part"—he braced himself over her on his elbows, lowered his mouth to her neck—"where you find yourself in a truckload of trouble."

He wasn't sure, but he thought he heard a breathless "Oh, goody," as he crushed his mouth over hers and she sank into the mattress beneath him.

Wasn't sure. Didn't care.

He was too far gone. She was far too willing. And he'd been wondering about that soft, snug heat between her thighs for far too long.

This wasn't going to take long. He was about to explode. And the restless way she moved beneath him, the frantic way she clutched at his shirt then stripped it up and over his head before dragging his mouth back to hers might just make it happen before he had his pants off.

Then it hit him. Condoms. He didn't have any fucking condoms.

He sucked in a deep brace of air. Rolled painfully to his back. Pressed the heel of his hand against his throbbing dick and covered his eyes with his forearm. Then he tried not to whimper like a dog.

"This isn't happening," he finally managed when he could draw a breath that wasn't fueled by testosterone, lust, and stupidity.

The mattress shifted when she popped up on an elbow. "What, are you crazy?"

He pushed out a humorless laugh. "Gettin' there. It's your lucky day, hotshot. No protective gear."

Stillness. Then a flurry of activity and he was alone in the bed with the stuffed dog. He lifted it, glared at it, then tossed it to the floor.

The light went on.

He lifted his arm, glanced across the room to see her rummaging furiously through her handbag. Seconds later she was back on the bed and astride his lap, sporting a smile as wide as the lanes on *Avenue 9 de Julio*.

"What?" He regarded her with equal measures of hope and dread as her long red hair tumbled around her face like a halo on a wild, reckless angel.

"You're the one who's lucky." She produced a foil packet and presented it to him as if it were the key to the city. "Any more problems we need to take care of?"

Not waiting for an answer, she made quick work of his belt, slid down his zipper, and using more care with his injured leg than he would have taken time for, stripped off his pants.

"Only one." He reached for the hem of her T-shirt. "This has got to come off."

15

She helped him peel off her soft cotton shirt then rose to her knees and undid the snap and zipper on her shorts. Gabe stopped her hands when she would have pushed them down her hips. He watched her face as his big rough hands spanned her waist—because he'd been wondering if they could. And because he'd been wanting his hands on her skin for so damn long.

Wanting to feel the creamy smoothness, indulge in the pliant softness. Wanting to watch her eyes go blind with pleasure as he unhooked her bra and feasted on the sight of her bare breasts.

Damn, it had been eons since he'd taken the time to take pleasure in a woman, and in her scent. She smelled like sex and a salvation he'd go to hell for seeking.

He took pleasure in the sight of her—she belonged on canvas, with her breasts bare like this, full and round, her areolas velvet soft, her nipples ridged and berry pink.

Pleasure in touching her—she let him mold her in his hands, let him brush his palms against her nipples and feel them harden with arousal.

Pleasure in tasting—she let him coax her down and draw a full, perfect nipple into his mouth, let him suck and indulge and feed a hunger he'd denied for so long and now wondered how he'd survived without.

He consumed her, felt consumed by her when she pushed herself upright, took his hand in hers, and guided it to the open placket of her shorts.

"Please," she whispered, her gaze—misty and aroused and just this side of desperate—locked on his. "Please, please, please."

Covering his hand with hers, she slid it across the quivering flesh of her flat belly then farther down, inside the V of her open zipper.

Her breath caught, her hands fell to his shoulders, fingers gripping, when he tunneled beneath her panties and caressed damp, downy curls.

"Gabe." A whisper of need in the dark.

"Gabe." A plea for more contact as he found the hot, wet heat of her and slipped two fingers inside.

Sleek.

Tight.

Wet.

Warm.

The way she moved. She was something to see. Exotic, erotic, one-hundred-and-fifty percent involved as she moved against his hand like a dancer, rode with his caress to a sultry beat, pushing herself toward release and him past the point where anything but deep, deep penetration was an option.

"Take 'em off." Holding her gaze with his, he slowly withdrew his hand, giving special, lavish attention to the plump, pulsing bud of her sex and triggering another low, pleasured groan.

"Take 'em off," he ordered again, when she gripped his hand and held him there, riding against the friction, begging for more of his touch.

It would have almost been worth it to make her come that way. To watch her shoot over the top. Her eyes were closed in pleasure, her lips parted, her breasts bare and bouncing, her amazing nipples tightened to diamond-hard tips.

Almost worth it, if self-control hadn't become a commodity in dangerously short supply.

With a low, feral growl, he gripped her waist, lifted her, and laid her flat on her back. Before she could react with anything but a gasp he got rid of her jeans and panties, wedged a knee between her thighs, suited up, and drove into the very core of her.

Drove deep. Drove hard. Once. Again. Measuring his strokes. Pacing his need.

Until he lost it.

Lost his head, lost his control, lost his ability to think, feel, breathe, live for anything but the heat and the silk and the tight wet wonder of her body.

He couldn't remember ever needing this badly. Ever wanting this much. So much that he pounded into her with all the finesse of a bull. Even when he realized how rough he was, he couldn't rein himself in.

He tried to ease up. He really did. But she'd wrapped her long legs around his hips, locked her ankles together, and met each slamming stroke with a breathless, pleading, "Yes."

Control became a distant murky memory. Eternity became these few moments he was entrenched in her.

She was so damn tight. So hot and slick and as out of control as he was as she locked her fingers around his neck and dragged his mouth down on hers. She bit his lip like a tiger, thrust her tongue inside his mouth, and possessed it as he pounded in and out of her, mimicking his hip action, driving him to the brink with her mindless need and uninhibited responses.

They were both drenched in sweat as he hooked an arm behind her knee, tucked it into her chest, and took penetration to a whole new depth.

She cried out as her body opened to him, stretched for him, gave to him. On a gasp of breath, she screamed his name, then convulsed around him, going rigid with the force of her release.

He was vaguely aware of her teeth digging into his shoulder, of her nails finding purchase on his back as he rammed into her one final time . . . and his conscious world shattered like glass.

He shot into her like fury, rode an orgasm so rich and rare and explosive that his muscles tensed, locked, then shook violently with the force of it as he milked every last surging, electric sensation.

Too soon, it was over. And the "little death" that had claimed him took its toll. Boneless, he collapsed on top of her, his breath labored and heavy, his heart slamming and thundering, his head reeling from the ride, from the rush, from the uncensored and giving responses he'd found in the wonder of this woman's body.

In the wonder of this woman.

This woman who was the last good thing that should have ever happened to him.

This woman who meant far too much to him.

Far too much for him to do anything but get the hell out of her life after he was certain she was safe.

You're doing a damn fine job of protecting her too, aren't you, asshole?

Talk about leaving them both vulnerable.

With his last reserve of strength and a will he hadn't known he possessed, he pushed up on an elbow, released her leg, and guided it back down to the bed.

She was like warm, pliant clay as he slid his palm back up the length of her thigh, her body damp with perspiration, her arms limp on the pillow on either side of her head. Only the rapid thrum of her pulse when he checked it indicated she was even alive, let alone conscious.

He watched her face with concern. Seconds ticked by and she remained motionless. Not even a flutter of an eyelash. He was about to ask if she was all right when a small smile curved her lips and a huge, contented sigh eased between them.

"*Our* lucky day," she murmured sounding smug and satisfied and not at all concerned that they'd just committed an act of unforgivable stupidity.

Stupid because they had no future and his gut told him she wanted one. Stupid because being with her made him wonder if maybe he was wrong. Maybe she was the one woman who could handle who he was and the things he'd done. Stupid because she made him want things he couldn't have. A normal life. A clean conscience. A fresh start.

Which was so not going to happen.

"Gabe?"

Her voice was whisper soft, concerned, and a little uncertain.

She wanted something from him. A word. A touch. An indication that they'd just shared more than their bodies. Shared more than hot, amazing, sweaty sex.

He couldn't give it to her. Just like he couldn't give her anything else she wanted.

So he gave her nothing.

He rolled away.

Rose from the bed.

Mentally cursing himself and his injuries that gleefully reminded him there were many levels and many kinds of pain, he limped to the bathroom and shut the door.

Jenna somehow found the energy to roll to her side and watch as Gabe eased out of bed then limped, in all his naked glory, to the makeshift bathroom.

She felt—God, she felt amazing. Wasted, sated, boneless, and . . . amazing.

So he hadn't uttered words of love everlasting. So he hadn't whispered sweet nothings and wrapped her in his arms for a little post-coital snuggling.

It wasn't as if he'd been a willing participant in this. Well, at least not at first. She'd taken him by surprise. That went both ways. She *had* been asleep. She *had* been dreaming. Dreaming about making love with him. About feeling the weight of his strong, scarred body pressing hers into the bed. About the length and the strength of him hot and heavy in her hands, thick and pulsing inside her body.

And the next thing she'd known, she was all over him.

Then she was awake. And she *was* touching him, and amazing, beautiful man parts were changing size and shape and, well, hell. In for a penny, in for a pound.

Make that two hundred twenty pounds—give or take.

Big man. Big, big man, she thought with a smile and felt a renewed stirring of arousal heavy and low in her belly.

Big, rough, raw, take charge, take control, take her to the limit man. Who had just had sex—and nothing but sex—with her. Sex the way she'd imagined sex would be with him. Hot. Primal. Perfect.

With one exception. His heart hadn't factored into the equation.

That was the reality of what had just happened.

Deflated, she rolled to her back again and flung her arms above her head. So she'd hoped for more. Yeah, she was disappointed, but now she knew the rules. The ones that said sex was as much as he wanted from her.

Fine. She was a big girl. A big girl who should go back to sleep and let him sleep too because if certain unknown threats had their way, she might not live to see another morning.

There was the kicker. She turned her head, glanced toward the closed bathroom door and the faint light that peeked out beneath it. Could she live with herself if she let things go at this? At one amazing, mind-blowing bout of incredible, scorching sex with an amazing, mind-blowing man?

A man she was growing more and more certain she was in love with.

A man who, in all likelihood, would walk away without a backward glance if they were both still alive when this was over.

The shower went on.

She contemplated all of ten seconds, then she strode naked across the room and opened the bathroom door.

She shoved aside the shower curtain.

His eyes were blank when he met hers. His look as closed and sealed as a vault.

He wanted her to go away. Too bad.

She slipped up against him under the spray.

He stiffened. "Jenna—"

"Shh."

Yeah, he wanted her to go. At least he thought he did. That was all going to change in about ten seconds.

"Let me. Just . . . let me."

He watched her face as she took the soap from his hand. Sucked in his breath when she rubbed it across his chest, rubbed it across her breasts.

His eyes glazed over. And against her thigh, she felt the burgeoning presence of his arousal.

The water was hot and pulsing as it sluiced across her shoulders, through her hair. The shower stall was slippery and hard against her knees as she knelt before him.

"Jenna, don't."

She didn't listen. She knew what he wanted. Knew what he needed. She took him in her hands. With deliberate care, a provocative touch, she cleaned, caressed, finessed him to the point where he was thick and heavy and hard in the loose circle of her fist.

Oh, he wanted her there now. His hands were already moving in her hair, his big body clenched in anticipation as she brushed her lips against the very tip of him, flicked her tongue across his head and tasted salt and sex and desire.

With both hands surrounding him, she gently squeezed, slowly stroked, delicately sucked, teasing, teasing, *teasing* until he groaned and swore and battled to keep himself under control.

Finally, she opened her mouth and took him inside. His hips were already moving as she cupped his testicles and possessed him there.

"Jenna."

No protest now, but a plea. An adulation. An expression of the pleasure he took in the pleasure that she gave.

And gave, and gave, and gave.

Because she loved him.

Because she knew he was eventually going to leave her.

Because that knowledge hurt. Hurt her pride. Hurt her heart.

Because for this one moment, she needed the power. Needed him to know that she was aware she possessed it and could bring him to his knees if she wanted to.

And because, she thought, as tears mixed with the water cascading down her face, she wanted to make certain he never, *ever*, forgot her. And that he'd be damn sorry when he let her go.

16

It was still dark, closing in on four a.m. They dressed in silence. Gabe had insisted they get dressed in the event they had to leave in a rush. In the meantime, they both still needed sleep before they faced a morning that would arrive with the same unanswered questions.

Who was trying to kill her and why?

Then they both lay down on the bed. On their backs. On their respective sides of the mattress. Staring at their respective spots on the ceiling.

Silence was a third entity in the safe room, a huge, hulking bull of a division between them.

It wasn't as if Jenna had expected him to experience some sort of epiphany, she told herself as she forked her fingers through her damp hair so it would dry on the pillow. Wasn't as if she thought he might offer an explanation, or the ever popular "It's not you, it's me" speech. Or the "You're an amazing woman, but . . ." speech. Men like Gabe Jones didn't offer explanations or excuses or attempt to soft-pedal the gritty truth.

She understood. Just like she understood that to him, what she'd offered was sex. She hadn't asked for strings. Wouldn't ask.

Would *never* ask. She had just enough pride left to hold that line. Just like she had grown far too cynical to expect he'd make any effort to justify, clarify, or sanctify.

So when his voice, a gruff, near whisper, filled the silence, her heart reacted with a jump and a dive.

"I met Angelina three years ago."

Angelina.

Of all the things Jenna hadn't wanted in this bed with them, it was Angelina's ghost. Yet somehow, she'd known it would come down to her. Just like she knew his statement begged a response of some kind. For the life of her, she couldn't say anything. She couldn't process the fact that he'd voluntarily opened up a very raw wound, or speculate about his reasons for doing so.

So she said nothing. She just waited, heart in her throat, breath caught in her chest, waited for him to go on.

"I'd been working another detail," he continued finally, "tracking down a network of gun runners.

"One thing you learn about bad guys." His voice was void of emotion, his tone hesitant, as though he were feeling his way through a field of land mines. "They always have sidelines. This crew was also into child porn and prostitution. In the process of rooting them out, I ran across a stable of children. It . . . it was bad."

He paused then and an unholy image formed in Jenna's mind. She'd seen, firsthand, the horrors of child prostitution rings in Thailand. She'd been instrumental in exposing and shutting one particularly bad operation down.

It would have been gratifying if she hadn't seen the haunted faces of those children and known that many were beyond saving. If she hadn't also known that another operation had probably taken its place in a matter of days.

"There were five of them," Gabe said, bringing her back to this moment. "Sick. Scared. Abused. I couldn't leave them there."

Another man might have. A man who was as mercenary as Gabe wanted her to believe he was.

She turned on her side, facing him, her damp hair hanging heavily behind her. His eyes were open, fixed on the ceiling. "What did you do?"

"I'd heard about a network that funneled children who were victims of this kind of abuse out of the country—an underground railroad that operated outside the scope of the law."

"Let me guess. Because there was a little payola going on with some government officials in return for turning a blind eye to their little dealings?"

He closed his eyes. Nodded. She felt the same disgust as he did for that type of corruption—the kind that preyed on the weakest and the most vulnerable.

"So you took the children to safety."

"I took them to Bahia Blanca. To Juliana and Armando Flores."

She didn't know what she'd expected him to tell her, but he'd just surprised her. Then again, when she thought about it, it made sense. "You took them to their clinic. For medical attention," she surmised.

"Yes, that, too."

In the following silence it dawned on her. "Juliana's involved with the underground railroad?"

"She and her husband, Armando. They used to run it together."

She took a moment to digest this information and to wonder exactly what had happened to Armando Flores. But she'd let Gabe tell her if that's what he intended to do. "No wonder you want me to stay away from a story on her."

"She doesn't need any extra attention drawn to her."

Jenna agreed. "It could jeopardize the operation. I see that now. So her medical clinic—it's a cover. At least in part."

"In part. Yeah."

He didn't speak for long moments. She suspected she knew the reason why, so she decided to make it easier for him to go on. "That's how you met Angelina?"

The lump of his Adam's apple rose and fell as he swallowed. "That's how I met her."

And fell in love.

Jenna didn't need to hear him say it. It was easy enough to put together.

"After that first time," he said after another lengthy silence, "whenever I had an opportunity, I helped them out. I had the means of ferreting out information on locations and drop points, had the contacts to help intercept and scoop some of those kids out of that hell."

All this from a man who was only in it for the money. But now was not the time to point out that his humanitarian efforts did not spell mercenary in anyone's book.

"Angelina . . . she played a big role in the underground network. We . . . we had no secrets. She knew I was working on an op to take down MC6."

Again, he paused, this time to wipe his palm across his jaw. Then he stared endlessly at the ceiling again before picking up on his conversation.

"When Angelina suspected there were children being victimized inside the MC6 compound, she wanted to investigate." He breathed deep. "I didn't want her involved. Refused to even talk with her about the possibility. It was too dangerous."

There was emotion in his voice now. Anger. Regret. Guilt.

"But she was determined," Jenna offered, afraid she already knew what happened next.

He lifted his arms, folded his hands behind his head, but he moved out of restlessness, not in an effort to get comfortable.

"A child had been abducted from his parents in El Bolsón. She strongly suspected that he was being held in the compound."

Again he paused, exhaled deeply.

"I had to leave on an op. I told her we'd figure something out when I got back." He raked a hand through his hair, down his face. "I made her promise that she would wait, that she wouldn't do anything."

His heart was thundering. She could see the rapid thrum of it in the thick vein running the length of his neck. Her own pulse picked up.

"She didn't listen. Wouldn't wait. After I left, she infiltrated the compound by applying for a position as domestic help in the main house."

"Oh, God." The exclamation slipped out before Jenna could stop it. The brave, foolish woman. A lamb among the lions.

"Her plan was to . . . hell, I don't know. Smuggle out information? Grab the kid and run? I don't know. I don't know what she was thinking."

"She was thinking," Jenna said reacting to the sheer torture in his tone, "that she had to do something. She was thinking that she had to help."

"Yeah, well, when I got back to Buenos Aires a week later, there was a message waiting for me. It was from Erich Adler."

Now Jenna closed her eyes, wishing she didn't know what was coming next.

"He'd caught on to her. Took great pleasure in telling me in the letter that he'd tortured her into telling him who she was working for."

Tears stung her eyes. "Oh, Gabe."

"She was a smart girl." His words were stilted now, abrupt with pain. "Even when he'd drugged her and . . . and done things to her, she didn't give her parents away. She protected them. She gave up my name instead because she knew I was her best chance of getting out alive."

Jenna felt her heart beating in her throat now, pounding through her ears as she thought about the horrible things the MC6 leader must have done to Angelina.

"So you went to the MC6 compound."

He didn't respond for a moment. It was like he was lost in his own thoughts about the pain Angelina had experienced.

Finally he shook his head. "Adler made it clear I wouldn't find them there. He'd taken her north."

He scrubbed his face with his hand again, as if he could scrub away the horrible truth. "The sick bastard made a game of it. Gave me clues leading me to where I could find them, made sure that every hour I delayed in getting there was another hour of agony for her."

Jenna's heart broke for him. She swallowed thickly, knowing she couldn't even begin to comprehend the agony both Gabe and Angelina had gone through.

"He made it clear I was to come alone. Said that when I arrived he'd trade Angelina for me."

"Surely you didn't believe he would let her go."

"No. I didn't believe him. But what choice did I have? What chance did *she* have if I didn't go?"

Of course he would go. He loved her. "So you figured out where she was."

"Yeah. He'd taken her to a stronghold near Iguazu Falls, well away from the areas the tourists have access to. He wanted to make sure we weren't anywhere near civilization, so that no one would hear her screams."

"It was a trap," Jenna conjectured when she could speak past the lump in her throat.

He slowly nodded. "I knew that going in. Armando, Angelina's father, insisted on going, too. He was a doctor. Angelina would need him. I couldn't . . . I couldn't stop him."

"He was her father. Of course you couldn't stop him."

A deep breath, harsh and serrated and unsteady, slowly pushed out. "We choppered as close to the area as we dared, went the rest of the way on foot. And as I'd expected, we were ambushed by Adler's men and captured just short of the camp."

His voice had become a monotone again, an unconscious attempt to distance himself from the memory. "They executed Armando immediately. Made Angelina watch while she screamed for them to show him mercy."

Another deep breath. A breath he needed for fortification to go on. A breath Jenna needed to brace herself for the rest of this nightmarish story.

"Then they went to work on me. Another show for Angelina's benefit, yet one more way to make her suffer."

Jenna's chest felt tight, like a metal band had been cinched around it and was cutting off her air supply.

"They'd beat me unconscious then revive me over and over again. After a couple of hours, Adler got tired of playing that game. So he had his men tie me spread eagle to a tree. Then he made me watch as they started in on Angelina."

Oh God, oh God. Jenna covered her mouth with her hand. She felt violently ill. But she forced herself to settle. If he had found the courage to tell her, she had to find the courage to listen.

"I listened to her screams," he said with so much torment in his voice that she wondered if he was even aware that she was in the room at this point. "I still listen to her screams."

He became very still. Entrenched in the horror. Engulfed in the pain.

"I had to watch them beat her, burn her . . . Jesus . . . I had to watch them cut her. They shot her. The fucking bastards shot her. Shot her so she'd bleed. Shot her so she'd hurt, avoiding anything vital so they could drag out her agony."

Tears welled up in his eyes. "And they did. They dragged it on and on. I begged for them to stop. Pleaded, groveled, screamed for them to stop.

"Finally . . . they did."

"They killed her," Jenna whispered, stunned and horrified.

"No," he said and the world stopped turning. "I did."

Jenna couldn't speak. Couldn't make herself believe she'd heard him right.

He turned his head on the pillow. Met her eyes and yet seemed to look right through her. His eyes were glazed now, and she knew he'd gone back there. Back to that horrifying moment in time.

"I was given a choice. Watch as they tortured her for hours more until the pain and the shock finally killed her, or end her suffering myself."

Oh God. Oh, sweet merciful God.

Tears, silent and hot, fell from her eyes, while everything inside of her turned ice cold.

"They untied one of my hands. A dozen of them stood with rifles pointed at me. They gave me a pistol with one bullet." He looked away. "And I used it."

Jenna flinched as if she were the one who'd been shot.

She heard the crack of the gun.

Saw Angelina's body crumple and fall.

Saw the broken and bleeding man who had not only lost the woman he loved but had been forced to take her life.

He was still broken.

Still bleeding.

He'd relive that horrible moment for the rest of his life.

He had to live with the fact that not only had he not been able to save her, he'd been the one to pull the trigger that ended her life.

It didn't matter that he'd done it out of love. It didn't matter that he'd been half-dead himself. What mattered was that every day, every waking hour, he carried that weighty burden as guilt.

Jenna said a prayer for Angelina. Another for this man, this tortured, guilt-ridden man who had been given a choice that had been no choice at all. There was nothing, *nothing* she could say that was remotely adequate. And yet, she felt compelled.

"I am so, so sorry."

He said nothing.

And his silence deepened her sorrow and enriched a love growing stronger and bigger and more hopeless every moment.

She laid a hand on his arm. Human contact in the night.

A reminder that he wasn't alone with his pain and his guilt and his nightmares.

A promise that he could trust her to know what to do with all three.

An invitation to lean on her, to be weak with her because he'd borne the weight of his burden alone for too long.

But he didn't turn to her. Instead, he turned away. Physically, emotionally, he shut down, shut her out.

He left her lying alone in the dark, more alone than she'd ever felt. Yet the tears she shed were for him, not for herself.

She had no clue how to help him.

No idea how to reach him.

And no hope that he'd ever divorce himself from his past to consider that she might be the one thing that could save him from a future of more suffering and misery and pain.

"Enter."

A door opened, then shut quietly.

El Diablo glanced at the clock beside his chair. Three-thirty a.m.

Only one person would dare disturb him at this hour. Ramón appeared before him in the dim light.

The pain, a constant, pummeling entity, had grown like a virulent disease as time wore on and he'd received no word of the Archangel.

Ramón risked more than he realized by coming here.

"Report."

"The transmitter is now operable. We're receiving a signal."

A fissure of something other than agony snaked through his blood. At last, something had gone right. "Then you've located them?"

"We have."

He rose slowly from the chair, anticipation momentarily outdistancing the excruciating process of standing. He met Ramón's gaze in the diluted light of the darkened room.

"Do not disappoint me this time. I will not tolerate another failure. Not from anyone."

"They will not escape us again."

"Let us hope that your confidence is well placed. Now leave me."

He needed to prepare.

There was much he wished to share with the Archangel. Even more excitement planned for the woman.

She didn't quit. Even in sleep, the woman just didn't quit.

Gabe had known the moment Jenna had given in to sleep. Heard the subtle transition in her breathing.

Exhausted, worn down, tapped-of-energy sleep.

And still she reached for him. A hand on his arm. Gently caressing.

The touch wasn't sexual. It was something infinitely more intimate. Significantly more profound. All the more so because of what he'd just told her.

And what he'd told her, he'd told no one else. No one knew the exact circumstances of Angelina's death. Not even Juliana. No one knew that it was Gabe, not Adler, who had killed her.

And killed her and killed her over and over again in his mind, in his sleep, in the middle of an op, on a brilliant sun-drenched day. It would come over him. Consume him. Remind him that he'd not only failed her, he'd killed her.

He'd killed her.

And yet Jenna reached out for him. Tears burned his eyes.

Fuck.

He roughly brushed them away. Sucked in huge, steadying puffs of air to get control of himself because, damn it all to hell, he would not bawl like a freaking baby.

He didn't get it. Didn't understand why all this . . . *shit* . . . all these *feelings* were boiling up inside him. He didn't *do* feelings. He didn't *have* feelings. Ask any of the guys. To a man they'd tell it straight. He was a machine. Stone cold. Mechanical.

So no, he didn't have any fucking feelings.

But the woman hadn't run. She hadn't turned her back. Hadn't recoiled.

He'd expected shock, horror, at the least revulsion, even fear at the worst. What he'd just told her was the worst of him. The very worst of him.

And yet she reached for him.

What the hell was wrong with her?

Nothing.

There was not one damn thing wrong with Jenna McMillan. Except that she might be thinking that she was in love with him. Even now, now that she knew.

Her fingers tightened on his arm.

It was all he could do not to gather her up against him and hold her close, even knowing the biggest threat to her health and safety was him.

Or maybe not.

He stiffened, listened as a low *beep, beep, beep* sounded from the panel by the door.

Shit. Someone had tripped the perimeter alarms he'd set outside the building.

17

"Jenna."

Her eyes flew open when Gabe shook her awake.

"We've got company," he whispered, covering her mouth with his hand to ward off any sound.

She struggled to get up.

He held her down. "Easy, okay?"

She nodded.

"You got it together?"

She nodded again.

He lifted his hand from her mouth, put a finger to his lips, and eased out of the bed. Snagging his Butterfly, he sheathed it on his belt.

Stoked on a surge of adrenaline and oblivious to the pain in his leg, he hustled to the door and shut off the alarm. His cell phone vibrated in his pocket just as he reached for it.

"How many?" he asked, knowing it would be BOI HQ on the other end. Their security monitors would have picked up the activity.

"Low-light cameras put them at about twenty, carrying rifles, at least one shotgun, and submachine guns, moving in an assault formation." Mendoza's lightly accented voice and deliberately calm tone underscored the urgency of the situation. "Sit tight. We'll be geared up and there in less than ten."

The clank and grind of elevator cables from outside in the hall bled into the room. Gabe figured they had three minutes max before the bad guys started pounding on their door with the neighborly sound of buckshot. These guys weren't amateurs. They'd have a special breaching load for the shotgun to break down the metal door.

"That's a big negative. They're already in the building. We need to beat feet. And we're going to need a little help from a higher power."

"Roger that," Mendoza said. "Got you covered, man."

Gabe disconnected, pocketed his phone, and headed for his go bag. Jenna was already on her feet beside the bed.

"What's happening?"

"Grab the rifle and the pistol," he told her as he dug around inside the duffel. "There's a chain hanging down the wall by the window. Pull it."

She was a smart woman. She didn't ask questions, she moved and moved fast. She grabbed her things while he retrieved smoke and frag grenades and a Claymore from his bag. He hooked the pineapples on his belt along with a thirty-foot length of coiled rope, then tucked two extra magazines for his pistol in his pants pockets.

He could hear the rattle of the chain behind him as Jenna grunted and strained to pull down the ladder suspended from the ceiling on hinges.

"Be ready to move."

He headed for the door, undid the lock, and pulled the pin on a smoke grenade. He rolled it out into the hall and relocked the door in under five seconds.

Then he set a tripwire on the door, giving it plenty of slack so the majority of the bad guys would be in the room before it triggered the Claymore that he set carefully on the card table where it would have maximum effect. There wasn't time to rig it for a remote control, but if all went as planned, the kill zone would not only cover the room, it would reach out into the hall.

Regardless, whoever was in front of this bad boy when it went off would either be dead, or dying and wishing like hell they were somewhere else. Hopefully he and Jenna would be well on their way to a different zip code.

After a final check, he hot-footed it over to the ladder as fast as his leg allowed and relieved Jenna of the pistol. He shoved it in his belt before slipping the rifle sling over his neck.

"Like glue," he said, wanting her to stick with him as they climbed the ten feet to the window.

Footsteps—lots of them—and coughing sounded in the hall outside the door.

"Cover your head." Using the rifle butt, he shattered the window. Glass shards flew in every direction as he shoved and bent the meshed wire out of the way so they could climb through.

Ignoring the blood running down his arm from a glass cut, he swung around to the back side of the ladder so Jenna wouldn't have to wrestle her way around him. "Go."

Again, she reacted like a good soldier and hopped to.

"Watch your hands," he warned as she hauled herself up to the concrete and metal ledge.

She swung a leg outside. "Ohsweetjesusgod. It's a long way down."

"That's why we're going up," he said. Nothing like a bird's-eye view of a four-story drop to get the old heart racing. "Don't look down. Sit tight. I'm right behind you. And tie that to your waist," he said, nodding to her bag of things. "You're going to need both hands free."

Just then their new friends opened fire on the door. A deafening, steady volley of shotgun blasts rang through the room.

Gabe snagged the frag grenade from his belt, held it in his teeth, and joined Jenna on the ledge, riding it double like they would a wild bronc.

The room vibrated with the continued salvo of shotgun blasts. The door started smoking. Wouldn't be long now before they were through.

Gabe hooked a finger in the ring, pulled the pin on the pineapple, and let go of the spoon.

"One Mississippi, two Mississippi, three Mississippi—"

The metal door slammed open and a dozen heavily armed men burst through, guns firing.

Gabe tossed the grenade then wrapped himself around Jenna to protect her from flying shrapnel.

The grenade exploded before it hit the floor. Then, right on cue, the Claymore blew. Gabe hung on like hell as the concussion shook the building, blasted their ears, and scattered debris and bodies through the air like confetti.

He shut out the screams of wounded and dying men and tossed another smoke grenade toward the bed to add cover for the next wave.

"Don't think about it," he said gruffly when he saw the horrified look on Jenna's face.

Her eyes, wide and round with shock, sought his.

"Just don't think about it."

She nodded like an automaton as thick, gray-black smoke billowed through the room and the bed they'd just vacated went up in flames.

"Don't check out on me now, hotshot. We're a long way from home free. Are you with me?"

She swallowed. Nodded.

"Good girl."

"Who . . . who are these people?" she stammered as he unhooked the rope then leaned out the window and searched for something on the edge of the roof to attach it to.

"Now would not be the time for formal intros." He quickly made a knot and a loop on the end of the rope.

He visually measured the distance to a metal vent pipe extending from the corner of the roof one story above them, as the sound of the elevator cables came to them through the remnants of the blast. The second wave was on its way up.

Concentrating, Gabe swung the rope in ever widening circles, checked his timing, let it fly.

And missed.

He quickly gathered it in, started his swing again, shutting out the crunch and rattle of the elevator making its ascent. He figured they had a minute, minute and a half max. "Don't suppose you ever took a calf-roping class back at the ranch."

"Real cowboys don't need classes," she said with that old sass he'd been hoping would show up again.

But when he missed again, her shoulders drooped and she dropped the F bomb.

"You do surprise me, Ms. McMillan." He wasn't normally a talker, but she was still teetering on the edge here, both literally and figuratively, and he needed her with him so he kept her engaged. And kept himself calm.

"Just throw the damn rope," she sputtered, then held her breath as he tossed it again.

It caught.

"Thank you, God," she breathed and he resisted pointing out that God—if there was a God—had nothing to do with it. For that matter, no God he knew had anything to do with him.

"Please tell me you were a good Girl Scout and went rappelling when you were a kid."

"Got the merit badge to prove it."

Okay, if there *was* a higher entity, Gabe would have considered thanking him at that moment.

He quickly tied the dangling end of the rope around Jenna's waist as a safety precaution. "Now climb," he ordered and helped her to her feet on the window ledge. "It's only about ten feet up from here. When you get to the top, toss the rope back down to me."

"They're going to be here any second," she protested even as she gripped the rope in both hands and planted her feet on the outside wall of the building.

"With a little luck, we won't be, so climb. Don't stop for anything, including gunfire. I'll be right behind you."

But first he wanted to give them a little edge.

With no choice but to leave her to her own devices, he turned his attention to the ladder. Without leverage, it was a bitch working the chain over the pulleys. When he had it halfway up, he unhooked a third smoke grenade, activated it, then tossed it to the floor to add to the confusion and buy them a little more time.

On cue the second wave flooded into the room, rifles blazing.

Gabe shouldered the M-16 and opened fire. Bodies were still flying, and he was still firing when the rope hit him in the back.

Give a man enough rope and he just might save himself.

He emptied the magazine as he stood, then threw the rifle like a lance. On a deep breath, he grabbed the rope and swung outside.

And felt the calf muscles in his injured leg give out.

Fuck.

Hand over hand, foot by miserable foot, he hauled himself up the side of the building. His hands were burned raw and slippery with sweat and blood by the time he reached the top and fell, in a heap, over the gable.

Jenna was there to pull the rope up behind him. "What took you so long?"

He knew how she felt. A six-minute firefight could feel like six hours if you were the one being shot at. "Glad to see you, too. Now help me the hell up."

Jenna was revved on adrenaline and fear as she grabbed Gabe's outstretched hand and helped him to his feet. Her hand came away sticky with blood.

"Oh, God, Gabe—"

"Glass cut," he said. "No biggie." He wiped his hand on his pants.

Just as a rock came winging up and landed on the roof. It rolled to a stop at their feet.

Before Jenna could assimilate that the rock was really a grenade, Gabe had tackled her and sent them rolling across the corrugated metal roof.

His big body covered hers as the frag grenade went off with a concussion of sound and a shower of debris.

Her ears were still ringing when she lifted her head and assessed the damage. Other than a bruise on top of the bruise on her butt, she was fine.

Or she would have been if she hadn't seen a heavy forked hook attached to a metal cable fly over the gable, land, and catch.

"Gabe."

He glanced at her then in the direction of her gaze.

"Fuckers don't know when to quit," he muttered and rolled off her. "Let's move."

Okay. Dawn hadn't yet broken, they were on the top of a roof, and they were going to have company any moment now. The kind of company who didn't come for tea and cookies.

Where the hell were they going to move to?

She didn't question him. He said move, she moved, even though she saw approximately zero possibilities for where they could go. And not a lot of hope of getting there fast when she realized how badly he was limping.

She understood how bad his leg really was when he let her sling his arm over her shoulder and take on some of his weight. They were both winded from the exertion as they made their way to the far end of the building where they ran out of room and out of roof fifty yards later.

"What now?" She dragged her hair away from her face, glancing frantically behind them. So far, they were still alone. If she didn't know that could change at any second she might have breathed a sigh of relief.

Then it did change. A head popped over the side.

Before she had a chance to tell him, Gabe spotted the new kid on the block.

"Over there." He nodded toward a satellite dish perched on the corner of the roof. It was one of those first-ever models, a hulking metal monolith of a saucer, ten feet in diameter, two inches thick. Thick enough to stop automatic weapons fire, she hoped, as Gabe checked the magazine on his 1911–A1 and decided on his defensive position behind the dish.

Jenna peeked out from behind it. Two more heads had joined the first one. Even in the dark she could see the silhouettes of automatic weapons.

Gabe had a knife and a pistol, and a few more grenades, she realized as he unhooked the three remaining canisters from his belt and laid two at his feet.

She covered her ears when he pulled the pin, then held her breath as he waited, waited, *ohmygod*, waited for an eternity before he heaved the damn thing.

The explosion never came. Instead, smoke billowed up in a thick high line between them and the bad guys. Automatic weapons fire, wild and blind, rent the night as Gabe sent a second then a third smoke grenade flying, one to their left, one to their right. All around them smoke lifted and shifted, ringing them in a little pocket of relatively clear night and hiding them from their attackers.

It was then, in the midst of the gunfire pinging off the satellite dish that she heard the unmistakable sound of a helicopter.

Gabe's words when he was talking on the cell phone came back to her. *"We're going to need a little help from a higher power."*

She looked skyward—and there it was. The cavalry had arrived in a Little Bird.

For the first time since Gabe had awakened her she felt a heartbeat that jumped with joy instead of stark, raving fear.

She'd read *Black Hawk Down*. Seen the stunningly accurate movie version of the book. So she recognized the stealthy Little Bird whose heroic crews had kept the Somalia rebels pinned down and helped extract both Delta and Rangers in Mogadishu.

"I don't even want to know how you managed it," she yelled above the roar of bullets bouncing off the dish and the *whoop* of the chopper blades. "But I do want to know how they're going to land that thing."

It was dark. A network of phone and electric wires crisscrossed in a maze across the rooftops.

"If Reed's at the controls, he can dodge mailboxes and ice cream trucks, and pick petunias with the skids if he has to."

She didn't need petunias. She just needed off this freaking roof. As the smoke from the grenades cleared, she saw six more reasons why. And they were closing in fast.

"Gabe!"

"I know." Sweat poured down his face as, with a two-handed grip, he sighted down the barrel of his pistol and fired until the clip was empty.

Two men went down. The others kept coming as Gabe ejected the empty magazine and reloaded to automatic rifle fire, muzzle flashes, and the *whump, whump, whump* of chopper blades, sounding closer now. Close enough that Jenna's hair started to whip all over the place from the rotor wash.

She shielded her eyes and glanced up. And could have cried.

The Little Bird hovered no more than ten feet above them, and sticking out of the open bay was their means of getting out of here alive.

Sam hung out the open cockpit with what she thought she recognized as an M-203 grenade launcher fitted under the barrel of his M-4 rifle.

"A lotta boom to go with the bang," a ranger had once told her when she'd asked him why the scope was mounted on the bottom of his rifle. Then he'd proceeded to show her that it was a grenade launcher, not a scope, by blowing a hole in the ground big enough to swallow a small truck. It had made an impression. Just like it was making an impression now as Sam aimed the M-203 directly at the guys who wanted them dead.

She turned to Gabe to tell him, but he was busy sighting down the barrel of his pistol. He squeezed the trigger, and the far end of the roof suddenly exploded as if a new corner of hell had opened up.

Gabe glanced from the carnage to his gun. "What the—"

Jenna tugged on his arm. Pointed upward.

His grin was spontaneous, stupendous, and absolutely stunning. "Do you want to catch this bird or wait for the next one?"

"You pick the damnedest times to be a comedian."

"Like I said, it's all about timing."

Without wasting another second, they moved out. All it would take was one lucky shot and the chopper would be out of commission. Gabe leaned on her for support yet still managed to shelter her with his body while firing behind them and providing cover.

Eyes squinted against the rotor wash, Jenna hustled to the Little Bird where it had dropped to hover a couple feet off the roof. A strong hand reached down and hauled her inside—Sam.

"I've never been so glad to see anyone in my life!" She turned with him and, together, they helped Gabe inside. They were up and away before she'd caught her breath.

"Took your damn time, Reed," Gabe grumbled, but since he was grinning when he said it, Jenna highly doubted anyone took offense.

Johnny, covered from head to toe in black flight gear and helmet, flipped Gabe the bird without bothering to turn around.

"And I've gotta tell ya," Gabe added, covering a grimace of pain as he shifted his leg, "your customer service sucks."

Sam stared at Gabe and frowned.

"What?" Gabe asked.

"You been accessorizing at Toys R Us?"

Gabe followed Sam's glance down to his waist. He actually looked embarrassed as he tugged something out from under his belt and tossed it toward Jenna as if it was a hot potato.

She caught it. Knew from the feel of it what it was before she even looked down, disbelieving and unreasonably happy that he'd rescued Nugget.

When she met his eyes he shrugged a shoulder, tough-guy code for "No big deal, I don't want to talk about it."

"You seemed attached to it," he said, sounding grumpy.

And because it was a *very* big deal that he didn't want to talk about it and because she didn't want to make him wish he hadn't bothered, she blinked back tears and hugged the stuffed dog to her breast. "Yeah. I'm very attached."

18

Hovering on the brink of a huge adrenaline crash, Jenna watched over the rim of a steaming mug of rich black coffee as Gabe reluctantly let Doc Holliday clean and bandage his hands then tend to his leg—again.

The six of them, Sam, Johnny, Doc Holliday, Gabe, Jenna, and Raphael Mendoza, whom Doc had just introduced her to, had gathered back at their base at the cantina in what Gabe had referred to as the situation room.

Apparently, she'd convinced Gabe and company that she wasn't a threat to their operation because they'd finally given her free rein to move around their base as she pleased.

She, Gabe, and Sam sat at a well-used metal conference table. Doc squatted in front of Gabe, muttering under his breath as he repaired Juliana's work on Gabe's leg. Mendoza leaned against a counter, and Johnny made a second round with the coffeepot.

Outside daylight had broken. Inside, fluorescent lights lit the windowless room while computers, printers, phones, fax, security surveillance monitors, and an assortment of high-tech, high-ticket electronic equipment Jenna couldn't begin to identify blinked, hummed, beeped, and whirred, radiating heat and fighting with the air conditioning that marginally cooled the room.

At this moment, however, the coffee maker in a small kitchen area in the corner out-valued all of the pricey state-of-the-art gizmos. And Johnny had proven, once again, that he was more than a pretty face and a kick-ass chopper pilot by brewing a pot of high-octane coffee that he referred to as lifer-juice.

God bless him.

It had been almost an hour since Sam and Johnny had extracted her and Gabe from the roof of the warehouse. Everything had been pretty much a blur after that.

They'd raced across the night sky to a small airport at the edge of the city, left the chopper for someone on the ground to stow away, then jumped in two separate vehicles and taken different routes back here.

Now the cars were tucked away in the underground garage, and Gabe hadn't even offered to try to tuck her away in the quiet room. Good thing, because regardless of how bushed she was, she had no intension of being quiet or *tucked*. Whoever was behind these attacks was a whole lot pissed.

Well, guess what. She was a whole lot pissed now, too. She was ready to find some answers for the reason why, in the past few days, she'd survived a bombing, a shotgun blast, tear gas, scaled the side of a building, dodged grenades, and been shot at.

Oh yeah, and there was that issue that she'd made love to a man who hadn't so much as looked her in the eye since.

It hurt. And yet she'd expected both Gabe's physical and emotional withdrawal. He was in combat mode now, and he was like a stranger again—a stranger whose body she now knew as intimately as she knew her own. A stranger who had shared his deepest, darkest secrets.

She couldn't think about him without aching for him and all that he'd endured. And he—he couldn't even look at her.

Not the time, she thought. *Not the place to deal with a broken heart.* There'd be plenty of time to lick her wounds later. Staying alive was the top priority at the moment.

"Okay." Gabe glanced around the room as Doc, finished with his patch work, packed up his kit. "What the fuck is going on, who are these people, and how do they keep finding us?"

Had to appreciate the man's bluntness. Jenna couldn't have phrased it better herself.

"Unfortunately, Doc and I were a little outnumbered on the ground," Mendoza said with a nod toward Holliday. "The best we could do was give you a diversion so the chopper could pick you up."

"Sorry, Gabe. We were hoping to engage and persuade some of those goons to spill their guts," Doc added. "The few remaining on the ground must have heard the grenade launcher Sam brought to the party. They ran like hell."

Gabe leaned back in the metal chair. "So we've got nothing."

"Actually, we've got a lot." Johnny refilled his own coffee mug. "While you were sandbagging at Bahia Blanca," he said, earning a grunt from Gabe who otherwise took no exception, "Sam and I went back to the bomb scene. Place was still crawling with the local and grounds *policía* so we had to keep a low profile, but we ran across something interesting."

"Let's hear it."

Reed talked over the top of his coffee mug. "The shooter at the Congress? You'd think if he was aiming at Maxim that the street by the armored car would be pocked with bullets—same thing with the Mercedes. But guess what? All the slugs we found, we dug out of the street where you'd been staked out," he said, nodding at Gabe, "or out of the outside wall by the front doors of the building."

Gabe went still. "Which side of the front doors?"

"The same side you're thinking they were on. The side where Jenna was standing."

Jenna glanced up from her own mug, the mix of caffeine and shock over Johnny's findings perking her up from a slow slide toward exhaustion. "Which means what? He was a really bad shot?"

"It means," Sam said, "that Maxim wasn't the shooter's target. You were."

Jenna glanced from Sam's grim face back to Johnny, looking for a denial. She didn't get one.

"You're serious."

"As a heart attack," Johnny said, looking sympathetic.

A huge part of her still didn't want to believe she was a target; her mind pulled every denial card it could conjure. "But there were slugs found near Gabe, too, right? So why aren't you saying *he* was a target?"

All eyes turned to Gabe. "I was."

She blinked. "Seriously?"

His hard stare was the only answer she needed.

"Okay," she said. "Don't you think it's time you guys told me what *you* were doing there?"

Johnny looked at Gabe.

After a long moment, Gabe nodded then Johnny confirmed her suspicions.

"We were hired to protect Maxim."

"We?" Now, she decided, was the time to push. "Who is *we* exactly? And why would you be protecting Maxim?"

"We. The Agency. Protection is what we do," Gabe said, then effectively blocked any follow-up questions with another one of his own. "What about the bomb?"

Johnny scratched his head. "Yeah, well, it seems the bomb actually *was* meant for Maxim. Sam and I shook a few trees and, *hel-lo*, as we suspected, a couple members of the Argentina Alliance fell out."

Gabe turned back to Johnny. "So how hard did they fall?"

"Hard enough. The upshot was, they didn't know anything about a shooter, but they owned up to the car bomb."

"So that's good news, right? The bombing wasn't meant for me." Jenna stopped when she realized how ridiculous that sounded. She shook her head. "But then again, dead is dead whether it's a bullet or a bomb that gets you."

God. She dropped her forehead into her palm and tried to regain her balance. "So let me get this straight. There were two separate attacks at roughly the same time. Two *different* attacks on two *different* targets coming from two *different* factions."

"That about sums it up, yeah," Johnny said.

Jenna glanced at Gabe. "Kind of makes mince meat out of your 'there are no coincidences' theory, huh?"

Once again, he did not appreciate her humor.

"Which means I've been figuring this wrong." Gabe scowled around the room. "All along, I've been pegging the shooter as a diversion and the bomb as the main event."

"One more thing," Johnny said, setting the coffeepot back on the burner. "Our happy bombers got a real bad case of diarrhea mouth when we convinced them that their life expectancy was nil if they didn't give us something we wanted." He grinned. "Sam let me play the good cop."

Sam grunted. "They finally volunteered something interesting. Someone had paid them off to keep them from staging an attack on Maxim."

"Yet the Alliance took the money and went with their bomb plan anyway," Gabe concluded, thoughtful. "They give up a name on the money man?"

Johnny shook his head. "I don't think these guys knew who the money person was. Sam—who makes a damn fine bad cop, by the way—had 'em pretty well freaked. Too freaked to lie to him."

"So if the Alliance is telling it straight," Gabe put in, "not only did they have nothing to do with the gunman, they weren't even supposed to make an appearance."

"Okay, wait a minute." Jenna glanced from Johnny to Gabe, who had grown very quiet. "That's got to be relevant here, don't you think? The deal about someone paying off the Alliance *not* to bomb Maxim?"

Doc was the first to come up with a theory. "Maybe whoever hired the shooter wanted some insurance from the Alliance that nothing would foul up their plan to take you out."

"Or wanted to ensure that it looked as if they were after Maxim but Gabe and Jenna were the real targets all along," Reed added.

"Which would mean our bad guy knew Maxim would be there at the same time you were." This from Mendoza.

Jenna was still dealing with the bluntness of Doc's statement—*their plan to take you out*—when Gabe broke into her thoughts.

"We need an ID on the shooter." Gabe glanced at Mendoza. "See if we can link him to Maxim."

"Already got it. Name was Hector Lopez. Low-life local thug." Mendoza started digging around in the refrigerator. "Ring any bells?"

Apparently it didn't because all of them looked blank.

Mendoza set eggs and bacon on the counter.

"Food? Real food?"

Several heads turned Jenna's way. "Oh, sorry. Did I say that out loud?"

Johnny made a big show of sympathy. "Have you not fed this poor woman?" he groused at Gabe.

"Ask the man who stocked the warehouse with peanut butter and jelly," Gabe countered as he absently checked his cell phone, which, from the looks of it, was no longer in working order.

"Something else worth noting," Sam said, looking at Jenna. "Besides the CS we found in your hotel room, we found a small canister the lab ID'd as knock-out gas."

"Knock-out gas?" Jenna blinked at Sam.

"That's significant because it means they weren't out to kill but to disable," Johnny clarified.

"That would have done it, and then some," Doc said with a shake of his head. "Shit's wicked. Russians tried to use it a few years ago when Chechnyan terrorists took over a theater. They ended up killing over two-thirds of the hostages they were trying to help because it's so difficult to titrate and they overdid it."

"Titrate?"

"Measure the dosage so it's not fatal," Doc said, addressing Jenna's question.

She felt faint. She put her head between her knees.

Doc was beside her in an instant. "You okay?"

"Yeah. Yeah, I'm fine." After several deep breaths, she lifted her head. Forced a smile. "Just thanking God for small favors.

"Why disable me?" she asked abruptly as a new thought struck her. "If they don't want me dead, what do they want me for?"

"If we knew the answer to that question, we'd know all the answers," Sam said quietly.

"Okay. So the only thing we know for certain at this point," Gabe said, quickly masking the concern she'd seen on his face, "is that the bomb was meant for Maxim. We know who did it and we know why. That problem's solved.

"What we still don't know is who is after Jenna and possibly me and why and how Maxim fits into all of this. Or why someone broke into Juliana's villa last night and if it's connected to this."

"Wait," Jenna tore her gaze away from Mendoza and all that food when Gabe's words registered. "Someone broke into Juliana's house?"

"About the same time we were dealing with the situation in your hotel room," Gabe said, looking grim.

"You got a phone call," she said, remembering his cell ringing while she was still dealing with the residual effects of tear gas and her ruined hotel room. "That was about Juliana?"

He nodded.

My God. Gabe had been right. Juliana had been in danger all the time they'd been there. And apparently, that danger hadn't ended when they'd left. "Is she okay?"

"She's fine." His expression remained grim. "At this point it makes sense to assume that whoever broke into Juliana's villa was looking for you there. Has anyone heard from Nate, by the way? My cell's KIA."

"Not a word," Mendoza reported as he turned the heat on under a skillet.

"Okay, back to the beginning. How did these jokers know Jenna was going to be at the Congress Building that day?" Doc asked, steering them back to the puzzle. "You broadcast your trip over radio free Argentina, or something?"

Jenna shook her head. "No. No one but my editor and my parents knew I was trying to catch up with Maxim. They wouldn't have said anything to anyone. They wouldn't have had any reason to."

"Just out of curiosity, how did that come about, anyway?" Sam asked. "That you ended up covering a story about Maxim?"

She related the same information she'd told Gabe last night, about Maxim's people contacting her—which now, in retrospect, was very suspect.

"What was the plan?" he persisted.

"With Maxim? I was to meet him on the Congress steps that day. He even specified a time."

The men shared meaningful glances around the room.

And Jenna blew like a geyser. "Okay. That's it." She shot out of her chair. "You guys know something you're not sharing. And it's way past time to play nice."

Gabe pinched the bridge of his nose, heaved a resigned breath. "We can link Maxim to Rashman Hudin."

It took a moment for his words to register. When they did, she sank back down in her chair. A lengthy silence told Jenna that every man in the room knew about Hudin's involvement with MC6. They may keep what they do a secret, but they kept no secrets from each other.

If she hadn't been good and worried before, she was now. "You think Hudin is behind this?"

"Starting to look like it, yeah."

Gabe sat up straight in his chair. The look on his face made the hair on Jenna's arms stand up.

"He and Maxim are business partners," Gabe said.

"There's another connection," Mendoza added. "I dug this up last night. Maxim did business with Erich Adler in the past."

Jenna's gaze locked on Mendoza's face like a laser as he told them about the info he'd found tying Adler, MC6, Maxim, and Hudin in bogus cattle deals.

"It's still a stretch," she insisted, digging deeper into denial.

"What? To figure Hudin may be using Maxim to get to both of us? You don't think he'd want to retaliate for the loss of the MC6 operation here in Argentina? What better motive is there?" Gabe pointed out.

"You're forgetting one thing. There were no survivors that day," Jenna said.

"She's right about that," Sam agreed. "We planted enough C-4 to take out a small country. We blew that hellhole off the planet."

"Plus no one knew it was us." Johnny looked around the room. "Hudin would have no idea that either of you were involved in destroying the compound, and anyone who could have told him is dead."

Gabe leaned back in the chair, dragged a hand over his face. He looked as weary as Jenna felt. "Adler could have gotten word to Hudin before the attack. He knew we were coming. He was waiting for us."

Jenna's hunger had been replaced by a sick, heavy sensation of dread. Their arguments made too much sense.

"If it is Hudin, he won't stop with us." She sought Gabe's gaze across the table. "We need to warn Dallas and Amy. They could be in danger, too."

Gabe nodded toward Johnny. "Better safe than sorry."

"Already on it." Johnny picked up a phone.

"I need to get in touch with Nate," Gabe said.

Jenna's head was spinning at how fast they'd mobilized. She'd heard the name before but couldn't make the connection. "Nate?"

"Nathan Black," Mendoza said. "Our boss."

Jenna's stomach did a flip-flop. She was going to meet the head honcho, the one who called all the shots.

"Better throw in another pound of bacon," Johnny said with a nod toward the skillet as he waited for the call to go through to Dallas Garrett in Florida. "We've got a starving woman on our hands."

She didn't bother to tell him that she didn't think there was a prayer that she could actually eat.

19

Bahia Blanca, Villa Flores
5:45 A.M.

Juliana had just gone upstairs to shower when Nate's cell phone vibrated in his pocket. He didn't have to look at the display to know it was Gabe.

"Good timing. We've been tied up the past few hours with the local *policía*. They just left with my new best friend," Nate said, thinking about Juliana's intruder.

"What's happening?" Gabe asked.

"I was about to call and fill you in. But bring me up to speed on what's happening there first."

Nate listened, growing more concerned by the moment as Gabe told him about the assault on the safe house and their narrow escape.

"Jesus," he swore when Gabe outlined the conclusions they'd drawn about Maxim and Rashman Hudin possibly being behind the attacks. "I can see why you made the connection, but if Hudin wanted to retaliate, why wouldn't he have done it before now? And why follow Jenna to Argentina? He could have had her picked off anywhere."

"Yeah, that's what I've been thinking. Drawing a blank on that front. In the meantime, I don't think we can rule him out."

"Agreed. Let me put out some feelers to my contacts at the State

Department. See if they've picked up any chatter from that quarter lately."

"Your turn," Gabe said after giving Nate a moment to process, "how is Juliana's break-in connected? *If* it's connected."

"I think it's a pretty good bet it is," Nate said. "Our guy goes by the name of Eduardo Caesare. He didn't want to talk much at first, but we came to an understanding. Tried to tell me he was hired to find you and report back if you were here. Then I tried to tell him that filing a recon report didn't generally require breaking and entering with an AK-47 in tow."

"So who won the argument?"

"I'm insulted you'd even ask. Anyway, by the time we finished our talk, he was bawling like a baby and begging me to have him arrested."

"Must have been some talk."

"Hell, I never laid a hand on him. He was scared shitless, but it wasn't of me. Said that when his boss found out he'd been caught, he would be tortured to death for his failure."

"So did he give up this benevolent boss's name?"

"El Diablo. Seriously, that's all I got. Guy is convinced he's working for the devil. I couldn't get anything else out of him. I'll let him cook in the city jail for a few hours then have another go at him. So what's Maxim have to say for himself?"

"That's the next step. I'll let you know what we find out."

"Roger that. Watch your six, Gabe. Whoever they are, these guys mean business."

Thoughtful, Nate pocketed his cell phone just as he heard Juliana enter the kitchen. When he turned and saw her, as always, it was a sight that damn near knocked the pins out from under him.

It was close to zero six hundred hours. Juliana had been up all night, and by the looks of her, she was wavering somewhere between exhaustion and a caffeine buzz from the two pots of coffee they'd killed. But in spite of the fatigue and stress, she was stunningly, strikingly, *undeniably* the most beautiful woman he'd ever seen.

Aside from the physical response Nate had to her, there had always been a quality about her that tapped something basic and bone deep inside him.

Something that made him question who he was: A loner.

Question what he'd always been: Alone.

"Was that Gabe?" she asked crossing the room, dressed for the day in a big, boxy shirt and a pair of loose trousers made of raw silk. Both were the color of violets. She should have looked—hell, he didn't know—sloppy, even genderless in the unstructured garments, but she couldn't hide those curves. And he couldn't stop thinking about what the silk fabric would feel like against the silk of her skin.

"Nate? Was that Gabe?"

He snapped to when he realized he was staring and that she was waiting for a response. He was forty-six years old, for Pete's sake. Most of his life was behind him. And there was much that he'd done in those years that would shock, horrify, or disgust her. Which was why he'd never do anything but wonder about the softness and sanity a woman like Juliana could bring to his life.

"Yeah." He walked to the sink and dumped the dregs of coffee out of his cup. "It was Gabe."

"Is he all right?"

Nate nodded. "Says he's fine."

"Which tells me nothing," she said, sounding worried.

He understood. They both knew that Gabe wouldn't cop to a gunshot wound if he were bleeding to death.

"And Jenna?"

"Yeah." He offered her a tight smile when she turned back to him. "She's okay. A little shaken, but okay."

Her shoulders relaxed in relief. "What's happening?"

Nate told her what he knew—everything Gabe had shared with him, including Maxim's connection with Hudin—while she walked to the refrigerator, pulled out a bowl of fresh fruit and a covered casserole, and set them on the counter.

"What do you think it all means?"

He cupped the back of his neck with his hand, trying to rub away the tension of the long night and his reaction to the supple stretch and flex of her body as she reached into the cupboard for plates.

"Honestly? I don't know what to think."

The shelf was a little high. Before he knew he'd even moved, he was behind her, close behind her, his hand over hers on the heavy stoneware plates.

In a moment of intense awareness, he cataloged a thousand sensations. Her heat. Her softness. Her scent. The texture of her hair.

Her hesitation when she realized just how close he was.

For a long moment they simply stood that way. Bodies touching. Hearts beating. Silence heightening a tension that arced between them like heat lightning skittering across a summer sky. Subtle. Fragile. New.

And totally wrong.

Even as she turned her head, looked up at him through those huge dark eyes and he wanted to kiss her more than he wanted to breathe, he knew it was wrong.

"I've got 'em," he said, relieving her of the plates and backing away. Way away. Only seconds had passed, yet it felt as if his entire world had changed.

Juliana's cheeks were flushed. Her hands fidgeted as she turned but couldn't quite face him. "You . . . you should be there. In Buenos Aires. With Gabe."

He shook his head and shoved away the visual and tactile memory of what had just happened between them.

And what *had* just happened?

Nothing. At least not on her part. It was all him. He'd imagined her response. Had to have. She wasn't the only one who'd overdosed on coffee.

He should leave. But she'd insisted she wanted to feed him breakfast after her shower. Besides, he had a responsibility. He was not leaving her by herself until this was sorted out and he was certain she was safe.

"The boys are on top of it," he assured her as she set the casserole in a microwave oven and programmed the touch pad. "They'll figure it out. If it turns out Maxim is a key player, he's already neutralized. Trust me. If he has any information, they'll get it out of him."

She crossed her arms beneath her breasts, closed her eyes. She looked pale. The look on her face, more than any words she could have uttered, told him what a fool he was for even imagining that a woman like her could ever see anything redeeming in a man like him.

He was a product of his profession. He took down bad guys. In the process, he often had to be a bad guy himself.

"David—I'm sorry, I mean *Nathan*—"

"It's okay," he said, anticipating and wanting to avoid an awkward conversation about him getting the wrong idea. "You don't have to say anything."

She met his eyes then. "I think I do. I think I need to thank you again for being here for me. You're . . . you're a very brave man."

He blinked. Blinked again. *Brave. She thought he was brave?* He, who knew how to employ a number of not so nice methods to extract information from other human beings? Bad human beings, barely human beings, but human beings just the same.

"It makes me realize just how much of a coward I am. I'm not very proud of myself. I . . . I pretty much lost it last night when I realized someone was in the house."

He was still processing the fact that she was expressing gratitude instead of revulsion. "You called me. That's not losing it. That's reacting with a clear head. That's smart thinking."

She smiled. "No, that was panic when faced with the possibility of my own death. It made me . . ." She hesitated, tears filled her eyes. "It made me think of Angelina. The horror she went through before they finally killed her. She was always so brave. And last night . . . all I could do was hide. I was such a coward."

"Never," he whispered and went to her when he saw that she was about to let down in a big, big way.

She let go with a sob when he gathered her in his arms and held her while she cried, understanding intuitively that it was not for herself, but for her daughter.

He didn't think about whether he should have kept his distance. Didn't care that he'd crossed a line he'd drawn for himself in his mind.

He only cared about the woman and that she found comfort in his arms.

He pressed a kiss to the top of her head, ran his hand down the silk of her hair. "It's okay," he whispered. "It's okay."

And there they stood. In the middle of her kitchen, with the morning sun slanting in through the east window and the shadows of last night still lurking in the hall.

Finally spent, she lifted her face to his. Her dark lashes were spiked with tears, her cheeks streaked with them. He used his thumbs to wipe them away.

"I realized something else," she began in barely a whisper. "There've been times since I lost her and Armando that I haven't wanted to live."

His heart broke for her. "Don't think that. Don't ever think that."

"Last night, alone in the dark, waiting and knowing I might die . . . I realized how badly I want to live. And I realized how long it's been since I felt alive. "

Her eyes searched his as her arms went around him. As she melted into him and told him what she needed even before she put voice to her plea. "I need to feel alive again."

Jesus.

Jesus.

He needed to back away. Give her time to put her world back in perspective. And he tried. Damn it, he tried.

"You don't really want this," he whispered but his hands were already in her hair as she arched against him and her sweet breath mingled with his.

"Don't make me think about it. Please . . . you saved my life last night. Save me again. Please, please save me again."

Buenos Aires, BOI HQ

Breakfast was a grim, but necessary affair. Jenna had to force herself to eat.

Then she had to force herself to accept the truth. "So. Hudin's using Maxim to get to us."

Gabe lifted a shoulder, but the answer was written all over his face. Yeah. He thought Hudin was coming after them for taking down the MC6 compound at El Bolsón.

"What'd you find out about the Hudin-Maxim connection?" Gabe asked

Mendoza as Johnny started clearing plates and placing them in the sink.

Mendoza shook his head. "Not a lot more than we already knew. Maxim and Hudin have done business together—cattle deals, supposedly. But as far as an exchange of money, no big amounts show up, no recent contacts that would be suspect. If they are working together, they're working way, way off the grid. As a matter of fact, Hudin hasn't been seen for close to a year. Not sure what that says, but there it is. Something else to think about."

"Did Maxim know where you were staying?" Colter asked abruptly as he made a round with a fresh pot of coffee.

The segue caught Jenna off guard. "Well, yeah, just in case we missed our connection."

"Did he have a mechanism in place to contact you?" Colter pressed. "Like did he send you a dedicated cell phone or a pager or anything like that?"

She shook her head absently as a niggling thought she couldn't quite isolate poked like a tack in the back of her mind. "No."

"Okay," Doc said then tossed something else into the mix. "Maxim contacted us, too, right?"

"To make certain that we—or maybe specifically *you*," Mendoza said with a nod toward Gabe, "were also at the Congress the same time Jenna was there."

Gabe's gaze moved slowly around the table. "If we were to buy into that idea, we'd also have to assume that Hudin and Maxim know I work for BOI and that I'd be working the detail that day." He shook his head. "That's not possible."

"Unless security was somehow breached." Johnny said what none of the others wanted to. Even Jenna knew what that meant. If their security was blown, they were all in deep trouble.

"At this point, I think we have to operate on the assumption that it is. Otherwise, how could they have found us at the safe house?" Sam put in.

"Okay, let's say we peg Maxim as the pawn. Hudin is using him to get to Jenna and Gabe. We can figure Hudin's motive. But what's in it for Maxim?" Doc asked, playing devil's advocate. "He's already got more money than God so it's got to be something else."

Gabe glanced sharply at Sam. "Time we get him over here and ask him."

"I think I might like this part," Sam said with a sinister smile. "Green and Savage will be relieved, although they'll hate to leave their cushy digs."

He was referring to the Alvear where they still had Maxim in "protective" custody.

Johnny grinned. "Maxim's been trying to fire us—ungrateful bastard—but Papa Bear and Mean Joe, they've kind of convinced him we're going to finish the job he paid us to do."

"Wanting to bolt, is he?"

Johnny nodded at Gabe. "Itchy as poison oak. Almost makes a man think he might have a guilty conscience. A nervous Nellie like that—hell, probably won't take much more than a friendly little sit down to get him to spill the beans."

"I'll give the boys a call." Mendoza moved toward the phone, a dishtowel in hand. After a brief conversation, he told them, "They'll be here with the big man in about twenty."

Jenna felt ill. That pesky little detail that she hadn't been able to pinpoint finally became crystal clear. It was all coming together now. And only one answer made sense.

"Jenna?"

She snapped her gaze to Gabe's, aware suddenly that he was watching her.

"What is it?" he demanded, apparently realizing she had something on her mind.

The sick sensation doubled when the final piece fell into alignment. "I think I know how they found us at the safe house."

She scrambled for her purse, fished frantically inside, and finally came up with the memory stick. "Maxim didn't send a cell or a pager, but he did send this. I never thought anything of it until now. It's filled with BS and propaganda he sent to supposedly help me prep for the interview."

"How long have you been carrying it?" Doc held out his hand.

She gladly gave it to him. "I brought it with me from the States, but I left it with my laptop in my hotel room. So until last night, when we came back from Bahia Blanca, I wasn't carrying it," she added. "But I've had it on me ever since we left the hotel."

"Yep," Doc said after quickly dismantling the cigarette lighter–sized stick. "Here's our culprit." He balanced a tiny chip on his fingertip. "They tracked you to the safe house with this transmitter." He glanced at Gabe. "What do you want me to do with it?"

"Get it the hell out of here. And fast, before they regroup and track us back here."

"How do you know they haven't already got a bead on our location?" Jenna wanted to know. They'd been back for close to an hour sorting things out.

"They could have. That's why I want it out of here. Let's make them think we're on the move again. Go," Gabe repeated with a nod toward Holliday. "But don't disable it," he added as an afterthought. "Dump it someplace far enough away and remote enough that they'll have trouble getting to it. That'll steer them off course and buy us a little time."

And time, Jenna knew, was suddenly a very precious commodity.

20

Emilio Maxim was sixty-two years old. He told himself on a daily basis, while making it a point to observe his image in a full-length mirror, that he didn't look a day over fifty. He kept his body conditioned, didn't smoke or drink to excess, and had been fortunate enough to inherit his father's thick, coarse hair. Only a hint of gray touched his temples. Otherwise, his hair remained a lustrous, blue black.

His tailor-made designer suits, regular manicures, and five-hundred-dollar haircuts lent a suave sophistication to his overall appearance. As did his Argentinean heritage, a rich mix of European bloodlines heavily influenced by his Spanish ancestors.

While he prided himself on his appearance, he was no fool. He understood that it was his business acumen and self-confidence, his shrewd eye for investments and bold action, that had gotten him where he was today. That and a total lack of conscience. The meek may inherit the earth, but Emilio Maxim planned to own a good portion of it while he was still alive.

Already, he controlled a small empire. His holdings were vast; his fortune was, indisputably, one of the largest in the world. He'd been careful over the years. He'd chosen his alliances with caution; allies had been integral to his success.

He had made few mistakes. One of those mistakes, however, had come back to haunt him.

He sat on a battered metal folding chair in a locked room located he knew not where. He told himself that these men could not touch him. Nor did they frighten him.

The blindfold they had used while transporting him here had been disconcerting, of course. They'd meant it to be. And when they'd removed it, it was all he could do not to shudder in relief. But he'd held his composure. Would not allow it or them to rattle him. He would remain extremely, meticulously vigilant. He would protect the secrets that could harm him. He did not intend to allow anything or anyone to topple his empire.

These men were no match for his intellect. They were no match for him.

So he waited, unimpressed by his surroundings, refusing to be intimidated by the lengthy wait before they interrogated him, unconcerned that they held any power over him.

He knew how to deal with these kinds of thugs. He'd always known. Money was the equalizer. Money made problems go away. And money would ensure that he'd be out of here and on a flight to Boston before lunch.

Bahia Blanca
7:00 A.M.

Juliana understood silence: The silence of the midnight hour when sleep was as elusive as daylight; the silence of sorrow that struck without warning and made a shambles of a moment previously without pain; the silence of solitude in a life that should have held two.

The silence that joined her in this bed with Nathan Black in the aftermath of their lovemaking, however, echoed through the crystalline clear morning like the pound of a judge's gavel. But no judge could have been as harsh with punishment as she was at heaping it on herself.

She drew the sheet up over her breasts, stared at the ceiling, and listened to the deep, even breaths of the man lying beside her.

An amazing man.

A gentle man.

A tender and generous lover.

She did not regret the pleasure she'd taken from his body. Not for herself. She'd needed the touch of a man's hand, the weight of a man's body, the raw, needy strength of a man to remind her that a woman's blood still ran through her veins. That she hadn't known how *badly* she'd needed it, still came as a shock. That she'd selfishly used this man to satisfy that need, however, riddled her with guilt and left her feeling a hollow satisfaction. She was not ashamed, but disappointed that she'd so easily disregarded the repercussions for him.

He might have expectations. He might read more into what had happened between them than there was.

"So . . . this would be the awkward moment after."

She turned her head, smiled an apology when she met his sleepy smile. "It is a bit awkward, isn't it?"

He turned to his side, propped himself up on an elbow, giving her an unobstructed view of a broad chest lightly dusted with dark hair, of the corded muscles in his arms that he'd successfully hidden all these months.

He'd also been hiding the scars of a warrior. She recognized a long-healed bullet wound on his shoulder, another on his left pec, stopped looking when it became too painful to think about the difficult recoveries he must have gone through or how he might have encountered those wounds.

"I was hoping it wouldn't be. Awkward," he clarified when she met his gaze again. "I'm sorry if you're second guessing yourself."

She looked away. "What I'm sorry about is that I really gave you no choice."

"Yeah, well, a wimpy little guy like me didn't stand much of a chance against the likes of you."

He'd actually managed to make her laugh. "Thank you for that. And . . . so there's no misunderstanding . . . it was lovely, Nate. Truly . . . lovely. Thank you for that, too."

"You may not have noticed, but I wasn't just along for the ride, Juliana. You were amazing."

"I was desperate," she said then groaned. "That didn't come out right."

"It's okay. I know what you meant. I've been a desperation fix before. Don't sweat it. Everyone's entitled to a meltdown now and then. I'm glad I was here to help you through it."

My, weren't they being civilized. Two people, little more than strangers lying here naked after sharing the most physically intimate of acts.

"Juliana."

Embarrassment almost kept her from turning her head and facing him.

"Don't overthink this, okay? It happened. It was amazing. No guilt. No regret. No expectations. Let's just let it settle. If there's supposed to be more, it'll happen."

And there was the problem. There would never be more. Armando had been her one and only love. She'd chosen her path and now that he was gone, she would walk it alone.

No matter how charming, how giving, how exceedingly attractive she found Nathan Black, this was where it ended between them.

Buenos Aires, BOI HQ
7:30 A.M.

"Pompous bastard."

Gabe grunted in agreement as he and Jenna observed Emilio Maxim from behind a two-way mirror.

"He hasn't so much as shifted position since Reed stashed him in the room an hour ago."

"That's because he's trying to convince us he's not rattled. He's not as confident as he wants us to think he is. The man is sweating," Gabe said with a nod toward the damp stains under Maxim's armpits.

"Yeah, it does look like he's cooking a little."

"Time to stick a fork in him and see if he's done."

Leaving Jenna outside, Gabe entered the room.

"Mr. Maxim," Gabe said with a respectful nod.

Maxim glanced up, his face expressionless. "I don't believe we've met."

"Are you finding your accommodations to your liking?" Gabe intentionally avoided addressing Maxim's pointed request for an introduction.

"The Hotel Alvear is a favorite of mine. This . . ." He lifted a hand, a gesture that encompassed the time-cracked ceiling, peeling paint, and bare cement floors, "this is substantially below my usual standards."

"My apologies. I'll try to make this as brief as possible so you can return to your comfort zone."

That finally got a small rise out of him.

"I am mystified why the very agency I employed to provide protection is now holding me hostage."

"Hostage? You misunderstand. You narrowly escaped death at the Congress two days ago. We're merely fulfilling our contract and providing security during your stay in Buenos Aires."

Maxim's smile was tight and totally without warmth. "Considering it was my wish to leave the city yesterday, you'll understand why I will stand by my original claim. I demand you release me immediately."

"Obviously there's been a gap in communication. We understood you wished to have in-house protection at the Alvear while a second meeting with the Congress was arranged."

"Now you know otherwise."

Gabe pulled out a chair, sat across from Maxim. "And yet we're compelled by duty to advise you it may not be safe for you to leave just yet."

Maxim stared without blinking. "What do you want?"

Gabe smiled. "Excellent. I was hoping we could cut right to the chase. Why did you lure Jenna McMillan to Buenos Aires then arrange for her to carry a tracking device?"

The slightest shift of Maxim's dark eyes told Gabe he'd hit pay dirt. "I have no idea what you're talking about."

"Why did you hire our agency to provide personal security when you have a trained staff at your disposal twenty-four–seven?"

Maxim seemed to consider the consequences of replying, then must have decided he risked nothing by responding.

"It seemed more convenient to arrange for an on- site security detail."

"Specifically, a detail that included me."

Another tight smile. "I don't know who you are, remember?"

"Oh, I think you do. And I think it's time you start answering my questions."

Maxim made a big show of appearing bored. "I grow weary of this game. Your insolence and your assumptions have crossed the line. And you have highly underestimated my power to presume that you can hold me here and question me about things I know nothing about."

"Jenna McMillan," Gabe repeated with force. "Why did you arrange for her to come here?"

Maxim didn't budge. "I intend to report your actions to the U.S. government immediately."

"Good luck with that. I'm guessing you'll find the U.S. government never heard of Black Ops, Inc. Likewise, if something," he paused, as if searching for the right word, "*unfortunate* should happen to you down here, the government, sadly, will never know about it. Men have been known to just disappear."

For the first time, Maxim's bravado wavered. "You dare to threaten me?"

Gabe shrugged. "I'm just saying. Shit happens. And down here shit happens all the time."

Were this a chess match Gabe had just placed Maxim in check. He waited as if he had all the time in the world. In the end, he knew Maxim would break because the miserable excuse for a human being was just a little man who played at being tough and powerful.

"I have powerful friends," Maxim said after a long moment.

"Glad you brought that up. Why don't you tell me about them? Let's start with Rashman Hudin."

The introduction of Hudin's name into the conversation clearly shook Maxim.

"What does Hudin have to do with this?"

Gabe pinned him with a hard look. "That's what I want to know."

Maxim swallowed thickly; the sweat rings under his arms, Gabe noticed, had grown larger.

"If you're thinking that Hudin is one of those friends who can help you," Gabe said, leaning back in the chair, "I think you've overestimated his power. He tell you about what happened to his little operation down in El Bolsón last year?"

Maxim squirmed, caught himself, and resumed his rigid posture. "Again, your words are lost on me. I have no idea what you are talking about."

"Hudin found out he's not invincible," Gabe went on, undeterred by Maxim's denials. "Neither were the assholes who ran the place. And yeah, we know you were tight with Adler, too."

Maxim's gaze sharpened before he could catch himself.

"Too bad Adler's not around, right?" Gabe went on. "Maybe *he* could help you out. But we all know what happened to him, don't we? He died."

Just like you're gonna die if you don't start talking. The implication was clear. It didn't have to be said.

"Now tell me something I want to hear. Tell me why you're after Jenna McMillan."

A thin sheen of perspiration had broken out on Maxim's forehead. "I cannot speak of something of which I know nothing."

Gabe kept his temper in check. And waited.

"All right. Let's get to the bottom line." Maxim said at last, his composure restored, his businessman persona firmly in place. "How much is my freedom going to cost me? I'm certain we can arrive at an agreeable sum."

"I'm about done being agreeable," Gabe said with meaning. "So I'll tell you what. Why don't you think about my questions for a little while? I'll leave you here to ponder. Maybe something will come to you. For your sake, let's hope it's something I want to hear."

Gabe rose; the metal chair legs screeched across the concrete floor in ominous warning. *Let the sonofabitch chew on that for a while.*

"You can't get away with keeping me here," Maxim said, a generous measure of both heat and anxiety in his voice.

"Yes," Gabe said flatly. "We can."

Then he turned and left the room, locking the door behind him.

"Do you believe him?" Jenna asked when Gabe joined her by the mirror.

"Do you believe the moon is made of green cheese?"

She crossed her arms under her breasts and stared at Maxim. "Not so much, no."

"Well, there you go."

Her green eyes were troubled and weary when she looked up at him. And now was not the time to get lost in them.

"So what now?"

"Now we let him sweat for a while."

"And if he doesn't give up any information?"

"Trust me. He will."

El Diablo stared at the bloody remains of what had once been a human being.

He'd acted in haste, perhaps. A haste he may later regret. But examples must be made. And the rage, as brittle and unforgiving as the fire that burned through his ruined body, could only be contained incrementally. The lust for vengeance, the hunger for retribution had come upon him. He'd lost control.

He would miss Ramón's reliability. The man had served him well.

Until he had failed him.

Regret was not a luxury a commander of an army could afford. Not if he wanted results.

He glared at the men standing around him. Their eyes revealed their thoughts. He revolted them. The way he looked. The way he doled out punishment.

They thought he was mad.

El Diablo. A ghost from hell.

Their own ignorance and superstitions were his insurance that they would follow.

"Find them," he uttered as Ramón's blood ran across the floor.

Then he turned and struggled back to his bed.

Where he renewed himself by thinking of all the ways he would extract pain, excruciating, unrelenting pain, from those who had sent him to this living hell.

He *was* the devil.

He *was* invincible.

And he *would* have justice from the blood and the flesh of his enemies.

21

Gabe had never brought anyone here. Not the boys. Not Nate. Not a woman.

Yet Jenna McMillan stood in the middle of his apartment, her gaze bleary, her eyelids heavy with fatigue as she took it all in and clearly found it lacking.

He didn't usually think about it. But now he saw what she saw: the stark, plain furnishings; the utilitarian austerity; the total absence of anything indicating connection, roots, stability.

It was the equivalent of living out of a suitcase. He could pick up and leave anytime, with no regrets, no footprint that he'd ever been here.

Much, he thought, like the rest of his life. *No one would know he'd ever been.*

He tossed his keys on the small kitchen table, wondering where all the morbid introspection was coming from.

It was the look in Jenna's eyes, he supposed. She felt sorry for him. Felt lonely for him. Felt *for* him.

It was all there. And it made him wish he'd never brought her here. *Thank you, Doc.* Colter had badgered Gabe into it.

"She's a big girl," Gabe had stated emotionlessly when Doc had pointed out that Jenna looked like she needed a time out.

"Yeah, she is," Colter agreed, sounding impressed with the way Jenna had handled things. "But even big girls have a saturation point of violence and mayhem. Jenna's reached hers. We've got this under control. Maxim's not going anywhere. Take her someplace where she can get horizontal for a while and recharge her batteries."

Yeah, Gabe regretted bringing her here, but it was by far the safest place he knew.

Or, on second thought, he decided watching her face, maybe it was exactly the right thing to do. Let her see that this was who he was. This was *all* he was.

"This is where you live?"

He laid his newly assembled go bag on the floor where he could get to it easily. She was starting to get the picture.

"This is where I sleep."

He saw in her eyes that she did understand. He lived for the job. The job was all he had.

"Doesn't it ever get to you?"

He limped over to the ancient fridge. Dragged out two beers.

"I mean, I wigged out after what happened at MC6. Lost my—I don't know. Fever. My thirst. Mostly my nerve," she added, sounding disappointed in herself.

He twisted the tops off both bottles, handed one to her.

"I don't think about it." He sank down on a well-worn sofa. Beige. Like the walls. Like the chair that almost matched. "That way it doesn't get to me."

"That's one of the reasons I agreed to do the Maxim story. It was my chance to get back on the bicycle. Maybe find that backbone I seem to have lost down here nine months ago."

Backbone? The woman had it in spades. Sure, she'd freaked a time or two, but she'd pulled it together. That took guts.

"You're holding up fine," he said before he could check his urge to reassure her. He did manage to keep himself from asking her about the other reason that had brought her back to Argentina.

"Maxim will give us the goods sooner or later. In the meantime, just relax. It's under control."

She shook her head, took a sip of beer. Then she dropped down beside him on the sofa and went completely limp—eyes closed, head leaning back against the cushions, hair tumbling down to her shoulders.

She looked exhausted and vulnerable. He couldn't take his eyes off her. The delicate arch of her throat, the rise and fall of her breasts beneath her T-shirt, the slender length of her legs.

Less than twelve hours ago, he'd held those breasts in his hands. Drawn them into his mouth. Claimed that hot secret place between her thighs.

And her mouth. That had been his, too. Until she'd turned the tables and taken him by storm in the shower.

It had been a mistake to let it happen. An amazing, mind-numbing, life-altering mistake.

And if he sat here much longer, so close, so goddamn close that he could smell her, see the tantalizing flutter of her heart beating at her throat, almost touch the incredible weight of her hair—he was going to do something really, really stupid.

He started to rise. Jenna's voice, relaxed yet intense, stopped him.

"I couldn't do this. I couldn't do what you do. I don't even pretend to understand how you or Sam or Johnny or any of the guys for that matter, can live on the edge all the time."

Deep breath. Look away. Get it the hell together. "It's that money thing we talked about."

"Bullshit."

He glanced at her sideways, thinking how much he appreciated her spunk. "You do have a mouth on you."

"It's still bullshit," she said again, her face red with anger as she hitched a bare foot up under her so she could face him. "I could almost buy that you do it for the adrenaline rush. I could *almost* buy that you do it for personal satisfaction. But you'll never convince me that you do it for the money. Try again, Rambo."

He slouched down into the sofa. Silently sipped his beer.

"You should get some sleep," he said because he didn't want to try again. He didn't want to talk about it. Didn't want to think about it.

"I'm too tired, which means I'm too wired. I couldn't sleep now if I tried."

He drew a deep breath. The woman was not easy.

"Is it about them?" she asked abruptly. "About the guys? You're a team. You do this for each other."

"Yeah," he said because she wanted to hear it and because it was true. And because he *was* tired and he just didn't have it in him to fight her. "We're a team."

"For how long?"

He told her about joining the army at eighteen. About moving on to Spec Ops, and Task Force Mercy and Nate and the boys on the team. He even told her about Bryan Tompkins, how his death had affected all of them.

"The Task Force was important to you."

He nodded, finished off his beer.

"So was the military. And yet you left."

"And yet I left," he echoed. "Want another beer?"

She shook her head.

And he stayed put. He sensed something intimate and alarming growing between them and knew he should nip it off. He hadn't talked this much since . . . hell, he couldn't remember ever talking this much and yet every time he was alone with her, she somehow got him to sing like a canary.

"Why did you leave?"

"The military?"

She nodded.

"Because I was fed up to my eyeballs with the political games that hamstrung our missions," he said, giving in to her again. "The political games and the stupidity."

"Armchair generals?" she speculated.

He grunted. Boy had she gotten that right. "War should be waged by warriors, not lawyers in senate seats who don't have a clue how to fight a fight, let alone win one. Senate seats occupied by men like my old man," he added as an anger simmering just below the surface broke through. "His vote belonged to the special interest group that came up with the most green."

"Your father is a senator?"

He cradled the empty bottle between both hands, rolled it back and forth. "Was. He lost his re-election bid a few years ago. It was only afterward that I found out that it was his campaign targeting the subcommittee on defense appropriations that was responsible for pulling the plug on projects like Task Force Mercy."

Her brows pinched in confusion. "Why would he do that?"

"Because he was ignorant and greedy. Because cuts in the defense budget netted him appropriation money for the lobbyists who bought him off. Because he knew he'd be cutting me off at the knees."

He hadn't talked to anyone about his old man in years. He didn't have a clue why he'd let her drag him into talking about him now.

"I'm sorry," she said at long last. She sounded the part. "Do you ever see him?"

"Saw him once a few years ago," Gabe said thinking back. "Ran into him at LAX. I looked up. There he was."

He'd never forget the look on his father's face. Shock. Then anger. Then denial.

"Let's just say it was less than a heartwarming reunion."

In truth, it had been no reunion at all. His father hadn't even bothered to acknowledge him. He'd just turned and walked the other way. Their exchange pretty much summed up their entire relationship.

"What happened between you? To make things so bad?"

What happened? What happened was that from the time Gabe could remember his father had pushed him in one direction and he'd pulled away in the other. What happened was that he'd been a disappointment of epic proportions.

"Let's just leave it at we didn't see eye to eye on things. He expected more. I gave him less. I figured it was an even trade. End of story."

She took the hint. Let it drop.

"So how did you end up with the guys again?"

He needed another beer. She laid a hand on his arm, stopped him from standing.

"I'll get it. You need to rest that leg."

Yeah, the leg. Sucker hurt like a bitch. Felt like it was on fire. Something had popped when he'd swung out on the side of the warehouse and tried to rappel up to the roof. Something that would just have to wait. A refill on the antibiotics he'd lost somewhere between Bahia Blanca and Buenos Aires would also have to wait.

"Thanks." He reached for the beer when she held it out to him, accidentally brushed her fingertips in the process—and experienced a vivid, tactile memory of her hands trailing across his bare skin, her nails digging into his back.

He jerked his hand away like he'd been bitten by static electricity, though there was no static here. Humidity hung in the air, thick and cloying and earthy. Just like the heat.

"You were telling me how you ended up with the guys."

"No," he said as she dropped down beside him again, his fingers still tingling from her touch. "You were pimping me for information."

She shrugged. "You say toe-may-toe, I say toe-mah-toe."

She was like a dog with a bone. And what the hell. It wasn't any big state secret.

"The CIA recruited me after I separated from the army. Turned out to be more of the same BS. When Nate contacted me a couple of years later, I jumped at the chance to work for him."

"BOI," she said as if something had just occurred to her. "I saw it on a letterhead back at your base. Black . . . something . . . something?" she speculated.

"Black's Operators, Inc."

"Nice play on the whole Black Ops thing."

Better than Black's Obnoxious Idiots, he supposed. "Yeah, well, I joined them several years ago."

"And you've been working out of Argentina since?"

"Pretty much."

"It's better than working for Uncle?"

"It's better. We play the game the way it needs to be played. We make the rules. It evens the odds."

It *was* better. And yet . . . sometimes . . . sometimes he got tired. Sometimes he wondered what he'd given up when he'd walked back into the fray instead of walking away.

He glanced at Jenna. Her eyes were closed again.

Now was his chance. Fade to silence. She'd be out like a light within a minute.

And yet he had to ask.

"What was the other reason?"

Slowly she opened her eyes. Her heavy lashes fluttered against her cheeks as she blinked to rouse herself. "I'm sorry . . . what?"

"You said *one* of the reasons you came down here was to see if you could find something you lost. What was the other reason?"

Her eyes searched his face, seeking, considering before she finally looked away. "I don't think you want to hear the other reason."

No, he didn't suppose he did. And yet he figured he had his answer.

The way she'd looked at him pretty much told him why she was here. Just like the way she'd made love to him—with her heart, with her soul, with an uninhibited yearning—had spelled it out in capital letters.

She'd come back to find him.

He wiped his palm over his jaw. Closed his eyes. And felt his heart beat in places he'd thought were dead.

She'd come back to find him. Because she'd been curious. Because she'd been intrigued. Because she wanted to find out if there was something more than heat between them.

He had a real problem with that. A huge problem.

He hadn't wanted to be found. Hell, until she'd shown up in his life again he'd been perfectly content being exactly where he was—which was as lost as a man could be.

Jenna had a crick in her neck. Her foot was asleep, and her bruised butt was complaining bitterly.

Shifting carefully, mindful of the stiffness, she finally opened her eyes—
to beige.

Gabe's apartment.

Sluggish with sleep, she wiped her eyes, got her bearings and willed
herself awake, which was a surprise because she didn't remember falling
asleep. Apparently, she'd slept for a while, too, because the last time she'd
noticed, the sun had been beating against the closed blinds in the window
to her left. Now heat radiated from behind the shaded window to her right.

She was still sitting up on the sofa, which accounted for the stiff neck.
Beside her, still holding a half empty bottle of beer—or half full if she were
feeling optimistic—Gabe slept sitting up as well.

So much for getting horizontal.

The cobwebs were slow to leave as she sat there. Eventually, her mind
cleared enough to set her on edge again with vivid reminders of the events
of the past three days.

Shower, she told herself, not wanting to dwell on any of it. She needed
a shower. Careful not to disturb Gabe, she eased off the sofa and went in
search of a bathroom.

She hand-washed her bra and panties, used her finger to brush her teeth
with his toothpaste, then spent ten blissful minutes paying homage to the
gods of water as it washed her grogginess and stiffness away.

When she wandered back into the living area several minutes later, her
under things were hanging over the shower curtain rod drying and she was
wearing a pair of baggie white boxers and a size XXL black T-shirt she'd
found in a drawer of Gabe's equally stark bedroom.

Sometimes practicality won out over decorum or she might have felt a
twinge of guilt for rifling through his things. Not that there'd been much of
anything to rifle through.

The man lived like a monk.

And made love like a sinner, she thought as a little shiver of awareness
rippled through her.

The T-shirt smelled like him. The well worn, much washed cotton felt
soft against her bare skin. And as she stood beside the sofa and watched him

sleep, she found herself wanting to know all kinds of mundane, everyday things about him. Like, did he do his own laundry? Did he cook? Did he sleep on his side or his back?

Did he dream? That one stopped her cold.

Nightmares, she suspected, thinking of Angelina, were more likely.

A surge of tenderness washed through her for this big, hard man who had suffered so much. Did he ever let down, she wondered? Did he ever give in to the pain? Did he ever wish he had a soft place to fall?

She wanted to be that place. It hurt her heart to know that he would never allow it. Never give her the right to say, "Come to me. Fall into me. I'm a safe, steady place for you to land."

He looked so uncomfortable sitting there, his head tilted toward his shoulder, his hands propped on his lap, the beer bottle tipping sideways. She reached for the bottle, intending to slowly slip it out from between his fingers so it wouldn't spill.

The next thing she knew, she was flat on her back on the floor, her hands manacled above her head by one of his. A knife was pressed against her throat and over two hundred twenty pounds of hard-breathing, wild-eyed male pinned her down like she was a tissue.

22

"Jesus," Gabe swore when he realized where he was, what he was doing, and whom he was about to do it to.

Jenna could barely breathe, let alone speak as she felt the sharp edge of the knife balanced like a guillotine directly over her windpipe.

"Jesus," he repeated, that one oath riddled with anger and awareness and something very close to fear. "Don't *ever* do that again," he said, carefully lifting the knife.

Jenna finally sucked in a breath that smelled of spilled beer. Let it out on a ragged sigh. "Trust me. I won't."

He propped himself above her on both elbows. "What the hell were you thinking?"

Okay. He was mad. At himself, she suspected, as much as at her. He was also hurting. He winced when he moved his leg.

"What was I thinking? That you looked uncomfortable? That the beer bottle was about to tip and I didn't want it spilling all over you?"

His eyes were still wild as he searched her face. "Did I hurt you?"

"I . . . um . . . possibly my pride's a little bruised."

"Damn it, Jenna. You're lucky that's all that's bruised."

He sucked in a breath. Another. Steadier now, he started to move off her.

She stopped him with a palm on his chest. Just a touch. A touch that she couldn't stop.

"Possibly," she said, her eyes never leaving his, "you . . . you *might* have bruised my jaw."

His brows pulled together. He searched her face, more suspicious than concerned. "Really."

She swallowed. Nodded. "Yeah. Absolutely. My jaw. And maybe . . . maybe my mouth needs a little attention, too."

He became absolutely still as an acute awareness arced between them. The weight of his body pressing against hers. The thunder of their heartbeats. The sharp, heady longing as their bodies remembered what it had felt like to join and meld, to give and take.

"I'm not asleep this time," he said.

"I noticed." She slowly moved her hips against the erection straining between them.

He closed his eyes on a groan. "This is really enough for you?"

"If that's all there is," she whispered, knowing she should be ashamed for settling for so little when she wanted so much, "if that's all there is . . . then it has to be enough."

She told herself it would be. Assured herself it could be when she saw the apology in his eyes.

Apology and hunger.

"Where, on your jaw, exactly?" he whispered, lowering his head to hers.

She cupped his head in her hands, guided his mouth to her jaw where he pressed a hot, heady kiss.

"Better?" he murmured as he brushed his lips toward hers.

"Umm."

"And your mouth." His breath was warm and rich as he gently bussed her lips with his, then nudged them open and slipped his tongue inside.

Electric sensations, hot and wild and rare, shot from that simple contact of tongue on tongue and licked like flames all the way to her belly.

"Feeling better yet?" He pulled his head back, gently nipping at her lower lip then tugging with unimaginable tenderness.

"Gettin' there." She sighed and opened for him, wanting his tongue again, *craving* his tongue suddenly with a wild restlessness that grew from deep inside—heart deep—and consumed her in need.

"This floor is too damn hard," he growled and the next thing she knew she was on her feet beside him, clinging to him as they tore at each other's clothes between hot desperate kisses.

Naked, they devoured each other, hands caressing heated skin, fingers exploring secret places, mouths seeking flesh with a hunger that stole her breath.

He pushed her to the sofa, knelt down between her knees. "All or nothing," he growled and, cupping her hips with his big hands, he dragged her forward.

She met his eyes, saw the fire and the need.

"All," she sighed, swollen and wet and throbbing with anticipation as he draped her legs over his shoulders.

Jenna bit back a cry as his fingers dug into her inner thighs and he buried his face between them, parting the folds of her vulva with a bold sweep of his tongue.

And indulged them both.

He devoured her. Destroyed her. Owned her.

Stole her breath, her power of speech, her ability to think of anything but the heat of his mouth as he lavished attention to her sensitized clitoris with the same fierce dedication he employed to protect her.

Sumptuous, abundant sensation consumed her, shot through her body like summer heat as he took her higher and hotter, relentlessly driving her to heights she never knew existed.

And then, unbelievably, he took her higher.

She gasped when he slipped two fingers inside her and caressed, moving them in concert with his tongue.

It was too much.

Too good.

Too powerful.

She flew apart with a cry, climaxing with a sob when he sucked her sensitive nub until the intensity of the pleasure flirted with a pain that left her breathless and weightless and shattered.

She was weeping softly when he eased away, placing open-mouthed, biting kisses on the inside of each thigh, then returning to her core for one last, lingering kiss there. Like he couldn't get enough of the taste and the scent and the essence of her.

"Come here," she whispered when she could form the words.

Cupping his head in her hands, she guided him to her mouth. As she melted to the taste of his desire and her orgasm on his lips, he entered her.

Strong.

Hard.

Full.

She'd never felt so full.

Never loved so deeply as, on his knees before her, he moved to a rhythm that was steady and slow and as profound as life itself, as sacred as a promise.

He called her name when he came. Holding her tight, his arms locked around her ribs, he pressed his face into her breasts and surrendered to the moment, to the madness, and, she told herself as she, too, slipped gently over the edge again, to the need to be wrapped in her arms.

There they stayed. Her arms tight around him. Their bodies entwined. Their hearts beating madly. His breath feathering her breast.

A tear trickled down her cheek that got lost in the heat of their bodies.

And she tried to convince herself, once again, that this was enough.

Somehow they made it to the bedroom, though neither of them slept.

Jenna felt raw and exposed and, despite the best sex of her life, ramped up and edgy.

Proximity made her brave. Lying here, in Gabe's bed, with nothing but his big scarred body wrapped around her, she found the courage to revisit what had once been only his ghosts but now haunted her, too.

"How did you live?" she whispered into the quiet. "How did you get away from them?"

She felt an infinitesimal stiffening of his big body, and was grateful when he didn't pull away from her.

He understood what she was asking, and considered whether he was going to answer. Just when she thought he was going to tell her to leave it alone, a deep breath soughed out.

"Adler had had his fun," he said, his voice low, his words slow. "Angelina . . . was dead. And he'd broken me. He knew I was as good as dead, too.

"So he left me there. Tied to that tree. With one last taunt that it would be his pleasure to know I would rot there as I watched Angelina's corpse rot before I died."

Jenna wrapped him tighter in her arms, knew she would forever see a gruesome picture in her mind of Gabe bleeding and broken and tied to that tree as Angelina's lifeless body lay in a pool of blood before him.

"But you didn't die." Her voice was barely a whisper as she pressed her lips against the top of his head.

"The boys came on a search and rescue, guns blazing. Adler and his men cleared out. They got away."

He ran a rough hand down the length of her bare back. "I don't remember much after that. At least not for a while. I'm told that I buried Angelina and Armando. That I wouldn't let anyone else touch them. That I insisted Juliana could never see them this way."

He squeezed her hip then untangled himself from her arms and rolled to his back. Stared at the ceiling. "Like I said, I don't remember. The next time I came to, it was over a week later. One of the many slices Adler had taken out of me had become infected. Juliana kept me sedated for another week."

Jenna folded her hands beneath her cheek, watched his profile, waited.

"When I finally had my strength back, I went to ground, disappeared for several months, healing, recovering, planting a rumor that I'd been killed in a drug raid gone bad in Columbia.

"Then I waited and I made plans to take Adler and MC6 down."

She swallowed hard. "Then I came along and almost screwed things up. No wonder you hated me on sight."

He turned his head, met her eyes. "I didn't hate you. I just didn't want you there."

"And now?" she ventured, her heart beating wildly. "What about now?"

His eyes were bleak, distant even before he looked away. "And now you need to understand. I *did* die that day." His voice was so cold Jenna felt a chill run through her. "I did die," he repeated. "Inside. There's nothing left."

Then he sat up and swung his feet to the floor, turning his back to her, leaving her feeling raw and exposed. And alone. Like he hadn't only turned his back, but he'd left the building.

Left her with her mind reeling over all the things he'd told her . . . and all the things he hadn't.

She understood him better now, though. Understood the harshness in him. The hardness. Understood why so much of what she felt from him was anger and pain. Why he lived his life the way he did. He *did* have a death wish.

As she lay there, something else became clear.

"That night, in the safe house," she said. "Why did you tell me? About Angelina? About how she died?"

He lifted a shoulder. Shook his head. "You asked."

"No, I didn't ask. Not then. Not after the first time we made love. You simply started talking."

Another shrug. "I thought it was important for you to know."

"Because you wanted sympathy? Because you wanted to get it off your chest?" she asked abruptly, intentionally goading him, knowing that neither was the reason.

He heard her anger, chose not to react. "If that's what you want to think."

"No. That's not what I want to think. That's not what I *do* think. Wanna know what I think? Good," she cut him off when he looked over his shoulder to say no, "because I'm going to tell you."

She rose to her knees beside him, dragging the sheet with her and wrapping it around her. "I think you laid bare your deepest, most painful memories, I think you told me things you've never told anyone else, because you felt like you were getting too close to me and decided you needed to warn me away.

"I think," she went on, refusing to be cowed by the anger creeping over his face, "that you figured you'd make me run because then *you* wouldn't have to. Because you know what? You care about me. What's happening between us . . . it's about way more than sex.

"I'm not finished," she said, cutting him off again when he would have grumbled out a denial. "I think the reason you insist that I don't pin anything on what's happening between us is because in your addled brain, you don't think you have anything to give."

She went on, standing, jerking the sheet angrily out from under the mattress where it was stuck. "I think that you feel the need to remind yourself that not only are you incapable of love, you don't deserve to be loved either. And I think," she continued, her voice softening when she saw the devastation on his face, "that you're full of shit."

Damn it, she was going to make him admit the real reason instead of letting him get by with writing them off before they ever had a chance to make things work. She was going to fight for what she wanted—a chance to make him see the possibilities.

"Think whatever you want," he said standing and pushing by her limp toward the bathroom. "But it's not going to change a thing. When his is over," he said, referring to the Maxim issue, "we're over."

"Because you're dead." She threw his words back to him, praying she'd make him realize how wrong he was. "Because what you're telling me is that I just made love to a ghost."

No response. Which was the same as an affirmation.

23

No one made Emilio Maxim wait.

But these bastards had made him sit in this locked, airless room for four fucking hours.

He started to wipe a hand over his perspiring brow. Caught himself when he realized his hand was shaking.

He wouldn't give them the satisfaction of knowing he was rattled. They were watching him. He knew they were. That mirror didn't fool him, he'd seen his share of two-way mirrors. Had utilized them himself.

One of those mirrors had landed him in this difficult situation.

He had certain . . . tastes. Tastes that Erich Adler had been more than willing to satisfy when Emilio had visited the El Bolsón *estancia* several years ago.

Adler had understood. Adler had confided that he too, had proclivities for lovely young boys. He'd allowed Emilio to experience the special viewing room in his personal residence.

To whet his appetite. Emilio understood that now.

Just as he understood the motive behind Adler's accommodating nature. The German scientist had been more than happy to provide Emilio with "company" each night of his stay at the *estancia*. Then the bastard had secretly videotaped each night's romp, kept them, shared them with his superiors.

Those damn videotapes had come back to haunt him now. He was being blackmailed with them. Not for money. Money would have been easy.

Arranging for Jenna McMillan and Jones to be at the *Congreso de la Nación Argentina*—that had been the price. That and planting a transmitter that the McMillan woman would be certain to carry so she could be tracked.

The price was turning out to be too high.

But the consequences of that tape getting out would be higher. It would devastate his family. Ruin his reputation. Destroy his chances of running for public office.

He rolled his shoulders, focused his mind. These men would not kill him. They would not go that far.

He must merely wait.

They would eventually come up with their price.

He would meet it. Then he would get on with his life, his obligation met and this nasty business behind him.

2:00 P.M.

Reed looked up from his laptop when Gabe and Jenna walked into the situation room five hours after they'd left.

"You look . . . rested," Reed said, sounding as though he questioned that assessment.

That's because he'd lied. What they looked was edgy. At least Jenna did.

Her usual sass and sizzle were nowhere to be seen. Her green eyes were flat and lusterless, her bearing defeated, defensive, and distant.

She was hurting. Gabe was the reason why.

Couldn't be helped, Gabe thought as he tossed his go bag on the floor and limped over to the coffeepot. She'd known up front what the deal was. She'd come on a fool's mission if she'd thought he was capable of giving her anything but grief.

"What's happening with our guest?" Gabe asked, pouring himself a cup of coffee then cursing the fire in his leg as he limped to the two-way mirror.

He liked what he saw. Maxim paced the room like a caged rat. His perfectly styled hair looked like he'd combed it with a rake. His silk designer shirt was wrinkled and rumpled and sweat-stained.

"Man's got one strong bladder, I'll say that for him," Reed said watching Jenna with concern before he glanced at Gabe.

His frown said it all. *What the hell did you do to her?*

Leave it alone, Gabe warned him with a look.

Which the former marine promptly ignored.

"Did he feed you, darlin'?" Reed asked Jenna, sounding all mother-henny.

Gabe shot him another glare. A wasted effort.

"I'm fine." She crossed her arms under her breasts and leaned a hip against the counter.

Reed rose and went to her. Touched the back of his fingers to her cheek and gave her an affectionate stroke.

Gabe gritted his teeth.

"You look like you need a little dose of Johnny D, baby. Come on. Give us a hug."

She laughed at that.

Because he was god damn ridiculous, Gabe thought biting back a snarl. Then he damn near broke his coffee mug when Reed pulled her into his arms.

And held her way too close, the fucker. And way too long.

You're a dead man, he mouthed over his coffee mug when he was sure he had Reed's attention.

The bastard grinned and slid his hands in a slow glide down Jenna's back, let his little finger brush the curve of her ass.

The sonofabitch was taunting him. Thought he was being cute. Thought he was doing Gabe a favor by opening his eyes to how much he cared about her. Laying on the crap in the equivalent of a dare. *You want her? Come and get her.*

Because Reed knew what it would do to Gabe. And like an ass, Gabe was rising to the bait.

"Where's Sam?" Gabe asked because if he didn't get himself together, he was going to use his Butterfly to relieve Reed of his dick then shove it down his throat. "I didn't see him when we came in."

"Off to Honduras with Savage," Reed said, still holding Jenna, fussing with her hair, bussing his nose along her temple, one eye on Gabe to make sure he was watching.

Gabe turned to the two-way mirror, bit back his irritation.

"Honduras?"

"Got a new lead on Fredrick Nader, a guy they've been tracking for a while now," Reed said, answering Jenna's question. "Came up quick. Sam said to tell you he was sorry he had to bail on you."

It was nothing new for the BOIs to be spread thin. They were a small agency and their services were in high demand.

"Maybe it's time we resume our friendly chat with Maxim." Pointedly ignoring Jenna and Reed, Gabe limped back to the counter, set down his mug.

Then he left the room before Reed could provoke him anymore.

But not before he caught the look in Jenna's eyes, a look he'd put there. And no amount of well-intended goading on Reed's part was going to take it away.

Reed thought he was a fool.

Maybe he was.

Maybe he was walking away from one of the best things that had ever happened to him.

But he *was* walking because he sure as hell wasn't going to saddle Jenna McMillan with one of the *worst* things that could ever happen to her.

Gabe walked into the room where Maxim was sitting. He could smell the man's sweat, and a little twinge of fear. *Little* was going to change to *big* real soon.

"You have answers for me?" This part was for show. Gabe knew before he asked what Maxim's response would be.

The older man met Gabe's eyes. "I told you. I don't know what you're talking about."

Gabe didn't even blink. "Last chance to play nice."

Maxim looked away, that twinge of fear swelling to something more substantial. "Name your price."

Gabe turned around and walked out of the room.

When he came back, Doc and Mendoza were with him. Now Maxim was about ready to piss his pants with fear.

"Take Jenna into the other room," Gabe said to Johnny before he shut the door behind them. "I don't want her to see this."

Maxim's eyes went wide. "What are you doing?"

Gabe nodded to Doc and Mendoza. They flanked Maxim and grabbed him by the arms. Doc twisted one arm painfully behind Maxim's back, immobilizing him, hardly bothered by Maxim's struggle.

Mendoza pinned his other arm on the table, forced his palm flat, his fingers wide.

Eyes hard, Gabe withdrew his Butterfly. "One finger for each answer that doesn't satisfy me."

"You're mad!" Maxim shouted, thrashing around in a futile attempt to get away.

"I'm past mad. I'm royally pissed. I gave you a chance to do this the easy way. You chose not to take it. Now we do it the hard way."

He unfolded the Butterfly's four-inch blade from the Titanium billet handles. The fluorescent light overhead glinted off the razor sharp edge of tempered, carbon steel.

Maxim squealed like a pig when Gabe laid the lethal length of it over his finger. He nicked it lightly. Drew blood.

"For God's sake! Don't do this!" Maxim begged, his face red with terror, spittle flying from his mouth as the stench of piss flooded the room.

"Who sent you after Jenna McMillan?"

"Adler!" Maxim sobbed, folding like a tent in a high wind. "Erich Adler."

The room fell deathly still. The only sounds Gabe heard were of Maxim's sobbing and the ringing in his own ears.

"Adler is dead. He died when his chopper went down in El Bolsón last year."

Maxim shook his head vehemently. "No. No. He's alive! It wasn't him in the chopper!"

"Try again, asshole." Gabe pressed the knife harder against Maxim's finger. "I saw his body."

"You saw a double! Adler lived through the blast. He hid in a bunker!" Maxim was bawling like a baby now. "For God's sake, I'm telling you the truth! Adler is alive. I swear to you . . . he's alive."

Gabe glanced from Doc to Mendoza before turning his attention back to Maxim.

"Talk," he ordered. "Start from the beginning. And make it good."

Jenna was ghost pale when Gabe returned to the situation room.

He didn't have to ask if she'd watched. The look on her face told him that she'd not only watched, she'd heard. Erich Adler was alive.

Jenna she was shell-shocked by the news. The proof of it was apparent when the door opened and Nate and Juliana walked in. Jenna barely batted an eye.

"You're ill," Juliana said by way of greeting and rushed straight to Gabe's side.

Gabe scowled over her head at his boss.

"She insisted on coming," Nate said. "And I figured you could use the extra body," he added referring to himself.

"I'm fine," Gabe insisted as Juliana touched the back of her fingers to his forehead.

"You have a fever. Damn it, Gabe. You haven't been taking the antibiotics."

It wasn't a question so Gabe didn't bother to answer. They both knew she was right on both counts. He'd lost the antibiotics somewhere. And yeah, he was sick and getting sicker. In the past few hours he'd started to feel like shit.

"I'm fine," he repeated as Juliana, muttering under her breath, gave Jenna a quick hello hug then rushed out of the room, no doubt in search of Holliday and his stash of medical supplies.

"Nathan Black. Jenna McMillan," Gabe nodded between the two as he made introductions.

"It's Nate," his boss said extending his hand.

"Jenna," she said quietly and returned his handshake before walking, robot-like, to the empty coffeepot. Her hands were shaking as she searched the cabinets for the makings of a fresh pot.

Gabe shook his head when Nate frowned at him over Jenna's reaction. It was a silent signal that said he'd explain later, which proved to be a mistake because Nate switched his attention to study Gabe.

"Juliana's right," Nate said. "You don't look so great."

It was neither here nor there. Gabe didn't have time to deal with it now any more than he had time to deal with his leg, which had swollen so tight it felt like his skin could break at any moment.

"I'm fine," he insisted again then rolled his eyes when Juliana rushed back into the room like a tornado.

"Sit," she ordered as she came at him with a cotton swab, a bottle of alcohol, and a syringe.

"It's an antibiotic," she said when he glared at the syringe with suspicion. "Roll up your sleeve."

The coffee started perking in the background as he sat and did as Juliana asked. It was much easier than fighting her.

"This is going to hurt," she warned him.

Yeah, he knew. IM antibiotics hurt like hell.

"And it's going to take a while for it to work. Now let me see the leg," she demanded when she'd finished.

"The leg is fine," he said through gritted teeth.

"Gabe—"

He cut her off, took her hands in his. "Juliana. We don't have time for this. I have some hard news. I'm sorry, but you need to be strong."

Juliana stilled instantly.

Then Gabe took the one thing away from her that had made it less difficult to cope with the deaths of her husband and daughter.

"There's no easy way to tell you. Erich Adler is alive."

Her reaction was instant and heartbreaking. Her fingers gripped his; her face paled to chalk.

Nate came to her side instantly, his hands cupping her shoulders, steadying her when she swayed.

"Sit," he said.

She sat.

Nate never left her side. His eyes never left her face, his entire bearing possessive, protective and . . . and *Jesus*, Gabe thought, as a fleeting truth hit him. *He's in love with her.*

"H . . . how can this be?" Juliana's voice was as unsteady as her bearing. "Adler is . . . dead. Gabe. You told me he was dead."

Her eyes were pleading when they met his, and Gabe felt the weight of Angelina's and Armando's deaths settle like lead on his shoulders.

Jenna slid a cup of coffee in front of Juliana, offered one to Nate, who shook his head.

Jenna sat down beside Juliana, laid a hand over hers, and squeezed.

"She needs to hear it. All of it," Jenna said, glancing at Gabe, apparently sensing that he was debating how much Juliana could take. Steadier now, Jenna held his gaze, nodded in encouragement.

On a bracing breath, he repeated what Maxim had told them.

"The man who went down in the chopper the day we destroyed the MC6 compound wasn't Adler. He was a double, a safeguard Adler had put in place years ago employing dozens of plastic surgeries."

He paused, waited for the devastating news to settle with her. "Adler survived the blast in an underground bunker, although Maxim says he was badly burned and disfigured.

"Apparently," he went on, "Maxim feels that Adler's injuries affected him mentally. Maxim claims that Adler is insane. That his sole reason for living is to destroy me, Amy Walker, Dallas Garrett, and Jenna."

"Revenge," Juliana said softly.

Gabe nodded. He was still dealing with that himself. Dallas could take care of himself and Amy. Gabe could take care of himself as well. But knowing that Jenna was the target of a madman tapped something deep inside him. Something primal and protective and profound that rocked him to his core.

"In any event, Adler has a hold over Maxim." This information, Gabe would spare her. Juliana didn't need to know about Maxim's revolting taste for young boys. "He used it to blackmail Maxim into arranging for both Jenna and me to be at the Congress that day.

"Adler's plan was to have his men wound both of us then bring us to him so he could, per Maxim, extract his revenge."

"That's insane," Juliana said, sounding defeated.

"Which would support Maxim's statement. And I agree. Adler would have to be insane to think he could pull off an abduction like that in broad daylight."

"So the break-in at Juliana's," Nate interjected thoughtfully. "How was that part of this?"

"Your new 'friend' was sent by Adler to see if Jenna or I were there." Gabe would tell Nate later that the secondary part of the plan had been to kill Juliana in order to make Gabe suffer even more.

"Now it works," Nate said with a nod. "All the mumbling about El Diablo."

"It would seem he has half the lowlifes in the country scared loyal. They'll do damn near anything to avoid falling out of favor.

"Anyway," Gabe went on, "Adler instructed Maxim to contract with BOI for protection. He made certain Maxim had contacted Jenna's editor to ensure she'd come down here on the pretense of covering a story about him."

"What about Rashman Hudin?" Nate asked. "He still figure into this?"

"According to Maxim, Hudin has no direct involvement. Quite possibly, Hudin doesn't even know about Adler's grand plan. MC6—again, according to Maxim—cut off all communication with Adler.

"The flip side to his plan is Adler thinks that once he delivers the news to Hudin that he's killed us, he'll fall back into favor with MC6. He'd regain his standing in the organization, which has apparently considered him persona non grata since we destroyed the El Bolsón complex."

"Jesus." Nate scrubbed a hand over his face. "So the bottom line is, you've got a nut case on your trail. One, I'm thinking, who won't stop until he gets what he wants.

"Which means you'll be looking over your shoulder for a helluva long time," Nate added. "Adler's got contacts and connections all over the world. He won't stop until he gets what he wants."

"That's why we need to smoke him out," Gabe said. "If we don't, he'll go to ground and bide his time until he thinks we've let down our guard."

"There's another possibility," Jenna said, looking up from her coffee mug. "He could shift his attention to Dallas and Amy."

"We need to find him," Gabe said. "We need to find him now."

The room became as silent as a tomb.

"Or he needs to find us," Jenna said.

All eyes turned her way.

"He wants me. Let's give him what he wants."

24

Jenna watched as Gabe fought a barely controlled rage boiling just below the surface. "No. Fucking. Way."

"Wait. Just listen," she insisted when he rose and limped over to the counter. He jerked open a cabinet door, snagged a mug, then slammed it down.

"I'm not listening because we aren't talking about this." He sloshed coffee into the mug then spun around to face her. His face was red with rage, his stance combative. "So just forget it. I will not use you as bait."

"And I won't live the rest of my life wondering if each day is going to be my last," she shot back. Jenna dragged a hand through her hair, gathered herself, trying not to read things into Gabe's violent reaction that would give her hope. It wasn't that he didn't care about her. She knew he did. He cared deeply. He didn't want to see her hurt or dead. But he was still going to walk away from her when this was over.

"Look," she said reasonably, "I'm not stupid. I'm sure as hell not a martyr, and I'm no Braveheart. This monster has me scared to death. But I want this over. I want it over," she restated firmly. "If making Adler think I'm easy pickings will draw him out, then let's just do it."

"How do you see this going down?" Nate asked quietly.

"For chrissake, Nate!" Gabe growled. "You can't seriously be considering this."

"Let's just hear her out."

Jenna nodded her appreciation to Nate. "Adler doesn't know you have Maxim, right? Right?" she repeated when Gabe silently glared.

"I'll take that as a yes," she said and went on. "Have Maxim contact Adler. Tell him he's figured out a way to deliver me. That he's already contacted me and that I've agreed to meet him. Have him tell Adler—I don't know— tell him that he's promised me the goods on Hudin. Something that would be plausible enough to make me want to risk it."

"No. No. And no," Gabe repeated vehemently.

"You know the city," she continued, ignoring Gabe and appealing to Nate. "Put me outside somewhere. In a park. Or at a public café. Whatever. Someplace you and the guys can watch and be all over in seconds. When Adler's men come after me, you move in.

"I've seen your powers of persuasion." She directed that comment to Gabe. "You can *sweet* talk them into leading you to Adler. You grab him. Then it's over."

Silence blanketed the room.

"It's not bad," Nate said at last.

Gabe swore roundly. "It reeks of a cluster fuck."

"You have a better idea?" Jenna challenged.

"Yeah," Gabe said, eyes hard. "We give him me."

"He'll never rise to that bait." Nate shook his head, looking grim. "He'll smell a rat the size of an Abrams tank. No. He won't go for it. Then you'll be back to playing a waiting game with Adler making all the rules."

"I want this, Gabe," Jenna said, meeting his eyes.

"Yeah, well, we all want things we can't have."

"No one," she said making certain he understood her meaning, "knows that better than me."

Except for the tick of the utilitarian clock hanging on the wall above the sink, the small room was silent.

Gabe stared. Glared. Then finally headed for the door.

He stopped with his hand on the knob. "All right," he said, never turning around. "We do it your way. But I will micro-manage this op down to every breath you take. And so help me, Jenna, you will do everything I say, no questions asked, no hesitation. Got it?"

Oh, she got it, all right. He was afraid for her. Well, so was she. But she wanted to eliminate Adler as a threat and get on with her life.

Which meant getting as far away from Gabe Jones as she possibly could.

"Yeah," she said, softly, already regretting the possibilities she would leave behind her in Argentina. "I got it."

7:00 P.M.

It was taking too long. Gabe watched, never taking his eyes off Jenna as she sat alone across the street at a table outside the café.

She'd been right. He and Nate did know the city. They'd debated long and hard about the location and finally settled on LaBoca. The oldest and most authentic neighborhood in Buenos Aires was partly an artist's colony but mostly a working-class neighborhood.

Caminto — little path — was the main street, the center of activity and host to a number of outdoor cafés and street vendors. From Gabe and Nate's perspective, it provided multiple venues to watch over Jenna without being detected.

He still didn't like it. Had that itchy twitchy twisting feeling in his gut that told him this was a catastrophe in the making.

He rarely ignored that feeling, and wouldn't have ignored it this time if he hadn't been suspicious that the fever invading his system had set him off stride and was clouding his judgment. That and his feelings for Jenna.

First rule of operation: Never become personally involved.

Fuck. He was way past worrying about that.

A string of traffic went by, trucks honking, engines racing as he hunched behind an easel, absently splashing color on a four-foot-square canvas that worked as both foil and partial concealment.

Doc, Mendoza, Reed, and Nate were similarly disbursed along the street. Doc read a local newspaper and sipped coffee. Nate haggled with Mendoza over the price of today's fish catch. Reed flirted casually with every skirt that walked by.

Dusk was closing in.

This was taking too damn long. Gabe felt the physical strain to his bones. The antibiotic hadn't taken hold like he'd hoped. He felt like shit. Sapped of strength. Lightheaded. Dizzy.

He shook his head. Worked to shake it off. Cursed when another wave of dizziness swamped him.

It had been four hours since Maxim—more than willing to comply with their instructions in exchange for keeping his precious digits—had made the contact with Adler, dangling Jenna as bait. The bastard had jumped like a great white on fresh kill. They'd had Maxim set up a time and place.

Too damn long, Gabe thought again, edgy with the compulsion to pull the plug and back the hell away.

He knew Jenna. She'd defy him, because that's what she did best. He didn't care. He'd give it five more minutes then they were out of here.

He tensed when a man approached her.

Flirted. Tried to pick her up.

The wire worked perfectly. He could hear every word as Jenna let him down sweetly and he moved on down the street.

Gabe's heartbeat settled after the false alarm while his head continued to pound with fever.

Gabe had personally wired her then reviewed her instructions with her until she'd dug in and put an end to it. He'd taken every precaution he could think of, including making her memorize his cell phone number on the very off chance she needed to contact him.

"I've got it, Gabe. I've got it all, already. I'm not a moron. I'm not going to do anything stupid. I just want to get this over with."

Brave green eyes had regarded him with determined defiance. A defiance that often cost her.

He knew that. Just like he knew she wanted more from him than he could give.

"Let's just do this," she'd said. "Then we can both get on with our lives."

On two separate continents. Two separate worlds. He sure as hell didn't belong in her world, and he could never ask her to be a part of his.

"Anything?" He tucked his chin and spoke into his commo mic.

He got a chorus of "Negative"s.

"Okay," he said with a mixture of annoyance and relief. "The bastard isn't coming. Let's call it qui—"

An ear-splitting blast cut him off, rocking the street with a concussion that toppled his easel.

"What the fuck?" Johnny's voice echoed in his ear.

The sound of terrified screams filled the air as fire licked twenty feet high and smoke billowed from the shop beside the café. Lots of smoke. Crawling at street level, obscuring his view of Jenna.

"Move in! Now!" Gabe shouted.

He shot toward the street, battling the four lanes of traffic to get to her. He couldn't see her through the smoke. Couldn't hear anything but screams and honking horns and squealing breaks.

An urban bus, followed by a utility van followed by a dump truck crawled to a stop in front of him.

Fighting the urge to panic, Gabe dodged the bus, almost went down when he got cut off by another van.

Frantic now, that feeling he'd been trying to ignore raising the hair on the back of his neck, he ran at a limping gait down the line of bumper to bumper traffic, trying to get to her.

"Jenna!" he shouted her name into the mic.

Nothing.

An eternity passed—in truth only seconds—until he vaulted over the front bumper of a cement truck and broke through to the far side of the street.

And his heart stopped beating.

She was gone.

25

The bastard had her. The sonofabitch had her!

Gabe leaned against the outside wall in the alley to keep from falling over. Two hours had passed since Jenna had disappeared. In those two hours he'd searched like a man possessed.

He had to find her. He had to fucking find her. He pushed away from the wall. Felt the world tilt and spin. He dug for the strength to fight the fever and the fear.

In his mind, he saw Adler torturing her. He could hear her screaming. See her bleeding.

Fuck. Oh, fuck. This couldn't be happening again.

"Gabe."

Nate's voice reached him through a fog.

He opened bleary eyes. Struggled to focus. "I'm okay."

"You are like shit. You've hit the wall, man. Get back to HQ. Have Juliana give you something before you drop."

"I have to find Jenna."

"Son, you couldn't find your ass in this condition. You're sick. Your eyes are glassy. You're burning up. And right now, you're more of a liability than an asset. I'll have Mendoza drive you."

"I'm not going anywhere."

"That's an order, Jones. You aren't going to be any good to Jenna or to me if you pass out cold. We'll keep looking. You can catch up with us later."

"Later, she might be dead."

"We'll find her." Nate clapped him on the shoulder. "It'd be nice if you were alive when that happened."

9:00 P.M.

Juliana had known something was wrong. As the hours passed while she waited at the BOI headquarters for word, she knew that it was taking too long.

So when Raphael Mendoza walked into the situation room supporting Gabe, she knew the worst had happened.

Gabe, oh Gabe. He looked ill and exhausted and haunted.

She helped Raphael ease him onto a worn sofa in the corner of the small room. He dropped like a sack of flour, eyes closed.

She felt his forehead. He was on fire.

"What happened?" she asked Raphael as she hurriedly ran a dishtowel under cold water then rushed back to Gabe's side. "Where's Jenna?"

Mendoza shook his head, looking frustrated and weary. "They got her."

He told her about the bomb that had clearly been set as a diversion. About the traffic jam that had apparently been prearranged.

"Looks like they were waiting inside the café," Mendoza added while he hurried around the room, snagging equipment. "Slipped out the front door, grabbed her, disabled her mic—we found it on the sidewalk. They must have taken her out through a back door and into a delivery van or a truck waiting in the alley. Somehow they got her out there without us spotting her.

"We tore the city apart, searching," he said with a look on his face Juliana had never seen before—dark, brooding, angry. "And turned up nothing."

"She's out there," Gabe said, his voice close to breaking as he struggled to get back up. "That monster's got her. I've got to . . . find her."

"You're sick." Just how sick was evident when she was able to hold him down.

"So fix me up."

He wanted a quick fix. She couldn't give it to him.

"You need to be in bed."

"That's not happening."

"Half an hour," she begged. "Lie down for just half an hour. Give your body that small respite. Then I'll give you another injection."

"Do it," Mendoza said. "You can meet up with us later. We'll find her, Gabe," he added on his way out the door. "We'll find her."

BOI HQ
9:00 P.M.

The sound permeated his restless sleep like a fog horn. A door bell. A car horn. A phone.

A cell phone.

His cell phone.

Gabe forced his eyes open. The room spun.

Where the hell was he?

Finally it seeped through. BOI. HQ. The situation room.

Sonofabitch. He'd fallen asleep.

His phone continued to ring.

"Jones," he said groggily as he struggled to sit up, his pounding head forcing him to his back again.

"Gabe . . . Gabe . . ."

He shot to attention when he heard Jenna's voice, ignoring the pain ripping through his body. "Where are you?"

"He . . . he . . ." A gut-wrenching scream cut her off.

He gripped the phone in both hands. "Jenna!"

"You are very careless with your women."

It was a voice from the grave. Menacing. Evil. Rattling like old, bleached bones.

"Let me talk to her."

"You want to talk to her? You know where you can find her. And you will come alone if you want to see her alive before she dies. Then you can kill this one, too."

Deep in the Parque Nacional Iguazu,
near the base of Garganta del Diablo,
Argentina-Paraguay border
Five hours later, 2:25 A.M.

The moon hung like a spotlight, huge and white above the canopy trees in the rain forest that was flanked for miles by the meandering river and the legend that was Iguazu Falls. With every step Gabe took, the roar of water cascading with immeasurable force over a two-hundred-foot drop grew closer, louder.

Mist hung in the muggy night air in a blanketing vapor. It soaked Gabe's hair. Clung to the cammo paint he'd smeared on his face and hands. Cooled his fever—but not his fervor.

He had to get to Jenna.

He had to do it soon.

He'd called Nate from his cell on the way to the airport and told him where he was headed. Ignored his CO's orders to wait for them.

He couldn't wait. Based on the location they'd given him, Nate and the guys were at least twenty minutes behind him. So, no. He couldn't wait. Jenna couldn't wait. Every second that monster had her brought her closer to death.

The four-hour flight in the Little Bird had taken him north of Buenos Aires to the rain forest and the falls on the Argentina-Paraguay border.

You know where you can find her.

Adler's mind was sick, twisted, and predictable. That's all he'd had to say. Didn't matter. Gabe had known exactly where the bastard had taken Jenna.

He had walked this path once before. Felt the same urgency. The same gut-wrenching sense of doom. Had heard the rumbling thunder of the falls and the horrifying sound of Angelina screaming.

Screaming. Screaming. Screaming.

And now Adler had brought Jenna here, to the same place.

Gabe walked on, his night vision goggles delineating rock from shrub, his single-minded purpose blocking pain and panic as he fought through the fog of fever, focused on his goal.

He thought about certain truths. He'd lied to Jenna. He was not as mercenary as he wanted her to believe. He did fight for God and country. He fought for right. He fought against wrong. He fought from a base of justice.

But not tonight. Tonight blood lust ran through his veins craving vengeance, vying with the fever that threatened to consume him.

He wouldn't let it. And he would not watch the woman he loved suffer at the hands of a madman. Not again.

Adler would die long before Gabe let that happen. Gabe would die himself, before he let it come to that end.

He knew Jenna was still alive. The bastard would not have already killed her, it wasn't his MO. Adler wanted more than seeing her death. The monster wanted to make her suffer first.

And he wanted Gabe to witness it.

He didn't think about what Adler might have already done to her. Had thought only of finding her during the past hour as he'd hiked, feeling his way carefully and stealthily through the undergrowth.

No pain could slow him down. No fever could override the fire in his gut to see this through to the end of Adler's miserable life.

The falls were louder now. Closer.

He stopped, wiped the mist from the lenses of his NVGs. Got his bearing. He knew he should be coming upon Adler's encampment soon. A slight movement to his left confirmed that he was close.

He ducked down low, concealed himself behind a stand of ferns. Then he watched. He made himself wait, still as a stone, while two guards stood smoking, AK-47's slung over their shoulders.

His gaze locked on them, Gabe pulled the MSP out of its shoulder holster. He'd chosen the compact, two-barrel, single-action pistol for two reasons. One, it was completely silent. The Russians had known what they were doing when they'd developed it over thirty years ago.

Two, he needed something deadly at close range. The MSP gave him that. The stacked barrels were short but lethal.

He tensed when the static and squawk of a two-way radio broke through the relentless drumming sound of the falls.

The guard on the left answered, assured whoever was on the other end that all was well.

Gabe checked his watch. He figured he had fifteen minutes until the next radio check.

As soon as the guard disconnected, he cocked the twin hammers of the MSP and went in for the kill.

Two shots. Base of the skull.

Two dead.

No mercy.

No remorse.

He dragged the bodies deeper into the underbrush and quickly reloaded two cartridges bound together with a spring steel clip.

Then he resumed the hunt, moving in a clockwise circle. If Adler worked true to form, he'd have guards placed in a circular pattern surrounding him at two, four, six, eight, ten, and twelve o'clock.

As silent as the night, with his Butterfly between his teeth now, the MSP in one hand and a garrote in the other, he cut a wide arc, found the next two guards twenty meters away.

He popped one with the MSP. The second guard spun just as Gabe looped the garrote around his throat from behind, jammed his knee in the middle of his back, and yanked both ends. The man twitched in his arms, then after a couple of minutes went still.

Gabe was a machine now. He reloaded the MSP, moving fluidly through the underbrush to the beat of the pummeling falls and the tick of the clock in his head.

The next two guards were squatted down approximately eighteen meters from their counterparts. By the light of a small flashlight, they were playing dice, Gabe realized as he snuck closer.

Six down.

Six to go.

Less than five minutes before the next radio check.

Quick as a jungle cat, deep in the zone, he located then dispensed with two more guards without a struggle.

Two minutes.

He'd become one with the night. He flew through the forest, plotting his circular pattern, stalking and finding prey.

The next man, he shot. Broke the neck of the other with a quick, lethal snap. The last guard hadn't yet hit the ground when one of their radios squawked to life.

Gabe took off at a run, banking on the element of surprise to see him through the last outpost.

But he ran out of luck as he approached the final two guards.

A twig snapped beneath his feet.

Both men turned as Gabe closed in, AK's aimed in his general direction in the dark.

He kept running toward them. Fired the MSP when he was within five feet of the closest guard. One shot. Two. Was peripherally aware of the man dropping to his knees clutching his throat as his rifle fell to the ground.

Just as he was tangentially aware of a muzzle flash, the sound of AK rounds, something slammed hard into his side; a burning sensation flooded his left arm as he launched himself at the last guard, who fell with him to the ground.

They rolled across wet grass, wrestled over sharp stones. Gabe landed on top, wrapped his fingers around the guard's throat just as the man slammed a stone into Gabe's temple, dislodging the NVGs.

Blood ran into his left eye, blinding him as he reached for his Butterfly, slashed it hard across the guard's throat; he felt blood, warm, sticky, and wet, rush over his hand as the guard went slack beneath him.

Breathing hard, fading fast, he slogged through level upon level of awareness.

The passing of time.

The danger to Jenna.

The roar of the falls.

The excruciating layers of pain.

Winded, weak, he staggered to his feet, felt the sticky wetness of his own blood running down the side of his face, seeping through his shirt, trailing over his fingers as he sheathed his Butterfly.

Half-blind, barely conscious, he stood alone in the night, the scent of death heavy in the mist-shrouded air around him.

Jenna.

Every thought began and ended with her name.

Jenna.

He swayed, fell against a tree, battled to stay conscious and on his feet.

Had to find Jenna.

He lurched forward, snagged the still-smoking barrel of the AK-47 and stumbled toward the center of Adler's circle of death.

26

Jenna wasn't certain what roused her.

A car backfiring? Firecrackers? Rifle shots?

Didn't know. Didn't care. Each time she came to, it was to face a living nightmare.

Each time she regained consciousness, she prayed for the drug to take her under again. But whatever they'd used to knock her out when they'd abducted her in Buenos Aires remained only in a diluted dose in her system.

And pain was an enemy of sleep. Pain and the growl of the waterfall constantly pummeling its way to the river.

Bleary eyed, she raised her head from her chest, dared to look through the damp, filthy tangle of her hair and focus on her captor.

She'd known the moment she'd come to, lashed to a crude wooden cross like a human sacrifice, that the monstrous visage greeting her was Erich Adler.

He was grotesque. He was also insane as he'd raved on and on about payback and retribution and justice. She had no doubt in her mind that her suffering at his hands had barely begun.

She glanced toward the small campfire that flickered in the clearing. The coals glowed red hot. So did the branding iron that lay in the center of the flames.

She swallowed back a wave of nausea, fought the excruciating memory of Adler pressing the iron to her skin. The delicate flesh of her inner bicep still burned and throbbed in agony. She could only pray that she passed out before Adler made his next pass with the iron.

Her shoulders ached and burned, stretched in their sockets beyond mere pain. Her wrists were scraped raw from the rope that bound them, her hands numb from lack of circulation.

She tasted her own blood, felt the swelling in her cheek and her lower lip with her tongue. For the first time in her life she understood what made one human being relish the thought of killing another.

"Excellent. You're awake."

Involuntarily, Jenna's gaze sought Adler as the hoarse, grating assault of his voice startled her.

"I think the main event is about to begin." He'd dragged himself to her side. His breath smelled like death against her face as he drew his clawed hand down the side of her cheek. "Did you hear the gunfire? It would seem the Archangel has finally come for you."

She glanced up.

And there through the rising mist, she saw Gabe, bloodied and beautiful, and God, oh God, looking half dead as he broke into the clearing.

She cried his name as Adler picked up a fuel can and drenched her clothes with gasoline.

"Like Pavlov's dog," Adler said with a sneer in his ruined voice. "Conditioned to protect and defend. I knew you couldn't stay away."

Gabe stopped, frozen by the sight that met him. He could see nothing out of his left eye. But what he could see shot a jolt of panic through his system that almost dropped him to his knees.

Christ, oh Christ, the bastard had tied Jenna to a cross. Like Angelina.

Rage and revulsion rolled in his gut as he took in the sight of her; arms spread painfully wide, her face bruised and bloody, her arm burned, hair matted and filthy around her beautiful face.

Jenna's face.

Angelina's face.

He shook his head, willing away the tangled net of cobwebs crowding his mind—a legacy of pain, fever, and blood loss.

Not Angelina. Jenna.

Jenna.

Alive. She was alive.

No more than six meters away a ghostly apparition, cloaked in a black, hooded robe that hid his face, stood in the shadows beside her.

In one hand, Adler held a Glock that was pointed directly at Gabe. In the other grossly deformed hand he clumsily clutched a lit torch, waving it inches away from Jenna's breast. *The sonofabitch was going to set her on fire.*

"Drop the rifle."

Gabe glanced from Adler to Jenna's tortured expression. Instincts born during years of battle, imbedded over time into muscle, blood, and bone, kicked in to do his reacting for him.

He had no choice. He dropped the rifle.

"Now the pistol."

Slowly, he pulled out the MSP. Tossed it at his feet.

"She's in fairly good condition, don't you think?" Adler taunted. "I wanted to save the best for you to watch."

"Let her go." Marshalling what strength he had left, Gabe headed toward them.

"Stop. Now. Or she goes up in flames."

Gabe stopped, head spinning.

His stomach knotted when Adler used the muzzle of the Glock to shove back the hood covering his face and revealed the ruined vestiges of the human being he had once been.

Red, rubbery scar tissue ran in thick, melted clumps from his left temple, over his closed eye, and disappeared beneath the robe at his neck.

"She'll burn like I did," Adler promised, spewing out his hatred like bullets. "And you'll get to watch her fry."

Watch her fry . . . watch her fry.

Gabe reeled as if Adler had gut-punched him.

"You did this to me!" Adler roared above the pounding of the falls.

"Both of you. You destroyed my body. Condemned me to an existence of excruciating pain. Made me an outcast in the very organization I nearly died trying to defend."

His voice had risen to an eerie screech, his good eye bulging and wild. Spittle flew from his deformed mouth in a wide, arcing spray.

"And you think I would allow either one of you to leave? I have lived for this day and only for this day since I crawled out of that bunker charred and ruined by your hand. By *her* interference."

Adler stopped, visibly settled himself.

"Take him!" he yelled. Then he glared around the perimeter of his encampment when no one appeared.

"Take him!" he demanded again.

When understanding dawned, rage more than panic colored his voice. "What did you do with my men!"

"They're indisposed." Gabe took a halting step forward. "Looks like it's just you and me."

"And the woman," Adler pointed out, threatening with the torch again.

Gabe knew what he had to do. And he knew he had to do it fast. He was fading. Adler would soon fully grasp the reality that he had no one to come to his aid.

"Burn her and you're a dead man," he warned, advancing step by determined step.

Adler lifted the Glock and fired.

The bullet hit Gabe like a freight train, spun him like a top.

He slammed to the ground, clutching at the pain in his left shoulder. He tasted dirt. Heard Jenna scream. Felt the shattered bone shift in his shoulder, the warmth of more blood pouring out like rain.

On auto pilot now, he pushed himself to all fours, fell flat on his face again when a dizzying rush knocked him off balance. Again he fought to rise to his knees, groped for a rock lying beside his right hand.

He winged it in Adler's general direction.

Adler fired again. Wildly this time. Missed.

Now.

Gabe lurched to his feet and launched himself at Adler like a disabled missile. The impact drove them both to the ground.

Adrenaline took it from there. Adrenaline and rage and a blood lust for retribution.

Indescribable pain seared through his shoulder as Gabe pinned his left forearm against Adler's throat.

Eyes fixed on Adler's nightmare face, Gabe withdrew his Butterfly from its sheath.

"You can't kill me," Adler grated out in a tortured whisper. "No one can kill me!" Adler's smugness ran thick in his voice.

"Wrong." Eyes never leaving the monstrous face, Gabe shoved the Butterfly in for the kill.

He knew exactly where to place the blade. Above the fourth rib. Past the sternum. Slice toward the arm. The strike ripped open a lung and cut Adler's heart in half.

Jaw clenched, he watched the surprise register, then the understanding and finally the shock as Adler's blood warmed his hand where it flowed onto the hilt of his blade.

"M . . . mercy," Adler wheezed.

"I'll show you mercy. Just like you showed Angelina mercy. Like you showed Jenna mercy."

Gabe drove the blade deeper, twisted, watched without remorse as Adler's body jerked, spasmed, and he wheezed his dying breath.

Dead.

Finally, Erich Adler was dead.

Gabe rolled off his prostrate body, his adrenaline letting down with a blinding rush of pain.

He lay there. Gulping air. Staring at the sky. Wanting to feel elation. Wanting to feel justice.

Yet all he felt was weight, heavy and cloying and dragging him toward blackness.

"Gabe!"

Jenna's sob jolted him back toward consciousness. He had to get to her.

His legs felt like stumps, thick and numb, seeming unattached to his body as he pushed himself to his feet, stumbled to her side.

She was sobbing now. Sobbing his name. Sobbing in pain. Sobbing because she knew what he knew.

He was dying. He felt the life being sucked out of him in huge, greedy licks.

Eyes glazed, he searched her face through a bloody haze. Watched the tears trail from those amazing green eyes and run in rivers through the grime on her cheeks.

Her beautiful, beautiful face.

"Hey . . . hotshot. Helluva place . . . for a . . . party."

His words were slurred, his movements slow and disassembled as he cut the ropes binding her left wrist, then sliced the ropes on her right.

"'Sokay," he whispered when she whimpered in pain then collapsed against him. "You're . . . okay . . . now."

Then the world fell out from underneath him.

He was falling.

Tumbling through day then night.

Hot then cold.

The falls rumbled.

Jenna's voice floated somewhere out of reach. Somewhere between now and nowhere.

Don't leave me. Gabe! Don't leave me.

But he had to go. He felt it. Felt who he was, felt what he was, drifting away.

Realized, too late, that he didn't want to go.

Because it would hurt her.

Because he didn't want to leave her.

More voices.

Floated in.

Floated out.

Nate.

Reed.

Mendoza.

They shouldn't be here. He was the only one who was supposed to leave.

"Go . . . g . . . go." He heard his own voice through a barrel. Heard Jenna's from miles away.

"Got a pulse."

Doc.

Urgent.

Excited.

"God damn, I've got a pulse!"

Then he heard nothing at all.

27

Sanatorio Guemes Hosptial Privado, Buenos Aires
Twenty-five hours later

"You should get some rest."

Jenna roused herself from her vigil at Gabe's bedside. She opened her eyes to white on white and realized she must have dozed off with her head on the hospital bed.

"I'm fine." She lifted her head but held tight to the lax fingers of Gabe's hand. Searched his pale, drawn face.

Monitors beeped steadily in the background. Pain medication and antibiotics dripped into his veins through an IV.

Another line delivered a unit of plasma—one of the many units he'd been given since the Little Bird, with Reed at the controls, had set down in the hospital parking lot in Buenos Aires almost eighteen hours ago. Rusty colored fluid drained from a chest tube and from the site where surgeons had worked to repair his shattered shoulder.

She glanced at Juliana. "Any change?"

Juliana shook her head as she stood at the foot of the bed, perusing Gabe's chart. She hooked it back on the foot rail, offered a careful smile. "No. No change. But he's hanging in there."

Which in itself was a miracle.

Doc had saved Gabe's life in the field. The surgical trauma team had been amazed that Gabe had made it to the ER alive. Doc had field-dressed the gunshot wound in his shoulder and his side with the same kind of blood-clotting agent used by the military in Iraq. Then he'd inserted a chest tube and worked whatever kind of magic he'd had to, to stabilize him.

"Jenna, you really need to rest," Juliana repeated. "I'll stay with him. I won't leave him alone."

Again, Jenna shook her head. "It's okay. I want to be here when he wakes up."

She hadn't left his side until they'd forced her to stay behind when the trauma team had wheeled Gabe into surgery. Juliana had gently manipulated and cajoled her into having her own injuries treated, taking a shower, and dressing in some scrubs the staff had rustled up for her. Johnny had sweet-talked her into eating, though she'd barely picked at her food.

Then the waiting had begun. Eons of waiting under the stark sterile lights of the waiting room.

The boys had paced and brought her coffee, held vigil at her side in sullen supportive silence, all at a respectful distance. All but Reed, who had drawn her onto his lap, petted her hair, held her close, and let her cry.

"It could be hours yet before he comes to," Juliana warned her now.

It had already been hours. Too many hours.

Please, please, please, she willed Gabe silently, pressing her forehead to the back of his hand so Juliana wouldn't see her tears.

His fingers moved in hers.

She reared up. Eyes wide. Stared at his hand.

Still. It lay there, very, very still.

"What?" Juliana rushed to Jenna's side.

Deflated, she shook her head. "I . . . I thought he moved his hand."

"Talk to him," Juliana suggested gently. "Go ahead," she said with an encouraging nod. "He might be able to hear you."

Jenna suspected that Juliana was merely attempting to offer her hope, something to cling to. Even so, Jenna did as she suggested.

"Gabe . . . it's Jenna." She squeezed his hand. "You're in a hospital. You've had surgery. You're . . . you're going to be fine," she assured him.

Nothing.

Hours of fatigue, frustration, and worry—maybe even a delayed reaction to her own ordeal—finally took their toll. Her emotions, raw and frayed beyond the limit, gripped her heart, squeezed.

"Damn it, Jones." She cried, willing him to come around. "It's time to get your sorry ass out of this bed. I'm tired of seeing you lying around like a slug."

Juliana's hand gently caressed her shoulder.

"Fight!" she implored. "Please. Please. You have to fight!"

She went to pull her hand away from his, swipe at the tears running down her face—when his fingers moved again.

A sob escaped her. She hadn't imagined it.

More tears. Of promise, this time, not fear. "That's it? That's the best you can do, tough guy?"

He squeezed her hand this time. With the strength of a kitten, yes, but *he squeezed her hand.*

"He's trying to say something." Tears filled Juliana's eyes too when Jenna glanced over her shoulder at her then quickly back to Gabe.

His lips were moving. Jenna's heart did flip flops of joy as she stood and leaned close to his mouth.

"Got a . . . sm . . . art . . . m . . . mouth . . . on . . . you, hot . . . shot."

"God, oh God. Thank you. Thank you," she whispered skyward. "Damn right I do," she told him, pressing a kiss to his brow. "You're damn right I do." She was laughing and crying and containing herself from doing cartwheels around the bed. "And you're going to hear plenty from it before I'm through with you."

Bahia Blanca
Two weeks later

Arms crossed beneath her breasts, a soft smile on her face, Jenna watched from the doorway of Gabe's first-floor bedroom as Juliana fussed and Johnny and Nate gave Gabe grief about landing in the lap of luxury.

He'd been released from the hospital earlier today. The lot of them had then flown on the Angelina Foundation chopper to Bahia Blanca where Gabe would spend the next few weeks at Villa Flores recuperating.

Unfortunately, he'd had to go back in for a second surgery on his shoulder, but it was healing well now, although the cast and the dressings on both his shoulder and his chest needed regular attention.

Also unfortunately, his calf wound continued to be a problem. The infection wasn't reacting as well to the antibiotics as they'd hoped. Juliana said they would have to fight it aggressively to get him past it.

If he got past it.

Jenna was so worried for him. Because the odds weren't good. He could lose his leg below the knee.

"Clearly he's got more attention than he needs," Johnny said, seeking Jenna out by the door, leaving Nate and Juliana to fuss over Gabe. "How are you doing with all this, darlin'?"

Jenna smiled up at the heartbreakingly handsome blond. She thought fleetingly of how she'd misjudged this man in the beginning. He liked to play the rake, the scoundrel, the good-time boy, but there was much more beneath Johnny Duane Reed's I-could-give-a-damn smiles and cowboy swagger. Much, much more.

"I'm good," she said and let him drape an arm over her shoulder.

And she was good. Physically, she'd healed. Emotionally—well, she was dealing with the nightmares. "Now we just need to get him back on his feet."

Johnny squeezed her hard. "You don't have to worry about that tough s.o.b. Man has more lives than a damn cat."

"That's what I'm counting on," she said, pasting on a brave face.

"I'm going to go find me a beer," he said abruptly. "You want something?"

She shook her head, squeezed his hand before he left the room. She observed, with interest, the two dark heads on either side of Gabe's bed. Something . . . she couldn't pinpoint it, but she sensed that something was going on between Nate and Juliana.

There was nothing overt. No. Jenna had never seen any blatant interaction between the two of them that would even suggest . . . what? Attraction maybe?

She didn't know. But seeing them together during the past two weeks, she'd detected an energy of some sort humming between them. An occasional exchange of glances. The careful distance they religiously maintained.

She could see it, she decided finally. Nate and Juliana. She could see them together. She wondered if they even realized there was something in the wind.

"What's happening with Maxim?" she heard Gabe ask Nate.

She pushed away from the door, happy beyond measure every time she heard his voice after facing the very real possibility that she'd never hear it again.

"He's back in the States, singing every song he knows about Rashman Hudin to our friends in the State Department."

"And you accomplished that how?" Gabe asked, shifting carefully.

Jenna winced for him. Even though he never complained, she knew he was in constant pain.

"By convincing him he wouldn't much like the accommodations at Gitmo, which was where we could damn well make certain he'd end up if he didn't come clean," Nate said with a grin.

"So there's a good chance Uncle will be able to pin something on Hudin?"

Nate shrugged. "If not pin him, slow him way down. We found nothing, by the way, to suggest you or Jenna are even on Hudin's radar. Adler acted alone. Mendoza and Reed have been beating the bushes, flushing out any remnants of his band of miscreants. I don't think we'll be hearing from any of them again. Word on the street is they're damn glad El Diablo is dead. And yeah, we made sure to spread the word that he'd gone to hell for good this time."

"I know you two want to catch up, but I think the patient needs to rest now," Juliana said gently.

Gabe had already closed his eyes. The lines around his mouth were tight with fatigue and pain.

Nate squeezed Gabe's good shoulder. "Leave it to you to come up roses.

Not sure I would have gone to such extremes, though, to land myself in a feather bed just so two beautiful women could step and fetch for me."

Without opening his eyes, Gabe lifted his hand, flipped Nate the bird. "Sir," he added, which got a chuckle out of his boss.

Jenna found Gabe awake and alone later in the day when she peeked in on him. Which was a relief. Between the staff at the hospital, the boys, Nate, and Juliana, it seemed she rarely found a moment to be alone with him when he wasn't sleeping.

"Hey," she said, smiling as she walked into the room. "How are you feeling?"

"If I felt any better, I don't think I could stand it."

She crossed the room to his bed, fussed with his pillows. "Oh, so we can add delusional to your list of conditions."

He grunted. "I hate this."

"I know." She pulled a side chair up to the bed and sat. "Since patience isn't one of your strongest suits, I'm guessing you're about ready to climb the walls."

"Good guess."

Poor baby. In a week or two, he would be going crazy. Now he was too sick, too weak, and his body was still too far away from healing for him to give it more than a fleeting thought.

She couldn't wait for that day. Couldn't wait until he felt that good. She could envision him cross and cranky and giving both her and Juliana fits as they tried to keep him settled down. She smiled at the notion because she was just so damn happy to have him on the mend.

"When are the guys leaving for Buenos Aires?"

"Soon, I think." She poured him a glass of water. Helped him with the straw. "Nate said something about wanting to get back to HQ tonight. I'm sure they'll be in to say good-bye before they go," she added, deciding the chair wasn't close enough. She hitched her hip onto the bed instead. Smiled down at him. "Johnny wouldn't want to miss another chance to rag on you."

She'd expected a smile. Instead, he sobered, had trouble meeting her gaze. "Now would be a good time for us to say our good-byes then. Before they file back in here and it's time for you to go."

Jenna froze. Felt her heart jerk. Replayed his words, hoping she had heard him wrong.

When he looked away, purposefully avoiding her eyes, she knew she'd heard him loud and clear.

"Go? Why would I need to do that?" But she knew. She knew exactly where this was headed.

Her chest tightened. She had to tell herself to breathe.

Gabe stared at the ceiling. Swallowed. "Because you have a life you need to get back to." A life that didn't include him.

She closed her eyes. Let out a breath that made her chest ache. "You're not really going to do this."

He made a big show of looking puzzled, didn't quite pull it off. "Do what? Hey. I'm just saying. You got your story, right? I figured you'd be itching to get back to the States, get on to the next big assignment."

"What I'm anxious about is you."

"Well, hell. You heard Juliana. I'll be fine. Just fucking fine."

He looked away. His jaw hardened. And she realized what this was really about.

Her heart broke for him.

"This is about your leg, isn't it?"

Silence. Telling and cold.

"You've heard the reports," he said then, still not looking at her. "You know the score."

"Yeah. I've heard. I know. You could lose it. And I'd hate that for you. But give me some credit here. Whatever happens, it's not going to affect the way I feel about you."

But he thought it would. The hollow look in his eyes when he finally turned to her said it all. He thought it would affect how she felt about him because it would affect the way he felt about himself.

She could practically read his mind. He was a warrior. Now he saw himself as possibly becoming something less. *Less of a man. A cripple. An amputee. A disabled citizen.*

"Gabe—"

"I do not want your pity," he snapped when she made a move to take his hand.

"Pity is the last thing I would ever feel for you."

"Yeah, well, give it some time."

Anger. Pain. Hopelessness. It was all there.

"If the infection wins, we'll face that together."

"No," he said in a voice as hard as stone. "We won't. Get it through your head. I don't want you here. Just . . . just get the hell back to your life and leave me to deal with mine."

Her heart breaking, she bit her lower lip, shook her head. "Don't do this."

"Come on, Jenna. Get a grip." Mr. Macho was suddenly back. "We're both adults here. You knew from the beginning what I had to give," he said wearily.

"Yeah. You made that clear. Guess I should have made myself clear, too. Here's the deal. I love you."

It was a desperation move. It was the truth. And it didn't play.

He looked away again as she fought tears and rage and . . . God, oh God, he was really going to let her walk away.

"You care about me, too," she insisted.

Nothing.

Nothing but a cold distant stare followed by a barely discernible, "I'm sorry."

So was she. Sorry and frustrated and suddenly mad at the world. "You're sorry. Dandy. I'll tell you what else you are," she said. "You're a coward."

That earned her a glare.

"Yeah, that's right. You almost died for me. Because that's what you do, right? You save people. You're the big, brave, alpha warrior who comes charging in to save the day, but that doesn't take any guts, does it? That just comes natural. It's the right thing to do. Adler was right. You're like one of Pavlov's dogs, reacting to the hero stimulus."

A muscle in his jaw worked, but he remained stubbornly silent, angering her even more.

"But now something's not quite going your way, and you're the one who might need saving. I could do that. I want to do that. I'm the best damn thing that ever happened to you, Gabriel Jones."

Tears stung her eyes. And one more time, he looked away.

"Damn you." She hated herself for bullying him, hated him more for being so stupid and so stubborn. "I'm worth fighting for. Fight for me, damn it. Don't just lie there and let me go because you've got some misplaced notion that you're protecting me. I deserve better than that. You deserve better than that."

"What I deserve," he said without emotion, "is some peace and quiet. I think you'd better go now."

"Yeah," she said, struggling to hold it together. "Maybe I'd better."

She turned and headed for the door because damn it, she didn't want him to see her cry.

"Hey, hey," Johnny caught her as she bolted, head down, out the door.

She threw her arms around his neck, hung on tight.

"I'm sorry," he whispered into her hair.

She sniffed. "You heard?"

"Give him some time, Jenna. He's a hardhead."

"He's a stubborn fool."

"Quite possibly the dumbest fuck I know," Johnny agreed.

No, Jenna thought. She was.

She made it back to Buenos Aires in a daze. Spent the entire flight back to the States staring into space.

It wasn't until she walked into her D.C. apartment, felt the cold chill of the empty rooms and the silence of her future without Gabe, that she broke down.

She broke dishes. Broke glass. Damn near broke her big toe when she repeatedly kicked her bedroom door.

Broke her heart a hundred times over replaying the times they'd made love, the look on his face when he'd found her with Adler, the look on his face when she'd left him.

Bastard. Ignorant, pig-headed, rat bastard.

She was going to hate him for the rest of her life.

When she got over loving him.

When she got over missing him.

When she got past wondering about him.

When she quit aching for him.

Yeah. When she was done doing all that, she was going to hate Gabriel Jones forever.

28

"Passport," Jenna muttered as she rifled through her "important papers" drawer. "Where in the heck did I put that passport?"

She tucked her hair behind her ear, checked her watch. She was cutting it close. She had to catch a flight to Paris in less than two hours. The streets were slick with three inches of new snow with more coming down and she still hadn't called a cab.

"Crap," she sputtered when her doorbell rang. "I do not need this."

Distracted, she marched toward the door in two-inch black leather boots, tugging her fuzzy peach sweater down over her jeans.

"Whoever you are," she muttered as she reached for the doorknob, "this is going to be short and not so sweet."

But when she swung open the door, ready to bid the poor unfortunate soul a speedy "no thanks" to whatever he was selling, she almost reeled over backward.

"Whoa, there." Gabe's strong hand reached out, caught her arm, steadied her.

A million thoughts raced through her mind. God help her, she'd played out this scenario a thousand times in her head. Willed him to come to her.

Imagined seeing his face . . . his beautiful, dangerous face just one more time.

Now here he was.

Gabriel Jones. In the flesh.

And damn it, she hadn't worked her way up to hating him yet.

"So." He lifted a hand. "Hello."

"Um. Yeah. Hello." She couldn't stop looking at him. She told herself that was because it was impossible not to. He filled the open doorway, solid, strong, stunning.

Standing on two legs.

"How are you?"

He shrugged. "Getting there. You?"

She nodded back. "Good. I'm good."

That was the end of that brilliant and sparkling conversation. Silence, big and blank, yawned between them.

"Well, this is awkward," he said finally. He smiled. And broke her heart all over again.

What was he doing here? Why didn't he say something?

"Can I come in?"

"Oh. Oh," she repeated, finally realizing she was standing there staring at the deep brown of his eyes, at the breadth of his shoulders made even wider by the heavy wool jacket he wore. "Um. Sure. Come . . . come in."

She stepped back and he limped into the apartment.

Limped.

She'd wondered how he was doing. Every day. Every night. She'd wondered.

"You're leaving," he said after a quick glance around.

She followed his gaze to her open carry-on, the e-tickets lying on the table beside her purse. "Yeah. Catching a flight to Paris."

He nodded. "So. This is where you live."

"This is where I sleep," she said.

She could see that her choice of words was not lost on him. They were the exact same words he'd said to her when they'd ended up at his apartment in Buenos Aires.

Before they'd made love the second time.

She had to do something. Say something. Her heart was racing. Her chest was aching.

She still hadn't digested the fact that Gabe was really here, in D.C., in her apartment. Hadn't processed what it meant that he'd actually left Argentina. To come here. He must have had to do some digging to find out where she lived.

She knew what she wanted it to mean.

She knew what she *needed* it to mean.

So did her heart. It jumped around every which way in her chest, but she was too afraid to even go there. So she held her breath. Waited.

"Okay . . . how 'bout I cut to the chase?" he asked finally.

"How about you do that."

"You called me a coward," he said abruptly, not looking any too pleased about it.

That horrible ache eased to a dull throb. He'd been two weeks out of a surgery that had given him lousy odds to keep his leg. He'd been hurting and sick. So had she. And, yes, she'd called him a coward.

"Yeah, well. Sometimes I talk before I think."

"There's a news flash."

He smiled then. Smug and sexy, and what the hell was going on here?

"So you came all the way here to call me out?"

"Crossed my mind," he admitted.

She could feel her heart in her throat now, hear it in her ears. Didn't want to trust it to lead her to the wrong conclusions.

"Did you mean it?"

She tilted her head. "I might have," she admitted as he paid undue interest to a ceramic vase on an end table.

"Was I right?" she ventured as he touched a finger to the lip of the vase.

Finally he looked at her. Slowly nodded. "Yeah. You were right. About everything. And I really hate it when that happens."

He smiled again, crooked and cute and damn she was going to cry. Because now she knew. She knew why he was here.

"Everything?" She was damn near bursting with the need to get her hands on him, but she'd waited too long to let him off the hook now. "Like what, everything?"

"You're going to make me say it aren't you?"

"Oh, yeah. I'm going to make you say it."

"You're sure? Because this might take a while. Don't want you to miss your flight."

"Damn it, Jones," she shot back, her patience at an end. "Screw the damn flight, quit stalling and tell me that you love me."

His grin faded. His eyes filled. "I love you, Jenna." No hesitation. No doubt.

"Again."

"I love you."

Tears filled her eyes as she saw the truth and regret and pain in his.

"I'm sorry. Sorry I hurt you. Sorry I let you go. Sorry for . . . hell. Pick a reason."

She wasn't sure how she found it in her, but she took a quick step back when he reached for her. "Which is your bad shoulder?"

His brows knit together. "The left," he said carefully.

She slugged him in the right.

He staggered. Steadied himself. Grinned. "Is that like some weird Wyoming mating ritual thing I should know about?"

"Damn you," she cried, flying into his arms. Finally. "Damn you, damn you, damn you!"

He wrapped his arms around her, held her tight. "I'm sorry. I'm sorry I was such a coward."

She held his face in her hands. Kissed him with all the pain and love and longing she'd suffered the last two months. "If you ever let me walk away from you again, I'm going to make you wish you'd never been born."

Hands in her hair, he laughed as she walked him backward toward her bedroom. "Try to get away this time. Just try it. See where it gets you."

They made fast, frantic love. When the touching and the loving and the gasping and the desperation all eased to something manageable, they talked. About Juliana. About the BOIs, about how stupid he'd been.

Then they made love again. Soft and slow. Easy and sweet.

"So, guess that answers *one* question," Jenna said as she snuggled against his side, naked and warm and even softer than Gabe had remembered.

"And what question would that be?" He ran his hand lazily along the silk of her hip.

"You are *definitely* doin' fine."

Because he knew he was still a long way from fine, he didn't say anything for a long moment.

This was the part that was going to be hard for her to hear. Hard for him to say. He pressed a kiss to the top of her head. "Yeah. Lung's fine. Shoulder's healed better than even Juliana expected. The leg . . . you need to know about the leg."

She lifted her head, concern furrowing her brow when he paused.

"There's still a chance I could lose it."

"Oh, Gabe."

He rolled to his back and crossed his hands behind his head. Outside her bedroom window snow drifted down in huge, fat flakes. "So far the antibiotics haven't been able to knock down the infection."

"So what happens next?"

"It's a waiting game. We're still hoping the aggressive treatment will do the trick. The docs at Walter Reed are amazing."

She rose up on an elbow. "Walter Reed? You're being seen at Walter Reed?"

"For about a month now."

"You've been here for a month and—"

He pressed a finger to her lips. "Yes. A month. And no, I didn't come to see you before now. Look, Jenna, I needed that time, okay? I needed to get used to the idea of what my new normal might look like. And then there was that coward thing."

"You're not a coward." She snuggled back down against him.

He ran a hand up and down her back. "All these vets at the hospital, they come home from Iraq or Afghanistan. Some of them are pretty messed up.

"I've been spending a lot of time with those guys. Some of them are amputees. All of them are looking for hope."

He paused, squeezed her tightly. "I couldn't very well give it if I didn't buy into it myself."

She snuggled closer. "And now you do?"

"Yeah. Now I do." He tipped her head back so he could see her face. So she could look in his eyes and see the truth. "I was coming for you. Leg or no leg, I was coming for you."

Tears filled her eyes. "Because you're not a coward."

"Yeah, well, I had to prove you wrong, didn't I?" He ran a hand over her hair, searched her face. "No matter how hard I tried, I couldn't get you out of my head. You want to talk about scared? The idea of spending the rest of my life without you scared the hell out of me."

She kissed him. Everything in that kiss said she'd been scared, too.

"So," he whispered against her mouth. "Now you know it all."

She touched his cheek with her fingertips. "I have always known. I know I love you. I know that you love me. Other than that, nothing else matters."

"Maybe one thing does." He smiled into her eyes. "You have *got* to get a bigger bed if you expect me to spend any time here."

That brought her right back up on her elbow. Her green eyes narrowed as if she wasn't certain she could believe the implications of his statement.

"You figuring on spending a lot of time here, are you, Angel boy?" While her delivery was playful, her eyes showed her uncertainty.

He sobered suddenly. Because he understood. This was about commitment, long term and life changing. It was a huge step for him. One he'd never wanted to take before. One he wanted now with this woman. "Yeah. I am. Work for you?"

"Oh, it works." Her smile was at once joyous, devilish, and challenging as she rose to her knees. Gloriously naked, she leaned over him, planting a palm on either side of his shoulders. "But there will be expectations."

He chuckled as she swung a leg over his hips, straddling him. "Again? You trying to kill me?"

"That is so not what I had in mind."

She was so beautiful. That amazing red hair fell forward, brushing his chest as she lowered her upper body over him, kissed him . . . slow and wet and deep.

He reached up, caressed the bare hips that hovered above his lap. "Have mercy, hotshot. I need a little recovery time here."

"Recover all you want. All you have to do is lie there. I'll do all the work. There's this little game I've been wanting to play since the first time I saw you naked."

He laughed, thinking he was the luckiest sonofagun on the face of the earth. Sex. Laughter. Love. This was as good as it got. "Oh yeah? What kind of game?"

Then he groaned as she brushed the tips of her breasts against his pecs . . . sensual friction, velvet heat.

She touched her lips to his shoulder and his fresh scar. "Connect the dots. This scar," she whispered and moved on to his collarbone, loving him with the sweet wet caress of her mouth, "to this scar."

He groaned again and despite the fact that she'd worn him out, he felt himself swell as she used that amazing, busy mouth to lavish attention across his chest.

She moved slowly down to his abdomen, lingered over his hip. He was as tense as a wire, beyond combustible when her lips brushed his dick, teasing, whispering heat, promising heaven . . . before she began a slow deliberate path back up his body.

When she reached his jaw, she nipped him lightly, then pushed herself up and sat astride his lap. "So, how's that recovery thing coming along?" she asked with a smug, lazy smile after flipping her hair back away from her face.

He laughed, gripped her bare hips, and ground her against the long, hard length of him. "This the way it's going to be? You always getting what you want?"

She leaned close. Kissed him around his smile. "I think so, yeah. Just like I think you'll always manage to *rise* to the occasion."

She leaned into him again as he reached between them, guided himself home. Her eyes closed on a shivery sigh as she stretched to accommodate him, slowly lowering her body until he filled her.

He cupped her nape, dragged her down to his mouth, kissed her deeply. "My God, I've missed you."

"Never again," she promised between hot, probing kisses. "Never, ever, again."

Washington, D.C.
Six months later

"So, what's on your agenda today?" Jenna asked when Gabe walked into the kitchen, rubbing the sleep from his eyes.

She poured two glasses of juice, set them on the island separating the kitchen from the living room.

She loved the sleep-mussed look of him. The morning stubble. The way he smelled, still warm from the bed.

She went up on tiptoes and kissed him.

He hooked an arm around her waist and nuzzled her neck before letting her go and reaching for his juice.

"I want to get a run in."

She reached into the fridge for the bagels. "That a good idea?"

"Yes, Nurse Nightingale," he said injecting a gentle warning in his tone. "Doc says it's fine."

"Cool. Then I'll run with you."

He grunted. "You can't keep up with me, hotshot."

"That's not what you said last night." Last night she'd worn him out. And he'd loved it.

"You are such a gloater."

She flashed him a quick, smug grin. "I was born for the role."

"So when do we leave for Israel again?" he asked unfolding the morning paper.

They were a team now. Not a team like with the BOIs, and it was just temporary. When she went on assignment now, sometimes he went along. She did the reporting, he shot photos.

Horrible photos, she thought with a soft smile, but she wasn't about to tell him he was a lousy photographer. She suspected he was just doing that for show anyway. He went along to keep an eye on her. And because she shouldn't get to have all the fun, he'd told her with a grin the first time he'd joined her on assignment.

Her own personal bodyguard—when he wasn't consulting for BOI. She'd known he'd miss it too much to bow out completely. She gave him about two more months of healing before the itch caught up with him and he'd be off to Argentina in the thick of an op.

He was still a warrior, and too stubborn to let a little thing like a bum leg keep him from doing what he lived to do.

She also knew that he missed the BOIs. That was the bottom line because he sure didn't have to work at all if he didn't want to. He hadn't lied about the "lot of money" part. He had made buckets over the years, and had invested it wisely.

She popped two bagel halves in the toaster, loving the simple domestic rituals they'd fallen into since he'd moved in with her six months ago.

"We are leaving a week from tomorrow," she said after looking at the calendar and checking on the Israel trip. "You sure you're up for it?"

He lowered the paper, raised an eyebrow.

"Okay, okay. I'm fussing. I can't help it."

"I'm fine, Jenna."

Yeah, she thought, so proud of the way he'd handled everything. He *was* fine.

Not that long ago, he hadn't been. He'd woken up one morning five months ago with unbearable pain in his calf. They'd rushed to his orthopedist.

And gotten the bad news. The antibiotics were useless. Osteomyelitis had set in, infection in the bone. Despite their efforts and repeated operations, the surgeons couldn't get ahead of the infection and save the dying bone. It was either amputate below the knee or the infection could kill him.

When she'd cried for him, he'd held her tight.

"I don't need my damn leg. I've got what I need. I've got the girl."

Yeah, she thought as the bagels popped out of the toaster. He had the girl. And she had him.

"So, after we run, then what?" She smeared cream cheese on her bagel.

"Thought I'd check in on the guys."

She thought that might be something he'd want to do today. He still made a point of stopping by the orthopedic ward at the V.A. hospital each week, visiting with the returning vets.

She went with him sometimes. She was working on a piece about these brave young men and women for Hank.

"How's Rich doin'?" she asked, thinking of the young private who'd gotten hit by an IED.

"Getting there," he said. "He's getting there."

The phone rang.

Gabe reached across the counter, snagged the phone off the wall. "Yo. Oh, hello, Mrs. McMillan."

Jenna thought it was so cute the way he always called her mother Mrs. McMillan. After they'd both talked to her parents, they headed for the bedroom to get dressed for their run.

"So . . . you talked to my dad for a long time," she said, hoping he'd take the hint and fill her in on the conversation.

"Yeah. He's wondering when I'm going to make an honest woman out of you."

She threw her nightshirt at him then opened her dresser drawer. "He never said that."

"Okay, maybe I said that. When *can* I make an honest woman out of you?"

She froze with her running shorts clutched in her hand. She turned slowly to see him holding a little stuffed dog in his hand. Warmth flooded her.

"Nugget. I thought I'd lost him."

Then she noticed the red ribbon tied around his neck. A ribbon attached to a velvet ring box.

Gabe opened it, held it out for her to see the contents.

She glanced from him to the huge diamond twinkling up at her. "Seriously?"

He laughed. "God help me, yes."

She raced across the bed, snatched the ring from the box. Slipped it onto her finger. Then she turned sparkling eyes to him.

"You're in big trouble now, Jones."

"Yeah," he said, drawing her into his arms. "That seems to be a pattern with me."

EPILOGUE

Richmond, Virginia
One month later

"I'll see your five and raise you ten."

Damn, Gabe thought, glancing from his own poker hand to Reed, who had just upped the ante. He fanned his thumb over the edge of the cards. Jacks and tens. It was a borderline hand, but there'd been a lot of BS and bluffing at the table tonight so he considered calling.

He cast a glance around the table, tried to get a read on his opponents while Ann Tompkins strolled into the room with a tray stacked high with sandwiches. Robert was right behind her, loaded down with chips and dip and who the hell knew what else. No one went hungry at the Tompkins home.

It had been a while since the BOIs had all gathered here. It was good to be back again. Good for him. Good for the BOIs, most of whom had turned out for Robert's birthday celebration.

Gabe wished Sam could have made it. But he was back in Honduras, chasing down another lead on Fredrick Nader.

"You gonna bet or fold, Angel boy?"

Gabe glared at Doc, who sat with a fat unlit cigar tucked in the corner of his mouth and a stack of chips that would choke a horse piled in front of him.

"Yeah, Angel *boy*," a fourth player at the table taunted, with emphasis on *boy*. "You gonna stare the spots off those cards or you gonna stick around and run with the big dogs?"

Sparkling green eyes goaded him from behind a fall of thick red hair. Damn, the woman made him laugh. He hadn't been too sure how the boys would react when Jenna had asked if she could join the game. But Reed, being Reed, had welcomed her with open arms. He'd whipped off his dealer's visor, plopped it on Jenna's head, and pulled out a chair for her. After he'd kissed her.

Bastard, Gabe thought with a smirk.

"Fold," he said, tossing his cards face down on the green felt tabletop. "Too rich for my blood."

Jenna made clucking sounds.

Yeah. She made him laugh.

He shook his finger at her—a warning that she was going to get hers later. She blew him a kiss as he shoved away from the table.

"I like her," Ann said when Gabe wandered over to the bar for a beer. "She's got sass."

Gabe grunted. "Understatement of the year. So how are things at D.O.J.?" Recently, Ann had given up her lucrative private practice for a position at the Department of Justice. As usual, she was giving back.

"It's good. It was good move for me. And you—how are you?" Ann asked when he eased down on a tall stool and leaned back against the bar.

"Good," he said thoughtfully as his wife won the pot and celebrated with a whoop and a high five to Reed. "If you'd have asked me that a year ago, I'd have told you the same thing." He smiled into Ann's soft brown eyes. "I'd have been lying."

"But not now?"

He shook his head. "Not now."

Life was good. Life was excellent.

He missed his leg sometimes. Missed it a lot sometimes. Cursed the agility he'd lost. Worked to figure out ways to recoup it.

In the meantime, that wild woman he was married to didn't give him much of a chance to slide into the occasional funk. And the truth was, losing the leg had opened him up to thinking on a number of different levels. Who he was had always been tied to what he could do physically, and that had overshadowed what else he could be.

He was still learning about himself. He'd been pleasantly surprised to find out there was more to him worth finding.

"It's good to see all you boys here together."

Yeah, he thought, his gaze drifting around the room. Nate, Savage, and Green sat by the fire, deep in a hot discussion with Robert. Some of the other guys who worked out of the BOI office in Rome had even made it. Holliday and Jenna were in the process of cleaning them out at the poker table, too. Mendoza, who usually just watched and laughed, had even let Stephanie goad him into a game of pool. Probably because he had a small crush on Bry's pretty little sister, Gabe suspected.

More warmth than he'd ever thought he was capable of feeling filled his chest, made it ache in a good way.

These were his brothers. The Tompkinses were his family.

Only one other thing in the world made him feel this way, this complete. And she was currently at her obnoxious best as she accused Doc of hiding aces up his sleeve.

"So, Doc tells me you're back on board," Ann said.

He nodded. "Part time. I'm also consulting for a firm based in West Palm Beach."

Just last week he'd signed a contract with the Garretts and E.D.E.N. Securities, Inc. He and Jenna had flown down to visit Dallas and Amy. They'd ended up at a Garrett family gathering where they'd somehow gotten roped into a very wild and very strange game of cutthroat croquet. The next thing he knew, he'd had another job offer.

That worked for him. It let him split his time between Argentina and home and left him plenty of time to ride roughshod on the woman wearing the diamond he'd put on the ring finger of her left hand.

He glanced at Ann, who had become quiet beside him. Found her looking with a wistful sort of longing at the portrait of Bryan above the fireplace.

"He would have loved this," she said when she realized Gabe had caught her.

"Yeah," Gabe said, doing something he wouldn't have been capable of doing before that redhead had come into his life. He put his arms around Ann, rocked her in a gentle embrace. "He would have loved this. "Thank you," he said, pulling back to look down at her. "Thank you for making me his brother."

Ann nodded and he hugged her again.

Across the room, Gabe caught Jenna watching him. The tenderness and pride that filled her eyes touched him in a place that she had brought to life.

I love you, he mouthed for her eyes only.

Her smile was as brilliant and as vital as the future she'd given him.

I know, she mouthed back.

Then she swore like a drill sergeant when Holliday laid down a full house that beat her flush.

God save me from this woman, he thought, and in that instant realized that he and God had finally taken steps toward a tentative sort of peace.

TAKE
NO
PRISONERS

This book is dedicated to the men and women of the United States military, both active and retired. There are no words to adequately express my gratitude and respect for the sacrifices you and your families have made and for the losses many of you have endured to protect and defend our nation and our way of life.

ACKNOWLEDGMENTS

Special thanks to Kylie Brant and Roxanne Rustand, problem solvers extraordinaire—and a darn good time to boot :o)

Again, thanks to Gail Barrett for her excellent assistance with the Spanish translations.

Susan, Leanne, Glenna, Ben, Joe—you know I luv ya!

People sleep peaceably in their beds at night only because rough men stand ready to do violence on their behalf.

—GEORGE ORWELL (ATTRIBUTED)

1

~

A gecko, low slung, forked feet flying, skittered across the sill of an open window, hauling ass as if it actually had somewhere to go.

Lucky little bastard.

Sam Lang watched him through world-weary eyes—jealous of a damn lizard because at the moment, Sam had exactly *nowhere* to go. And nothing to do.

Nothing but sit here, slouched at a crude wooden table in a shadowed corner of a crumbling adobe cantina, like he'd sat here for the past three days. Nothing but amuse himself watching insect-eating egg-laying reptiles and wishing he were anywhere but Las Rosas, Honduras, on yet one more wild-goose chase.

No, he was not having fun yet.

While the action in the cantina was stagnant and slow, years of caution and force of habit had Sam sitting with his back to the wall. Thirst and boredom had his fingers wrapped around a lukewarm can of Polar. He wiped his cuff over the lip of the can, then tilted it to his mouth as the gecko shot away again.

Fast little sucker. Speed-of-sound fast compared to the rest of the populace in this dusty and rodent-infested hamlet where time crawled, stalled, and stopped dead in the noon heat of the Central American sun. The gecko obviously knew something Sam and the handful of patrons of this squalid, sweltering cantina didn't because, hell, even the flies didn't bother to buzz over pools of stale, spilled beer. Nope. Not a lot of action—with the notable exception of the gecko and the X-rated show taking place in the middle of what could loosely be called a dance floor, where a man and a woman performed what could loosely be called a dance.

Sam had known better. He should have dragged his partner, Johnny Duane Reed, out of this dive three hours ago when they'd officially decided their guy wasn't going to show. So far, the "tip" that they might get the goods on Fredrick Nader hadn't panned out. With each tick of a very slow-moving clock, it became more apparent that they'd run up against one more dead end.

Big surprise. Sam had been tracking the elusive German for months. He'd set trap after trap, harassed the hell out of Nader, whose "legitimate" international enterprises were merely fronts for every type of terrorist activity known to man. Drugs, weapons, bioterrorism— you name it, Nader was in it ass deep. Yet his blue-blooded lineage and the bottomless cache of payola that came with it kept every international agency off his back.

That's where Sam and Black Ops, Inc. came in. Nader was an off-the-books operation. Sam had finally found the man's Achilles' heel. The pompous bastard had a penchant for sparkly things—Nader craved stolen gems—which Sam was counting on to be Nader's downfall.

Last week in El Salvador, Nader had gotten a little sloppy and Sam had come within minutes of nailing him—only to lose him one more time. Just like this last attempt had turned out to be one more lost cause.

"We've been here for three frickin' days," Reed complained earlier when Sam had decided to give up the ghost and get the hell out of Dodge. "Another hour or two isn't going to change the course of the world. Besides, we deserve some R and R."

Deserve, in this case, was Johnny Duane Reed–speak for "I've been eating dust and drinking mud-thick coffee for three days and I'm ready for a beer—or ten."

Three hours ago, Sam had been hard-pressed to argue with Reed's stand, but that had been three long hours ago. Now he realized the error in that line of thinking.

He glanced toward the dance floor again. Shook his head. Reed was a pretty boy, but Sam knew from experience that there was strength in those broad shoulders, speed in those lean legs. He'd relied on the former marine despite his smart mouth, Rambo strut, and weakness for the ladies in more than one dicey situation. The kid had never let him down and he delivered few surprises. That's why it came as no shock that nothing good would come out of a situation when Johnny Duane Reed had time on his hands and a yen for alcohol and a woman.

A scratchy merengue played from a dusty jukebox as Sam watched Reed through dim light and a haze of sweet-smelling smoke. Both the smoke and the scent hung in the air like fog. No one mistook the scent for anything but what it was: prime Colombian weed. Just as no one mistook the woman with the swaying hips, barely haltered breasts, and sex-and-whiskey laugh for anything but what she was: a past-her-prime Honduras whore.

No one but Reed, who'd been without the company of a woman way longer than the cowboy liked. Give a fisherman a hook and he'll catch dinner. Give Reed a beer and he'll catch a hooker.

Kee-rist.

Reed was in lust. He was also *bolo*—drunk off his ass. It made for a perfect combination. Or a perfect storm.

If Sam didn't break the lip-lock the hooker had planted on the tall blond cowboy, whose hands were now kneading the hell out of her ass, dawn would find Reed rolled, robbed, and in need of a good delousing.

He heaved a weary breath, then couldn't help but grin at the cowboy's sloppy attempt at a salsa move. Sam tried to remember the exact point in time when he'd been appointed Reed's keeper. Somalia? Beirut? Sierra Leone? Hell. Could have been any one of a hundred third world hellholes. Years ago, as team members on Uncle's top secret Task Force Mercy, they'd saved each other's lives more times than Sam could count. More times than he wanted to.

Lot of years ago when they'd been lean and green and full of God and country. *Hoo-rah!*

Years ago, when they'd been soldiers.

He drew deep on his beer. At least Sam had been a soldier. He'd been Delta Force, U.S. Army. Reed was Marine, Force Recon and in or out of uniform, he'd be a marine—not a soldier, he was quick to point out—until the day he died.

Sam squinted through the smoke. They'd all paid a price through the years. Which was why, from time to time, they needed to let off a little steam. Case in point was stumbling around on the dance floor, probably not as drunk as he wanted everyone to think he was.

"You want to party, too, gringo? Maybe a private dance? *Vaya pues?* Okay?"

A pouty brunette had sidled up next to Sam and wrapped herself around him like a faded ribbon on a Maypole. Once upon a time he might have taken the *ladina* woman up on her offer. Once upon a time when she'd been young and pretty and he'd been young and stupid. A time when better judgment and discerning taste had been no match for randy youth, raging hormones, and the superior intellect that could be found in a bottle of tequila. Before control had become the name of Sam's game and the mantra that he lived by.

Sam wanted to ignore her, but his mother had taught him better manners. "Not tonight, darlin'."

While he'd thought he'd been gentle, he could see by the look in her eyes and the way she'd skittered away that he'd done it again. Scared the shit out of her with one hard look. Apparently it was the same look that Reed was always telling him was more intimidating than an M-16.

Whatever.

He headed for Reed. The cowboy may have tipped a few but that didn't negate the fact that Reed was still six lean feet of solid muscle and sinew. Thirty-plus years of stubborn warrior blood pumped through his veins. And he was horny.

This wasn't going to be fun.

And it wasn't going to be pretty.

But it *was* going to get done.

Sam tapped Reed on the shoulder. "Yo. God's gift. Time to roll."

"Fuck off."

Reed's response was typical and expected. It was also remarkably articulate given the fact that his tongue was buried halfway down his lady love's throat. "Get your own woman, Sammy. This one's mine."

"I said, let's go." Sam stood, hands on hips, waiting for it to seep into Reed's alcohol-soaked brain that he'd just been issued an order.

"Aw, come on," Reed actually whined when Sam didn't buckle.

Lolita, or Rosalita, or whatever the hell her name was, spewed a string of Spanish curses in Sam's direction when she realized her customer was slipping away.

"Yeah. Things are tough all over," he agreed and pried her arms from around Reed's neck.

"But our guy didn't show," Reed pointed out, hopeful it would buy him a little more time.

"It's not happening. Let's go."

As sure as two plus two equaled four, Reed drunk plus horny equaled belligerent. Lang had no expectations that either his math or his take on Reed were anything but dead-on right.

The cowboy didn't disappoint. "Fifteen minutes. That's all I need."

"No."

As only a drunk can, Reed squared off in front of Sam, bleary eyes narrowed. "You ain't the boss of me."

Sam couldn't help it. He grinned. "That's the best you can do?"

Reed sniffed. Cocked his chin. Shot for a glare. "I don't want to have to drop you, Sam."

This time Sam actually laughed. It was as much bluff as amusement because even drunk, Reed was one of the toughest, meanest, dirtiest fighters Sam had ever seen in action.

Sam pulled the older, meaner, wiser, bigger card out of the deck. "Yeah, that's gonna hap—"

He never finished his sentence.

A car roared to a screeching stop outside the cantina and grabbed his full attention, jarring him straight to red alert.

He was already diving for the dirt floor, dragging Reed down with him when the swinging cantina doors burst open to a hail of AK-47 fire. Together they rolled, overturning tables as they went, scrambling to reach their go bags, where Sam had stashed an H&K MP-5K and Reed had packed a mini Uzi.

Wasn't gonna happen. The gunmen's fire steered them in the opposite direction, where they finally found cover behind a thick wooden support post and a half-baked adobe wall near the bar. They bellied down on the floor behind it as the deafening burst of automatic-weapon fire sprayed through the cantina. The women screamed and everyone ducked out of the line of fire.

Beside him, Reed was all business now as he unholstered his gun. "What the fuck!"

Nothing like an AK to snap a man out of a drunken stupor.

Sam peered around the wall for a quick look-see, then ducked back behind it when another round of fire slaughtered the bottles lined up behind the bar, shattering them into oblivion along with the cloudy mirror. Gunpowder and *guaro*—rotgut whiskey—stank up the air as Lang cut a glance to Reed. Like Sam, Reed had flipped to his back with his pistol in a two-handed grip, waiting for a break in the action.

It came as fast as the barrage of gunfire.

Silence—acute and potentially deadly.

Unexpected silence, except for the ringing in their ears and the creaking swing of the cantina doors.

Car doors slammed, an engine roared, and a vehicle sped away.

Sam glanced at Reed. Nodded.

Sam rolled left, Reed rolled right, flat on their bellies, Sam's Kimber Tactical Pro 1911 Al and Reed's Sig Sauer 9mm aimed at the door—where they met nothing.

No one.

There was nothing in the cantina but residual smoke, broken glass, spilled booze, and quietly weeping women.

A single mason jar sat in the threshold beneath the cantina doors.

"Party's over?" Reed croaked, carefully assessing the bar for any remaining threats, his Sig still in a two-handed grip, muzzle pointed down and at the ready.

Sam stood slowly, did the same with his Kimber. "Seems so."

He glanced around the room. "Anyone hurt?"

One by one, figures emerged in the gloomy and hazy light. Except for a glass cut on the bartender's face there appeared to be no casualties. The conclusion was clear. With that much firepower, they should have all been dead, which meant the bad guys hadn't been aiming to kill.

They wanted someone's attention.

Reed nodded toward the dirty jar. "I'm gonna take a wild guess and figure that's for you."

Sam grunted, his footsteps crunching on broken glass as he walked across the room. He chanced a careful peek over the top of the chest-high doors. The walkway outside was littered with spent cartridges. Other than a boiling dust trail, the street was empty.

He stared down at the jar.

It was exactly what it looked like. An old, scarred, and well-used mason jar. He slipped his Kimber into his waistband, squatted down, got a better look.

"There's a note inside."

"There always is," Reed said, rubbing at bloodshot eyes.

Sam picked up the jar, cautiously fished out the sheet of paper and unfolded it.

All the blood drained from his face when he read it.

Jesus. Jesus.

Eyes wild, he sprinted for his go bag, unaware of the gecko scrambling for his life to get out of the way.

"What?" Reed pushed aside an overturned table, racing to catch up with him.

Sam shoved the note in the general direction of Reed's chest. "I need the SAT phone."

"Christ, Sam." Reed's eyes were watery with shock and disbelief when he finished reading.

Sam dug into his bag, shoved the H&K, ammo, and a dozen other pieces of equipment aside until he finally found the satellite phone. His fingers shook as he dialed the number, heart thudding, breath choppy.

"Dad." He forced himself to calm down when his father finally picked up. "Dad . . . it's Sam."

The moment of silence before his father spoke told the unthinkable truth.

"Sam . . ." His father's voice was weak. Shaken. Sam's chest tightened into a mass of white-hot lead. "I . . . I've been trying to . . . to get a hold of you, son." Then he dissolved into desolate weeping.

Sam gripped the phone tighter. Waited, eyes burning, while his father composed himself and confirmed what Sam feared.

Wild with rage and grief and guilt, he disconnected, then burst through the cantina doors, staggered outside.

So he could breathe.

So he could think.

Only when Reed touched his shoulder did Sam realize the younger man had followed him.

A dust devil spun down the debris-strewn street, scattering powdery grit in his eyes, burning until tears ran down his face.

"Come on, Sam." Reed's voice, painfully gentle and rock solid sober, made Sam's chest ache.

"Come on," Reed repeated and urged Sam toward their car. "We need to get you home."

Sam knew he was dreaming, did his damnedest to wake up. But he was mired in images and sensations that sucked him deeper into the nightmare.

He felt like he was swimming through mud. Slogging through quicksand. Watching a movie in slow motion through a distorted wall of glass. Behind the glass, traffic shot by on the bustling Las Vegas Strip. A blur of color and motion.

On the other side of the glass wall, he saw his sister, Terri. She was walking toward her car. Laughing at something his brother-in-law, B.J., had said. Love in her eyes. Fun in her heart. Completely unaware of the danger.

He had to get to them. But he couldn't get through the mud and the quicksand and stop them before it was too late.

"Terri!" Through an echo chamber he heard his sister's name.

A man's voice shouting. His voice. Begging.

Then roaring. "Stop . . . stop . . . for God's sake, stop!!!"

But she kept going. Straight for the car.

He could still stop this. Maybe he could still stop this.

"Terri!!!!!"

Frantic to get to them, he pushed through air as thick as foam and finally reached the distorted glass wall. Behind it four lanes of city traffic crawled in an eerie, choreographed dance. Cars sped then slowed, transformed to jeweled and painted carousel horses that danced and spun in a kaleidoscope of dazzling prisms, brass rings, and gilded manes.

Rhythm and light, glowing and golden—perfection out of place with the horror that was about to happen.

"Terri!"

He rammed the wall. Slammed hard with his shoulder . . . again, again, again . . . until finally, glass shattered and parted, flew around him in glittering, knifelike shards.

He sprinted past it. Sank into more quicksand. More mud, as Terri opened the passenger door and B.J. slipped behind the wheel.

Oblivious to his shouts.

Sweet and pristine and good with the sun on her face, the breeze in her hair, and the heat of the Las Vegas morning baking down.

"Terri! Terri!!!!"

Sweat trickled down his back, ran into his eyes as he dodged a minivan, then rolled over the hood of a fast and flashy red sports car.

Fast like life. His sister's life.

Red like blood. His sister's blood.

His sister, who he could see reaching for her seat belt as B.J. shoved the key into the ignition.

"Terri!!!!!!!!!!"

He ran faster, shouting her name, praying he'd still make it in time . . .

Then time stopped. Life stopped.

The car exploded in a blast of fire and smoke and a breath-stealing concussion that blew him off his feet . . .

• • •

Sam shot awake like a bullet. Heart hammering. Drenched in sweat. Aware of someone talking.

Talking to him, he realized after several moments.

He blinked. Blinked again, focused on the FASTEN SEAT BELT sign lit in red on the bulkhead in front of him. Heard the clunk and shift of landing gears.

"I'm sorry to wake you, sir."

A sense of time and place finally assembled. He was on a plane. On a flight from Tegucigalpa, Honduras, to Vegas.

"We'll be landing in a few minutes. Please return your seat to the upright position."

He dragged an unsteady hand over his jaw, nodded absently to the cabin attendant, did as she asked.

"Someone special?"

He glanced up at her. Barely noticed nice blue eyes, a cover-girl complexion. Her name tag identified her as Dana. She was smiling at him. Expectant. Flirtatious.

"I'm sorry?"

"Terri? You were calling her name. While you were sleeping. Is she someone special?"

He felt himself go cold beneath the clammy layer of perspiration dampening his back.

Dana must have taken his silence for affirmation. And a rebuff. "Well . . . hope she knows how lucky she is."

With a wistful, regretful smile, she headed down the aisle.

. . . how lucky she is.

Sam stared at the seat back directly in front of him. He fought the burn of tears that had been pushing since he'd talked to his father yesterday.

. . . how lucky she is.

Yeah. Terri was lucky.

Lucky enough to be dead along with her husband.

Lucky enough to be buried in two days.

Lucky enough to have been killed by a bomb delivered as a message for Sam to back off.

He reached into the breast pocket of his shirt. Unfolded the dog-eared scrap of paper delivered with the help of AK-47 fire and a fucking mason jar.

He reread the words that still made his heart lurch, his breath catch, his hatred coil like a snake in his belly.

"Better call home. Boom, boom. She's dead."

Guilt washed through him. Weighty. Desolate. Acute.

His sister was dead. Because Sam had pissed off the wrong person.

Fredrick Nader.

There was no question in Sam's mind that Nader was behind Terri's and B.J.'s deaths. Nader's signature was all over the hit.

Nader wanted Sam to back off. When he wouldn't, and because Nader couldn't get to Sam, he'd found a way to hit Sam where it hurt the most.

The bastard murdered Sam's kid sister with a fucking car bomb.

As a warning.

As a means to ensure that Sam understood: Back off or Nader's organization could get to any of his family members anytime he wanted and Sam couldn't do a damn thing about it.

Not one thing but bury his kid sister.

2

"What about yours?"

Abbie Hughes glanced up from her chocolate malt and pressed at the sharp pain in her temple where the ice cream had shot her into a temporary brain freeze. "What about my *what*?"

"What about your qualifications for the ultimate male?" Crystal Debrowski reminded Abbie of their current topic of conversation. "I told you mine, now you tell me yours."

Abbie fiddled absently with a French fry. Outside the window, neon flashed, sirens screamed, and people of every age and ethnic heritage ambled along the street, laughing and talking, limping and exhausted. It didn't matter that it was nearly 1:00 a.m. It was bright as noon twenty-four-seven, three-sixty-five, on the Vegas Strip.

Crystal glared impatiently at her friend. "You may think you've gotten good at practicing avoidance, but, my dear, it doesn't work with me."

Abbie grinned at Crystal. Well, she'd tried. With Crystal for a friend, Abbie practiced avoidance a lot. Not that practice made perfect—and not that Crystal ever let her get away with it.

Abbie dragged her gaze back to Crystal. "Why is it that every time we get together the conversation eventually drifts to men?"

"Because," Crystal said with the patience generally reserved for the mentally challenged, "conversations about men always lead to conversations about sex—and sex is my all-time favorite subject."

Abbie lifted a brow. "I have no idea why that logic escaped me."

Crystal snorted. "Yeah, well, I do. It's because you're too busy to think about sex, let alone participate in it. The way I see it, I'm your best chance to live vicariously since you obviously have your priorities all screwed up."

Priorities. Well, there were those, Abbie thought, and tried not to worry about her kid brother, Cory, who should have returned home last night. Not only was Cory a no-show, Abbie hadn't heard word one from him about where he was or why he'd been delayed.

It wasn't that Cory hadn't pulled something like this before. Before and often. Cory wasn't exactly known for his reliability and good judgment. She just kept hoping that he had finally found a little stability in his life.

So much for what she'd hoped.

Reminding herself that it was his life, not hers, and that she had to literally stop trying to be her brother's keeper, she tuned back into what Crystal was saying.

". . . later?"

Abbie grinned sheepishly. "I'm sorry. Later what?"

Crystal slumped back in the booth, expelled an elaborate sigh. With her pixie features, spiky red hair, and fairy-green eyes, Crystal had to work hard to look stern, but somehow she managed it. "I said, do you want to go casino crawling later?"

"I don't know how to break this to you, Tinkerbell, but one, it *is* later. Two, I just came off a double shift, which means that I just *crawled* out of a casino. And three, I can't think of a single incentive strong enough to compel me to crawl back into one."

Chin in her palm, Crystal swished her straw around in her glass. "How do you ever expect to meet men if you don't go out and party with them?" She looked and sounded put out.

"I've met plenty of men. You may recall I was even foolish enough to have married one."

Not that Don was the yardstick by which Abbie now measured all others, but once had been enough, thank you very much. She'd given it two good years. The problem was, Don had only given it one. By the time Abbie found out he was sleeping around, it was all over but the shouting anyway.

Yeah, Abbie had regrets. She'd loved Don. She'd planned on making a life with him. She hadn't suspected that he'd had the fidelity of a tomcat and the integrity of a Kleenex. And she hadn't banked on being such a poor judge of character. That was probably what upset her the most out of the whole deal.

Her confidence in herself had been badly shaken. Confidence in her judgment, in her self-worth. In monogamy in general. True, she'd been only twenty-three when she'd married Don. Twenty-three was young. She recognized that now, yet two years after the divorce, she still didn't feel that she had fine-tuned or adequately honed the skills required to fight the good fight again.

"You probably haven't even noticed the hunk in the booth across the aisle from us," Crystal said in a low whisper and with a little head hitch to the right. "He's been checking you out ever since he got here."

Abbie glanced across the aisle. She'd noticed the guy all right. It was hard not to. Hair too long and too blond, eyes too blue, body too buff, jeans too tight. Oh, yeah, let's not forget the heavy five o'clock shadow and snakeskin boots. She knew the type. Don had been just like him. Pretty and petty, with an ego the size of Lake Mead.

"Do not—I repeat," she uttered under her breath with an I-mean-business glare at Crystal, "do not make eye contact. Do not encourage him. Do not even think about playing dating service."

She glanced involuntarily at Mr. Blond and Blue, ignored his "I like what I see and I'm interested" grin and fired Crystal another warning glare.

"You are sooo not fun," Crystal muttered with a roll of her eyes.

"You like him? You go after him."

"Why bother?" Crystal sighed. "He's probably gay anyway." Another sigh. "Or a cowboy. Or a cop. One's as bad as the other."

Abbie pushed out a sympathetic laugh. With anyone but Crystal, it would have been a difficult leap of logic to follow. But, since Crystal had fallen for all three types and had gotten her heart broken each time, Abbie understood. She also understood that Crystal talked big about sex but the truth was, she was monogamous in her relationships. That's not to say she didn't take very seriously the old axiom of love the one you're with and practice it with enthusiasm.

"I suppose you have class tomorrow," Crystal muttered, looking and sounding as disgusted as if she'd just said, "I suppose you have foot rot."

"I suppose I do." Between Abbie's job at the casino and her accounting classes at UNLV, her free time was short. So was her sleep time. "Which is all the more reason for me to head home and get to bed."

Abbie slid out of the booth to Crystal's mumbled, "And we all know what that means for you."

"Yeah. Sleep. I need it."

As they walked to the register to pay for their burgers and fries, Abbie was aware of the sidelong looks they got, not only from the cute, blond, gay, cowboy cop who was still sitting in the booth watching them with his bedroom-blue eyes, but from the other patrons of the little diner. They'd been getting those looks for years. Individually, the two of them were each capable of turning a head or two. Together, they never failed.

It wasn't that either of them was a raving beauty, although one of the most common lines Abbie heard as she dealt at her blackjack table five nights a week was that she was striking. The same could be said about Crystal. As a pair, though, they presented ample cause for curious stares.

While Crystal was green-eyed and tiny—in her four-inch platforms she had to stretch to make five foot five—Abbie's eyes were so brown they were almost black. And she was tall. Put *her* in a pair of four-inch platforms— and Lord knows, Crystal had tried—and Abbie pushed six feet. In addition, while Crystal's fair skin would fry to a crisp under the Nevada sun and she wore her fiery red hair short and spiky, Abbie had been blessed with a Mediterranean complexion.

Her olive skin loved the sun. She wore a perpetual honey-colored tan that complemented the hair she'd inherited from her mother. Sable brown, thick and lush, she wore it in a simple cut, the same length all over. When she wore it down, it hit just between her shoulder blades; when she wore it up, which she had tonight, it added another couple of inches to her height.

Where Crystal bounced when she walked—all round jiggling breasts and saucily swinging hips—Abbie had been told that she glided, her figure lean and fine-tuned from the five miles she ran every morning.

"See you, toots," Abbie said as they walked out the diner door. "And be careful out there," she added in her best warning-cop voice.

"Wish I had a reason to offer you the same advice." Crystal fluttered a wave over her shoulder.

Abbie just smiled, headed for her car, and drove straight home, enjoying the new-car smell, the luxurious leather, the quiet purr of the smooth-running engine. Lord, she loved this car. Her very first *new* car.

Once home, she engaged her security system,   double-checked the locks, and before she went to bed, spent too much time worrying about her brother and wondering about the boxes that arrived a couple of times a week from Honduras.

"Relax," Cory had said the last time he'd called and she'd asked what was in them. "It's nothing illegal. You think I'd stick you in the middle of something like that? Give me a little credit."

Abbie had been giving Cory credit for most of her life. Most of her life, though, he'd disappointed her. Yet she chose to believe him because she loved him and because of all they'd been through together. If she didn't believe in him, no one else would.

"Check 'em out if you want to," he'd said, sounding wounded. "All you're going to find are trinkets. Native craft items I picked up for a song in Honduras. You know. Drums. Baskets. Knockoff Mayan figurines. As soon as I find the right wholesaler, I'm going to make a small fortune off that stuff."

Cory was always going to make a small fortune off something. Of course, Abbie hadn't checked the boxes she had stored in her garage. Cory needed that from her. Needed to know she trusted him.

She hoped it had been the right choice.

She checked her e-mail before she went to bed, just in case. Nothing from Cory. Before she finally fell asleep, she was still thinking about him, worrying about where he was and how he was. And yeah, she spent a little time wondering about the blond Adonis who had all but followed them out the door. Cowboy? Gay? Cop?

Cop, she decided finally. Despite the obvious invitation in his eyes, he had an edge to him. What didn't make sense, though, was why he'd seemed so interested in her, and that had her wondering about Cory's boxes and fretting again about where he was as she drifted off.

San Pedro Sula, Honduras

Cory Hughes sat behind the wheel of the rented Jeep, tapping his fingers restlessly on the steering wheel.

"Sit and wait. Sit and wait," he muttered. He spent half of his life on the sit and wait.

It would be different if he could afford to. As it was, he was living on borrowed time.

He felt it. Just like he sensed the clock ticking. Just like he knew that if he didn't get out of this cloak-and-dagger crap he was going to end up sliced and diced into little pieces and scattered like chum bait from the Gulf of Honduras to Cuba.

Exhaust fumes and jet fuel clogged the sweltering air as he sat and waited for Derek Styles outside the San Pedro Sula airport, trying to figure out how he'd come to this. One day he'd been selling his knockoff Honduran artifacts on a Vegas street corner. The next thing he knew he'd agreed to do a favor for a friend in exchange for a free ticket to Honduras, where he could select his inventory firsthand instead of relying on long-distance contacts. All he'd had to do to earn the ticket was bring a package back with him to Vegas.

How could he say no? All his life he'd been scrambling to make a dime. The job market was slim to none for a high school dropout. He'd needed rent money. He'd needed to eat. And he'd promised himself he wouldn't hit up his sister for cash again. So he'd made the delivery. End of story—or so he'd thought.

God, he'd been stupid. He should have known there was something illegal going on. Turned out the package had contained drugs—something he'd fought all his life to stay clear of. It also turned out that his so-called friend had been an enforcer for an international criminal and warned Cory that if he didn't continue to play along and deliver the occasional package, bad things would happen to him.

He didn't want bad things to happen, so now he was in the stew up to his neck and barely managing to stay afloat. He knew without a doubt that if he crossed these guys, he'd end up dead.

That fact became crystal clear six months ago, when he'd been taken to meet Mr. Big in Puerto Cortez. Fredrick Nader had asked to see him. To be introduced to the "promising young protégé," as he'd put it.

Cory had never been anyone's promising young anything. Knew he wasn't now, even when a limo had picked him up and driven him to the docks, where a cigarette boat right out of *Miami Vice* had run him out to Nader's yacht.

And Nader—he acted like royalty or something. Looked like it, too. The dude was old—fifty-, sixty-something. Thin and fit. Hair as white as his pants. Cory had never seen pants so white. Shoes so shiny. Nader had been getting a manicure when Cory had been introduced to him while a crew of servants had stepped and fetched him pricey wine in a glass so fine and thin he was afraid it would break in his hand.

Then things had gotten real. Cory had been shown what happened to someone who "opted out" of Nader's employ. The man—what was left of him—had fallen out of favor with Nader and under the blade of Nader's muscleman, Rutger Smith, a guy with a real skill with a knife.

Cory had been scared straight ever since that night. Just like he'd been looking for an out ever since.

"Hey, man."

Cory jumped when Derek Styles, another one of Nader's mules, jerked open the passenger door and threw his duffel into the back. "How's it shakin'?"

He tried to look cool. "You're late."

"Bitch to the airline."

Derek was tall and scrawny, his hair a shaggy, dirty brown. He smelled like sour sweat and sweet weed as he crawled into the passenger seat and slammed the door behind him. "Home, James."

Cory grunted, checked the rearview mirror, and pulled away from the terminal and into traffic.

"Big deal going down," Derek said, tapping his fingers on his thigh.

Yeah, in this business, there was always a big deal going down. "Don't want to know about it."

Derek shook his head in disgust as they headed for open highway and the wind dragged his hair back from his ferret face.

"Nader—he's got more money than God, you know?" Derek said, ignoring Cory. "Me, I'd spend it on women and blow. But Nader has this thing for diamonds."

Didn't surprise Cory. Nothing about Nader surprised him anymore. Nader's main business involved cocaine and heroin, stolen arms, and chemical weapons. That Nader also had a thing for diamonds just stood to reason. Diamonds and stolen art and anything else that was hard to come by and illegal to own fit the MO.

"That's why I'm back in Honduras," Derek went on. "To move hot rocks for the Man."

"Must be some diamonds." Cory's curiosity got the best of him when Derek told him how much Nader paid for the diamonds. "How do you know what they cost him?" It wasn't like Derek was in Nader's inner circle.

"I overheard Smith make the final transaction on the phone."

Cory suppressed a shudder when he thought about Rutger Smith. He was one big scary dude. Carried one big scary knife.

"Package arrives tonight. Coming into port at Muchilena."

Muchilena was a small Gulf of Honduras port less than an hour north of San Pedro Sula. Nader liked to mix up the drop spots. Last pickup had been on the Caribbean side.

"You know, we could get there first. You and me. Beat Smith to the transfer."

Cory stared at Derek like he was tripping on E when he realized what Derek had in mind. "Are you nuts?"

"Come on, dude. Get a backbone. Don't you ever get tired of being Nader's errand boy?" Derek taunted. "Don't you ever wonder what it would be like to have the lion's share of the sale instead of groveling for table scraps?"

"Hell, yes, I wonder. But I'm not crossing him. No way."

"Not even for a cool half of five mil? You really think you're going to make anything but chump change with those native craft knockoffs you keep sending back to the States?"

Those knockoffs were Cory's bid for legitimacy. He bought them for a song down here and shipped them back to his sister in Vegas. And, yeah. When he finally figured a way out from under Nader's iron fist, his little stash of merchandise was going to set him up in business. Rich Americans dug that kind of stuff. He'd get twenty times his cost once he broke into the market. He could finally leave this life behind and get back to being legit.

Not that half of five million dollars wasn't tempting as hell. But so was living. "A little hard to spend if you're dead."

Derek snorted. "With that kind of coin, you can go to ground for a year. Buy yourself a new face. New ID. Nader can't kill a dead man."

Cory checked his mirror. Switched lanes. "I don't want to talk about it."

So he didn't. Didn't say another word as he drove Derek to a cheap motel and dropped him off.

"Don't do it," he warned when Derek got out of the Jeep.

"Last chance," Derek baited him.

Hands raised, Cory shook his head, then drove away. Hoping to hell that if Derek was lame enough to attempt his idiotic plan, Nader wouldn't come looking in his direction for an accomplice.

He decided right then and there that he had to figure a way out.

2:00 a.m.

Cory shot up in bed, jolted out of a dead sleep. Someone at his door, he realized as a muffled pounding had him scrambling to his feet. He stumbled into a pair of cargo shorts and scrambled across the room.

"Who is it?"

"Le' me in."

Derek.

Cory cracked the door to the hostel room he rented by the day. Deadweight pressed against it, then Derek fell into the room. Blood soaked his shirt.

"Jesus. Jesus." Cory caught him, broke his fall. "What the hell happened?"

He stared into unfocused, feverish eyes. Derek struggled to breathe.

"Damn. You did it, didn't you? God, Jesus God." Panic slammed to the beat of his heart as Derek coughed up blood and folded into himself. "You stupid bastard."

"So s-stupid I'm carrying . . . m-millions of dollars in . . . diamonds."

"And you brought them here? Led Nader to me?"

Derek's breath rattled. "Lost 'em. Those . . . fuckers who shot me . . .lost 'em."

"Yeah," Cory wailed. "For now. Fuck. You need a doctor."

He started to rise. Derek grabbed his arm, stopped him.

"My pocket." Derek wheezed with the effort to even whisper. "It's all . . . there. The goods. The d-deal I set up. Your . . . d-deal . . . now."

Then the bastard died.

Died.

Holy God.

For a moment, all Cory could do was stare. He was frozen with panic, stunned by what had just happened. Derek wasn't a friend. But he was a human being. And now he was dead.

Heart pounding, Cory stood, stared at the body, dragged his hands through his hair. Knew the door was going to burst open any moment and Nader's thugs would blast him, too.

That's what he had to think about now. No matter which way he sliced this, Nader was going to kill him. Even if he went to Nader and told him what Derek had done, Nader would figure Cory was in on it but that he'd gotten cold feet. If he ran, Nader would just find him. He always found who he was looking for.

He stared at the blood on his hands. At the body on the floor. Then his survival instincts kicked him in the ass.

His hands shook as he fished around in Derek's pockets. Finally, he pulled out a blue velvet pouch. He turned it upside down. A necklace of the biggest diamonds he'd ever seen poured out into his hand.

His mouth dropped open.

Shit. Oh, shit. He'd seen this necklace before. On the local news on TV. Big theft from the Honduras National Museum last week. A national treasure. Once belonged to some Honduran priestess or something. He couldn't remember.

What the hell did it matter anyway? He had the diamonds now. If he turned them in to the government, it was just one more guarantee he'd signed his death warrant. Nader wouldn't take kindly to having what he, no doubt, considered his stones given back to their rightful owners.

Five million dollars worth of stones.

Five. Million. Dollars.

It didn't matter that he didn't want anything to do with them. Like it or not, they were his now. All he had to do was figure out a way to live long enough to reap the profit.

He glanced back down at Derek. He had to have had a buyer set up. Someone who was a guaranteed quick score, because Derek would have needed a quick score to get out of Honduras.

He dropped to his knees again. Frantically searched the rest of Derek's pockets. He finally came up with a piece of paper with a name and phone number.

It took him a while to puzzle out the letters but he made himself take his time. When he finally pieced the words together, he didn't want to believe what he saw.

Desmond Fox.

Oh, Christ.

This was where Derek had planned to sell the diamonds? To Desmond Fox?

Cory wanted to fall to the floor and bawl like a baby.

If Nader was a cobra, Fox was a pit viper. The two men were archrivals. There was no love lost or honor held between these two murdering thieves and Cory was now firmly caught between them.

He clawed a hand through his hair again. Finally laughed. Shit. It was either that or curl up in a ball and wait for Smith to come after him with Mr. Knife. Or Fox to come after him with an AK-47.

"Think. Think, dammit!"

He stood, paced the floor, stumbled over Derek's body. Wondered who would stumble over his when they found him.

"What choice do you have? What choice do you really have?"

He stared at the phone number on the paper, drew a breath, and picked up his cell to make the deal with Fox. His fingers shook as he dialed the number. A voice, heavy with a Spanish accent, answered on the third ring.

"Tupacka." Cory had labored over the letters, spoke them now, according to the instructions on the paper. As soon as he said it aloud he made the final connection. Tupacka — that was the name of the Honduran priestess. The diamonds had been hers — a wedding gift from some Spanish dude a couple hundred years ago, according to that same TV news report.

"Hold, please," the contact said after a short silence.

Cory waited. And paced. Bouncing with nervous energy and fear. Until finally, he was given a time and a place for the meet. The connection ended.

His gut knotted with fear. Five days. The meet was set for five long days from now. Swearing, he started throwing his few things into a backpack. He carefully packaged the diamonds, deciding what he had to do to protect them and hopefully protect himself until he made the deal.

He got all the way to the Jeep, had the engine started, hand on the gearshift, and just couldn't do it. He couldn't leave Derek there. Styles was a thief and a druggie but somewhere, someone might care. Just like somewhere, someone cared about what happened to Cory.

Swearing, he sprinted back to his room, wrapped Derek's body in a blanket, and hauled him out to the rented Jeep. He stopped at the first church that popped up — there were hundreds of them in San Pedro Sula — and pulled up out back where it was dark. Making sure no one was around, he unloaded Derek's body by the back door.

Then he raced the hell away, ditched the Jeep, and took off on foot. He never looked back. He made himself disappear in this city of close to a million people. Five days from now he'd either be rich or dead. Providing he could stay alive in the meantime.

3

"I get the picture, okay?" Without turning away from the screen on his laptop, Sam interrupted Reed's monologue about some woman he'd just met. "She brushed you off like a piece of white dog hair on a black dress."

"Yeah. She did for a fact." A big grin spread across Reed's outrageously handsome face. Somehow, he'd managed to slouch all six feet and one hundred eighty pounds of cover-boy looks into the black leather club chair facing the desk in Sam's office.

"The woman said no. To me," Reed continued, oblivious to Sam's dark scowl. His golden grin flashed a set of perfect white teeth and a pair of dimples that made the old ladies coo and the young ones lie down and smile. "God, what a set of balls."

"Having a little trouble with *that* picture," Sam said drolly as he turned his attention back to the pedigree of the quarter horse stud he was considering buying to improve the line of the breeding program at the ranch.

Reed laughed. "You are not taking me seriously, here." He stood, started prowling the office.

"Ya think? You met her on a flight. You'll probably never see her again. End of story."

God only knew what Sam had been thinking when Reed had called him from the airport and Sam had told him to come on out for this impromptu visit—the third in the three months since Sam had resigned from Black Ops, Inc.

He wanted Reed and Nate Black and the rest of the BOIs to leave him the hell alone. The chances of that happening were about the same as Reed giving up women. Just like the chance that Reed had shown up again was so he could catch Sam up on his love life.

Sam put up with Reed's semimonthly visits for one reason. He understood that his leaving Black Ops, Inc. hadn't merely broken up the team. That's because they weren't just a team. Black Ops, Inc. was a family. They were brothers, not by blood, but by ties forged in the trenches that were as tight as the coordinates on a precision bombing run.

Several years ago, Nathan Black, the CO of Task Force Mercy, had grown tired of being hamstrung by D.C. legislators who didn't know their ass from a frag grenade and knew even less about waging war, covert or otherwise. So Black had formed his own private contracting firm. When he'd parted ways with Uncle, so had most of the Task Force Mercy team. Sam had been one of the first to join, along with Gabe Jones, Raphael Mendoza, Luke Colter, Wyatt Savage, and Joe Greene—to name a few. Once they'd served out their hitches, they had separated from their various branches of the military and joined Black Ops, Inc.

For a lot of years now, they'd worked for Nate like a family.

Sam watched absently as Reed walked around the room. Most of those years had been spent down in Argentina. All of them chasing bad guys whose names law-abiding Americans would never know, pulling off ops that would never make the paper, and never be recorded in any annals of American history attached to the U.S. war machine.

Through it all, they hadn't just worked together. They'd lived together. Fought together. Grieved together.

Sam thought back to Terri's and B.J.'s funerals. Not only had the BOIs come to pay their respects, so had Ann and Robert Tompkins, who had "adopted" them all several years ago. The Tompkinses also knew what loss was. They'd paid the ultimate price. Their son, Bryan, had been a member of Task Force Mercy. He'd been killed on a mission in Sierra Leone, fighting as a warrior who knew the stakes, knew the risk, accepted the danger.

Sam stared into space. Clenched his jaw.

Terri hadn't been a warrior. Terri hadn't signed on for any risk. She and B.J. had been innocents. But to Fredrick Nader, Terri had been a means to an end. Collateral damage, a necessary tactic to get Sam off his back.

Well, Nader had gotten what he wanted.

Sam was done. Finished. He'd resigned from BOI the day he'd helped bury his sister. Nader's message had been clear. Back off or someone else Sam cared about would die.

So he'd walked away.

Yeah, it ate at him. Ate at his gut, ate at his soul, ate at his will until there was no fight left in him. He was done. Done trying. Done fighting.

Nader had won.

He would not risk anything else happening to his family.

"How do you handle this?" Reed had moved to the window. He stared out at the horse barns that snuggled up to the slow rise of the foothills and the low riding mountains beyond.

Sam spared him a glance. He'd known this was coming. It was the opening line to the "aren't you ready to come back to BOI?" spiel.

And the "this" in question was life on the ranch. Sam had grown up on Rancho Royale, breeding and selling quarter horses with his dad. "I'm handling it just fine."

"It's so friggin' quiet." Reed turned, planted himself in front of Sam's desk. Head cocked, he frowned, looking genuinely perplexed. "Don't you miss it?"

Sam looked up. He met Reed's eyes with a direct stare. Did he miss the action? The adrenaline rush? Breaking bad boys and their toys and putting them out of commission?

He couldn't afford to miss it. Just like he couldn't afford to let Reed see that he did. "Nope."

Reed hunkered down on his haunches, crossed his forearms over the edge of the desk directly in front of Sam. Those baby blues studied Sam from behind lashes as thick and blond as his hair. "Not even a little?"

Sam blinked. Turned back to his laptop.

"You know, if it's the conditioning that's stopping you," Reed continued, "it wouldn't take much to whip you back into shape. Hell, it's only been three months. And thirty-five's not *that* old—you're still close to fightin' weight. Not that anyone would ever expect you to keep up with me. Not that you ever could," he added with a baiting grin.

Sam gave him a benign look. "And the horse you rode in on."

Reed laughed. Sam didn't.

He wasn't going back. Reed knew why.

Yet here Reed was. Again.

"So," Reed said, sober suddenly, "it probably wouldn't interest you to know we've got a line on Nader. No smoke and mirrors this go-round. Something solid. We can nail his ass this time."

Sam forced himself to remain perfectly still. Reed was every bit as still. His good-ole-boy grin had dissolved into a grim expression.

"I mean it, Sam. This could finally be the break we need to take him out," he said with a soft but steely resolve. "Mendoza's been in Honduras since you left, digging around, setting up contacts, working on leads, but it's been your op from the beginning. Your hard work. You deserve to make the strike and take this bastard down."

Sam closed his eyes, made himself breathe as fists of anger clutched at his chest and pummeled at his control.

What he deserved.

This wasn't about what he deserved. His sister was dead. His brother-in-law—dead.

Because Sam had been bearing down on Nader's ass.

He wanted Nader more than he wanted to breathe. But he couldn't. He just couldn't.

He pushed back in his chair, steepled his fingers over his mouth, and glared at Reed. He wanted to shout at him to get the hell off his property and drag the bait along with him.

Forty pounds of giggling energy burst through the door of the study and forestalled anything more toxic than a glare. "Uncle Sam!"

Oblivious to the tension zipping through the room, as only a six-year old can be, Tina scrambled up onto Sam's lap.

"Hester's foalin'," his niece announced breathlessly. She smelled of little girl sweat and hay and sunshine. It was painfully sweet to see her smile after listening to her cry herself to sleep most nights. "After waitin' and waitin' it's finally time. This baby's mine, right, Uncle Sam? Mine and Hester's."

Sam smiled into Tina's dancing brown eyes. Love for this beautiful child overwhelmed him. She looked so much like her mother had at this age. Terri had been as bright and as bubbly as the ginger ale she'd loved to drink. Tina sparkled with the same effervescent energy.

Fredrick Nader may be the reason Sam was helping his parents raise his sister's little girl, but Sam was ultimately the one responsible. Just like Tina and his mom and dad were the reasons he couldn't risk going after Nader.

"Right, Uncle Sam?" Determined to get his full attention, she tugged on the dog tags he still wore.

"You betcha, baby." He pressed a kiss to her forehead. "Everything going okay in the barn?"

"Um-hum. Caesar said Hester's doin' just fine, but he wanted me to run and tell you 'case you wanted to call the vet or somethin'."

"Hey, babycakes," Reed said when he could get a word in edgewise. "How's my darlin'?"

"Johnny Duane!" Tina squealed.

In a flurry of scuffed boots and honey-brown pigtails, she scooted off Sam's lap and ran into Reed's outstretched arms. "What'd you bring me?"

Reed laughed and scooped her up for a smacking kiss. "You women are all alike. Greedy little wenches, that's all you are."

"So what'd you bring me?" Tina persisted, playing the game they'd played since Reed had charmed her on his first visit, a female secure in her element and her power.

Reed dug in his hip pocket and produced a set of handcuffs.

"Wow!" She snatched them away like a little thief. "Just what I always wanted!"

"Wish all the girls were as easy as you, shortstuff."

"Are you staying for supper?" she asked hopefully as she slid down to the floor and experimented with the latch on the cuffs.

Reed glanced at Sam, took his cue from a stone-cold glare. "I don't think so, darlin'. I think I'll head back to town and try my luck on the Strip. I just stopped by to give your Uncle Sam a piece of news." He slid an envelope out of his breast pocket, tossed it on the desk.

Sam's gaze shot from Reed's to the envelope. He knew there would be information on Nader inside. Very slowly, Sam rose, turned his back on the desk and any discussion involving Nader. "Come on, Tina. Let's go check on Hester."

"Call me," Reed said when they'd walked outside. The sun beat down like hot lead, weighty and oppressive.

Sam kept right on walking. Everything that mattered to him now was right here on this ranch. He wasn't leaving them alone and defenseless ever again.

The first thing Sam saw when he stepped into his office at 6:00 a.m. the next morning was the unopened envelope Reed had left on his desk the day before. He glared at it through bleary eyes, set a steaming cup of coffee beside it. Then he sat down in the leather chair and dragged a hand over his face, rubbing at the stubble.

He'd been up all night with the mare. Turned out she'd had complications after all and he'd had to call in the vet. All was well now. Both the mare and a foxy little filly were doing just fine.

He wasn't.

He stared at the envelope.

Swore.

Picked it up.

Tossed it down again.

He glanced outside. Through the branches of a cottonwood framing the office window, he could see all the main buildings. The stud barn sat on the north, the foaling barn dead ahead. A large enclosure full of yearlings opened wide to the east, just beyond the pasture of broodmares turned out with their foals.

His mom stood by the paddock fence, a protective hand on Tina's back as Tina stood on the third fence rung, her little cowboy boots hooked over the rail so she could get a better view of the mommas and their babies.

As loving and giving as his mom was, as nurturing and careful as she was with Tina, the picture was all wrong. It should include Terri.

A soft knock on the door broke into his thoughts.

"Am I interrupting anything, son?"

Sam forced his shoulders to relax. Just as he forced a smile. "No, Dad. Come on in. And since when do you have to knock on your own office door?"

His dad walked into the room, glanced out the window. "It's your office now." Tom Lang turned back to Sam, offered a smile that didn't manage to conceal the strain Terri's death had carved into his face.

"Always hoped you'd come back home. Take over the ranch someday." He compressed his lips, shook his head, and Sam could see he was fighting tears. "Never thought it'd be like this."

Sam swallowed hard. He hated seeing his father like this. Haggard. Broken. Always on the edge of tears.

For as long as he had memories his dad had been like a god to him. Strong. Proud. Invincible. Young for his years. Loving life.

Terri's and B.J.'s deaths had changed all that.

Sam had never felt helpless in his life. He felt it now. Marrow deep. Like he felt the churning deep in his gut to hunt down Nader like the dog he was and make him pay for what he'd done to Terri. To little Tina. To his mom and dad.

Helpless because, to keep his family safe, Sam had had to let the murdering bastard walk away.

"You need to fix this."

The hard edge in his father's voice startled him. For the first time in weeks, Sam saw something other than profound grief in his father's eyes. They were fired with anger and conviction.

"You can't let him get away with what he did to Terri and B.J."

His father knew, of course. One night over a bottle of Jack Daniel's, Tom Lang had called his only son out. "Let's hear it," he'd said. "Let me hear it all."

Sam had never lied to his dad. Had never been able to keep something from him when it was eating at him. Terri's death had been tearing into him with shark's teeth.

So he'd told him. Slouched back on the leather sofa in this very room, with a half-empty glass in his hand, tears in his eyes, and midnight striking on the clock, he told him that Fredrick Nader had killed Terri to get to Sam.

"Sam."

His dad's voice snapped him back to the here and now.

"You *need* to fix this."

Sam was so tired. Of living with the guilt. Of resisting the urge to do exactly what his father was asking him to do. "I can't. You know why I can't."

His dad eased down into the club chair, met Sam's tortured eyes across the desk. "I've given you time. Knew you needed to get yourself grounded again. Needed to grieve. But now it's time for revenge."

Sam looked away, heartsick. His dad was a gentle man. Like Sam, he was also a quiet man. Tough but fair. Honest to a fault. A believer—in God, in goodness, in his fellow man. Sam's hatred of Nader ascended to new heights as he sat here and listened to his father talk about revenge.

"I can't," he said again. Pleaded with his eyes for his dad to understand. To let it go. To move on.

Like Sam was trying to move on.

Tears filled his father's eyes. "You can't not."

Tears. From this proud, proud man.

Sam's fault.

"You think I don't want to take this bastard out?" Sam's voice broke. He settled himself. "Jesus, Dad. It's all I think about."

"Then take care of it."

He lifted a hand. Let it fall. "What? And take a chance he'll come after you next . . . or Mom? What if he targets Tina? I can't live with another death on my head."

His father straightened. "I may be getting older, son, but I can still take care of my own. He won't blindside me or mine again. No one else is gonna die on my watch."

Outside, the sky was a brilliant, crystalline blue, the air hot and arid and scented of the desert. Inside, shadows filled the room—shadows of his sister's ghost that cooled the air to a grave-damp chill.

Tom Lang stood, walked to Sam's side, and laid a hand on his shoulder. "You owe it to Terri. More, you owe it to yourself. I know you. This is going to eat at you until there's nothing left but a hollow shell of the man you are. Then you'll be as gone from me as Terri is."

He squeezed, dropped his hand. "I can't lose you both."

Then he walked out of the office, closing the door behind him.

Sam sat in the ringing silence for almost an hour before he picked up the envelope Reed had left. He ran his thumb along the creased edge. Finally opened it.

Read it. Read it again.

He glanced out the window to see his dad walk out of the stud barn toward the driveway. His shoulders were stooped, his gait labored.

Sam breathed deep, then he slowly reached for the phone.

Reed answered on the second ring.

"I'm in," he said and hung up, knowing he'd just done the equivalent of stepping out of a Blackhawk without a parachute or a rope.

4

"Do you think I should be worried about Cory?" Abbie asked Crystal as the two of them stood back and assessed the placement of Abbie's new sofa and chair.

"I think you should be enjoying your new furniture. My Lord, this leather feels like butter." Crystal Debrowski sank down on the luxurious sofa with a humming sigh.

"Yeah," Abbie agreed, grinning at her friend. "It *is* pretty cool, huh?"

"More than."

"Looks good," she said, glancing around the room, approving of the arrangement after she and Crystal had moved the furniture several times.

"Looks great!" Crystal agreed.

For accessories and paint, she'd gone for soft, soothing colors to complement the buff-colored leather. With her hectic and packed schedule, she'd wanted a calm and inviting place to land when she had a moment to unwind. Sage and moss green, sand and desert browns interspersed with the occasional punch of a watery blue made this room the oasis she needed.

"So what do you think about Cory?" Abbie persisted, plopping down on the sofa beside Crystal. "He was supposed to be back in Vegas two days ago. I still haven't heard from him."

"And this is out of character?"

Abbie lifted a shoulder. "Okay. So maybe it's not."

"You're not his mother, Abbie," Crystal said gently. "And you're not his keeper."

Yeah. Crystal was right. Abbie needed to quit stewing.

"Right. Thanks. And thanks for the help." She checked her watch. "Oh, man. I've got to scramble or I'll be late for work tonight."

"Say no more. I'm off like a dirty shirt." Crystal headed for the door. "See ya when I see ya."

Abbie hustled for the shower, mentally calculating the time and wondering what corners she could cut and not be late for her shift, all the while fighting desperately not to worry about her brother.

"That's her. Second table. She's just coming back from a break."

Sam had met Reed at the Casino New Orleans ten minutes ago, where the two of them had taken up residence at a bank of Lucky Seven slot machines. Since then, they'd waited for a blackjack dealer named Abbie Hughes to return to her table.

According to Reed, Abbie Hughes was their pipeline to Fredrick Nader.

Sam fed the machine and tried not to second-guess a decision that had placed everything he loved at risk. He was back in this now. He was in it to the end.

Nader was going to die. For Terri. For B.J. For his dad. Sam would use whatever means available to make certain that happened.

He cast a glance away from the slot, sized up Cory Hughes's sister.

"She's a stone-cold fox, huh?" Reed sat at a slot beside him. "Begs the question, what's a woman like her doing mixed up in Fredrick Nader's shit?"

Over the years, Sam had learned that life begged a lot of questions. In this case, Sam's questions were the same as Reed's. Out of years of practice, he sized up Abbie Hughes with a cold, critical eye.

Reed's assessment was spot-on. The woman was stunning. She was also tall—five-eight, maybe—and willow slim. Vegas was filled with beautiful women. Wannabe models, wannabe actresses, wannabe famous. Sam's initial impression was that Abbie Hughes didn't appear to want to be anything but what she was, as she chatted easily with the players at her table.

That was his first inkling that she might not be exactly what she seemed. Yeah, Abbie Hughes made a pretty package. Sam had learned long ago not to judge a package by its wrapping. Just like he'd learned that women as beautiful as this one always had bigger, better, bolder things on their agendas—wide, guileless eyes and easy smiles notwithstanding.

Her sable-brown hair swung around her shoulders, glossy and girl-next-door natural. Though she had an athletic body, the curves were all there, too—all the more effective because of their subtlety.

She looked wholesome and centered and sexy, and if she were faking innocence, she was damn good at it, because if Reed's intel was right, Abbie Hughes was knee-deep in international crime just like her brother. That made her Sam's best lead to flush Nader out of his lair.

Still, Sam wondered as he turned back to the machine. "You sure she's in the mix?"

"Shame, huh? But yeah. Everything points straight to her door."

Yeah. It was a shame. Because if she were involved with Nader, she was fair game. As such, Sam would use her to get what he needed and walk away from the wreckage without a backward glance or an ounce of remorse.

"Fill me in." Sam hadn't wanted Reed to brief him over the phone. Old habits were hard to break. The landline at the ranch house wasn't secure and he didn't want to take a chance with his cell. While the report Reed had left for Sam addressed the key points regarding Cory Hughes and his sister, it hadn't offered specific details.

Reed smacked the side of the slot machine and swore when he just missed a jackpot. "Abbie Hughes. Twenty-seven. Divorced. Accounting student at UNLV. Deals here five nights a week. The brother, Cory Hughes, is twenty-two. Single. No visible means of support."

"That much I got. Why'd you look at him in the first place?"

"That watch list you'd been tracking on Nader? Cory Hughes's name started popping up with a bunch of known accomplices shortly after you left the team."

Sam dropped more money into the machine. Punched the button. The *ding-ding-ding* and whirl of bells joined the unending cacophony of sound resonating through the crowded casino and insulated their conversation. "Can you pin him with anything specific?"

Reed shook his head. Swore again when he just missed another jackpot. "What we do know is that Nader likes to play cat-and-mouse with U.S. customs. He's scrambled the paper trail, but Hughes looks good as a facilitator."

"So you're tagging Cory as one of Nader's mules."

"Low level. At least until recently. Like I said, Hughes has never had steady income. It looks like Nader hooked him hard with drug deliveries. Mostly out of Central America. Specifically Honduras."

Nader's favorite playground. Sam's biggest nightmare.

"Hughes was spotted in San Pedro Sula within the last week," Reed continued.

Which meant the trail was fresh. It also meant they needed to start moving on this fast before it went cold.

"Other than the fact that family is usually the first line of resistance, what points to the sister?"

"First, it would figure that an 'entrepreneur' like Cory Hughes would have an accomplice on the inside, right? Someone he could trust."

Sam glanced at Reed. "Yeah, it would figure. But you've got to have more than that."

Reed scowled at the machine, dug into his pocket for more change. "Couple of things. Little brother rents a flop in Northwest Vegas—just past Circus Circus. Nice neighborhood—if you're a rat. Lots of rent-by-the-hour or -day or -week motels. Plenty of meth labs."

"I take it you paid a visit."

"And wouldn't you know it, the door to his room just sort of swung open when I got there."

Yeah. Sam knew how handy Reed was with a pick kit. Lots of doors "just sort of swung open" for Reed.

"Anyway, like I said, the place is a dive. Nothing there but roaches, and there's no room to store anything. But I did find a slug of shipping orders tucked in a locked desk drawer."

"That drawer fall open like the door?"

Reed grinned. "Go figure. Anyway, guess whose address was on those shipping orders?"

"The sister."

"That would be a big blackjack. So, I checked out her place."

"Jesus, Reed. How many laws you going to break?"

Reed effected a wounded look. "I do not break laws. I take advantage of opportunities. But in this case, not so much. Part of town where she lives is several steps up from her brother's digs. Not high end but respectable. Small house. Modest suburban bliss. Lots of security. A suspicious amount, in fact. Gated lot. I also spotted a couple of cameras on the roof. Kind of makes you wonder what she might be hiding. Add that to the neighbors who are plentiful and nosy and I didn't get inside.

"But I did watch it for a few days," he added to the *ding* of his machine making a small payoff. "She gets a lot of deliveries. Gotta make you wonder what's in them. If they're from the brother, they could contain anything from drugs to laundered money to stolen gems."

"And if that's the case, we might be able to convince her we're on to them and that she's in deep weeds if she doesn't tell us what she knows," Sam surmised.

He cut another quick look at Abbie Hughes. Her table was full. She flashed her gamers a killer grin as she shuffled multiple decks, offered the cut card to the first-base player, then expertly slipped the cards into the shoe. Sam watched as she dealt around the table. He found himself wishing she would turn up clean, even though it would mean they'd hit a dead end.

"Anything else?" he asked Reed.

"Odds are she's cashing in on the brother's merchandise. The pretty lady has a brand-new shiny ride. Bought it just last week. Top of the line. And check out the sparkly hanging around her neck."

While she was wearing it over a pristine white shirt that buttoned at the throat to accommodate a black tie, the necklace was what Sam called a cleavage piece. The rock of a diamond hung from a gold chain. It didn't take much imagination to figure that if she hadn't been wearing that shirt, the diamond would hit just at the point where Abbie Hughes's breasts squeezed together above her bra cups.

Sam dragged his attention back to the slot and away from her breasts. "Maybe they pay their dealers well here."

"Yeah, right," Reed said. "A little above minimum plus tips."

"Did you run her credit history?"

"One card. Zero balance. And there's no lien on the car."

Which begged another one of those questions that Sam couldn't discount as coincidental: How did a minimum-wage dealer who was also paying tuition come up with the coin to buy a new car and a hunk of carbon that could choke a horse?

If Reed was right, Abbie Hughes could do it because she was working with her brother, who was working for Nader, who was a badass with a penchant for—among other things—stolen gems.

Gems like the diamond hanging around Abbie Hughes's neck.

"By the way," Reed said as he worked the machine, "Mendoza sent some info today that adds a new wrinkle to the report I left with you."

Raphael Mendoza, like Reed, still played on the BOIs team with Jones and Colter and the rest of the guys. Mendoza had been nosing around Honduras for the better part of three months looking for an in with Nader.

Sam waited.

"You did *read* the initial report, right?"

"Yeah. I read it." The Tupacka diamonds—a necklace valued in the millions, had disappeared from the National Museum of Honduras a week ago. Aside from it being worth upward of five mil, it was also a national treasure, complete with an ancient legend attached. While they had nothing concrete, Nader's fingerprints were all over the heist. Of course, Nader would never do the actual hands-on dirty work, but he'd sure as hell facilitate it. "What's the wrinkle?"

"Desmond Fox's name is surfacing on that deal now, too. Seems they both have a yen for the diamonds."

Sam grunted, not all that surprised. "This is turning into a regular bottom-feeder convention."

Desmond Fox and Fredrick Nader were both spawned from the same swamp. Fox had been on the BOI's radar almost as long as Nader. There was no love lost between these two thieves. No honor either. They competed for the same markets, undercut each other at every opportunity. So it stood to reason if they competed over drugs or weapons they'd mix it up over hot ice.

"Of course, we could get lucky and they'll do each other in," Reed pointed out. "Save us all a lot of trouble."

"Don't believe in luck. And I want Nader for myself."

Reed nodded. "So how do you want to play this?"

Sam glanced at Abbie Hughes again, rubbed a thumb over his lower lip.

"We could lean on her," Reed suggested after a moment. "Scare the info out of her."

Sam shook his head. "Let's save that for plan B. Don't want to take a chance that approach would backfire. She might clam up, warn off little brother, and that would be the end of that. We'd lose them both."

No. This called for a more subtle approach.

"You said she's single?"

Reed shoved more coins into the slot. "Divorced."

"Boyfriend?"

"Not from what I've gathered."

"So maybe she needs one."

"Don't look at me." Reed sounded disgusted. "I arranged to run into her the other night, thinking maybe we could get chummy, you know? Got shut down without so much as a hi, how are ya. I gave her every opening and she set up nothing but roadblocks."

"And you're up and around after that kind of hit to your ego?"

"Hey, I can't help it that most women find me irresistible—or that this one has no taste. Speaking of no taste . . . maybe *you're* her type."

Ignoring the dig, Sam glanced toward Abbie Hughes again. "Yeah," he said, prepared to do whatever it took to bring Nader down. "Maybe I am."

Abbie spotted the gay cop cowboy the minute she came back from break. It was hard not to. The guy was incredible looking. While she felt a little kernel of unease that he'd turned up again—where she worked, this time— she wasn't going to let it throw her off her stride.

The Vegas Strip wasn't all that big. Not really. There were only so many places for people to eat, sleep, and gamble. When he drifted off twenty minutes or so later without so much as looking her way, she chalked it up to coincidence. Just as she found it coincidental that the tall man with the dark eyes and short dark hair who'd been playing the slot beside the golden boy ambled over to the blackjack tables.

Big guy. The western-cut white shirt and slim, crisp Wrangler jeans told her he was a real cowboy. The kind who made his living in the saddle, not the kind who just dressed the part. He was confident but quiet with it, she decided, as she dealt all around to her full table then cut another glance the big guy's way.

He stood a few feet back from the tables, arms crossed over a broad chest, long legs planted about a shoulder-width apart, eyes intent on the action on the blackjack table next to hers. On any given night there were a lot of lookers in a casino, so it wasn't unusual that he stood back from the crowd and just watched. What was unusual was that between deals, her gaze kept gravitating back to him.

What was even more curious was that when one of her players scooped up his chips and wandered off, leaving the third-base chair empty, Abbie found herself wishing the tall cowboy would take his place.

What was up with that? And what was up with the little stutter step of her heart when he ambled over, nodded hello and eased his lean hips onto the chair.

"Howdy," she said with what she told herself was a standard, welcoming smile.

He answered with a polite nod as he reached into his hip pocket and dug out his wallet. When she'd paid and collected bets all around, he tossed a hundred-dollar bill onto the table.

Abbie scooped it up, counted out one hundred in chips from the chip tray, then spread them on the green felt tabletop for him to see. After he'd gathered them in and stacked them in front of him, she tucked the hundred into the slot in front of her.

"Place your bets," she said to the table of seven, then dealt the first round faceup from the shoe. When all players had two cards faceup, she announced her own total. "Dealer has thirteen."

Her first-base player asked for a hit, which busted him. When she got to cute, quiet cowboy, he waved his hand over his cards, standing pat with eighteen.

You could tell a lot about a person from their hands. Abbie saw a lot of hands—polished and manicured, dirty and rough, thin and arthritic. The cowboy's hands were big, like he was. His fingers were tan and long with blunt, clean nails, not buffed. Buffed, in her book, said pretentious. His were not. They were capable hands. A workingman's hands, with the occasional scar to show he was more than a gentleman rancher. Plenty of calluses. He dug in.

She liked him for that. Was happy for him when she drew a king, which busted her. "Luck's running your way," she said with a smile as she paid him.

He looked up at her then and for the first time she was hit with the full force of his smile. Shy and sweet, yet she got the distinct impression there was something dark and dangerous about him.

Whoa. Where had that come from? And what the heck was going on with her?

Hundreds—make that thousands—of players sat at her table in any given month. Some were serious, some were fun and funny, some sad. And yeah, some of them deserved a second look. None of them, however, flipped her switches or tripped her triggers like this man was flipping and tripping them right now. It was unsettling as all get out.

"Place your bets," she announced again, then dealt around the table when all players had slid chips into their betting boxes.

Whereas the blond poster boy had been bad-boy gorgeous, there wasn't one thing about this man that suggested boy. Abbie pegged him for midthirties—maybe closer to forty, but it wasn't anything physical that gave her that impression. He was rock solid and sort of rough-and-tumble-looking. Dark brown hair, close cut, dark, *dark* brown eyes, all-seeing. Nice face. Hard face. All edgy angles and bold lines.

Maybe that was where the dangerous part came in. He had a look about him that was both disconcerting and compelling. A presence suggesting experience and intelligence and a core of solid confidence that needed no outward display or action to reinforce it.

He was the quintessential quiet-hero type. Clint Eastwood without the steely squint. Matthew McConaughey without the long hair and boyish charm—and *with* a shirt on, something McConaughey was generally filmed without. Although, the cowboy *did* have his own brand of charisma going on because sure as the world, he was throwing *her* for a loop.

"Cards?" she asked him now.

"Double down."

Smart player, she thought, and split his pair of eights. She grinned again when he eventually beat the table and her on both cards.

"I think maybe *you're* my luck." He tossed a token in the form of a red chip her way.

"Tip," she said loud enough for her pit boss to hear, showed him the five-dollar chip before she pocketed it. "Thanks," she said smiling at him.

"My pleasure."

He spoke so softly that the only reason she understood what he said was because she was looking right at him. The din of the casino drowned out his words to anyone else at the table as the rest of the players talked and joked or commiserated with each other.

The next words out of his mouth—"What time do you get off?"—stopped her cold.

She averted her gaze. "Place your bets," she told the table at large, thinking, *Hokay. Quiet doesn't necessarily equate to shy.*

The man moved fast. Which both surprised and pleased her because it meant that all this "awareness," for lack of a better word, wasn't one-sided. It also made her a little nervous. Her first instinct was to give him her standard, *Sorry. No fraternizing with the customers.*

But then she got an image of a devil sitting on her shoulder—a red-haired pixie devil with a remarkable resemblance to Crystal. *Don't you dare brush him off. Look at him. Look! At! Him!*

She chanced meeting his eyes again—his expression was expectant but not pressuring—and found herself mouthing, "Midnight."

A hint of a smile tugged at one corner of his mouth. "Where?"

She didn't hesitate nearly long enough. "Here." *God, what was she doing?*

"Cards?" she asked the table.

He gave her the "hit me" signal when she came around to him.

He broke twenty-one, shrugged.

"Sorry," she said, liking the easy way he took the loss. "Better luck next time."

"Counting on it." He stood. "Later," he said for her ears only; then he strolled away from the table.

"Dealer pays sixteen," she said absently as she paid all winners and surreptitiously watched what was arguably one of the finest Wrangler butts she'd ever seen get lost in a sea of gamblers.

5

The rest of Abbie's shift dragged by but, finally, a little past midnight, she'd pulled down fifty-five dollars in tips, squared her cash drawer, checked out, passed through her standard security check, and retrieved her purse from her locker—after she'd checked her hair and freshened her lipstick.

She was way too excited about meeting the cowboy. *Way* too excited. When she walked back into the casino toward her table, she wasn't feeling nearly as sure of her rash decision to meet up with him as she had earlier. Making quick dates with strangers was not her style. Making *dates* was not her style.

Get over it, the devil on her shoulder—sounding amazingly like Crystal again—whispered in her ear.

About one thing, Crystal was right. Abbie *had* been out of circulation for a long time. Maybe it was time to test the waters again. And yeah, it made sense that at some point a guy would come along and finally get to her, make her want to step out of her comfort zone and open herself up to new possibilities.

Yeah. It made sense.

"All but the part about going out with a man whose name you don't even know," she muttered as she neared her table.

She spotted him watching the action where Bill Gates—yeah, that was really his name—had taken over for her. A lot of cowboys played at the Vegas casinos and she hadn't imagined it earlier. None of them filled out their Wranglers the way this man did.

"Hi," she said, before she lost her nerve and bailed on him.

He turned, slowly uncrossed his arms, and smiled, looking pleased. "Hi."

Then he just stood there, as if he were waiting for her to say something. As if he already knew she had something she wanted to say. Which she did.

"Just so we're straight on something." Abbie stared at his throat, not quite able to meet his eyes but liking the fact that she would have actually had to look up a bit to do it. "This is a first for me. Letting someone pick me up at my table."

Okay, now would come the part where he would say something like, *A gorgeous woman like you? Not used to pickups? Come on. You must have to beat them off with a stick.*

Or some such line that was supposed to make her gush all over. She'd heard plenty of them. But she didn't hear one from him. He just watched her with those dark, intense eyes, then nodded. "Okay."

Well, that surprised her. So did his unassuming gaze. So she hit him with a stop sign he couldn't possibly misunderstand.

"And so you know, you've used up your quota of luck for the night."

His grin was slow and full of amusement. "Not even enough left to find a good cup of coffee?"

Score more points for the cowboy. No disappointed frown. No casting about for excuses to find greener pastures—or in this case, a hotter, more willing date.

She finally relaxed, returned his smile. "I think I can take care of that."

"Name's Sam, by the way." He extended his hand. "Sam Lang."

His introduction was all formal and sweet and if he'd been wearing a hat Abbie was pretty sure it would have been white and he'd have tipped his fingers to the brim.

"Abbie." She returned his handshake, far too aware of the strength and energy radiating from his big callused hand and of an underlying sexuality made all the more unnerving because he seemed so totally unaware of the potent effect he had on her.

"Abbie Hughes," she said, feeling suddenly self-conscious. "Let's go get that coffee. I know just the place. It's a short walk from here."

Abbie took Sam to Benny's, a small mom-and-pop diner a couple blocks off the Strip.

"I used to bus tables here when I was in high school," she told him as they slipped into a booth. "Sure you're set on coffee? They make a mean chocolate malt."

"Another time, maybe. Tonight, coffee works just fine."

Everything was working just fine, Abbie thought as she sat across from him in a booth. He filled every space he occupied, it seemed. His white shirt against the faded red upholstery emphasized how broad his shoulders were. His big hands cupped around a mug of strong, rich coffee underscored the strength in them. And yet, nothing about his demeanor said he'd ever come on too strong.

"Haven't seen you in the casino before." She was curious about that.

"Haven't been back for very long. This is the first chance I've had to check out the action. Strip's changed, man, a *lot* while I've been gone."

"Gone?"

He nodded. "Grew up on a horse ranch just outside of town." He grunted. "Town's almost grown out there now."

"No way. Are you telling me you're a native?"

"Born and raised."

She grinned. "Me, too. We're a rare breed considering all the transplants."

"Rare's a good word," he agreed, his smile extending his meaning to include her.

Oh, man. She could get into a guy who thought she was rare, as in special.

"And gone's a big word," she prompted.

"College. Then the military. After that private work." He shrugged again. "Time passes and one day a man realizes something's missing."

"Home," she concluded.

"Yeah," he said after a moment. "Roots. They mean more as a man grows older."

He, it seemed, was rare, too. Special. "So . . . you're back on the ranch."

He lifted his mug, drank. "Yep. Taking over for my dad."

That was nice. Keeping things in the family. "I'm sure he's glad to have you home."

He smiled politely at the waitress when she swung back by the table and refilled their mugs. Abbie couldn't help but notice the strong lines of his neck, the defined curve of his jaw as he glanced up and nodded his thanks.

There was nothing about this man that didn't appeal to her.

"What about you?" he asked.

"Not much to tell. Afraid I never made it past the city limits. But it's okay. I like it here. Like the climate, have friends here."

"Family?"

Not like his, she was sure. "My brother."

If he wanted to ask more, he restrained himself. She appreciated that because she wasn't at the point where she was willing to share too much personal information. She'd experienced a little too much disappointment in her life to open herself up to someone who was essentially a stranger. And she had plenty of reason to protect herself.

"So, when you're not dealing blackjack, what do you like to do?"

Get Acquainted 101. It was sweet and something more to like about him. She liked it a lot that he wasn't prying too deep or coming on all strong and macho and, let's face it, sexual. The chemistry was there—had been from the moment they'd become aware of each other at her table tonight—but it was nice that he was taking the time to get to know her, too.

"Well," she fiddled with the handle on her coffee mug, "I'm an accounting student at UNLV, so when I'm not working, I'm either in class or studying."

"All work, no play . . ." He let the line trail off.

"Makes Abbie a dull girl," she filled in for him.

His gaze touched her face. "Not from where I'm sitting."

As flirting went, it was subtle. It was also very effective.

"So you're a cowboy." Suddenly she felt like flirting, too.

"Yes, ma'am."

He grinned when he said it and that made her smile. Again. In fact, she'd smiled a lot tonight. Smiled more than she'd smiled with a man in . . . well, she couldn't remember how long.

"So, other than saying things like 'git along little dogie' and 'yee-haw,' what, exactly, does a cowboy do?"

"Well, we *do* get to say that a lot," he agreed. "But we also do things like refine breeding lines, break and train the stock to ride. My dad has always done some showing. I might get back into that."

She could see him astride a horse. Big and brawny and bold against a sweeping vista.

"You ever ride, Abbie?"

"Actually, yeah. I have. Not that I'm expert. Had a friend once who had horses. I was enthralled by them."

"It seems to be a girl thing," he said with a sage nod.

Yeah. It was a girl thing, she agreed. All that big, bold beauty—much like the big, bold, and beautiful man smiling at her.

"What?" she asked, sensing he had something on his mind.

"Blackjack dealer. Student. Lover of horses. You still haven't told me what you like to do for fun."

"I run," she said.

"Run?"

"Five miles a day."

"In the army we called that PT—physical training—but we *didn't* call it fun."

She laughed. "Depends on your perspective, I guess. It's my self time."

He nodded. "Okay. I see that. My self time is on the back of a horse these days."

"I like roller coasters," she added, because she did and because for some reason she wanted him to know she wasn't as dull as dishwater.

"Ah. A thrill seeker," he said with a lift of his eyebrows. "What other kind of thrills turn you on?"

Okay. From any other man, that would have been sexual. And maybe it was, just a little, but his face never gave it away. He was either a very good actor or the most forthcoming man she'd ever met.

"The Space Needle. But it's been years since I was on it."

"Skydiving?" he suggested, almost as a dare.

"Not yet. But I'd like to."

He sat back in the booth, considered her through narrowed eyes. "What are you doing tomorrow night?"

"Tomorrow night?" She probably should have at least consulted her calendar, made some kind of a show of considering what her answer would be. His lack of pretense just wouldn't allow it. "Nothing. I work the early shift."

"Spend it with me."

Her heart did a little stutter step. "Doing?"

Something as close to devilish as she'd seen darkened his eyes. "How about I surprise you?"

All he'd ever done since she'd met him was surprise her. Just like she surprised herself again when without hesitation she took the leap. "Got to love a good surprise."

"No freaking way!" Crystal couldn't hide her shock when Abbie called her the next morning before class. "You? On a date? With a man?"

"It wasn't a date. It was coffee." Good coffee. Good company. She'd smiled a lot. For a while, she'd even quit thinking and worrying about Cory, who still hadn't called or e-mailed.

"It was a major breakthrough, that's what it was," Crystal insisted. "Details. Now. Start with what he looks like."

Abbie walked into her bedroom and reached for her jeans. She wedged her phone between her ear and shoulder and wiggled into them. "He looks like a cowboy."

"Well, can I hear a yee-haw, sista?" Crystal crowed. "So what kind of cowboy? 'Big hat, no cattle' cowboy or the 'real deal' cowboy? And please do *not* tell me he rides rodeo."

Abbie laughed. There were working, breathing, living the life "real deal" cowboys. There were rodeo cowboys who didn't have much more than their rigging bag and a beat-up pickup and several broken bones to their name. And then there were the "big hat, no cattle" cowboys. Men who played at being something they weren't.

It came as no surprise to Abbie that Sam Lang was exactly who he appeared to be. He wasn't full of himself. Wasn't on any mission to impress. She'd really liked that.

"Real deal," she said, working her arms out of the sleeves of her nightshirt.

"How real?" Crystal wanted to know.

"Born on a working horse ranch outside of Vegas."

"Get out."

"Went to college, did some time in the military, then some sort of private sector work, and now he's moved back home to take over the ranch for his dad, who's ready to retire."

"Solid, stable citizen. Caring son. I'm liking this guy."

Abbie was liking him, too. So much that she had to keep reminding herself to chill.

"So . . . when are you seeing him again?"

"Tonight. After work." Okay. So that wasn't exactly "chilling," but she'd wanted to say yes so she had.

"I am so proud," Crystal whimpered, playing thrilled mother.

Abbie laughed. "It's not that big of a deal."

"Sweetie, this is bigger than Botox. My little girl. Going on a date."

Abbie rolled her eyes.

"Where are you going? What are you wearing? Underwear. Oh, God. *Pleeeease* tell me you own something other than white, cotton, covers-your-entire-ass underwear."

Abbie sank down on the bed, grinning. "I didn't say I was sleeping with him, so my underwear is not an issue. I said I'm going on a date with him. And I don't know where we're going. He said he wanted to surprise me."

"A date. How sixties is that?" Crystal wanted to know.

"I think it's kind of sweet. Look. I've got to run or I'll be late for class."

"You made my day, Abs. This sounds promising. Really promising."

"I repeat. It's just a date."

"It's an act of God, that's what it is."

"Bye, Crystal." Abbie flipped her phone shut.

"Just a date," she repeated to herself as she finished dressing for class.

Just a date with just a man who just happened to be a really nice guy who just happened to turn her on like a strobe light.

She checked her watch. Saw that she was running about five minutes ahead of time and decided to check her e-mails. Still nothing from Cory. While it was like Cory to take off for days at a time, it wasn't like him not to keep in touch, even though she knew it was hard for him to read and type.

"He's a big boy," she reminded herself. Just because he was dyslexic didn't mean he was disabled, although it sure made life hard from him. She'd always been proud of him for making do. He could take care of himself— something that was hard for her to remember because for the longest time, she'd been the one taking care of him. Abbie felt more like his mother than his sister. That was because she was the one who had protected both Cory and herself from their father.

No good would come from dwelling on how rough they'd had it as kids. Especially Cory. He always took the brunt of Dexter Hughes's tirades. Their father had dealt out more than physical punishment and Cory was still searching for his path because of it.

Abbie immediately drew herself away from those memories. What was past was past. Since she still had a little time—and because she was basically a careful person who didn't believe in "too good to be true"—she did what she'd promised herself she wouldn't do. She Googled Sam Lang plus Rancho Royale, which, he'd told her, was the name of his ranch.

It was the smart thing to do, she assured herself. The safe thing. Even if it was intrusive, in this world, a person couldn't be too careful.

"Well, damn," she muttered when she got a hit. An old newspaper article— one of a dozen local-interest pieces the *Vegas Sun* ran every year—profiled Tom Lang and his family. A son, Samuel, and a daughter, Terri.

Sam hadn't mentioned that he had a sister. Abbie quickly scanned the article and felt a sudden clutch at her heart when she hit on another link to Sam Lang. At first she thought it was unrelated. Then she saw the name Tom Lang.

"Jesus. Oh, sweet Jesus," she whispered when an obituary came up.

She read through the obit, her eyes filling as it chronicled the short life of Terri Cooper, daughter of Tom and Vivian Lang. The photograph showed a vital, vibrant, smiling woman.

"She is survived by her parents, one brother, Sam Lang, and a daughter, Tina Cooper."

"How?" she wondered. Then she found it.

A car bomb had killed Sam's sister and her husband only three months ago. Right here in Vegas. In fact, Abbie remembered reading about it. She'd never made the connection with Sam until now because of Terri's married name.

Heart hammering, she read the article. Found an update. The case remained unsolved. Speculation was it was a mob hit but a case of mistaken identity because the Langs were model citizens.

Abbie was numb with shock when she forced herself to power down and head for class. She breathed deep, grabbed her keys, and then set her security system. Another push of a remote closed and locked the gates surrounding her property as she backed out of the garage.

No wonder Sam hadn't mentioned his sister, she thought as she zipped down the street. The pain he must be experiencing. The loss he must feel.

You don't know him well enough to get this invested in his life, she told herself staunchly.

But she knew. She was already invested. The proof was in her uncharacteristic desire to trust him. Her first instinct, in fact, had been to trust him and that was something new for her.

So yeah, she was invested. She couldn't hurt this badly for him if she wasn't.

6

"How'd it go with the Hughes woman?" Reed asked when he called.

Sam stared out his office window as his father drove by in the pickup, hauling a load of hay on a rack behind it.

"It went," he told Reed.

"Need to move on this, Sam," Reed reminded him.

Time was the enemy where Nader was concerned. Abbie Hughes was the key.

"You let me worry about that," he said and hung up.

He was meeting Abbie Hughes for their "date" tonight.

He thought about last night. Sharing coffee. Sharing smiles. Had to remind himself that she wasn't as innocent as she seemed. Tonight, he'd move a step closer to finding out just how deep she'd sunk into the mud with her brother.

Like the man, Sam's pickup was big and sleek and powerful.

"Sorry about the truck," he said when he helped her inside. "Haven't gotten around to buying a car yet."

Abbie smiled and buckled up her seat belt as he settled in behind the wheel. "You get a whole different perspective of the world from up here," she teased.

"Well, there is that," he agreed and made Abbie smile again, like she'd smiled when he'd called her earlier and told her to make sure she wore jeans.

"So, are you going to let me in on where we're going?"

He drove like he moved. Natural and relaxed with understated confidence, which was more appealing than any strut or swagger. His big hand rested on the gearshift knob, steady, sure, sexy as all get out.

"It's a surprise," he reminded her.

She laughed. "Yeah, I got that part."

"Then you'll get the part about if I told you where we were going it wouldn't be a surprise."

"Got me there," she agreed and settled in for the ride.

He was a man of mystery and he seemed to like it that way. She thought about his sister. She'd like to tell him how sorry she was about what had happened, but that would require telling him that she'd been snooping into his life. It wasn't exactly the kind of thing you wanted to reveal on a first date. Plus, he seemed so relaxed and lighthearted. She didn't want to break the mood.

So she decided to let it go. If she got to know him better, the subject was bound to come up. She wanted to be there for him when it did, she realized, and reminded herself to slow down, breathe deep, and keep the engine firmly ahead of the caboose.

The lights of the Vegas strip whizzed by as he drove. Throngs of people packed the sidewalks and wandered in and out of casinos. Laughter, the distant ring of slots and the constant buzz of thousands of conversations drifted on the warm night air.

"Look like fun?" Sam asked with a nod toward the roller coaster as they approached the New York-New York casino complex.

"You know, it does. I've never managed to find time to ride this one."

"Good to know," he said with a sly smile. "Because tonight's the night."

She jerked her gaze toward his, unable to hide the delight in her eyes. "Are you serious?"

"As a heart attack," he said, looking and sounding pleased with himself.

She grinned from him back to the coaster that looped and wrapped and rose and fell around the casino. "Cool!"

"You're a screamer," he accused an hour later when they tumbled out of the coaster—he'd insisted they ride in the first car.

"Hey. It's allowed," she laughed around a deep breath as she pulled herself together. "I read it in the rule book. I didn't see anything about laughing, though, and you seemed to do that all the way through the ride."

"Your fault," he said, dropping a hand on her shoulder. "Can't wait to hear you on the Space Needle."

He just kept surprising her. "No."

"'Fraid so, yeah."

She screamed her way through that ride, too. Was still catching her breath when they climbed back into his truck and headed out again.

"This has been fun," she said as he turned onto Convention Center Road. "Serious, serious fun."

"Good. But we're not done yet."

"No more roller coasters," she pleaded, feigning dread.

"No more roller coasters," he promised.

They rode in companionable silence for a while before she turned to look at him. His face was cast in shadows and light from the night and the neon. She was struck again by how ruggedly handsome he was. Just like she was struck by something else. She liked this man. "You're a really good time, you know that?"

"Same goes for you."

"Tonight reminds me of when I was younger." She didn't have a lot of happy memories from her childhood but the ones she did have stuck in her mind. "I used to spend a lot of time with my friend Crystal and her mom and dad when we were kids. They were always up for things like this. We'd go to county fairs; they'd take us on campouts. They even sent us both to a weeklong summer camp. That's where I learned to ride horses, by the way."

He braked for a light, glanced her way. "And weave baskets?"

She grinned. "I'll have you know I was darn good at it."

Yeah. She liked being with him. Being around him not only resurrected the kind of memories that made her feel good about herself, but made her believe that maybe she had a lot of memory making ahead of her.

Okay, so that was a huge leap, but it had been a long, long time since she'd thought about anything but work and school or done anything but worry about finances and Cory.

"Really?" she said when he pulled into a parking lot and she realized what he had in mind. "We're really going to do this?"

"You said you always wanted to skydive."

She made a gulping sound. "I talk big."

"You telling me you're not up for this, Hughes?"

She stared at the building that advertised indoor skydiving, swallowed hard. "Okay, now you're baiting me."

"Is it working?"

She frowned at the building again. "How far do we fall?"

He laughed as he got out of the truck. "All the way to the ground, sunshine. All the way to the ground."

"A. Ma. Zing," Abbie gushed after they'd completed their first dive. They'd both shrugged out of their indoor flight suits and met back up near the entrance. "The real thing must be the biggest rush in the world."

"It's a rush, all right. Especially when you dive out of a plane at fourteen thousand feet in the dark targeting an LZ the size of a pinhead."

"LZ?"

"Sorry. Landing Zone."

"In the dark?"

"More often than not."

"What? Were you a paratrooper or something?"

"Special Forces," he said, but she got the feeling there was much more to the story. "How about a bite to eat?"

Subject change. Okay. She could understand and respect that. She'd met some returning veterans. Hadn't talked to one yet who was eager to share his military experiences.

"Sure. I'm starving. All that adrenaline rush made me hungry."

"How about I pick the place tonight?"

"You're three for three so far. Who am I to question that kind of batting average?"

"You like baseball?"

She laughed when he jumped on her sports analogy. "Figure of speech. Seems a little slow-moving to me."

He smiled again.

"What?"

He shrugged. "Should have known you like your action fast."

Okay. Was that a come-on? Probably. Although she couldn't tell by looking. He drove eyes ahead, expression unreadable.

What if it was a come-on? she wondered. What would she do about it?

She was pretty sure she knew the answer to that and the fact was, it was as exciting as it was scary.

"Why did I not know about this place?" Abbie asked later as they gorged themselves on the juiciest hamburgers, the saltiest fries, and the most amazing chocolate malts that rivaled Benny's for excellence.

"I was just glad to see it's still going," he said, eyeing her French fries.

She sat back, shoved her plate toward him. "Help yourself. I'm stuffed."

"I'm impressed, though. You can pack it away for a girl."

She chuckled. "I think I've just been insulted."

He had the presence of mind to look embarrassed. "Sorry. That didn't come out right."

"But it happens to be the truth, so you're forgiven." She smiled at him then. "Thanks, Sam. Thanks for a really great night."

"You're welcome," he said, his dark eyes locked on hers. "I had a great time, too."

Yeah. It had been an excellent evening. So when he walked her to her door later and left without so much as a buss on her cheek, she wasn't only puzzled, she felt utterly and undeniably bereft.

"What," she muttered as she locked up behind herself, "just happened?"

Muchilena, Honduras
Close to midnight, one day later

Cory swiped a damp palm over the thin stubble covering his jaw. As he stood there, alone in the dark outside the cantina, he didn't kid himself. He could die here. Like Derek had died.

He shivered despite the cloying heat. No one would ever know. All that would be left of Cory Hughes would be a face on a wall with hundreds of other missing-person posters.

He leaned his head back against the scarred cantina wall as a runnel of sweat trickled down his back. Only one person in the world would give a damn if he ended up missing or dead. Abbie. His sister would care, even though all he'd done his entire life was give her grief.

"Swear to God," he whispered heavenward, "if I get out of this alive, I'm a changed man."

He would make it all up to Abbie. All the worry he'd caused her, all the guff he'd given her. All the crap he'd dished out over the years.

From inside the cantina, a blistering *punta*-rock beat blared out of a tinny-sounding radio and vibrated into the midnight silence. Muffled and raucous laughter leaked through an open doorway, punctuated by a woman's husky squeal.

Somebody was getting lucky. For ten bucks, you could get damn lucky in this village, where the dogs outnumbered the men and the men outnumbered the women three to one.

He dragged his tongue over dry lips. Derek's lifeless eyes haunted him. Nader scared him, made him feel like that helpless, snot-nosed little kid who used to cower in a corner and wait for the old man to kick the crap out of him in a drugged-up rage.

Cory wasn't that kid anymore. He was twenty-two years old. Chicks dug him, he thought, mustering a swaggering pride to beat away his apprehension. They liked his lean, lanky body, his long dark hair and baby blue eyes, liked his smile. It had always made him feel like a man when he could make a woman smile. They smiled best for cash, though.

His heart damn near crashed out of his chest when a stray cat scurried around the corner and leaped into a Dumpster. He swiped a hand over his face, told himself to get a grip.

"Just get through this and you can go as straight as the Vegas Strip," he promised himself, smiled nervously at his little joke, then concentrated on several more deep breaths.

Of course, he'd have to disappear for a while. That would make Abbie cry. Not knowing what had happened to him. He felt bad about that. But he'd feel worse dead.

"Come on, come on, come on," he muttered, jerkily pressing the glow light on his cheap watch and checking the time again.

Where the hell was his contact? Fox's contact, a guy named Juan, was supposed to have been here fifteen minutes ago. Right. Like Cory could trust anyone who wouldn't give their full name and agreed only to a night meet in this alley.

He swiped a damp palm over his face, tried to ignore that it was shaking. That's what was making him so skittish. Fox came with a new set of ground rules—and with a new threat: the wrath of Fredrick Nader.

"Nader doesn't know," he reminded himself. Nader didn't know about Derek's double cross. He might suspect something was off when Derek hadn't shown up with the diamonds, but Nader didn't know that Cory had them now. Not yet.

"*Hola*, gringo."

"Jesus!" Startled, Cory shoved away from the cantina wall. He whipped his head around expecting to see a *ladino* known as Juan. But it wasn't a native Honduran who stared back at him.

It was Rutger Smith.

Oh God.

The night shadows played across the grim, unsmiling eyes of Fredrick Nader's hired muscle. Light from the moon accentuated the shiny baldness of Smith's round head and the mean scar that ran like a scythe from the corner of his left eye to the corner of his mouth.

If there was an emotion buried behind the blank, obsidian eyes that stared into his, it was twisted amusement. If there was blood that flowed in the heart beneath that broad, steroid-inflated chest, it was ice cold. Cory had read a book once about this sadistic killer who liked to watch his victims bleed out while he chopped them up in little pieces. Rutger had always made him think about that book. Rutger always made him think about blood. Lots of it.

"Let's go, Hughes." The tip of the stiletto pressed in against Cory's ribs, then pricked his skin through his T-shirt—just enough to make him yelp. Just enough to make Rutger smile.

Cory swallowed thickly, felt his heart drop to his gut, and knew two things with ultimate certainty. One, he should have trusted his gut and gotten the hell out a long time ago. Two, unless he could convince Nader that he was more valuable to him alive than dead, he was fish food.

7

"All set for tonight?"

Sam glanced up at Reed, then went back to scanning the updates on Nader's activities that Reed had brought with him to the ranch. While Nader hadn't been spotted, his man, Rutger Smith, had turned up in San Pedro Sula. It was a guarantee, then, that Nader wasn't far away.

"All set," he said absently.

"So . . . what's she like?" Reed asked after a moment.

Sam knew Reed was referring to Abbie Hughes. Just like he knew that Reed had been biting his tongue the past couple of days to keep himself from asking about her.

"Like a means to an end."

Nothing but a means to an end, he assured himself because that was the only way he could afford to think about her. It had been four days since he'd taken her out for coffee. Three since they'd gone thrill riding. He'd taken her to a movie last night. Was seeing her again tonight.

In short, he'd been rushing like a running back, trying to find an in. He'd recognized that she got off on the quiet, sincere cowboy type and he'd played that angle. He hadn't so much as touched her, a feat that had been harder for him to accomplish than it should have been and that he knew both intrigued and puzzled her.

Yeah, it puzzled him, too, just like it pissed him off that he let himself be distracted. Still, the strategy was working. She'd finally asked him to pick her up at her house tonight.

She was starting to trust him, which was exactly what he needed her to do. He wanted her trusting him. Talking to him. About her life. About her family. About her brother. Because he still had a kernel of doubt that she was involved in Nader's business, Sam would much prefer to finesse the information he needed from Abbie Hughes than force it out.

So far, though, he'd gotten nada. And the clock was ticking. Nader wouldn't take a chance of staying in one place too long. The fact that he was still in or near San Pedro Sula suggested only one thing: He was waiting for something. Sam was banking on that "something" being the Tupacka diamonds. It was the only thing that made sense.

Just like it only made sense that Abbie's new car, serious bling, and elaborate security all pointed to her brother throwing some of his action her way. Cory Hughes could be the weak link in Nader's organization that would finally lead to Nader's downfall.

That's why Sam needed desperately to know what Abbie knew. That's why he was relieved he was finally getting a chance to check out her house. He could get lucky, stumble over something incriminating. If there were stolen goods or drugs in the mix, he could end up using them for leverage to get the info he needed on Cory from Abbie. Nothing spoke to a beautiful woman like the threat of jail time.

If it turned out he found nothing on her, well, one way or the other, he needed to make something happen tonight because Desmond Fox's appearance on the scene wasn't the only new fly in the ointment.

Reed had lobbed the latest news at him yesterday:

"We've lost Hughes."

"Lost him how?"

Reed had shrugged. "Puff of smoke. Flash of light. Gone. Hell. I don't know. He just dropped out of sight."

Which could have meant damn near anything. "Maybe he's smarter than we thought," Sam had suggested. "Maybe he made Mendoza as a tail. Figured he needed to fall off the radar for a while. Then again, he could have pissed someone off, caught himself a bullet."

"Funny you should mention that," Reed had added. "About the same time we lost Hughes, another one of Nader's mules—dude by the name of Derek Styles—also dropped off the grid."

"Something's not right," Sam had agreed.

Which had brought them to tonight. Now with two of Nader's mules missing, it could mean they had run into a buzz saw. All the more reason Sam needed to get something concrete from Abbie or he might miss his shot at Nader again.

"Time's getting short," Reed said now as he prowled Sam's office. "I know it's tough duty, being she's such a *dog* and all," he said, clearly meaning the opposite, "but you might have to take one for the team, get her into bed and fuck the info out of her."

Sam glared at him, came within an inch of shoving a fist in the pretty boy's face. When the haze of anger cleared, he recognized the look in Reed's eyes. He was intentionally trying to goad him.

"Oh, hell." Reed looked like he'd just confirmed his worst suspicions. "I don't believe it. She got to you."

Sam clenched his jaw.

"You like her, don't you?"

Sam glanced up from the report. "What I like is that she has the potential to lead us to Nader."

"But you *like* her," Reed insisted as he dropped into the club chair in Sam's office. He laced his hands over his belly, squinted through narrowed, knowing eyes.

Sam tossed the report on his desk. "What is this? High school? Look. I know what I need from her. And I know what she means to this op. She's a conduit. End of story."

The fact that Reed was right, that Abbie came off as sincere and straightforward and yeah, Sam liked that about her, had no bearing on the op. Or on what lengths he would go to, to get what he needed. If she was in as deep as all indicators said she was, then he'd take her down along with her brother and Nader. No regret. No remorse.

He worked his jaw. Disgusted with himself for wanting to believe the sincerity in her eyes and the innocent act she had perfected. Tonight, he planned to capitalize on the obvious. She was attracted to him. He'd seen it the first night he'd sat down at her blackjack table and nothing had changed his mind since. If that's what it took, then he'd exploit the instant chemistry and use it to his advantage.

Tonight was do or die. If he didn't get the information he wanted by playing nice, then the game was going to get dirty.

"What time are the boys coming in?"

Reed checked his watch. "Their flight lands in two hours."

Luke "Doc Holliday" Colter, former Navy SEAL and the BOI team medic, and Wyatt "Papa Bear" Savage, general operator and former CIA, were flying in from Buenos Aires to help with the sting—if it came to that— then join Sam on the trip to Honduras to flush out Nader.

"You sure you're going to be okay with this?" Reed asked.

No, Sam wasn't entirely okay with it, but he was left with little choice. "Yeah," he said. "I'm okay with it. We'll use the boys as a last resort. You wait for my nod."

"Just work it. You'll have her eating out of your hand," Reed said.

"Yeah. I'm a regular Joe Cool," Sam grumbled, telling himself it wasn't guilt hammering at him over using Abbie. He glanced at Reed. "So, you finished pimping me?"

Reed gave him a long assessing look. "Yeah, I think I've pretty well covered it."

"Then get lost."

"Getting lost," Reed said with a sharp salute and headed for the door. "This is good, Sam," he said, suddenly serious. "What you're doing. Whatever you have to do. It's right. And it's righteous.

"It's right," Reed repeated when Sam said nothing. Then he left, closing Sam's office door behind him.

Sam leaned back in his chair, stared into space, tried to buy into Reed's words.

Tried to make what he'd said true.

But this had nothing to do with right or righteousness. God knows he'd tried to convince himself that it did. Had tried to believe that what he was doing had to be done.

Done for his father, who wanted retribution. For his mother, whose heart would never fully heal. For little Tina, who still cried at night for her mommy and daddy yet soldiered on with her brave little eyes and her mother's spirit.

Yeah. Sam had tried to convince himself this was for Terri and B.J.

He stood. Walked to the window. The truth was in the reflection that stared back at him in the glass. In the hollow eyes. In the brooding rage.

This was about him.

About wanting to sleep one night—*one fucking night*—without seeing Terri's car explode in flames.

About waking up in the dark, drenched with sweat, his jaws clenched against a scream and the suffocating weight of guilt pressing on his chest like a tank.

It was about finding a way to live with himself knowing that his sister would be alive, that Tina would have a mother and a father, that his parents would still have their daughter, if Sam hadn't let the violence of his life bleed into theirs.

If he hadn't fucked up.

If he hadn't blown chance after chance to take Nader out of commission.

If he'd done his goddamn job.

So, no. This wasn't about them. This was about him. The one thought that mobilized him was knowing he had a chance to make Nader pay.

Which brought him to Abbie Hughes.

He checked his watch and headed for the shower.

Did he have any doubt about Abbie Hughes's involvement? Yeah. He did.

Did it matter? No, he told himself, lifting his face to the hot, pounding spray. It didn't matter.

All that mattered was getting to Nader. And guilty or not, Abbie Hughes was going to get hurt in the process.

"You look great."

Abbie smiled up into Sam Lang's serious brown eyes as he stood at her front door, long and strong and smelling clean and amazing—some subtle, sexy blend of sandalwood and sage.

As usual, his shirt was white and backlit against the dark of night outside; it made his shoulders look even broader. The silver chain holding his army dog tags winked out of the open collar of the shirt he'd tucked into the narrow waist of crisply creased jeans that he wore with a natural ease. If Calvin K and his cronies got a look at him, they'd be salivating over the idea of Sam posing for a *GQ* cover.

Just looking at him had Abbie experiencing that jolt of anticipation, excitement, and arousal that had knocked her off kilter the first time she'd seen him and that she'd hoped would lessen with exposure.

But here it was. Their fourth date, and if anything, her reaction to him had escalated.

"Thanks," she said, finally having the presence of mind to speak. She'd worn a dress tonight. It was black with a low, scooped neck. It was also sleeveless and short. It made her waist look small, her boobs look big, and her legs look a million miles long.

It was what Crystal called a "fuck me" dress and it was a first for Abbie. She felt both empowered and manipulative and she hadn't yet reconciled her motive for wearing it with her inherent instincts to proceed with care.

Until she saw the look in Sam's eyes.

Then manipulative and empowered felt just fine. So did a little reck-lessness.

"You're looking pretty good yourself," she added, stepping back so he could walk into the house.

As excited as she was to see him, she was still a little nervous. This was the first time she'd invited him to her home. She was a cautious woman. A careful woman, a care that had been nurtured by an alcoholic mother and an addict father. She'd learned to lock her bedroom door early on; she'd been locking doors both metaphorically and literally ever since.

So, taking that step and not only letting Sam know where she lived but inviting him over—well, it was huge for her. Huge as in *since her divorce, she'd never invited a man into her home* huge.

Huge, as in *she'd spent enough money at Victoria's Secret this afternoon to make Crystal lie down on the dressing room floor and weep for joy* huge.

"K-Y and condoms," Crystal had said when Abbie had frowned at the unopened sack Crystal held out to her before they parted ways. "You've been out of circulation for so long you're going to need a little help."

"Oh, for God's sake. Just because I'm buying new underwear doesn't mean I'm going to sleep with him."

Crystal had just blinked.

"Okay. So I want to sleep with him," Abbie had admitted, snatching the sack from Crystal's outstretched hand.

"Go forth and multiple orgasm," Crystal ordered.

"Orgasm is not a verb," Abbie had pointed out with a laugh.

"Oh, sweetie, it is if it's done right."

Abbie had the very distinct impression that Sam Lang knew how to do it right. That didn't mean she wasn't anxious about where this night might be heading. It had been a long time for her. Sex had never been casual for Abbie. It wasn't casual now.

She liked this guy. Really liked him. That made it that much more important.

Okay. So she'd only known him for a few days, but if something physical didn't happen between them soon, she was going to burst a vein or something—if worry over Cory didn't do it first.

She didn't want to think about Cory now. Told herself her brother was fine and that when he finally showed his face, she was going to give him a piece of her mind—right after she hugged him until his ribs broke.

"Nice," Sam said, after a taking in her living room. He looked huge and handsome in the pale light from the lamps on her end tables and pleased with what he saw. "Mellow."

Sam, she'd learned, was a man of few words. She found it part of his charm. When he had something to say, she knew he put a lot of thought behind it and his concise comments were generally right on target.

"Thanks again," she said, inordinately satisfied with his reaction. The furniture, like her final lump-sum divorcee settlement, had been a long time coming. She could finally afford to redecorate and buy a few things.

"Get comfortable," she said as she unconsciously touched her fingers to the diamond that warmed between her breasts. "I opened a bottle of wine. Be right back."

She had to make herself walk to the kitchen with slow, deliberate steps. Once there, she cursed under her breath because her hands were shaking when she reached into the cupboard for a pair of glasses.

Get a grip.

She wasn't a kid. She'd been around the block—at least she felt like it after Don. He'd soured her. Soured her good. So yeah, it was damn scary that she was on the verge of opening herself up to whatever she was opening herself up to with Sam. It was even scarier that she wished he would open up to her, too. She kept thinking about his sister. Wondering how he was dealing with it.

Wanting—*God help her*—to help him deal with it. It was one of her biggest character flaws—her "need to save" gene. Of all the men she'd ever met, Sam Lang, solid and strong and self-assured, needed saving the way a lion needed rescue from a mouse.

Obviously, she was in a little bit of trouble with this man . . . and she was wearing the underwear to prove it.

Abbie filled two glasses with her favorite Cabernet, then drew in a bracing breath and headed back to the living room. Sam stood in front of her bookcase, his back to her, staring at a picture of Cory.

Lord, sweet Lord, she would never tire of seeing this man in a pair of jeans.

"My brother, Cory," Abbie said, handing him his wine.

He nodded, turned to her. "Good."

Her heart did a little backflip. She knew exactly what he meant, but she wanted to hear him explain it. "Good?"

One corner of his amazing mouth tipped up. "Didn't see a resemblance. So, yeah. It's good to know that he's your brother."

She sipped her wine, taking her cue from the look in his eyes. It was a look that invited, flirted, made suggestions—at least that's what she wanted to see, so she went with it. "As opposed to?"

He lifted his glass, watched her over the rim, his dark eyes serious suddenly and dangerously attractive in the diluted light. "As opposed to competition," he said before taking a slow, savoring sip.

The kind of slow, savoring sip she wanted him to take of her.

"No." Her voice was barely a whisper. "No competition."

That prompted another slow smile. Another gruffly murmured, "Good."

A man of few words, she thought again. Effective. Very effective because she was feeling very flushed all of a sudden.

"You don't talk about him much. Are you two close?"

He was talking about Cory, she realized, shaking off the haze of sexual awareness that made both her vision and her better judgment fuzzy.

Slow it down.

"Yeah." She averted her gaze to Cory's picture because if she looked at Sam one more second, she was going to jump him. "We are close. He's my kid brother, you know? I look out for him."

"Looks like a big boy to me."

She sipped her wine, saw Cory at four, eyes red from crying, tears staining his face as she pulled him, trembling and bruised, out of the closet. The unexpected memory overwhelmed her. "Our mom . . . well, she wasn't much of a mom. Liked her Jack Daniel's, you know?" She shrugged, touched her index finger to Cory's image. "Our father, on the other hand, liked his blow. And he was mean with it. Especially after Mom passed out for the day. That's when he went after us. Mostly, he'd go after Cory."

Abbie's thoughts drifted back there . . . back when she hadn't always been able to be there for Cory. When she was in school—that's when their dad would get him. Rail on him for being stupid, when it was Cory's undiagnosed dyslexia that gave him problems in class.

She became aware of Sam's silence. "Oh, man." She shook her head, embarrassed. "Sorry. Really. I'm sorry. Not sure what sent me back there. Talk about a mood killer."

She shot him an apologetic smile. Would have looked away if she hadn't seen the expression in his eyes. She saw more than sympathy and not an ounce of rebuke.

"Sounds rough," he said.

She squared her shoulders, shook it off. "Yeah, well, it was a long time ago."

"But not so long that you don't still worry about your brother."

She nodded, needed to look away because it would be so very easy to want to lean into this man and leach all the strength out of him.

"Like you said. He's a big boy."

"You see him often?" he asked after a moment.

"Yeah." She nodded. "He lives in Vegas so, yeah. We're in touch." Usually every day but she hadn't heard from Cory in so long.

Tears threatened. Damn and damn again. This was *not* where she wanted this night to go.

"He deal for one of the casinos, too?"

Okay, she told herself. He was trying to be nice. Attempting to show interest in her brother because he realized Cory was important to her.

"No," she said. "Cory's . . . well, Cory's sort of an entrepreneur."

He smiled as if he understood, then confirmed that he did. "So he's unemployed."

She glanced at him. Hard. "Would you like some more wine?" she asked, feeling a sudden and inexplicable discomfort with the conversation. So much so that while Sam's questions about Cory had given her an opening to ask about his family—specifically about his sister—she decided to let it pass.

She reached for his glass. Realized he was standing very close. So close, he was in her space. Space she hadn't let a man enter for a very long time.

It startled her. Startled him, too, apparently, because when their fingers brushed, he took a step back, actually looked apologetic.

For whatever reason, that small show of apology made her bold. Just like the electric brush of their fingers had made her hyperaware of the sexual energy crackling between them.

Just like the look in his eyes made her brave and bold and reckless.

"Are you ever going to kiss me, Sam?"

8

Breathless. Her own boldness made her breathless. So did Sam's nearness. His scent. His heat.

She managed to swallow, managed to stand her ground, to seek and discard a dozen arguments for why she shouldn't push this, let alone encourage what was about to happen. At least, she hoped it was about to happen.

They weren't talking about just a kiss. A kiss—their first kiss—would shoot them from zero to all the way gone. She knew it and so did he.

So, yeah, there were a dozen reasons why she should back away.

It was too fast. Too soon. Too hot. Too much. Too scary.

And there was only one compelling reason that made it right.

Him.

"I thought you'd never ask," he said finally.

Then God, oh, God, it was going to happen.

Hopefully sometime within her next heartbeat. Please, God, within her next breath.

But he kept her waiting. Kept her wanting. Kept her wondering what kissing him would be like.

He was very meticulous, Sam Lang. Her fingers were trembling when he lifted her glass from her hand, set it, along with his, on the bookshelf.

Very intense when he moved back into her, searched her eyes as if he were seeking the secrets to immortality there.

And he was very deliberate when he touched the back of his curled fingers to her cheek, making her tremble, making her breath catch, making her wish he'd put her out of her misery and just do it.

But he didn't.

Dark, searching eyes caressed her face as he lowered his head to hers. Warm, wine-scented breath fanned her cheek as he feathered the gentlest of touches there, then slowly trailed kisses across her jaw in a teasing, torturous seduction.

"Sam." She gripped his arms because he stole not only her breath but her balance. "You're driving me crazy."

"A lot of that going around," he murmured, before finally, *finally*, covering her mouth with his.

Some things were worth waiting for.

Some things were worth praying for.

Sam Lang's kiss, she decided, was worth dying for.

His lips were amazingly soft, his arms devastatingly strong, his heat wholly consuming. This man of few words spoke volumes without uttering a sound, telling her in a hundred different ways how much he wanted her.

The way his mouth opened over hers, the way his heart pounded against hers and his big body tightened and warmed beneath her hands told her things he never could have said with words.

Her hands found his hair, wanting close, needing closer, desperate for skin against skin.

The promise to make it all happen was there, in his touch, in his taste, in the shudder of his big body and the hard length of him against her belly . . . so it stunned her when he lifted his head.

She made an involuntary sound of protest. Involuntary because she was lost in him, suddenly obsessed and needing his kiss like breath.

"Shh." He pressed her face against his shoulder. "Just . . . shh," he soothed again, his arms tight and fast and strong around her.

She could feel his heart slamming as he held her that way, gulping air, working for an even breath.

"Sam?" A desperate whisper.

"Yeah." He squeezed her tight then loosened his hold. "I know." Another fractured breath. "Maybe . . . hell. I didn't mean for that to get so intense. Maybe we should . . . go to . . . dinner."

Abbie lifted her head, beyond confused. "Do you *want* to go to dinner?"

He pushed out a frustrated laugh, let his head fall back. "You're kidding, right?"

Relief rushed through her. She pushed up to her tiptoes. Kissed his throat, savoring the warm, salty taste of him.

"Abbie—"

"Sam." She cut off what she recognized as a precursor to a warning and smiled into his eyes. "Shut up and kiss me."

She'd wanted a smile from him, too. Didn't get one.

His eyes were far too serious as they searched hers. "This was not my plan when I came here tonight."

"Make a plan. God laughs," she murmured and moved into him again.

Again, he pulled back. "Seriously, Abbie. Maybe . . . maybe we should slow things down."

The erection pressing against her belly told her he was so not on board with that idea. "I don't want to slow down." She kissed him again, open-mouthed, hot and hungry.

He groaned. Gripped her arms. "Make sure this is what you want. Make damn sure because one more kiss like that and I won't be able to stop."

"God," she said, matching his sober scowl, "I hope not."

As Sam laid her down it fleetingly crossed Abbie's mind that she'd never done anything but sleep in this bed. As he slowly undressed her it occurred to her that it had been two years since a man had seen her naked.

Two years since she'd worn underwear with anything but utilitarian use in mind or bought something black lace and satin with the singular intent of watching a man's eyes darken with desire when he saw her wearing it. When he took it off of her.

Two long, lonely years since she'd felt confident enough to want a man in her bed. In her body. Filling her head the way Sam filled her head right now.

The look in his eyes, oh Lord, the look in his eyes as he peeled black lace away from her breasts, made her tingle and burn and arch to meet him when he lowered his head and drew her nipple into his mouth.

His mouth.

His mouth was amazing. Hot. Wet. Wild for her.

And hungry. She felt such hunger in him, a hunger that stoked her own as he kissed her and kissed her, then left her lying there wearing nothing but her black panties and a flush of desire.

She indulged herself in the look of him when he rose to his knees above her and started unbuttoning the cuffs on his shirt. He was so . . . beautiful. There wasn't any other word for it. Not just the package he came wrapped in—the breadth of his chest, the tightly knotted abs and narrow hips, the smooth tanned skin—but the intensity in his eyes, the need in his tightly coiled muscles that told her how hard he was reaching for control.

He jerked open his shirt and she shivered. He was still shoving the sleeves down his arms, his dog tags lying flat and warm against bare skin, when she reached for his belt buckle, lowered his zipper. He froze with one broad shoulder cocked. His ab muscles sucked in tight when the backs of her fingers brushed the light dusting of hair there. There where he was hot and lean and the tip of his penis felt satiny soft and damp against the back of her fingers.

The look in his eyes as they met hers made her daring, made her yearn. The catch in his breath when she slowly lowered his zipper the rest of the way down made her restless and reckless. The low groan of pleasure when she burrowed her fingers under the waistband of his shorts and finally found the long, thick length of him intensified the ache low in her belly.

With reluctance, she released him, impatiently shoved his jeans, shorts and all, down his hips. Then she lay back and watched as he got rid of everything that got in the way of hot skin against hot skin.

Everything but her panties. Her black, lace, barely there panties.

Before tossing his jeans, he reached into a pocket, withdrew a condom, and laid it precisely over her navel. She didn't let herself wonder about the implications of him coming prepared, was only grateful that he had. Thankful that he was prepared and perfect and naked.

Completely, gloriously naked—and yet, she felt exposed suddenly.

Until he smiled.

And when he smiled and pressed a knee into the bed and the warmth of his thigh connected with her hip, she lost that last vestige of inhibition. The physical connection overrode any last-second surge of insecurity. She reached for his hand, laced their fingers together and, watching his face, drew their linked hands down to the small patch of lace covering her mons.

Electric anticipation shot through her when he rubbed their joined hands against her then urged her to part her legs before disentangling their fingers and cupping her there. Caressing. Enticing. Driving her to a level of arousal that would have been frightening if she hadn't trusted him so completely.

The fact that she *did* trust him amazed her. Opened doors leading to hope and optimism and expectations—all elements she'd given up on after Don. Essential elements that bridged the gap between doubt and her decision to take this leap of faith with Sam.

She was wet and achy and all but begging for a deeper touch when he skimmed a finger under the scrap of black lace and brushed her damp curls.

"Sam." She sighed his name, telling him with the undulation of her hips that his touch was wonderful . . . and not nearly enough.

He enclosed her completely then, the heel of his hand poised on her pubic bone as he finessed her lips apart, found the slick, swollen flesh of her clitoris, and stroked her.

She sucked in a breath, bucked, and scrambled to remove her panties so she could open wider for him, indulge more freely, experience more fully the exquisite rush of sensations she'd denied herself for so very, very long.

"Open it." He handed her the condom. "Cover me."

Her fingers shook, were clumsy with excitement as she struggled with the foil packet. With a sound of exasperation, she finally ripped it open with her teeth. She was half laughing, half whimpering as she reached for him, rolled on the latex, and made room for him between her thighs.

Where the sensations began again.

Stronger. Sharper. Deeper. And devastating.

So devastating, she cried out when he drove deep and seated himself there, the muscles of his buttocks bunching beneath her palms, his biceps knotting as he held himself above her.

"Don't. Move," he groaned between clenched teeth when she rocked her hips to meet his. "Just . . . don't move," he repeated, lowering his head to her throat, where he nuzzled and kissed her neck before moving to her mouth. "You feel incredible," he whispered.

"Yeah," she smiled against his mouth. "I do."

He played with her mouth . . . nipping, sipping, sucking on her lower lip before easing his tongue inside.

She opened for him, met each questing thrust, loving the taste of him, the lack of haste as he slowly began to rock his hips to the rhythm of his tongue.

In. Out. In. Out.

"So good." He felt so good. His weight. His heat. His strength, which surrounded her but never overpowered her, never made her feel dominated or defenseless. Instead, she felt unbelievably powerful as he taught her things about sensation she'd either forgotten or had never known.

She let him take her completely. Had never thought she could trust this way again, trust to follow his lead, trust his reactions to her touch, trust the rightness of it all. She marveled in the freedom, then stopped thinking altogether when he increased the speed of his thrusts, and the intensity of his rhythm, and let the night dissolve into nothing but tactile, torrid pleasure.

Time, place, even reality blurred, then suspended while he drove her closer to climax.

Relentlessly.

Ruthlessly.

Until she couldn't delay the inevitable. She let go. Let herself free-fall into an orgasm so sharp and fierce she cried out from the sheer intensity and wonder of it. She gasped for breath, cried out in joy and shock and even a little delicious fear as he took her on the ride of her life. Held him tight when he joined her, burying himself deep one last time as his big body stiffened with his own release.

Her nails bit into his back as their slick bodies tensed and pulsed. Heat sought heat as the release rocked through them like a seventh wave, huge and forceful and dangerously consuming.

She clung to him, held on for life while she fought for breath and clarity, all the while wishing the rush would never end.

When he could breathe, when he could gather some semblance of muscle memory to make his arms move . . . when he could think beyond the lush and giving heat of her body and the rush of sensation, Sam forced himself to roll off of her.

He lay on his back in the deepening darkness. Listened to her breathe. Catching his own breath in the ringing aftermath of something that never should have happened. Something that should have been just sex but felt like a helluva lot more.

His conscience slammed recriminations to the beat of his heart, berating him for what he'd just done.

Jesus. He hadn't meant to go this far.

Had he?

No.

Yes.

Hell, he didn't know.

But it was done. The proof of it lay wasted and spent on the sheets beside him. She was decimated. Physically. Sexually. And, if he didn't miss his guess, emotionally.

He turned his head on the pillow. To find her eyes closed. Her breathing slow, deep, even.

Asleep. She'd fallen asleep. If it wasn't so telling, it'd be funny. It was a man's job to fall asleep after sex. Unless the woman was exhausted. School, job, worrying about her brother. Yeah. She was exhausted.

Fighting the wave of tenderness washing through him, he dragged a hand over his jaw and eased slowly to a sitting position. He glanced over his shoulder when she didn't stir. A delicate little snore purred from between her parted lips.

Another rush of feelings sucker-punched him.

Like the need to get her naked and horizontal had sucker-punched him. Like the need to be inside her had robbed him of reason—but not restraint. No, he'd kept a handle on at least that much control. This woman . . . this woman made him want things in a way that threatened that control. Because he didn't know what he was capable of taking if he let himself go, he'd held back. Kept the leash on needs that still pulsed deep in his groin.

That was the worst part, the very worst part, he realized as he slowly stood; he wanted to start all over again. Wanted to kiss her awake, caress her to awareness, finesse her back to arousal, and take them both to the limit and beyond.

"Take one for the team and fuck the information out of her."

Reed's words rang loud and strong in his head, and not one bit amusing. What had happened in her bed hadn't been about gathering information. It had been spontaneous and demanding and real.

It had also been one of the stupidest things he'd ever done in his life. He'd just wanted information. In absence of something concrete, he'd wanted to get a look at her alarm system, figure out a way to breach it without bringing the entire Vegas PD down on them if he and Reed decided they needed to make an "unannounced" return visit. But one thing had led to another, then another, and . . .

Disgusted with himself, he found his jeans on the floor and carried them with him toward the door. Pausing with his hand on the doorknob, he cast one more look over his shoulder to make sure she was sleeping . . . and got sidetracked in the lush look of her lying there. Her long dark hair spread like silk over the white pillow. The peak of a perfect pink breast was cast in silhouette in the darkened room. The length of a long, supple leg splayed wantonly on the sheets. The gold chain that held her diamond lay warm and close against her skin.

He clenched his jaw. Turned away.

What he wanted from Abbie Hughes wasn't supposed to have anything to do with anything but the bottom line.

And the bottom line was getting Nader.

With grim determination, he closed the bedroom door softly behind him. Then he dragged on his pants and started his search, feeling like the lowest piece of scum on the earth for breaking her trust this way.

Until he walked into her garage.

It was clean, neat, uncluttered. Like Abbie.

A black tarp ran the length of the far wall. He drew it aside and found various-sized boxes stacked three deep and six high. It didn't appear that any of them had been opened. He couldn't make out the return address so he flipped on an overhead light. Checked the postmarks.

Honduras. Every last one of them was postmarked Honduras.

Sam swallowed back both regret and guilt. Neck deep. She was in this neck deep.

His cell phone vibrated in his pocket. He checked the readout. It was Reed.

"What?"

"Can you talk?"

Sam glanced toward the kitchen door, where he'd entered the garage. "Make it fast."

"You know that other missing mule—Derek Styles? Well, he turned up yesterday. Dead. Someone dropped the body at a church."

"Fuck."

"Double it. Something's going down. We need to speed this up or we're going to lose Cory Hughes, too, if we haven't already. And that means Nader will be out of reach again."

Sam didn't need Reed to tell him. He knew all too well that time was slipping away. He didn't need a conscience either, but his worked on him anyway when he made his decision. He'd like more time with Abbie. More time to talk, maybe even determine that she was innocent in all this.

But they were out of time and he was fooling himself about her innocence. New car, bling, and Honduras postmarks did not equate to innocent.

"The boys make it in?" he asked Reed.

"Yep. They're locked and loaded. Just waiting for the word from you."

He had the goods; now he just needed to turn the screws and get her to talk. His gut knotted when he thought about how Abbie's face would look when she realized he'd used her.

"Sam?"

"Yeah," he said when Reed prompted him. "Do it."

He stood in the silence for a moment after he disconnected. Then he walked back into the kitchen, found the security panel, and disabled the house alarms. Abbie was still sleeping when he walked back into the bedroom, blissfully unaware that her world was about to come crashing down around her.

He quietly gathered the rest of his clothes from the floor. Cast one long, lingering look at the woman he was about to betray. And felt a surge of longing and regret so strong it made his chest ache.

He could fall for her. Jesus. Was too damn close to falling for her.

Because you're thinking with your dick, he reminded himself angrily and walked out of her bedroom.

He had no business feeling guilt or remorse. He needed to quit thinking about what this would do to her. About the sounds she'd made when she came. The scent of her. The taste of her.

Instead, he needed to focus on what Nader had done to his family. He needed to remember that Abbie Hughes and her brother were, at the least, guilty by association, at the most, accessories to murder.

"Come on, come on," he muttered, hooking a finger in her living room drapes and searching the street for the boys. He wanted this over with. A black SUV pulled up in front of the house a few minutes later.

On a relieved breath, Sam headed for the door. Nodded a grim hello to Colter and Savage as they piled out of the passenger seats wearing FBI jackets and caps, shoulder holsters, and, he was certain, fake badges in their wallets to match the rest of their phony gear.

It had been three months since Sam had seen Luke "Doc Holliday" Colter, the BOI team's medic, and Wyatt "Papa Bear" Savage. While Holliday was former SEAL and Savage former CIA, both went back to Sam's Task Force Mercy days. Both had forgotten more about weaponry, covert warfare, and guile than most men had ever known.

Sam hadn't seen or talked to either man since Terri's funeral. Hadn't let himself dwell on the fact that he'd missed them until he saw the looks on their faces and understood that the feeling was mutual.

There was no time for sentiment right now as Reed, also wearing FBI gear, slipped out from behind the wheel and joined them outside the garage.

"In here." Sam let them in through the side garage door.

"Holy fuck." Reed whistled long and low when he got a look at the boxes. "Just like Christmas. All we need is some ribbon and tinsel."

"I have a feeling you're going to find all the trimmings you need when you open them up," Sam said.

"And if we don't?" Colter asked.

Sam glanced at Reed, who nodded, indicating he'd come prepared. "Then you know what to do."

Sam let himself into the kitchen and waited there for Abbie to wake up. The last thing they needed was for her to hear them in the garage, think someone had broken into her house, and call the cops.

Then he steeled himself for the look in her eyes when she realized he'd betrayed her.

9

The sheets beside her were cold when Abbie woke up. She stretched, stretched again, feeling sated and relaxed and new.

Crystal was right. And Abbie's memory of sex being highly overrated was dead wrong.

Or maybe it had just been her memory of sex with Don.

Sam had been . . . Her entire body reacted to thoughts of him with a huge, clenching shiver. Sam had been amazing. And thorough. The man had been very, very thorough.

On a lazy sigh, she rolled to her side, stirred the scent of man and sex and satisfaction, and found the dog tags he'd lifted over his head at some point so they wouldn't hit her in the face. *Sexy* and *considerate*, she thought, gathering the tags and the chain in her hand. She drifted on the sensual reminders for a moment, then checked her alarm clock. It was a little past midnight.

"Cripes," she muttered, sat up, and dragged her hair out of her eyes. She'd slept for almost an hour.

She could just hear Crystal. *"You had a man like Sam Lang in your bed—a man who blew the top of your head off with one of the finest orgasms you have ever had—and you fell asleep? Are you crazy???"*

For once, Abbie would have to agree.

She had to be crazy to fall asleep with Sam around.

So yeah, she was a little sleep deprived. Came with the territory. Between work, school, and studying it made for long hours. But to fall asleep. On Sam.

It was embarrassing. And now, he was apparently gone.

"Way to go, twinkle toes," she muttered and, naked, rose from the bed. "A sex siren you are not."

On a whim, she looped the dog tags around her neck, felt a little naughty, a little possessive even, wearing them. Crazy of course, but there it was. She reached for her short silk kimono, wondering if he liked blue. Wondering if she'd snored. Was mortified all over again.

"No wonder he left."

Then she heard a sound. Realized she smelled coffee.

Sweet, she thought, and tying the belt at her waist, she opened her bedroom door. He was still here, helping himself to coffee in her kitchen. She didn't know what to think about that but decided that maybe she liked that he felt comfortable enough to make himself at home. It implied something— something more than sex.

Finger combing her hair and purposefully giving it a little sleep- and sex-tousled look, she made sure the robe fell open to reveal both her diamond and his dog tags nestled between her breasts. Then she walked barefoot into the kitchen.

Sam was sitting at her table.

"Hi." She smiled when she saw him. Melted a little when she glanced at his hands, remembering how he'd touched her. Loving how he'd touched her.

He glanced up at her, swept her body with a look, his gaze lingering between her breasts.

Instead of a slow, appreciative appraisal of her long bare limbs and sexy smile, he averted his gaze to the cup of coffee sitting in front of him. "You might want to get dressed."

His voice was gruff. His look was all business.

She blinked, more than surprised by a scowl that absolutely did not say, "Come here, darlin', and give me some sugar."

"Wow," she said, confused by the tension she felt in him. "So, guess that answers my question about whether it upset you that I fell asleep."

As attempts for light and breezy went, it fell flat. Her first niggle of concern crept in.

Before she could puzzle out his reaction and the reason for it and her sudden unease, she heard voices coming from her garage.

Her heart jumped. Her gaze flashed to his.

"Someone's in the garage," she whispered urgently.

"I know. Go get dressed," he repeated.

Confusion mushroomed to panic in a single heartbeat. Wrong. Something was very, very wrong. "Sam? What's going on?"

She was already backing out of the room when he stood. Flashed a badge. "FBI," he said. "Just relax. No one's here to hurt you."

If he'd have said, "Jack the Ripper," or "Hillside Slasher" he couldn't have stunned or panicked her more.

"FBI?" She bunched her kimono tighter and higher over her breasts, suddenly feeling exposed and violated. "*FBI?*" she repeated, accusation and more than a little fear making her voice shrill. "I don't understand. What . . . what's going on?"

"Unless you want my men to see you like this," he said, his face void of all emotion, "go get dressed. I'll answer your questions then."

"You will answer my questions now!" Anger and humiliation hit her like a sledgehammer, outdistancing the fear and confusion. "Why is the FBI interested in me?"

The door from her garage opened. A man poked his head inside the kitchen. *Oh my God.* It was the gay cop cowboy.

Even in the FBI jacket and cap he looked like a poster boy. Only the smile was absent—and telling. He wasn't playing now. He was all business. For whatever reason, she appeared to be the endgame. Abbie could see a black nylon shoulder holster when the jacket fell open.

He cut a glance her way, did a double take that had her clutching her kimono even tighter, before he turned back to Sam, hitched his head toward the garage. "You need to see this."

After another fleeting look at her, he disappeared into the garage again.

And just that fast, she knew. "Cory," she said, meeting Sam's eyes as a horrible dread sank through her. "Oh, God. Is this about Cory? Did something happen to him?"

Tears filled her eyes as worry for her brother overshadowed the confusion and disappointment of Sam's betrayal.

"Yeah," Sam said at last. "This is about Cory. Did something happen to him? I don't know. I was hoping you could tell me."

"Tell you? Tell you what?" She was beyond trying to cope with or control her emotions now. She was confused and scared and needed Sam to say something that she could make sense of. "I haven't seen or heard from Cory in days. And I don't understand any of this. FBI? *You're* FBI?"

He glared at her, his eyes hard and angry and impatient. "Dammit, Abbie. For the last time. Go get dressed. We are not going to have this conversation until you do."

She just sort of deflated then. Helplessly shook her head. "Is that what we had before? In my bed? Was that . . . *conversation*, Sam? Or was that an interrogation?"

His jaw clenched and she actually saw a trace of guilt.

"Why didn't you ask?" Her voice was so soft, the silence in the kitchen rang loud around them. "If you had questions about Cory, why didn't you just ask me?"

She swiped a finger over her cheek. Angrily wiped away the tear that had escaped when she finally accepted the truth. "You didn't have to *fuck* me, Sam," she said, her crudeness intentional and full of accusation. "Nail screws would have been just as effective."

And less painful.

She searched his face. Saw nothing.

"I'll wait for you here," he said after a long moment. "Stay away from the phone. And don't even think about trying to leave."

She turned then. Walked to her bedroom, shaking with rage and defeat and a hollow emptiness that took her back to her childhood. Her mother's indifference, her father's hard hand, and later, Don's infidelity—all paled in comparison to the pain Sam Lang had administered with lazy kisses, a gentle caress, and an implied promise that he'd never intended to keep.

• • •

"She buy it?" Reed looked up from one of the boxes they'd ripped open when Sam stepped into the garage. Packing material, clay pots and bowls, and primitive statues were strewn all over the garage floor.

Yet all Sam saw was the stunned look on Abbie's face—confused, accusing, hurting.

"Yeah," he said, pulling away from the way she'd looked, the way he'd felt about using her. "She bought it."

Reed was referring to their FBI scam. Just in case, though, Sam had unplugged her landline and fished her cell phone out of her purse so she couldn't make any calls. The last thing they needed was for half the Vegas PD to swarm the house.

That didn't mean they could afford to drag their feet. The X factor—a nosy neighbor, a passing cruiser— could throw a giant wrench in the works.

"What have you got?"

"Nothing." Wyatt Savage—a big man with a soft southern drawl he'd never quite kicked—glanced up from a stack of open boxes. "Nothing but clay statues, pottery pieces, shit like that. No drugs. No hot rocks. It's all penny-ante stuff."

Sam turned to Holliday. "Progress?"

Colter glanced up from the phone box mounted on a sidewall of the garage. "Almost set." He went back to work installing a tap on her line.

"If Hughes is shipping back illegal goods, I don't think we're going to find them here," Reed said, pulling a velvet pouch out of his pocket. "Not without a little help, at least."

Sam worked his jaw, not liking where this was going but knowing it had to be done. "Plant it," he said. "Wait for my cue." Then he walked back into the kitchen.

He poured himself another cup of coffee and waited for Abbie. He didn't have to wait long. She was dressed in jeans and a pale yellow long-sleeve T-shirt when she walked back into the kitchen. She was covered from head to toe—not even her feet were exposed, as, he ssuspected, *she* felt exposed.

Her eyes were dry, her posture straight and defensive. The look in her eyes when they met his relayed every emotion Sam would feel if he were in her shoes.

Anger. Betrayal. Confusion. Pain.

And hatred.

Above all, there was hatred.

He rose, poured her some coffee.

"Sit down, Abbie."

"I want to see that ID again." She crossed her arms and stood her ground on the far side of the kitchen table. Ignored the mug he held out to her.

Sam set the coffee on the table and reached into his pocket for his bogus FBI ID and the equally false search warrant Reed had taken care of this afternoon. He held out the badge for her inspection.

She wasn't stupid; she'd figure out the flaws in their con eventually. They had to work fast and keep the pressure on. She may not even be guilty or, for that matter, culpable in her brother's shady dealings, but Sam knew that if she were either, without the FBI ruse, they would get exactly nowhere. He didn't have time to sit and wait for her to talk. He'd wasted enough time already trying to finesse the information out of her. And look where that had gotten him.

"Okay?" he asked as she reluctantly sat down at the table.

"Nothing about this is okay." She shoved the badge across the surface toward him, and his dog tags along with it.

He picked them up. They were still warm from the heat of her body. He looked from them to her face, blocking the picture of her standing in the doorway, those tags nestled between her breasts.

"We need to know where your brother is." He cut to the chase, wanting to get this over with so he wouldn't have to look at the pain in her eyes.

"I don't know where he is." Her dark hair fell over her face as she stared at the hands she'd linked together on the tabletop. Hands that had driven him to the edge in the dark in her bed.

"When was the last time you heard from him?"

She lifted her head. "What do you want with Cory?" she asked instead of answering him.

"I think you already know."

Her irises darkened from brown to almost black. "This is what I know," she said, her voice brittle. "You're a lying bastard."

Sam closed his eyes. Breathed deep. And smelled her. And sex. "Look. I never meant for that to happen."

She made a sound that was both weary and wise. "Yeah, that's why you came prepared with a condom."

Guilty as charged. "I'm sorry."

"Oh . . . well, I didn't realize you were *sorry*. That makes everything all right, then, doesn't it?"

"Abbie. I understand. You're pissed—"

"You don't understand anything." Her eyes brimmed with tears. She blinked them back by sheer force of will. "I am far from pissed. I am mortified. I feel violated. And you and your 'apology' can rot in hell."

He wished she'd just slug him. Knock him flat on his ass. Maybe they'd both feel better. At least maybe he'd feel better. Because there was no fixing it, he made himself go on.

"Who does your brother work for?"

She looked away. "I didn't know he worked for anyone."

"What's he doing in Honduras?"

"I don't know."

"Fredrick Nader," he pressed on. "Name mean anything to you?"

She frowned. "Should it?"

"Nader is a known terrorist. He also dabbles in drugs, illegal weapons, and stolen gems."

"And I should care about this, why?"

"You should care about this because he's your brother's employer."

That finally got a reaction other than disdain. Her eyes lasered in on his. "Let's add 'delusional' to 'bastard.' Cory is a lot of things but he's not a thief. And for God's sake, he might not always show the best judgment, but he would never associate with a terrorist."

Sam had to work his damnedest not to offer her reassurances. He gave her a hard look. "I'll ask you again. What's he doing in Honduras?"

She sniffed. "Why don't you tell me, since you have all the answers."

"Okay. Fine. He's working as a low-level mule for Nader."

"A mule?"

"A courier. Delivering packages. Packages containing all sorts of things Uncle Sam frowns on—drugs, laundered money, stolen gems—like the packages he's been mailing to you."

"Those *packages*," she said, contempt dripping from each word, "are full of Mayan knockoffs . . . primitive pottery, native crafts . . . things like that. Cory's been buying them and shipping them to me to store so he'll have an inventory when he comes home and sets up his retail business."

"And you know that because you checked them out?"

She glared at him. "I know because that's what he told me was in them. And unlike with you, I can believe him."

"For the record, I never lied to you."

"No. You just screwed me for fun and profit."

"I never meant for that to happen."

"Yeah. I can see how hard you were fighting it."

Sam pushed away from the table. Walked to the door that led to the garage and opened it. "Reed."

The blond agent followed him back to the kitchen.

"Show her," Sam said.

Reed held one of the Mayan knockoff statues in his hand. It was about the size of a wine bottle. He held it up to the side of his head. Shook it.

"This one's a little heavier than the rest," he said. "What do you think? Should we check it out?"

"Just do it," Sam said.

Reed rapped the soft plaster on the side of her table. The piece broke in half. The inside was hollow.

Sam reached inside, pulled out a tissue wrapped package that Reed had planted there. He tossed it on the table in front of Abbie.

She looked from him to the tissue, her brows knit, her dark eyes questioning.

"Open it," he said.

She slowly shook her head. "What? So you can get my fingerprints on whatever's inside? I don't know what your game is but don't expect me to play nice," she said defiantly.

"I'll do it." Reed unwrapped the tissue paper to reveal a quart-sized plastic bag filled with white powder.

"Now, what do you suppose we have here?" Reed lifted the bag, held it in front of her.

Abbie stared at the bag as if it were poison. Reed sliced the bag open, dipped the tip of his little finger into the powder, then brought it to his nose. Sam could see that she knew what it was. Or what it was supposed to be. She'd told him her father was a drug addict. He figured she recognized blow when she saw it.

"He didn't know," she insisted, her gaze flying from Sam to Reed. "Cory *couldn't* have known. He isn't a dealer. And he wouldn't do this to me."

"Wouldn't do what? Make you an accomplice to illegal drug smuggling?"

She shot up from the table so fast her chair teetered and almost toppled over. "I'm not an accomplice in anything. And I told you. Cory wouldn't *do* this. How many ways can I say it? For that matter, how do I know you didn't plant that bag? You're good at games, right, Sam? Excuse me—you're good at games, aren't you, *Agent Lang*." She made a sound of frustration. "Or is that even your real name?"

"It's my name," he said.

She challenged him with a cold look. "Whatever. I don't understand why you targeted me."

If she was lying, she was damn good, Sam thought, as guilt hammered away at his conviction.

The door to the garage opened. Savage and Colter walked into the kitchen. They were about to level the killing blow.

"The boy's been busy," Colter said, holding a broken statue. "Wanna guess what we found inside this one?"

Abbie went pale when he pulled out a blue velvet pouch covered in plaster dust. He spilled the contents into his hand. An emerald necklace sparkled against his palm. It was one of the best paste re-creations Sam had ever seen. They had Joe Greene—another one of the BOIs—and his connections back in Buenos Aires to thank for that.

"What do you want to bet someone's looking for those little baubles?"

Colter held a thick manila folder marked FBI. He opened it up, thumbed through it, finally found what he was looking for.

"Here we go." He pulled a sheet of paper out of the stack, a photocopied picture of the fake emeralds that had been doctored with a date stamp of six months ago.

"Yep." Savage fully disclosed the photo so Abbie could see it and compare it to the necklace. "That's them."

Sam turned to Abbie, steeled himself against the panicked confusion in her eyes. "You're in a world of hurt here, Abbie. You realize that, right? Tell us what you know so we can help you."

She swallowed. "Your concern is touching."

He ignored the pain that spurred her sarcasm and pressed on. "Drugs. Stolen gems. With all this evidence to back up charges, that innocent act is not going to play well with a jury."

He saw fear as well as pain on her face now.

"Jury? Jesus. You honestly think I had something to do with this?"

Sam glanced at Reed then back at Abbie. "New car. Flashy diamond. Nice digs. You tell me how a student and a dealer at a casino manages all that? And why all the security if you aren't hiding something?"

She went pale. "Do I need a lawyer?" she asked softly.

Sam leaned back, sensing he was close to getting what he wanted, feeling no triumph in the toll this was taking on her. "What you need is to talk to us. Tell us everything you know about your brother and his association with Fredrick Nader. You cooperate, we can cut you a deal. You don't give us what we need, you're facing federal charges for drug trafficking and jewel theft."

He needed to close this deal. Before the shock wore off and her head cleared. Before she started making phone calls. Started asking questions and found out their FBI act was a fraud. Before she figured out that they were grasping at straws here and that she was all they had to lead them to Nader since Cory had fallen off the grid.

She crossed her arms protectively beneath her breasts. "I keep telling you. I don't know anything."

"This says you do." Sam nodded toward the fake bag of drugs and the paste emeralds. "I don't want to have to take you into custody."

She leveled him a look. "Like you didn't want to have to take me to bed?"

There was so much venom and hurt in her voice, Savage and Reed looked away. And Sam's respect for Abbie Hughes rose another notch. She was tough. It had to hurt like hell to hang out that laundry in front of the other men. It took guts.

"Look," Sam said, going with his gut and counting on the wiretap and the certain knowledge that as soon as they left, she'd make some calls. "Why don't you sleep on it? We'll come back in the morning. But I'll warn you right now, if you lawyer up, which essentially means you clam up, any deal is off the table. I'll see to it you spend the next thirty-plus years behind bars. And don't kid yourself. We've got enough evidence here to make any charge we want to level stick."

She had nothing to say to that.

"You've got until eight tomorrow morning." He nodded toward Reed and Savage to retrieve the "evidence" lying on the kitchen table. "I'll be back then."

He stood, faced her. "Think very hard, Abbie. You can still save yourself if you make the right decision."

"Has it even crossed your mind that I might be telling you the truth? Or are you so used to lying to get what you want, you don't recognize the truth when you hear it?"

Yeah, he was used to lying. What he wasn't used to was feeling guilty about it. "If you're telling the truth, then you've got nothing to hide. If you're lying, then you're in more trouble than you ever bargained for. Either way, your brother is in the thick of this. He's playing with some bad boys, Abbie. If he falls out of favor, Nader won't so much as blink when he kills him. You help me find Cory before that happens and you're helping him."

A single tear trickled down her cheek.

Sam couldn't let that stop him. He walked to the door, aware of her standing stiff and in shock. Her voice, however, thick with heartbreaking disappointment, had him hesitate with his hand on the doorknob.

"So what was I to you in all this? A job perk?"

He hung his head. Breathed deep. Then he made himself turn and face her. "A casualty," he said with all the emotion of a rock. "You were a casualty."

She nodded. Kept nodding as another tear fell. "Well. Good to know it was nothing *personal.*"

Like it had been personal for her.

By the time Sam closed the door behind him, all he felt was numb. Forget second guesses, forget regret. Numb worked. Numb overrode the guilt that pummeled his conviction and tried to convince him that the means didn't justify the end. That nothing justified the pain he had caused this woman.

But something did.

Terri's death was all the justification he needed.

10

Abbie watched the door close behind Sam. Stared for long moments after he left.

Then she began shaking.

She planted her elbows on the table, lowered her head into her hands. Fisted her hands in her hair and tried to hold herself together.

Jesus.

Cory—involved in drug trafficking and stolen gem smuggling.

Sam—an FBI agent.

Sam—in her bed. In her body.

"You were a casualty."

She couldn't stall the tears any longer. They hit her like a truck. No matter how she struggled to keep them inside, she couldn't. She wept openly. Wept violently.

For Cory . . . God, what had Cory gotten himself into?

For herself . . . Sam's betrayal cut like glass. Cut her deep.

She was no stranger to pain. Physical. Emotional. But this. God. She'd been so stupid. She'd been on the verge of falling in love with him.

And he'd been using her. He wanted to send her to prison for something she hadn't done. For something she did not want to believe Cory had done.

She saw the bag of drugs in her mind. The emeralds they said were stolen.

"Cory," she whispered and laid her head on the kitchen table. "Where are you? And what have you done?"

Off the coast of Muchilena, Honduras
Same night

"Truly, there are few areas of Central America worth the C-4 it would take to blow them to dust, don't you agree?"

Tied to a metal chair, blood streaming down his bruised face, Cory Hughes didn't respond.

Fredrick Nader frowned with impatience as he sat in a plush club chair that his steward had carried to the starboard deck. The running lights glittered off the dark water as he observed Hughes's dazed eyes.

"I have, however," Fredrick went on conversationally, "always held a true appreciation for the warm waters off the Isla de Roatán."

Of course, local, low-level government corruption had netted him some rare gem acquisitions over the years and had contributed to his affection for his favorite mooring.

"Have you been there? No? Well, it's a beautiful little island almost true east of La Ceiba," he continued, then nodded at Rutger, who promptly threw a bucket of seawater into Hughes's bruised and bloody face. The boy winced and hissed out a pained breath when the salty brine bit into open wounds.

"In any event, I'd much prefer to be moored near Roatán than here at Muchilena. Very wrong side of the social strata. Too crude for my taste. And while it's been mildly entertaining interrogating you, frankly, your stubborn resistance to answer questions to my satisfaction is starting to bore me."

Fredrick inspected his nails, made a mental note to have Arturo arrange the return of that lovely young manicurist when they next visited Roatán. In addition to a decent manicure, the pretty Maria was a woman of many talents and beautiful breasts.

He got hard thinking about their last encounter. Took pride in the ready response of his prick. He was, after all, sixty-five. Credited his virility to his staunch German lineage and his fastidious determination to keep himself in excellent physical condition.

Hughes raised his head, squinted at him through straggly wet hair and swollen eyes.

"Ah. Good. You're with us again. Let's go over what we already know, all right?"

He rose then, walked over to Hughes, was careful not to step in any blood and stain his white deck shoes.

"Derek Styles stole something from me. Something I have coveted for years and went to great lengths to obtain. Do you know the legend behind the Tupacka diamonds?"

The beaten man blinked.

"No. I don't suppose you do. Well, allow me. Legend has it that a Spanish conquistador arrived in Honduras and fell in love with the high priestess, Tupacka. He was so besotted by her beauty that he commissioned the diamond necklace as a wedding gift. They were married and the conquistador set sail to take his bride with him back to Spain. Are you still with me?"

Hughes's chin lolled on his chest. His hands were tied behind his back. Fredrick nodded to Rutger, who once again doused the boy with salt water, making him gasp in pain.

"As so often happened during those difficult and dangerous voyages," Fredrick went on, satisfied his audience was once again conscious, "a freak storm came up before their ship cleared the reefs. The vessel went down; all were lost. The only thing of value recovered was the necklace the priestess was wearing when her body washed ashore."

He smiled. "Tragically romantic, is it not? And positively miraculous that the diamonds were recovered to be passed down along with the story over the years and ended up in the National Museum. Until I made arrangements to own them."

He walked directly in front of Hughes. Got right in his face. "I want them back. Styles stole them. You somehow ended up with them. If you want to live to see tomorrow's sunrise, you will tell me where they are.

"Rutger . . . you've been very patient," Fredrick said when the mule remained stubbornly and stupidly silent. "You may get your knife out now and play. Perhaps our young friend will find the slice of your blade more convincing than your fists."

"No. No please . . . don't let him c-cut me. I'll . . . tell you. Tell you."

Fredrick smiled, pleased that they had finally worn him down. "One moment, Rutger. We must hear what the young man has to say. Make it good," he said, all pretense of amusement eclipsed by the acid in his tone. "Your life depends on it."

"What do you want me to do with him?" Rutger asked one hour later.

Fredrick looked up from his glass of port. "Get him off the yacht. Take him to Peña Blanca," he added. He owned a small estancia there near the village. While he hadn't spent time at the ranch lately, he liked its close proximity to both the Guatemalan border, should he have need to flee Honduran authorities, and the El Puente Mayan archaeological site. He did so appreciate the Mayan ruins.

Thick, nearly impenetrable national forest fortressed the estancia to the west. Its location, on the southward slope of Montaña de la Crita provided outlook and defensive advantages.

"Alert the men that a guest is on the way."

By the time Rutger arrived with Hughes in tow, the estancia would be heavily guarded.

Not that Fredrick expected resistance from what was left of Hughes. Not that he expected Hughes to live that much longer. Just long enough to ensure he hadn't lied about the diamonds.

"And the merchandise?" Rutger asked diplomatically. "Do you wish for me to make the trip to Las Vegas and retrieve it personally?"

"Yes. No. Wait. On second thought, I have a much better idea." Why risk Rutger being detained and his passport being confiscated? Rutger was on too many U.S. government watch lists. Damn radical extremists had taken all the fun out of flying.

"Hughes is responsible for this. We'll let him take care of it."

• • •

When Cory came to, he was lying facedown on a dirt floor. He rolled painfully from his stomach to his back. He was inside a building. High windows. Hot and dank and dark.

He didn't remember leaving Nader's yacht. He didn't remember anything beyond the pain. The pain told him he was alive. The intensity told him that Nader had finally let Rutger loose with his knife.

His hands were tied in front of him now. His left hand throbbed, ached, burned. Was covered with a thick bandage.

To stop the bleeding.

He remembered then. As he fought for breath, fought for calm, he remembered what he'd told them when he'd seen the moonlight glint off Rutger's knife. He remembered what Rutger had done to him. Why his hand was bandaged.

His hand.

God, oh Jesus God.

"Abbie," he whispered into a silence broken by the wind outside the windows and the swishing, skittering sound of whatever night creature shared the floor of this squalid hovel with him. "Abbie, I'm sorry."

Hot, salty tears ran into his hair, stung when they trickled across his abraded skin. He'd never wanted to involve her in this, but because he was stupid and weak, he'd drawn her into it.

What choice had he had?

What choice?

The only reason he was still alive was because he'd stashed the Tupacka diamonds someplace safe. Because he had, they couldn't afford to kill him. Not until Nader got his diamonds back.

He'd thought it was a safe bet to mail the diamonds back to the States. Not to Abbie. No. Hadn't wanted her caught in the middle.

But then Rutger had brought out his knife, and Cory had told them everything. Now Abbie was in as much danger as he was.

"I'm sorry. I'm sorry. I'm sorry," he wept, and for the first time in his miserable life, he prayed.

"Please, God. Please don't let them hurt her, too."

Las Vegas

Abbie sat up straight. She glanced at the kitchen clock. It was 5:00 a.m. She'd actually fallen asleep at her kitchen table. She couldn't believe she'd slept.

Shut down was probably more like it. She rose abruptly, walked to the counter, and dumped the pot of coffee Sam had made. She didn't want any reminders of him in her house. With shaking hands, she made a fresh pot. Then she stripped and stood under the shower, running it as hot as she could stand it, needing to wash away the scent of him and of sex.

She cried some more.

Then she got mad.

She was still wrapped in her towel when she charged into her bedroom, ripped the sheets off the bed, and threw them into the washer. As the washer filled with water, she stood in front of it, staring at the utility room wall, locked in a battle of images.

Sam, kissing her.

Sam, questioning her.

Sam, lowering his mouth to her breast.

Telling her she could go to prison.

Telling her she felt incredible.

"Enough." She slammed down the lid to the washer and marched out of the small room.

She had bigger problems than Sam Lang's betrayal. Cory was in a world of trouble and she had no idea what to do or how to help him.

At this point, she had no idea what to even think.

Drugs? Stolen emeralds?

It didn't fit. It just didn't fit.

Yeah, she knew Cory struggled. Knew he was too proud to ask her for help—too proud to take it when she offered.

She sipped coffee, thought of him as a little boy. Tears stung again. He'd been so beautiful. So small. So vulnerable. And so damaged. Their father had abused him so badly.

"*Why all the security if you aren't hiding something?*" Sam had asked.

When you grew up the way she and Cory had, it became very important to know there was a safe place to hide. Locked doors weren't always enough.

They hadn't been enough tonight.

Cory. God, Cory. What was happening?

Yes, Abbie felt responsible for him. And yes, she felt disappointed for him, sometimes disappointed in him. But above all, she loved him. She had to find a way to help him.

She walked to her second bedroom that doubled as her home office and study room, stared at the computer, then booted it up.

"Please, please, please," she whispered as she sat down and waited impatiently for her e-mail to open up. "Please let there be an e-mail from Cory."

She needed to get in touch with him. Beg him to level with her and tell her what was going on.

Her heart pounded as she sat there, waiting for a handful of new messages to download. A sales notification from an online catalog. A couple of spams her filter didn't catch. Notification that her credit card statement was now available online.

A silly note from Crystal asking how the underwear had panned out.

She swallowed back a rolling nausea triggered by humiliation when she remembered how brazen she'd been when Sam had taken them off of her. She'd been so stupid. She'd actually thought . . . well, it didn't matter what she'd thought. Sam Lang had used her. End of story.

She waited for the last message to download, annoyed because it was taking so long. Probably from Fran. Fran was in one of Abbie's accounting classes at the U and no matter how many times Abbie had told her not to send attachments with jokes, Fran was certain Abbie could not live without seeing the latest chuckle.

She was about to close down her e-mail when the message finally popped up on her screen.

It wasn't from Fran. She didn't recognize the sender's address but the subject line drained all the blood from her face.

All it said was: Cory Hughes. According to the date and time, it had been sent three hours ago.

She couldn't open it up fast enough.

She read the message.

Disbelieving.

Horrified.

Breath caught in her throat, she read it again.

Wishing to God she was wrong. That she'd read it wrong. That she'd wake up and this would all be a bad dream.

But the sound of the wall clock ticking into the silence told her she was awake. The thickness in her throat reminded her she was alive.

With terrified reluctance, she opened the attachment as the e-mail directed her to do. When she finally comprehended who was in the photograph and what had been done to him, the horror began in earnest.

She shot out of the chair, stumbled backward, then ran on rubbery legs for the bathroom.

She fell to her hands and knees.

Retched violently into the toilet.

When she could breathe again, when her abdominal muscles stopped convulsing, she rose on shaking legs. Stared at her reflection in the mirror.

Her face was pale, her eyes wild with terror.

Like Cory's eyes had been wild with terror and pain. Staring back at her from a face that was pummeled and bruised and swollen to the point where she hadn't recognized him at first.

A Spanish-language newspaper lay on a table in front of him—proof of life, she realized—today's date prominent for her to see.

Much of the rest of the newsprint was soaked in blood.

Cory's left hand lay beside the date, fingers splayed wide. Three fingers and a thumb. Blood soaked the newsprint where his little finger used to be.

It lay beside his hand now. Detached. Drained of blood. Lifeless.

Like Cory would be drained of blood and lifeless if she didn't do exactly as she was told.

11

They'd given her fifteen hours, and three of them were already gone. If Abbie wanted to see her brother alive again she was to retrieve a diamond necklace from the Las Vegas post office box where Cory had mailed it, then bring it with her to San Pedro Sula, Honduras.

Fifteen hours. Each hour she delayed beyond that, Cory would lose another finger.

Her stomach rolled again. She swallowed back the nausea. She had to get it together. Not only that, she had to *keep* it together or Cory was going to die.

She printed off the instructions in the e-mail. Read them over and over even though they were crystal clear. Then she paced, wound tight on adrenaline and anxiety, her mind running at warp speed.

She had to think . . . to come up with something . . . a plan that didn't get Cory killed. For that matter, a plan that didn't get them both killed.

If Sam was right, if Cory was involved in something illegal with this man, Fredrick Nader, then while the ID of the sender was a mystery, it made sense that Nader was the one holding Cory hostage.

She scanned the note again, searching for something—anything—that would give her an edge. Found nothing.

When she arrived in San Pedro Sula, a car would be waiting for her, it said. The driver would be holding a sign with her name on it. He would take her to Cory. She would exchange the diamonds for him and they would be free to go.

Right. They had to think she was either too stupid or too frightened to comprehend that once they had what they wanted, she and Cory were both as good as dead.

Die. Dead. Killed. She could count the times on one hand she'd said those words in her life. Now, every other thought was filled with the stuff of thriller movies and bad dreams. It was all so far removed from anything she'd ever encountered, she felt as if she were drowning in a big glass fishbowl. Swimming for her life.

With the clock ticking—it was close to 6:30 a.m. now—she sat back down at her computer, Googled a travel site, and found an eleven-hour flight from Vegas to San Pedro Sula that left at 10:55 a.m.

She needed to be on that plane. And then what?

No matter how many times she'd worked it through in her mind, she couldn't come up with a way to get either of them out alive.

She needed help. But the e-mail had been specific about that, too. She was not to contact the police. She was to come to Honduras alone. Still, she knew she needed help.

But she didn't know anyone who would be able to help her.

She looked up from the computer abruptly.

"Yes, you do," she told herself as her heart rate picked up speed.

She *did* know someone. Someone who had a vested interest. Not in her. Not in her brother, but in stolen diamonds. And in Fredrick Nader.

A plan came to her then—unfolded like the pages in a book. She knew exactly what she had to do. She had to use Sam Lang the way he'd used her. Ruthlessly, unapologetically.

It could work, she realized as she thought it through.

It *would* work.

It would probably mean she would end up in prison, but she'd worry about criminal charges later. Right now all that mattered was getting Cory back.

For the first time since this nightmare started, her heart pounded with something other than a helpless, hopeless fear. She ran into the bedroom to find her purse and her cell phone.

Gone, she realized after a frantic search.

Sam. He must have taken them.

So she would have to use the landline, she realized. If Sam Lang hadn't blinked at taking her to bed to get information out of her, he wouldn't hesitate to tap her phones. That meant any call she made would be monitored.

"Bastard."

It couldn't be helped. She picked up the phone and dialed.

"It's . . . six frickin' o'clock in the morning," Crystal grumbled, picking up on the fourth ring. "This better be good."

"Crystal. It's me. Don't ask any questions. As soon as I hang up, boot up your computer and open your e-mail."

"What th—?"

"Please. Just do it." Abbie disconnected.

Sam and his buddies were, no doubt, monitoring her e-mail account too, so she went out on Yahoo and quickly set up a new account under a name only Crystal would recognize. Her hooker name: Jiggles Larue. It was a game they had played one night after a bottle of wine and a lot of laughs. The fake name on the new account wouldn't stop Sam and his FBI pals, but it would slow them down. By the time they found the new account with Abbie's instructions to Crystal, it would be too late for them to stop her. Her plan would be in play and she'd be closer to getting Cory back home or . . . She refused to think about what would happen if it didn't work.

Her fingers flew over the keys as she gave Crystal the short version of what was happening and instructions for what Abbie needed Crystal to do as soon as the post office lobby opened at eight. She ended the note with a caution to make certain she wasn't followed.

She hit Send, waited for what seemed like an eternity, but in fact was only a few minutes before she received Crystal's reply. "Count on me. Be careful."

Thank God for Crystal.

"You too," she typed back and sent off the reply.

Next she replied to Cory's captors, carefully selecting her words. Her heart felt like it would explode as she hit Send, then prayed she'd bought Cory enough time for her to get to him.

On a deep breath, she deleted all messages and the new account, shredded the e-mail she'd printed—all but the picture of Cory—then she picked up the phone again and booked the flight to San Pedro Sula.

With that done, she hurried into her bedroom, dug her passport out of the safe in her closet, and thanked whatever gods of fate had prompted her to have it renewed last year even though she hadn't been out of the States since her honeymoon with Don.

Next, she threw a change of clothes and a few toiletries into a backpack. Then she waited for Sam to show up. If she'd been right about the phone tap, it wouldn't take him long.

A few minutes later, a black SUV pulled up in front of her house and Sam got out. It was nice to know she could count on him for something . . . something other than the truth.

"Is this the part where I'm supposed to say, what took you so long?" Abbie asked when she opened the door to Sam's knock.

She'd been practicing the line in her head. Didn't want to stumble over it, let him know how difficult it was for her to see him again so soon after . . . well, so soon. She stepped aside so he could walk into the living room.

"You're not actually planning to go to Honduras."

It wasn't a question. It was a statement. It was also confirmation that she'd been right about her phone calls being monitored.

"Because I'd be crazy to think you wouldn't find out and try to stop me? I may be gullible, but that doesn't make me stupid. Just like you coming off as a straight shooter doesn't make you one."

A muscle in his jaw worked. It was the only indication that her barb had hit home.

"Cory's being held hostage," she said without preamble.

If he was surprised to hear that Cory had been abducted, he didn't show it.

She walked into her office, intending for him to follow. She'd planned this part out, too, and handed him the photograph she'd printed off, struggling desperately not to look at it. "I received this in an e-mail. Or like the phone tap, do you already have hackers online and this is old news?"

Sam's silence and the grim look on his face as he studied the photo told her he hadn't seen it before now. Which meant he hadn't yet accessed her e-mail. It also meant she still had a small edge until he and his FBI buddies hacked in and intercepted her message to Crystal.

"This is Nader's work," he said, sounding grim. "More specifically, it's the work of his hired muscle, Rutger Smith."

"He wants a necklace," Abbie said. "Something he referred to in the e-mail as the Tupacka diamonds. He says Cory stole them from him and he wants them back."

"I need to see that e-mail."

"That's not going to happen. I deleted it." She didn't want Sam to know the original location of the necklace even though—God willing and with Crystal's help—it wasn't in Cory's post office box any longer. "Look, I don't have time to play any more games with you. Neither does Cory. So here's what's going to happen."

Abbie ignored Sam's hard scowl and drew a bracing breath. "I don't know why Cory had the diamonds in the first place. All I know is that he mailed them back to the States several days ago."

He glanced at her sharply. "To you?"

"No. Not to me. He sent the necklace to a post office box here in Vegas for safekeeping."

He glanced at the photo again. "So, he stole from Nader, knew that if Nader caught him he was as good as dead, so he mailed the diamonds to the States as insurance to keep Nader from killing him."

Except for the theft part, that's the way Abbie had figured it. "Until Nader gets the diamonds back, Cory is still of value to him alive."

"And it's safer for Nader if he has you deliver them instead of coming after them himself."

That made sense to Abbie, too.

"Does Nader know where the diamonds are?"

"He did." She shivered when she thought of the methods they had used to get the information out of Cory. "But not anymore."

She saw the moment Sam realized what she'd done. "The phone call to Crystal. You had her move them."

"*My* insurance," she said. "I let them know that I have the diamonds now. That I've moved them to a new hiding place and if they kill Cory before I get to Honduras to give them the new location they'll never see them again."

"Jesus."

For the first time since she'd met him, she saw Sam Lang rattled.

"You have no idea what kind of scum you're dealing with here."

She glanced at Cory's picture, shuddered again. "Yeah. I do."

"Then you have to know you just signed your own death warrant."

Maybe. Probably. Yeah. She knew that. Except that Sam was her ace in the hole. "What I know is I want my brother back."

"You are *not* going to Honduras," he said, anger rich in each word.

"Because you're charging me with a crime? Hauling me off to jail?" she baited, sounding braver than she felt. "Fine. Arrest me. That's not going to get you what you want."

They both knew that he wanted Nader. Cory was small potatoes. Abbie had figured that out already. It was the big prize Sam was after.

"You think they're going to go easy on you because you're a woman?" He held the photo in front of her face when she remained stubbornly silent. "Look at it. Look at it!" he demanded when she averted her gaze. "These guys play for real. You're as dead as Cory if you go down there. Hell, if he hasn't already, Nader's probably sent a man to watch your house. Someone could be watching it right now, waiting for you to go to the post office and retrieve the necklace."

"Then it's a good thing I sent Crystal after it," she said, defiant. "Look. You think I'm not scared? Well, I'm scared, okay? I know what I'm up against."

"Then prove it. Tell me where the diamonds are, Abbie. No promises, but if you do that for me, I'll do what I can to get your brother back."

"Oh, I'm counting on that," she said slowly. "You *are* going to help me get Cory back. And once he's safe, you can have the damn diamonds."

He glared at her. Let out a breath. "Last I knew, you weren't in any position to bargain."

"See, that's where I think you're wrong. The way I figure it, the only reason the FBI is after Cory is to get to Nader. I mean, my brother is . . . how did you put it? A low-level mule? Low-level? Come on. It's not Cory you want. It's not even me. You want Nader. You want the diamonds. And we both know I'm your best ticket to getting both, just like you're my ticket to saving Cory."

He was really angry now. "I repeat. You do not know what you're messing with here. Nader will stop at nothing to get what he wants."

"Yeah. You'd know all about that, wouldn't you?"

She hated herself for letting the hurt he'd caused her creep into her voice. Refused to believe she actually saw regret in his eyes.

"This is my brother's life we're talking about. I'd think you'd be happy as hell to use me—again," she added just to watch him squirm. "I mean, I'm your best chance to get the bad guy and save the day. That's what you guys with the *white* hats do, right? You save the day. No matter who gets hurt in the process? No matter who you have to use? No matter how you have to use them." Tears stung her eyes. She blinked them back.

"Abbie."

"No." She held up a hand, backed a step away when he reached for her. She couldn't stand for him to touch her. Couldn't stand to think about how she might react. "No, it's all right. It's the way the game is played. I understand that now. I was just a . . . how did you put it? A casualty. Nothing personal."

A long silence passed. She had him over a barrel. He knew it and so did she. That didn't stop her from wishing he'd been what she thought he was.

And it didn't stop him from trying, one more time, to get what he wanted from her. "How do I know you really have the diamonds?"

Her computer dinged just then, telling her she had mail. God bless Crystal. Her timing was perfect.

"You know why clichés are used so often? Because they work. Like now. A picture is worth a thousand words," she said and opened up the e-mail. Just as she had instructed, Crystal had taken her camera with her to the post office and accessed the box with the combination Cory had given Nader. Then Crystal had snapped a digital photo of the necklace and e-mailed it to Abbie along with proof of today's date in the form of another newspaper.

"Holy God," Abbie said, when she saw the necklace for the first time.

The diamonds—hundreds of them—were set in an elaborate mounting that started in a choker, then spread outward and downward like a delicate cape of solid stones and gold.

She could almost understand why someone would be willing to kill for this.

"Tell me what Crystal did with them."

Sam's voice startled her. She dragged her attention away from the photograph after she hit the print button. "That would sort of defeat my purpose now, wouldn't it? As long as you don't know where they are, I've got what us Vegas types call a pat hand."

His gaze never leaving her face, Sam tugged his cell phone off his belt and punched in a single digit.

"Did you pick her up yet?" he asked without preamble.

He listened, then hung up. "Seems your friend has disappeared."

Abbie retrieved the sheet from her printer. She fanned it slightly so the ink would dry and blessed Crystal again for being so good at what she did. "Yeah, she does that sometimes."

"Four hours," Abbie had told Crystal in the e-mail. "Make yourself scarce for four hours. That's all I need to make sure the plane is in the air and I'm on it. If anyone approaches you after that, just play dumb."

"You're stooping a little low, aren't you? Involving a friend in your mess?"

His accusation hurt. But she was getting used to being hurt by Sam Lang. "That's the difference between you and me. I would never put someone I care about at risk. You're not going to charge her with anything. Just like you don't really care about Cory, you don't care about Crystal either. All you care about is the diamonds. And getting Nader."

She could see by his expression that she'd hit that nail on the proverbial head. "I can give you both. Lead you straight to Nader's door. If you do charge Crystal with anything when this is over, I'll testify that I threatened and coerced her into helping me. And trust me, I can be very convincing. You know all about being convincing, don't you, Sam?"

She grabbed her backpack. Called his bluff. "With or without you, I'm going after my brother. Lock up behind you. I've got a plane to catch."

It wasn't until she was in her assigned aisle seat, her backpack stored on the floor in front of her, that Abbie let herself think about the reckless danger of her plan. And it wasn't until the cabin attendant came over and told her she'd been upgraded to first class that she knew her strategy had worked.

She leaned out into the aisle so she could see up to the first-class cabin. Sam Lang stood there glaring, waiting for her to join him.

12

Pissed. Sam was totally, majorly, *royally* pissed.

He worked his damnedest not to clench his hands into fists as Abbie Hughes, head held high, looking poised and perfect in a yellow knit top and jeans, walked down the narrow coach-class aisle toward him.

He didn't know what he wanted to do more: Haul her off the damn plane or haul her off to bed. The first would get her out of trouble. The second would get him deeper into it.

He didn't get it. Didn't get one thing about his reaction to this woman — and the control she pushed to the limit.

Part of him wanted to punish her. Part wanted to protect her. But one hundred percent was on board with wanting her.

So yeah, he was pissed that she could fuck with his head like this. He was pissed because he hadn't needed another player in this game to get to Nader. It was never supposed to come to this. Sam had only needed Abbie for information, yet she'd managed to manipulate herself into a key position on the team. *His* team.

Dangling her as bait to flush Nader out of his lair had never been a part of the plan either. Her involvement was going to pose ten times more complications than Sam needed. Her little sleight of hand had placed her square in the middle of a deadly deception that could get her hurt or killed.

Bottom line, that's what was really eating at him. He didn't want anything happening to her.

He lifted a hand when she reached him, indicating she should take the window seat. The strain he hadn't seen on her face in the predawn light in her house was apparent now. A slight bruising of fatigue darkened to shadows beneath her eyes. Her olive skin was visibly pale.

He remembered that skin in the dark of her bedroom. The softness of it. The taste of it. The scent of her and sex. He couldn't look at her without remembering those long, sleek legs wrapped around him, the silk of her hair tangled in his hands.

What it felt like to be inside her.

Her shoulder accidentally brushed his when she eased past him, then slid across plush leather into the roomy window seat in the first-class cabin. The slight touch prompted an immediate physical response. His entire body clenched involuntarily, leaned toward her—like a missile seeking heat.

He backed away, made sure she was settled, then dropped down into the seat beside her. Cursed under his breath.

One touch. One brief touch and he was panting like a damn dog.

Mistake. Taking her to bed had been a big, big mistake. He wished . . . Hell. It didn't matter what he wished. What was done was done. There were much bigger things at play here than Abbie Hughes's feelings. He had a job to do. Whether he liked it or not, she was going to help facilitate it.

He buckled his seat belt. Closed his eyes. Got it together.

"You know, there's one thing that's been bothering me," she said.

He grunted, rubbed a hand over his face. "One thing? You're heading into a snake pit and you're bothered about *one* thing? I can think of about a hundred things that should be scaring the hell out of you."

"What's the FBI doing mixed up in international drug trafficking?" she asked, ignoring his sarcasm. "Isn't that usually handled by the Drug Enforcement Agency? And while I'm asking, what's the FBI doing working an international gem theft? Didn't know you guys crossed national borders."

Yeah. She was smart. He grudgingly admired her for that. Even though the jury was still out on how deeply she was involved in her brother's dirty dealings, he admired her for a lot of things, and that didn't sit well with him either.

"And why, if this is a federal investigation, are you and your road crew," she notched her chin toward Savage and Colter, who were a little hard not to spot sitting across the aisle from them, "not on a government plane?"

Sam could lie to her, shore up the FBI scam, but in the end, there was no longer any point. "We're not FBI."

She opened her mouth. Closed it. Shook her head. Like she'd given up on expecting any truth from him. "Then who are you? Wait. Never mind. Don't bother." She averted her attention to the window as the jet taxied down the runway. "You'd just lie again anyway."

Sam steeled himself against the urge to explain. To try to make her understand that what had happened between them hadn't been about her brother or Nader or the diamonds. It had just happened. He hadn't meant for things to go that far. Hadn't been able to stop when he should have.

"Look, there are issues at play here that you're better off not knowing," he said instead.

She made a sound that was half laugh, half snort of disgust. "Don't you think it's a little too late in the game to be worried about what I know?"

It was a little late in the game to be worried about a lot of things. Like whether or not there had been another way to get to Nader and leave Abbie out of the mix.

"For all I know, you're just another bad guy on the take," she added when he remained silent. "But you know what? I don't care. All I care about is getting Cory back."

"By putting your own life on the line? Great plan."

She breathed deep, looked away again. "Other than showing up in San Pedro Sula and climbing into a car with a man who is supposed to take me to my brother, I don't have a plan. That's what I need you for. You're the guy who wants Nader. I'll leave it to you to figure out the best way to use me to get him. Whatever you want, I'll do it. As long as you help me find Cory."

He considered her for a long moment. In addition to being intelligent, she was loyal to a fault. She knew the danger she faced, yet here she was. On a fool's mission to save her no-good brother.

"He's not worth it, you know. He's just not worth it."

Her gaze snapped to his, full of fire and fury. "Would you say the same thing about your sister?"

Sam went utterly still. "What do you know about my sister?"

"More than you know about my brother, so don't begin to presume you know his worth. You'd be wrong. Just like you're wrong about me."

She'd hurt him, Abbie realized. She wanted to feel some satisfaction in that fact, wanted to call it payback. That wasn't her. Never would be.

"I'm sorry about your sister," she said when he lapsed into a tense silence. "I read about it online. Didn't put it together until, well, until recently."

He said nothing. So much nothing it finally dawned on her.

"This is about her, isn't it?" It made sense. He wasn't FBI. Wasn't military. "Nader had something to do with her death."

When he finally turned to her, his face was void of emotion. "Like I said, there are things in play here that you're better off not knowing."

Then he leaned his head back against the seat and closed his eyes.

End of discussion.

The flight from Vegas to Houston lasted three long hours. Even the roomy first-class cabin felt like a tight fit with Sam sitting so close to her. Not just because he was a big man, but because he had such a big presence. And because the memory of him naked and needing her in her bed wouldn't leave her alone.

His slightest movement made her agonizingly aware of him. The accidental brush of their thighs. The bump of an elbow. The sage and citrus scent of him, barely there, but oh so provocative when he turned his head, or shifted his weight.

The confinement drove her crazy. Abbie couldn't wait to deplane at Houston. She planned to spend a little time alone waiting for the connecting flight forty-five minutes later that would take them to San Pedro Sula.

She needed to regroup. To reassemble her thoughts. So as soon as they landed and got the all clear, she shot out of her seat, slid past Sam—who was *not* FBI—and headed for the exit door.

She was still shrugging into her backpack when a firm hand gripped her arm and stopped her before she left the covered jetway.

"Slow it down. We need to find a quiet place and get a few things ironed out."

So much for alone time and her "new" plan to be unaffected by Sam Lang. His grip on her elbow was firm but not bruising. And like the brush of their shoulders when she'd sat down beside him, the humming awareness that ran through her system was as involuntary as it was electric.

She was still recovering from the shock of it when he brought her up to speed on the two men who'd flown with them.

"Wyatt Savage," Sam said with a nod toward the guy on her left as the four of them walked briskly through the terminal.

Savage, like Sam, was a big man, only where Sam was lean muscle mass on a big, athletic frame, Savage was big as in bear. In football terms, Sam was built like a linebacker. Savage was built like a lineman. With kind eyes that she suspected hid secrets she was better off not knowing.

"Ma'am," Savage said with a trace of the South in his voice that she might have found charming if he hadn't seen her wearing only a short silk kimono and understood that Sam had just been in her bed.

"Luke Colter." Sam nodded to the other guy who was quick to flash her a smile and tip his fingers to a Stetson that wasn't there but that Abbie could easily see him wearing.

"Everyone calls me Doc. Doc Holliday. You got a hangnail or a heart attack or a yen for five-card stud—you come to me, okay?"

Colter was tall and rangy and built more like a basketball player. He had flirty blue eyes and that easy smile going for him—and the company of Sam Lang going against him.

"So where's the pretty boy?" Abbie asked.

Doc chuckled. "Lady's got Reed pegged."

"He's a little busy right now looking for your friend." Sam herded her toward an empty corner near their departure gate.

Abbie put on the brakes. "I need to use the restroom."

"In a minute." Sam steered her toward a seat in the corner. The three men sat in a semicircle around her, effectively establishing a barrier between them and the handful of travelers waiting at their gate.

Abbie rarely felt intimidated—it was one of the advantages of being five foot eight—but these three men could make a sumo wrestler cow. It wasn't just their size. It was their presence. Behind Savage's slow, southern drawl and Doc's quick ready grin, both men had an edge about them that defined them as something more than the average guy.

There was crispness to the way they carried themselves, an awareness of their surroundings above and beyond average situational awareness. Not predatory, exactly but . . . vigilant, she decided finally. And capable. They all appeared to be capable.

"Military?" she asked, glancing around the circle of three. Sam had once been in the military. Maybe he still was. She liked that idea a whole hell of a lot better than drug cartel on a vengeance quest. "Is that what you are?"

"Once upon a time," Doc said. "I like this woman," he added with a nod toward Sam. "She plays heads-up."

"She's going to have to," Sam said, his face stern, "if she wants to get out of this alive."

A cell phone rang. Since they hadn't returned her phone, everyone but Abbie checked their pockets.

"Yo," Savage answered, stood and walked away from them, his head down, his voice low.

"How am I going to communicate with you without my phone?" she asked.

"Unless you've got a special chip, your phone wouldn't work once we got out of the States anyway."

No. She didn't have a special chip. Either way, she had no means of communicating. Before she could get too worked up over that, Sam drew her attention.

"Tell me what you know about Nader."

"I already have. I don't know anything. I'd never even heard his name until you told me about him."

For the first time, Abbie sensed a hesitance in his expression. Like maybe he was starting to believe her—although it was clear that he didn't want to.

"Okay, fine. For the sake of argument, I'll fill you in with the basics," Sam said in a voice so low Abbie had to lean in close to hear him. "Nader has a dozen legit businesses scattered all over Europe that front for his illegal activities. He has money in everything from electronics to real estate to coffee, dumplings to ethanol. All silver-spoon acquisitions.

"But that wasn't enough to satisfy him," Sam continued. "He fancies himself some sort of gentleman Mafioso type. His legit businesses bore him so he started dabbling in the gray areas several years ago. Now he's a major player in everything from selling arms to terrorists to drug trafficking—has his fingers in a lot of sour pies. He's got a network that rivals Al-Qaeda for sophistication and capital, although it's not as big in scope. His biggest failing is that while he delegates, he also likes to physically participate in some of his 'business' deals. Not the dirty work—he leaves that to Rutger Smith."

"Smith is Nader's personal hit man," Doc clarified, picking up the briefcase he'd been carrying and setting it on his thighs. He opened it up, drew out a photo. "So you'll know him when you see him."

He handed her a photograph that appeared to have been snapped when Smith wasn't watching.

"Somehow I can't see this guy blending into a crowd." Abbie congratulated herself when her voice came out strong, because she'd darned near swallowed her tongue when she saw Smith's picture.

Talk about supersized. Rutger Smith was big, he was bald, and he was scary as hell. A scar in the shape of a crescent moon ran from the corner of his left eye to the corner of his mouth. Yeah. He was scary. Even more imposing than his size were his eyes. They looked . . . soulless.

"Six foot seven, around three hundred twenty pounds of solid mean," Colter supplied. "Carries a knife and loves to use it. Has as much regard for human life as he has for a cockroach. But killing's not his specialty. Slicing, dicing, and playing with his catch is."

Abbie closed her eyes, thought of Cory, of what Rutger Smith had done to him.

Doc slid another photograph on top of Smith's image. This man looked to be in his late sixties. Thin white hair, slicked back over a deeply tanned face. Trim, physically fit. Distinguished. He could have been a doctor or a lawyer or a CEO of a Fortune 500 company, dressed to the nines in a white jacket and pants, diamonds winking from his ring fingers, gold choker around his neck visible between the open placket of his shirt. Eyes like a snake.

"Fredrick Nader?" she guessed.

Sam nodded. "Like I said, his biggest weakness is what he considers a strength. Sees himself as a general who leads from the front. Can't seem to help himself when it comes to showing up when a big deal is going down."

"And he takes it personal when someone takes something he feels belongs to him," Doc added.

"Like the Tupacka diamonds," Abbie said quietly.

"Yeah," Sam agreed. "Like the diamonds."

"His penchant for cigars—among other things—brings him to Honduras often. Major cigar operations there," Doc interjected. "Likes to moor his yacht, the *Seennymphe*, off the Isla de Roatán. In addition to his addiction to the *maduro habano*, he also has an obsession for the local women."

Abbie looked up from the photo, amazed by the detailed information they had on Nader. "Not FBI. Not military. But some kind of organization that has access to all this information. Who are you guys?"

"We're the good guys," Doc said with a grin she wanted to believe. "Huge leap of faith, I know, but it might be best to just leave it at that."

Shorthand for, *That's all the info you're going to get.* Abbie had little choice but to accept it.

Savage returned to their circle and flipped his phone shut. "That was Mendoza. He'll meet us at the airport with a car and gear."

"Mendoza? There are more of you?"

"Oh, darlin'." Doc's blue eyes twinkled. "If you only knew."

"Yeah, if only." She squelched an unexpected desire to grin back. Cute guy, nice grin or not, Doc was cut from the same cloth as Sam. She could trust him as far as she could toss a tank.

"We want to fit you with a wire," Sam said.

"A wire?"

"Your instructions were to arrive alone. That means you have to get off that plane alone. Nader's man can't know we're along so we'll need to keep a low profile. We have to have a way to track you."

"Oh. Oh, right. And no. I've never worn one."

But it appeared that she was going to. Just like it finally sank in that while she was headed into territory way beyond her comprehension or experience, to these men, it was status quo.

Her single-minded determination to save Cory had suddenly gone from nebulous idea to stark reality. It had been one thing to think about arriving in Honduras in sweeping, unformed terms. It was another thing entirely to face the absolutes: She was going out there alone. Leaving the relative safety of Lang, Colter, and Savage and riding away with a man under the command of a known terrorist. A terrorist who had had her brother beaten and brutalized and who wouldn't hesitate to kill Cory or her, too, if she so much as breathed wrong.

13

"How does it work?" Abbie asked when she'd gotten herself together.

Doc dug into his briefcase again. Pulled out a short, thin wire with a disc about the size of a small button attached to the end.

"You're going to thread this inside your bra strap. The mic will rest flush against your skin beneath the strap."

Yeah, she thought again. They had to have some connections to have such quick access to this type of sophisticated listening device.

"So," she regarded the device skeptically, "it's a real wire. I always thought that was just a term."

"Works on radio waves," Doc went on, showing her the receiver they would use to pick up the radio emissions and track her. "As long as we stay within a couple of miles, we can hear everything you say, everything anyone within three yards of you says."

"Can I hear you?"

Sam shook his head. "Doesn't work that way. If we could, we'd fit you with an earpiece but it would be too risky. They'd spot it right away."

"What's going to stop Nader's man from finding this?" she asked as Coulter handed her the device. She read enough thrillers and mysteries to know there was technology to sweep for wires.

"The same thing that's going to stop him from detecting this." He pulled out a square chip—maybe twice the size of a regular postage stamp. "GPS transmitter."

Even Sam looked surprised by the small size. "Nate must have sprung big bucks for that little piece of work."

"Brand-new out of the U.K. Smallest GPS tracking device in the world. Company that produced it asked Nate to test-drive it."

"Test-drive?" Abbie didn't like the sound of this. "This is an experiment?"

"No worries," Doc assured her with a smile. "We used it in the field last week. Worked like a charm."

"So where's the antenna?" Sam asked, examining the chip.

"Internal." Doc turned back to Abbie. "I want you to slip it in your shoe, fit it beneath the foot liner, right under your arch. Less pressure there."

Abbie nodded.

"We'll track you every step of the way, okay? And we can operate both the wire and the GPS with remote switches," Doc explained. "Once you meet up with Nader's man, we'll switch both off, give him time to do his sweep, and then switch it back on when we either have visual confirmation that you're on the move or when a safe amount of time has passed. From then on, it's a question of hanging back until you lead us to Nader."

Not for the first time since she made the decision to put her life on the line, Abbie battled back an ominous feeling of dread. She was really going to do this. She was going to set herself up for God only knew what could happen to her.

"Then what?" She had to concentrate to keep her voice from shaking.

"Then you trust us to know what we're doing." Sam's voice was heavy with conviction. "We'll get you out of there."

Trust. There was that word again. She needed to trust Sam Lang. Like she'd trusted him once before. Look where that had gotten her.

Sam must have read her mind. "You can back out any time, you know. Just say the word."

She met Sam's dark brown eyes. Understood that he didn't want her here. "I'm not backing out."

He held her gaze for a long moment, finally nodded. "Nader's patience is going to be shot," he went on, accepting that she meant what she said. "He'll expect you to give him the information he wants. You're going to do it. No resistance. No hesitation. No heroics, you understand? You straight-out tell him where you hid the diamonds."

"Isn't that the same as signing my own death warrant?"

Doc shook his head. "He's not going to kill the golden goose until he's satisfied he knows where you hid the twenty-four-karat eggs, okay? As long as you hold potential value to him, you stay alive. He knows that if he kills you before he has those diamonds in his hot, thieving fist and it turns out you lied to him, then he's back to square one."

"Just like he knows that if he kills Cory before he gets the diamonds back," Savage interjected, apparently anticipating her next question, "he loses your cooperation."

"Look," Sam said, drawing her attention back to him, "we're going to take him down long before he has a chance to find out one way or another."

"How, exactly, are you going to make that happen?"

"Because it's what we do," Sam said with an assurance that left no room for doubt. "We make things happen."

Yeah, Abbie thought. They made things happen. A few days ago, she was taking classes and dealing blackjack. Life was simple, predictable, and boring. Now she was flying blind toward an international terrorist on a mission to save her brother. It was like playing a role in a video game.

"You can take that restroom break now," Sam said. "And you'd better hurry."

She looked from Sam to the devices, nodded. Then she stood, surprised when her legs were steady, and headed for the women's toilet.

A thread-thin piece of wire and a postage stamp were going to be her first and only lines of defense if something went wrong.

If something went wrong? God. That was pretty much a given.

Something else became abundantly clear to Abbie as she locked herself in a bathroom stall, slipped out of her shirt and bra, and began the process of threading the wire into her bra strap.

No matter how she felt about Sam Lang, no matter that he'd used her, lied to her, she had to let it all go. Her life, Cory's life, now depended on this man and his "associates" for lack of a better word.

The only thing that mattered was finding Cory and getting them both out of Honduras alive.

La Mesa International Airport
San Pedro Sula, Honduras

"She'll be fine," Doc assured Sam at 10:04 p.m. as they watched Abbie walk off the plane alone in San Pedro Sula. "She's smart. She'll keep her head about her."

Sam breathed deep, gripped his seat's leather armrests, and fought to control an inexplicable surge of panic as Abbie walked through the exit and out of sight.

With nothing but a backpack for self-defense.

Yeah, they'd gone over the plan, such as it was. Over and over and over it. She was to take no chances. Do exactly as they'd told her. Count on them to know how and when to strike. She knew the drill.

Yet he couldn't begin to count the bad feelings he had about this.

He couldn't explain it but somewhere along the line he'd gone from not believing in her innocence, to wanting to believe. Then he'd crossed the final line.

He believed her.

And son of a bitch, if he still didn't want her.

He flew out of the seat, ignored Savage and Doc's startled looks, and bolted after her. He caught up with her just before she left the jetway tunnel.

She spun around like she'd been shot when he snagged her arm. When she realized it was him she sagged against the tunnel wall, found her breath. "You scared me half to death."

"I've changed my mind. You're not doing this."

Confusion furrowed her brows. "What are you talking about? We're here. Nader's waiting."

He cupped her shoulders with both hands. "It's too risky."

After she got over the shock of him touching her, she made a sound of disbelief. "Yeah. I got that part. In spades. But it's been risky from the get-go. So I don't . . . I don't understand." She searched his face, thoroughly baffled. "What's this about? Why do you all of a sudden care about the risk to me? As far as you're concerned, I'm a liar and a thie—"

"Goddammit," he swore. "I was wrong, okay?"

She blinked up at him, startled into silence.

"I was wrong," he repeated, more in control now that he'd quit fighting what his gut had been telling him all along: She was clean. "I made a mistake about you. I'm not going to compound it by letting you anywhere near that murdering bastard."

Her eyes were liquid and wary but bafflement slowly transitioned to something softer. Not trust. She wasn't nearly ready to take that leap.

"Why the change of heart?"

Yeah. That was the million-dollar question all right. One Sam couldn't answer for either of them. "Pick a reason. Doesn't matter. Bottom line, I can't let you do this."

She stared at him for all of a heartbeat. Firmly shook her head. "He's my brother. I can't *not* do this."

It all came back to Sam then. His father's face. Beaten, defeated. His father's voice when he'd begged him to go after Nader.

"You can't not do this."

"Just do what you said you would do." Her quiet conviction sealed both of their fates. "Just get there in time."

Sam forced himself to let go of her shoulders, still fighting the urge to drag her back onto the plane to safety. But he understood that he'd already lost this battle. Understood because he'd fought this particular fight himself.

Her eyes were dark and searching when he lifted his hand to her cheek, involuntarily drawn to her mouth. He leaned in. Pressed his forehead to hers.

Her fingers wrapped around his wrist. Clung. "Just get there in time," she repeated on a whisper.

"Count on it."

Then he kissed her.

Hard and fierce. As much claim as desperation. Without a single thought of control.

When he pulled back, her gaze was locked on his. Startled. Stunned. Seeking.

"Be careful," he said, hearing the gruffness in his voice. "Be goddamn careful."

She swallowed. Nodded. Eyes full of a heartbreaking mix of determination, apprehension, and good-bye.

Then she turned and disappeared into the terminal.

Abbie's heart was revved to triple time as she turned her back on Sam and walked away.

She was scared.

She was anxious.

But above it all, she was shaken.

"*I was wrong about you.*"

Too little. Too late. That's what she should have said. *Too late, too late, too late*.

Damn him.

Damn him for kissing her.

Damn him for looking at her like . . . like he'd looked at her that night in her bed.

And damn her own stupid hide for wanting to believe him—again.

She drew a bracing breath. Shook it off. Got her bearings in the busy terminal. This wasn't about her or Sam. This was about Cory. She had to keep her head if—

Oh, God.

She stopped short when she saw a hand-lettered sign with her name on it, held above the crowd by a meaty hand.

This was it. The point of no return.

Then she prayed for strength when she recognized the man holding it.

Nader hadn't just sent a driver. He'd sent Rutger Smith.

Abbie's knees went weak with fear. She fought through a wave of revulsion and shot right on to rage. Every cell in her body shifted from prey to predator mode.

This was the animal who had brutalized her brother. Even more than she feared him, she wanted to make him pay for what he'd done. First, though, she had to get to Cory. The only way that was going to happen was if she kept her head and kept right on walking.

He hadn't seen her yet. The terminal was full of travelers even at ten o'clock on this Central American night where outside heat and humidity seeped into the poorly air-conditioned building. She looked toward the floor, spoke softly. "I spotted my driver," she informed Doc, knowing he and Sam would be listening on the receiver.

Also knowing that if she told Sam it was Smith who Nader had sent to pick her up, he'd come charging into the terminal and drag her away.

She made sure that didn't happen.

"Stay close, okay? Just . . . stay close."

Fight or flight. She'd read about the gut-jarring instinct. Had never experienced it firsthand. But when her gaze connected with Rutger Smith's, it took everything in her to keep moving forward.

His picture hadn't lied. His eyes, when they locked in on her, were devoid of anything vaguely resembling humanity.

"I'm Abbie Hughes," she said, stopping a good three feet away from him.

Smith swept her with a look so cold and remote, she felt a chill in spite of the warm, tropical night. "My employer is expecting you. I have a car waiting."

"My brother," she said, when he turned to lead her out of the terminal. "I need to know about my brother. Where is he? *How* is he?"

Smith stopped. His soulless black eyes bore into hers. "You would be well-advised to simply accompany me. I'm to provide transportation, not answers. You'll have those soon enough."

"I need to talk to him," she persisted as Sam had instructed her. She wasn't to go anywhere until she had proof that Cory was alive. "I'm not setting foot outside this terminal until I know he's alive."

Smith regarded her with impatient disdain, the first sign that he even possessed an emotion. Abbie knew she had him over a barrel. Without her cooperation, Nader didn't get his diamonds. And as long as they remained inside the terminal, she was safe. He couldn't risk making a scene by trying to drag her away.

Without another word, he pulled a cell phone out of his suit pants pocket.

"*Ponga el gringo,*" he said after a long moment. Then he handed her the phone.

Heart hammering, she gripped it with both hands. "Cory?"

Silence. Then a hesitant and weak, "Abbie?"

Tears stung her eyes. "Cory. Baby. Yeah. It's me. It's Abbie."

She heard a shuffling sound. "Don't . . . don't come here."

"Cory—"

Smith jerked the phone out of her hands. "Satisfied?"

No, she wasn't satisfied. But at least she knew that her brother was still alive. Alive and hurt and scared. Scared like that little boy who used to hide in the closet.

Smith turned and headed for the exit.

Shaking with relief and rage and fear for Cory, Abbie resettled her backpack and, because she had no choice, followed.

Like a lamb, she couldn't help thinking as they headed for the exit doors, *being led to the slaughter.*

14

"She's shaken," Sam said, listening with Doc and Savage to Abbie's voice through the receiver.

"She's fine." Savage stared at him hard.

Doc just cocked a brow.

Sam knew they'd heard the whole conversation between Abbie and Nader's driver through the chatter and bustle of the busy terminal. Just like he knew they'd heard the conversation between Sam and Abbie in the jetway.

Neither Doc nor Savage had said anything. Sam figured they were thinking plenty. He knew what they called him. The quiet man. The ice man. Cool under fire. Professional to a fault. They'd never seen him react with anything other than emotionless efficiency. So they were either too shocked by his reaction to Abbie or too worried about how or *if* his feelings would affect the op to comment.

How he felt wasn't going to affect anything. He wasn't going to let it.

The minute Abbie had cleared the jetway, the three of them were on the move. They grabbed their go bags from the overhead compartments and sprinted off the plane. Once in the terminal, they headed in the opposite direction of the passenger pickup area. Sam couldn't take the chance of being spotted by Nader's man. He'd crossed paths with too many of Nader's henchmen before—and not over tea and crumpets.

"Ring Mendoza," Sam said, anxious to connect with him and get in position to tail Abbie.

"He's waiting in short-term parking," Savage said after a brief conversation. "Older-model SUV. Gray. Local plates."

Mendoza knew his stuff. They needed to blend in, not stand out, and a big-ass new suburban would stick out like a tux at a biker bar.

"Anything happening?" Sam asked Doc as they backtracked toward the exit.

Doc was monitoring Abbie through a headset now. He shook his head. "Traffic sounds. They're outside. Not a lot of chitchat. Wait." He stopped. Held up a hand. Then quickly switched off the tracker.

"He just asked her to hold her arms out to her side."

Which meant he was sweeping her for a wire. Probably also meant he was patting her down. Sam clenched his jaw, forced himself not to think about the bastard touching her. Or the fact that for now, they couldn't monitor her conversation. She was on her own.

Eyes dead ahead, he walked across the parking lot, searching for Mendoza. Raphael spotted them first. He stood in the open driver's door of a dinged and dented monolith of an SUV that looked like it had been through a war.

Mendoza, as always, looked like he'd just stepped out of a photo shoot. His thick dark hair was cropped military short. His black eyes—a product of his Colombian heritage just like his caramel skin—shone clear and intelligent under the security light. He was ripped and ready. Not as big as, say, Gabe Jones or even Sam, but pound for pound, Raphael "Choirboy" Mendoza was one of the toughest fighters Sam had ever seen in action.

"Nice ride," Doc said with a grin as they reached Mendoza.

"Kind of like you, Holliday." Mendoza grinned back. "Not much to look at but good in a fight."

"How's it going?" He turned to Sam, extended his hand in welcome.

Sam gripped his hand hard. "Thanks for signing on."

"Hey. We're still a team. Always will be." Mendoza's smile faded. "I'm sorry," he said simply.

It was the first time Sam had seen Raphael since Terri's death.

Sam nodded.

"We'll get the bastard," Mendoza added and when the moment became too intense, changed the subject by stating the obvious. "No Reed?"

"Not this trip," Sam said. "Needed someone back on the home front."

Sam hadn't been completely straight with Abbie about Reed's activities back in Vegas. For the most part, Reed was tailing Abbie's friend, Crystal Debrowski, hoping to get a lead on where she'd stowed the diamonds. He needed Reed in place in the event Nader sent one of his flunkies after the necklace. And he was there as backup for Sam's dad. If Nader sent anyone after his family, they'd have to get past Reed first.

"You're going to need these." Mendoza handed out cell phones all around after the four of them had piled into the SUV. Sam rode shotgun; Savage and Doc settled into the backseat. "Already programmed with each other's numbers."

"What other toys did you bring us?" Savage asked, pocketing his phone.

Mendoza's smile was quick and easy. "All your favorites plus a couple surprises."

Which meant that Raphael had acquired a Kimber Tactical Pro 1911 A1 pistol for Sam as well as an H&K MP-5K. He suspected there was also an M-16 rifle or two in the mix. As far as the surprises, Mendoza knew how to plan for an assault and there wasn't a man in the vehicle who doubted it would come down to that.

Sam was taking no chances this time. And he was taking no prisoners.

El Nuevo Porvenir, twenty kilometers north of
Peña Blanca, Honduras

A slow smile spread across Desmond Fox's face as he hung up the phone and settled back, naked on the bed.

It was perfect. Perfect irony. Perfect execution. Nader would never know what hit him because Nader had no idea that Desmond was aware of his Peña Blanca estancia. Likewise, the bastard German had no idea that one of Desmond's own men had infiltrated Nader's little detail holding guard over the man—Nader's unfortunate mule—who held the key to retrieving the Tupacka diamonds.

Mules and moles. Desmond liked the play on words, liked that there were animals among men, doing the dirty work. The thought made him laugh. As did the massacre his men would soon carry out at Peña Blanca.

"I know that laugh, *mi amore*." Juanita of the dark hair and lush breasts rose to all fours over him. Her naked body straddled his, her caramel skin and delicious curves willing and warm and wanting to please.

Beautiful. She was but twenty and already so wise. And so deliciously wanton. Of course, Desmond had schooled her well. At fifty, he knew exactly how to instruct a woman to pleasure him. He touched a hand affectionately to her long hair, then gripped it in his hand. With a slow twist, he dragged her close until her mouth hovered over his. Her breath, scented of sangria and sex, melded with his.

"What is it that you think you know about my laugh?" he asked, guiding her head down toward the pulsing erection jutting against his belly.

"It means someone is going to die," she purred, brushing her lips across the head of his cock, tantalizing, teasing, licking.

"One of the things I so love about you, pretty cat, is that you are as ruthless and bloodthirsty as I am."

"*One* of the things?" Her smile was coquettish and coy as she squeezed her generous breasts together, imprisoning his cock between them.

"One of many," he replied tenderly and gentled his hold on her hair. "Carry on, my darling."

Then he lay back, let Juanita work her magic, and rode the wave of her expert brand of pleasure.

Later, when she lay sleeping, her skillful hand pressed against his chest, her head resting on his shoulder, he congratulated himself on both his choice in women and his cunning.

He reached for a cigarette, flicked open his diamond-studded lighter, and drew deep on the first robust puff. Smoke drifted in the darkened bedroom. He let it soothe him. Retribution was near.

Nader had made a mistake when he'd crossed into Honduras uninvited.

The pompous German was in Fox territory now. Central America was his. Honduras was his native country, and he called the shots in this part of the world. Nothing got past his radar or his network.

Which was why, at this moment, his men were about to pay Nader's estancia a little visit.

Nader's infringement would not be tolerated, something Nader would soon understand. Just like he would understand how Desmond Fox dealt with those who destroyed what was his. Juan Montoya, one of his best soldiers, was dead. Dead because Rutger Smith had intercepted him before he'd made the meet to procure the Tupacka diamonds from Nader's runaway mule.

Smith had sliced Montoya from gut to gullet. Left him to bleed out in a squalid back alley, where his body hadn't been found until several days later.

No. Montoya's murder would not go unpunished.

And Fox would see to it that Nader would never see the Tupacka diamonds, let alone own them. He may be a thief and much more, but he was also a patriot. The Tupacka diamonds belonged to Honduras, not to Nader.

His eyes on the ground had told him about the arrival of the American woman, the sister of Nader's mule, and Desmond's ticket to retrieving the necklace.

Nader had sent Smith himself to deliver her from the airport to Peña Blanca. Smith was a bonus Desmond had not expected. If all went as planned, when Smith returned to Nader, it would be in pieces.

He glanced at his Rolex. Phase one should be well under way.

Adrenaline. The wonder drug. Someone ought to figure out how to package it in pill form, Abbie thought as she sat quietly in the backseat of a black Lincoln Town Car with Rutger Smith at the wheel.

He hadn't said a word since she'd climbed into the car and shut out the exhaust fumes that clogged the parking lot in thick sultry waves. Only the whine of the tires on the highway and a light rain that had turned into a downpour the farther they traveled broke the silence.

Despite the fact that she hadn't had any real sleep in over twenty-four hours, she was wired. Desperation. Anticipation. Fear. All fueled the restless energy that hummed through her body while the Lincoln sped through the city that was full of activity even at this time of night.

While still in the city they'd passed a donkey-pulled cart, dozens of broken-down vehicles, and been passed by tiny white compact cabs squashed full of people. If Abbie had been in a laughing mood, the American fast-food places dotting the roadway lit by streetlights would have made her smile. Pizza seemed to be very popular.

Doc had been right to be prepared for Nader's man to search for a wire. He'd scanned her body with some kind of a sweeping device—after he'd completed a humiliating but all-business physical pat-down.

Her skin still crawled at the memory.

That was over two long hours ago, before they'd headed out of the city on Highway 71.

She wanted this over. She'd also reached her limit of silent forbearance. "How much farther?"

She asked as much for herself as for Sam and his men. At least she was counting on them still listening and still being with her.

Hell, she was more than counting on it. She was betting her life on it.

"She just asked him how much farther," Doc said, relaying Abbie's latest and only voice transmission since they'd reactivated the GPS and wire two long fucking hours ago.

Sam glanced sharply toward Doc in the backseat and let out a breath of relief, the first one that hadn't felt like it had been jammed in his lungs for half a century. "And?"

Doc shook his head. "So far, no response."

Sam turned back to the squeak and slash of worn wipers that fought a losing battle with the deluge of warm, tropical rain pummeling the windshield. Breathing. The rustle of clothes. That's all Doc had heard during the entire trip. They'd been literally and figuratively in the dark. Not knowing if Abbie was drugged, hurt, or worse. Every cell in Sam's body had wanted to tell Mendoza to step on the gas, overtake the damn vehicle, and see what the hell was going on.

But he'd made himself hold it together. Barely.

It didn't help that he'd decided early on that he knew where they were headed. At least, based on the route the driver was taking, he had a pretty good idea.

"They should have just passed La Entrada," Sam said after flipping on the interior light and consulting the map he'd been using to do his own tracking. "They should be turning off the highway soon."

"Just did," Savage confirmed, monitoring the GPS. "Heading north. Dirt road, according to the markings. You were right. Looks like he's taking her to Nader's estancia at Peña Blanca."

There was little Sam didn't know about Nader's activities or holdings. "We're looking at less than ten clicks from the start of the side road. Cut the lights at two, okay?"

Mendoza stopped the soft singing that had earned him the handle Choirboy and grunted. "I live to fly blind."

Sam had filled the BOIs in on the setup on the drive so they all knew what they faced. The main buildings of Nader's estancia consisted of a small adobe ranch house and a gardener's shed. Nader spent little time here. The accommodations were Spartan, near rustic—too crude, Sam suspected, for Nader to tolerate for any length of time. The location, however, was ideal as a spot to say, hide something or someone you didn't want found. It was out of the way and remote. The estancia also butted up against a particularly steep slope of the Montaña de la Crita range that provided protection from the north. A lookout could easily spot an approach from the south.

The SUV rocked as Mendoza, following the Lincoln, turned onto the rutted dirt road and hit mud.

"They stopped," Doc said, listening intently while the rain pummeled the SUV's roof and the motor revved and whined along the slime-slick road. He held up a hand, concentrated on hearing.

"Switch to speaker." Sam willed the SUV to move faster as Mendoza herded it over the rough, slippery road. The SUV's wheels slid into deep ruts, threatening to hang up the undercarriage as Mendoza skillfully maneuvered through the mess.

"What's happening?" Abbie asked, her voice sounding reedy and a little thin.

"You wanted to see your brother? You're going to see your brother," Smith said. "Now get out of the car."

"No," she said staunchly. "You bring Cory to me."

Silence.

Sam held his breath, waited for Smith's reaction.

"Look, bitch," the driver snarled, impatience and anger heavy in his voice. "You don't call the shots. You do as I say. And you remember, the only reason you and your gutless brother are still breathing is because my employer needs information from you. You want your brother? You tell me where the diamonds are."

"So you can kill us as soon as I tell you? No. It's not going to happen that way," she said, her voice stronger now as she faced the man with a reckless defiance that drove Sam crazy. "What's going to happen is that you're going to get Cory, bring him to the car, then you're going to drive us back to the airport. I'm not telling you the location of the diamonds until then."

Goddammit, Abbie, Sam swore under his breath. He'd asked her to trust them. To go along with whatever they asked her to do and know that they had her back.

The driver had apparently had enough.

A car door opened, then slammed.

He heard Abbie's sharp intake of breath, heard her scramble, punching locks.

He closed his eyes when the sound of glass shattering cracked over the wire.

"Fuck," Doc whispered. "Sounds like he slammed his fist through the window."

They heard the *snick* of a car door being wrenched open.

"Out," the driver ordered.

More silence. Then the sounds of a struggle.

"Now walk," the driver demanded. Savage turned back to the cargo area and started digging weapons out from under a tarp.

Sam heard a grunt of sound.

Abbie cried out.

The bastard had hit her.

Sam heard her hit the ground.

He was dead, Sam vowed. Whoever he was, he was a dead man.

"Get up."

Another cry and Sam could picture the bastard dragging her to her feet.

"Walk," he ordered again.

There was no more talk then. Just the sound of Abbie, breathing hard. Rain in the trees. Soles crunching on the ground. They were walking uphill, Sam realized as her breath grew more labored.

"Can you fucking step on it?" he growled at Mendoza as Doc and Savage fixed full clips into their rifles.

Sam accepted the Kimber Savage handed him along with a Glock for Mendoza. The rifles came next, along with two M-16's and four extra thirty-shot magazines for each of them. The Kevlar vests followed. Like Sam and Mendoza, who herded the SUV down the treacherous road like a Formula One driver, they had their game faces on.

"Come on, Abbie," Doc muttered as he eased into his own vest, then Velcroed it shut. "Tell us what's going on."

The driver's voice came over the wire instead. "Wait here," he ordered Abbie, his voice gruff and scratchy as it vibrated over the speaker. "You run, your brother dies, got it?"

Several long, pulsing seconds passed as Sam waited, and waited.

"He's . . . he's about twenty yards ahead of me now," Abbie finally whispered, trying to keep Nader's driver from hearing her.

"It's Smith," she added, her voice sounding strained. "The driver is Rutger Smith," she repeated with emphasis.

All four men swore. Sam clenched his jaw, cursed again at both Abbie's stupidity and her bravery. She should have let them know right out of the block that Smith had her. Sam would have dragged her out of there before she'd ever left the airport terminal.

She'd known it, too. She'd intentionally kept Sam in the dark to keep him from doing just that.

"It's so dark," she whispered. "He's using a flashlight. Calling out names.

"No one's answering him," she went on, her voice suddenly rife with anxiety. "Something's . . . something's wrong. I'm going up there."

"Jesus, no!" Sam shouted, knowing she couldn't hear him and that she wouldn't listen to him if she could.

Her breath puffed out in harsh, hard pants as she ran up the hillside.

"Oh, God." She sounded frantic now. A high-pitched exclamation of pain. A helpless cry. "Oh, God, oh Jesus God."

Then she screamed. And screamed. And screamed until the roaring in Sam's ears and the growl of the SUV's engine and the pounding rain drowned out everything but the need to get to her.

15

Soaking wet, Abbie stumbled up the hillside in the dark after Smith, zeroing in on the beam of his flashlight. She'd come within ten yards of him when he stopped, disappeared inside the black hole of an open door of a small shed. She stopped, too. Between the rain and the pitch-dark forest, she couldn't see three feet in front of her.

Breathing hard, she waited, jumped when she heard a sharp snap, like the sound of a switch being flipped. The hillside was flooded with light, illuminating a scene straight out of a horror movie.

"Oh, God." She sucked in her breath, heard a sound, more animal than human, realized she had made it. She couldn't stop herself from crying. "Oh, God, oh Jesus God."

Blood. Oh, God, the blood.

Bodies everywhere.

And then she screamed. And kept on screaming, incapable of taking her eyes off the blood and gore.

"Shut up!" Smith growled as he stepped out of the building. He strode over to her, slapped her hard.

Her head snapped back from the force of the blow. She stumbled, fell. Landed on top of something soft and warm and wet. A body.

Still warm. Still warm. The body was still warm.

Horrified, she scrambled away, her hands slick with blood and rain and mud. She pushed to her feet on shaking legs, reeled when her own blood rushed south. She steadied herself, was peripherally aware of the sting on her check where Smith had hit her. Of her head throbbing from the blow. Of her sodden hair hanging heavy and dripping in her face.

Her full focus was riveted in morbid fascination on the bullet-riddled bodies lying where they'd fallen in the mud and the wet grass.

It was a bloodbath.

A massacre.

They'd been running.

Trying to get away.

She touched a trembling hand to her mouth. Felt the stickiness of blood and mud and gagged. Her stomach rumbled, revolted. She fell to her knees, retched violently, then watched, recovering her breath as Smith wedged a foot under the chest of a man who lay facedown in the grass; the back of his head was shot off.

Recognition crossed his face before he moved on to the next body, his expression growing darker and more furious with each man he found as rain soaked his suit, plastering it to his big, bulky body.

"Cory." Her brain finally engaged beyond the horror. She shot to her feet, reeled again from light-headedness, steadied herself until her balance returned. Oh, God. She had to find him. "Cory!"

Battling revulsion and terror and nausea, she started searching for her brother.

She fell to her knees, was gathering the nerve to turn over a body when she heard Smith speak in Spanish. "¿Quién hizo esto?"

She spun around, confused. Thought he was talking to her. But he was kneeling over a body. And then that body moved. She scrambled over beside them.

"¿Quién hizo esto?" Smith repeated urgently. Rain dripped off his head into the downed man's face.

Abbie's Spanish was rusty but she understood the question. He wanted to know who had done this.

"*Zorro*," the dying man wheezed through a gurgling breath. "*Zorro . . .
sus hombres. Em . . . emboscada.*"

Zorro. *Fox?* She couldn't have heard him right. He was delirious. But
then it hit her what he was trying to say. Not *a* fox but someone *named* Fox.
Fox's men had ambushed them, he said.

"*¿Dónde está la mula?*" Smith snarled. "*¿Dónde está Hughes?*"

Where's the mule? Where is Hughes?

Abbie's pulse spiked. She held her breath and waited.

The injured man lifted a bloody hand, gripped Smith's shirt.
"*Ayúdeme.*"

Help me.

Smith shoved the hand away, jerked the injured man up by his shirtfront.
"*¿Dónde está Hughes?*"

The man gasped, convulsed, then went limp.

Smith swore, looked beyond her, then grabbed her roughly by the hair.
"You bitch! You were told to come alone."

Abbie cried out in pain as he jerked her with him and shot to his feet.
He dragged her tightly against him, his beefy forearm wrapped about her
throat, choking her.

The prick of a knife bit painfully against her ribs. His belt buckle bruised
where it pressed against her back.

She gasped for breath, smelled wet wool and blood and death as she
frantically dug her fingers into his forearm desperate to loosen his hold. Her
head spun. Her ears rang. She saw a man materialize out of the veil of rain
and shadows. Wondered if she was hallucinating.

"Let her go, Smith."

It was Savage. Carrying a rifle. Doc and Mendoza stepped to his side,
both heavily armed. Which meant that Sam wasn't far behind.

Thank you, God.

Her relief was short-lived. Smith shifted, replaced his forearm with his
knife. The cold, cutting steel of it danced against her throat.

"Back off," he demanded in a voice so wintry it made her shiver in her
warm, wet clothes, "or she dies."

• • •

Sam crept through the forest. Silent, surefooted, even on the slick forest floor, he kept the pool of light flooding the area around the shack in his sights, worked his way quickly uphill toward Abbie.

Rain ran down his face, soaked his clothes. Mud clung to his boots, would have bogged him down if he hadn't been so single-mindedly focused on getting into position. The M-16 he carried wasn't a sniper rifle. But then the shot he planned to take didn't require accuracy at 2,000 yards. Thirty ought to do it.

The air was so thick and wet it felt like he was drowning in it as he drew closer, darting from tree to tree, finally spotting Smith in the relative open.

Open except for Abbie.

The animal had her. Was using her as a shield as Savage and the boys approached, stopped, waited for Smith to make the next move.

That's right, boys. Nice and easy.

Eyes on the prize, Sam shut out the rain. Shut out the splayed bodies littering the soaked ground. Shut out his own breathing. Shut out the terror and the blood smeared across Abbie's face.

He slowly lowered the rifle sling off his shoulder, dropped to his knees. He steadied the barrel against a solid tree trunk, wrapping the sling around his arm to help stabilize the rifle. Peered through the night vision scope.

Water from his sprint through the woods blurred the sights on the telescopic lens. Heart racing with adrenaline, he forced himself to quickly, carefully, tug the hem of his T-shirt out from under his vest and meticulously dry the lens.

Then he settled in again, positioned the butt of the stock against his shoulder, sited down the barrel. Honed in on his target.

Same drill.

The rain didn't exist.

The bodies didn't exist.

Abbie's life didn't hang in the balance.

Only the shot mattered.

He was one with his breath.

One with his craft.

Inhale.

Exhale. Squeeze.

Absorb the shock of the recoil.

Before he even heard the crack of rifle fire, or Abbie's scream, he saw Smith's head explode and blood and brain matter splatter and spread across the side of her face.

Savage and Doc were sprinting toward her before Smith's big body collapsed and Abbie fell forward. She landed on all fours, head hanging between her stiff arms.

Mendoza ran straight for Smith, rifle pointed at his head, taking no chances that the murdering bastard was no longer a threat.

Sam lowered his rifle, breathed deep. Only then did he let himself think about what could have happened if he'd missed. If he'd fired a hair to the left.

Abbie would be dead now, not Smith.

He walked out of the trees. Straight to her side. He handed his rifle to Savage and dropped to one knee beside her.

"You're okay," he said softly.

"Abbie." He lifted the hair away from her face when she didn't respond. "Smith is dead."

Finally, she moved. A slow, slight nod of acknowledgment, telling him she was still with him.

Then she started shaking.

Fuck it.

He drew her into his arms. Touched his hand to the blood and the mud and the gore covering her. And held her while she fell apart.

"Without stitches you're gonna have a helluva scar," Sam heard Doc tell Abbie as he walked back to the gardener's shed where they'd moved her under an eave and out of the rain. "Sorry, but we're going to have to make do with butterflies."

Under the glow of Doc's Maglite, Sam inspected the long narrow gash running from Abbie's shoulder to mid upper arm. Smith's knife had sliced her good when he'd fallen. It looked rough, yet Sam was relieved the blade had missed anything vital. Doubly so when Doc assured him that most of the blood staining her clothes wasn't hers.

"I'm just going to clean it up now, okay? The dressing will have to wait until we get back to the SUV and my medic kit."

Which was going to have to be soon. The rain had let up but they needed to head back or what was left of the road would wash out and they'd be stuck here.

Stuck with a dozen bullet-riddled bodies and no Cory Hughes.

"No," Sam said when Abbie looked up, her eyes questioning. "He's not here."

Sam had searched. So that was the good news; Cory Hughes wasn't among the dead. Unless Mendoza and Savage, who had widened the search around the perimeter of the ambush turned up something, the bad news was, Cory Hughes wasn't anywhere.

"Do you think he ever was here?" Abbie bit back a wince when Doc dabbed an alcohol pad to her arm.

"Sorry." Doc eased up. "It's gonna bite but we need to stall any threat of infection in this humidity."

"It's okay." She looked to Sam for an answer to her question.

Tough, Sam thought. She was much tougher than she looked. Much tougher than the woman who had come unhinged in his arms just five minutes ago.

She'd had plenty of reason to fall apart. Smith had slapped her around. The corner of her mouth was cut and swollen; her cheek was already starting to bruise. She'd stumbled into a bloody massacre, hadn't known if her brother was among the dead, and Smith had held a knife to her throat.

So yeah, she'd had a moment. But not for long. She was quiet but she was solid again. At least she was working her damnedest to get there.

"Someone was being held hostage here," Sam said. The gardener's shed was full of signs that he didn't need to share with Abbie.

"So . . . whoever did this . . . you think they took him?"

"It's looking that way." Sam squatted down in front of her. "Abbie . . . the rain garbled some of your conversation with Smith so we couldn't hear it all. Did he say anything? Anything that told you he might have a clue who had done this?"

"Actually, there was something," she said as if the memory had just come to her. "A man . . . one of the men . . . he was still alive. Smith asked him who had done this. He said the name Fox. That Fox's *men* had ambushed them."

Doc's face was grim when he glanced at Sam. "Had to figure he'd show up in the mix."

Abbie's eyes cut between Doc's and Sam's. "You know who Fox is?"

"Yeah." Sam nodded. "We know him. He and Nader swim in the same cesspool."

"They work together?"

"Not quite. Desmond Fox and Fredrick Nader hate each other's guts. Fox has been pissed ever since Nader got a toehold in the Central American arms trade a few years ago. Honduras is Fox's home turf. He considers Nader a squatter and a threat."

"What do you want to bet Fox knows about the necklace?" Doc suggested after a moment.

"More like Fox *wants* the necklace because he knows it would piss off Nader," Sam amended after he'd thought it through. "That's gotta be what this was about. The question is, how did he know about Cory?"

"I've got a live one over here!" Mendoza's shout came from behind the shed.

"Hold this." Doc pressed Abbie's hand over the gauze on her arm and headed toward the sound of Mendoza's voice.

Abbie started to rise.

"No." Sam stopped her with a hand on her shoulder. "You don't need to see this."

He could see in her eyes that she wanted to argue, but in the end, she sagged back down on the step. "For once, I'm not going to fight with you."

"First time for everything," he said and got the smile he'd hoped for. Not much of a smile but enough for him to know she was holding up.

"Yeah, well. Don't get used to it."

"Wouldn't dream of it," he said and started walking away.

"Sam."

Her voice stopped him. He turned.

She was looking at him, her poor bruised face tragically sad. "Thanks. Thanks for . . . well. Just thanks."

He knew exactly what she was thanking him for.

"Like I said. It's what I do. And you're welcome."

"Who do you work for?"

They all spoke Spanish but since Mendoza knew the local dialect, he did the questioning as the four of them huddled over the wounded man.

Savage shined his Maglite on the man's chest so Doc could work on him. Blood gurgled from several holes. Automatic-weapons fire. It was a wonder the mercenary was still alive, and Sam had no doubt that it was hired muscle they were dealing with.

"*Por favor. Por favor. ¡Me tiene que ayudar!*"

Sam glanced at Doc, who shook his head, telling Sam there wasn't enough help in the world to save this man. He was dying. He just didn't know it yet.

"Tell him we'll help. But we need information first. Ask him again who he works for."

"*¿Para quién trabaja?*"

The man gasped in pain. "Fox. Desmond Fox."

"Bingo," Savage said as Doc worked futilely to staunch the blood flow.

Although he could pretty much guess, Sam had Mendoza ask anyway. "Find out what happened here."

"*¿Qué pasó aquí?*"

"*Fueron mandados para . . .*" The merc stopped, wheezed, then continued, "*. . . emboscar a los hombres . . . de Nader y capturar . . . el americano.*"

"Apparently Fox sent men to capture Hughes and kill Nader's men."

"So Fox knew Hughes was here." Savage's conclusion prompted Mendoza to ask how Fox knew where Nader was holding Hughes captive.

"*¿Cómo supo Fox que el americano estuvo acá?*"

The man's eyes rolled back in his head. His breathing grew more labored. "*Me . . . infiltré en la guardia . . . hace meses. Para . . . espiar. Para . . . informar.*"

Mendoza glanced up at Sam. "He says Fox sent him to infiltrate Nader's guards months ago."

"So we have us a spy," Savage concluded with a nod. "A mole by any other name is still a rat."

A bloodied hand reached up, clutched at Doc's shirt. "*Por favor . . . por favor. Me muero.*"

That needed no translation. He was begging for his life. He was also barely clinging to it.

"We need to know where Hughes is now," Sam said, suspecting they were going to lose him soon.

Mendoza posed the question.

"*Por favor . . . me va a matar si digo más,*" the dying man responded with difficulty.

"Yeah," Sam said when the man expressed fear that Fox would kill him if he talked. "Make sure he knows we'll kill him first if he doesn't tell us what we need to know and tell us now."

Now, before it was too late—not only for the merc but for Cory Hughes.

"We've gotta boogie." Sam led the pack as the four men returned to Abbie's side.

She was beyond being startled as Sam took her arm, careful of her injury, and helped her to her feet. "What happened? Was he able to tell you anything?"

A cell phone rang in the eerie silence.

"Not me," Mendoza said. "Not you guys, either. I set all the phones I gave you to vibrate."

The phone rang again.

Savage headed for Smith's body. Started checking pockets until he came up with a phone.

It rang in his hand. "What do you want to bet that's Nader wanting a report?"

"Don't answer it," Sam said. "In fact, shut it off. Let the bastard stew until we figure out what happens next."

"What did you find out?" Abbie asked again as Sam guided her down the slippery slope toward the road. The beams of four flashlights illuminated the way.

"We'll talk in the car. Right now, we need to move. Take advantage of this break in the rain."

"Wait." She put on the skids. "You're going to just . . . leave him?"

Sam kept his eyes dead ahead. Kept on walking. "He didn't make it."

She glanced at Doc, who wouldn't meet her eyes. Understood then that they didn't want her to know the details.

That was fine. The truth was, she really didn't want to know either. She just wanted to know about Cory.

She was going to have to wait until Sam was ready to tell her, though, because the pace they set took all of her concentration to keep on her feet.

Sam was a hard man. A dangerous man. They all were. My God. Just look at them. Black rifles slung over their shoulders, pistols shoved in their belts. Light beams and shadows illuminated faces as rigid as stone. Eyes as blank of emotion as the night.

Had they seen things and done things that would make most men squirm? Yeah. Of that Abbie was certain.

Where they good guys? She wanted to think so.

The only thing she knew for certain was that Rutger Smith had been a bad, bad guy. And that his blood and part of his brains still clung to her hair.

She pulled up short when a fresh wave of nausea assailed her. She fought it, lost. Finally bent over and vomited.

Sam didn't say a word. He just held the hair away from her face, waited until she was steady again, then guided her the rest of the way down the slope.

16

Off the coast of Isla de Roatán
Aboard the Seennymphe

Fredrick Nader drew deeply on his *maduro habano*, savoring the rich, robust flavor as he stared off the port bow of the *Seennymphe* at the glimmering coastline of Roatán.

His impatience reaching flash point, he dialed Smith's number again as the water lapped gently against the hull and cigar smoke mingled with the salt scent in the air.

Once again, he was sent directly to Smith's voice mail.

He snapped his phone closed.

Clutched the bow rail.

Something was wrong.

He did not deceive himself. No man could be counted on for ultimate loyalty. Still, he had never figured Rutger Smith would turn on him.

For one thing, Fredrick paid Smith too well. For another, he gave the sadistic freak generous opportunities to play, no questions asked.

Fredrick's first thought, then, was that Smith had run up against unexpected resistance that had disabled him. It was a thought he was inclined to dismiss. Smith was not only a brutal opponent, he was exceedingly competent. Fredrick could not imagine any man gaining the upper hand.

Perhaps it was merely a question of foul weather. His onboard radar had detected heavy rain in the Peña Blanca area. Cell signals were notoriously unreliable in Honduras. Applying pressure to the inept regulatory body governing cellular service was something Fredrick had been considering for a time now. He would draft an offer of monetary assistance soon. It was always advantageous to acquire favors to enrich his coffers.

He breathed deep of the salt and sea air and cigar smoke, caught the sensual notes of a distant salsa beat drifting to the *Seennymphe* from the shore. He thought of sweet Carlota, the lovely manicurist, lying naked and willing in his berth below decks.

Tomorrow he would worry about Smith. No point borrowing trouble. The man had served him well.

So had Carlota. And so she would again.

La Entrada, Honduras

Abbie watched through the rear seat window as Mendoza sprinted through the lingering drizzle, heading toward a small house on a dark side street. It seemed that Mendoza had been in this general area for a few months on the hunt for Nader before the rest of them had arrived. He'd made contact with some of the locals. Money had changed hands.

Now it appeared that bit of groundwork was going to net them a place to stay for the rest of the night. At least that was the hope.

So they waited, the SUV motor running. The air conditioner didn't work so the fan merely pushed hot, damp air through the vents, increasing the steam factor instead of decreasing it. The steam heat was still preferable to the mosquitoes that had come out in droves once the rain stopped, so they sat there with the windows up in the dark of night.

Abbie was running on fumes and adrenaline and even the adrenaline had started letting her down. It shamed her to know that they were taking this break because of her even though the mumbled consensus among the men had been that there was nothing more they could do tonight. The roads were too bad. It was too dark. The rain was due to set in again before dawn. There was nothing for them to do but try to find a place to catch a couple of hours of sleep, grab a meal, then go on the hunt for Cory.

It also shamed her that she'd let down in front of Sam. Nothing spelled weakness like tossing your cookies in front of God—and in this case, Sam Lang. Nothing spelled misery like wet muddy clothes with a generous helping of blood and brain matter thrown in for good measure.

She couldn't think about that.

She could *not* think about that.

So she thought of Raphael Mendoza instead, whom a grinning Doc had introduced her to as the Dale Earnhardt Jr. of Honduras. She gave the gorgeous Latino credit. He'd maneuvered the lumbering SUV expertly down the mud-slick road and somehow managed to keep it and them out of the ditches, singing softly all the way.

She thought back to the conversation on the drive. Savage had joined Mendoza in the front seat; Sam had sandwiched her in the back between him and Doc, who had gone right to work dressing her arm.

"Cory," she'd reminded Sam when he seemed more interested in her arm than sharing information. "Did you find anything out about Cory?"

Yeah. They'd found out plenty. She thought she had it straight now but it had taken a while to sort out Sam's comments.

"Like I said," Sam began, "Fredrick Nader and Desmond Fox are blood enemies. Apparently, Fox had been in the mix on the hunt for the stolen diamonds, only Nader cut him out of the deal when he sent Smith to intercept Cory."

She hadn't said anything but she still didn't understand how Cory had gotten mixed up in this. At this point, it didn't matter why he was involved. What mattered was finding him.

"Fox had a mole infiltrate Nader's camp," Sam had added.

"And you know this how?"

"We know this because he was the guy who survived to tell us. When he relayed information to Fox that Nader had stashed Cory at the estancia, Fox decided to snatch Cory and kill as many of Nader's men as possible in the process."

"Nothing says pissed like a massacre," Savage had added over his shoulder.

"The plan," Doc added as he'd applied antibiotic ointment to her cut, "was that one man would stay behind to intercept you, then take you to Fox and Cory."

"The man you talked to?" she'd surmised.

"Yeah," Sam said. "That man."

Who was now dead. Like so many were dead.

"He stayed behind to wait for you to take you to Fox. He hadn't planned on one of Nader's men surviving the attack. He was searching the bodies— for money, probably—and got a little surprise when one of them was still alive and shot him before he could finish him off."

"So we still don't know where Cory is."

"Actually, we do."

The driver's side door jerked open, which sent Abbie's heart racing.

It was Mendoza. "They'll take us," he said settling back behind the wheel and shifting into gear. "We can park the SUV in that shed over there."

"Best Western, Honduras style," Doc said five minutes later, after they'd hidden the SUV in the ramshackle shed and spread a tarp over it for good measure. They'd grabbed their go bags and Abbie's backpack, and trudged toward a small, rustic house. "What do you think's on Pay Per View?"

Mendoza grinned at Abbie. "We like him despite the fact that he's a cockeyed optimist."

She was too numb and exhausted to appreciate either man's warped sense of humor as she all but staggered toward the open door of the house. A dim light shone through the threshold—a candle, she realized.

"*Señorita*," an older woman greeted her politely. Her black hair was heavily threaded with gray and pulled back into a loose bun. She pointed the way toward the back of the house.

Abbie knew she was supposed to follow. But somehow she couldn't make herself move.

"It's okay," Sam said. "You take the bedroom. We'll sleep in here." He nodded toward the floor of the room that appeared to double as living area and dining area.

Abbie nodded.

And still she stood.

The guys made themselves busy claiming various areas of the worn tile floor and working very hard not to notice that she'd frozen.

"Would you rather I slept outside your door?" Sam asked, his voice gentle.

Tears filled her eyes.

"Come on." Sam took her arm. "Let's go check things out."

She moved only because he propelled her forward. On a peripheral level she almost understood what was happening to her. It was because on a real and visceral level, she kept reliving those moments when Smith had had his knife to her throat, the rifle report, the splatter of blood . . .

"Hey."

Sam's voice brought her back. She blinked. Realized they'd moved to a small room lit by a candle.

"Don't think about it," he said, looking down at her, his eyes filled with a hard, intense concern.

"How do you . . . do it?" she heard herself asking. "How do you deal with all the blood and the gore and the—"

"Don't think about it," he repeated. "That's how you deal with it."

She breathed deep. Nodded.

"What about Cory? How are we going to find him?"

"We know where he is, remember?"

Yes. She remembered. Sam had said that Fox's dying man had told them.

"Then what happens next?"

"What happens next is that you rest. We can talk about Cory's rescue in the morning."

In the morning. There would be a morning. Something she had taken for granted before she'd seen the bloodbath in the forest at Peña Blanca.

"Come on," Sam insisted again. "Let's get you cleaned up."

Don't think about it.

Don't think about it.

Easier said than done but she made herself concentrate on anything— the scuffing sound of their footsteps as they walked down the tiled floor of a short hallway; the primitive conditions of the bathroom; the promise of fresh water and soap, which finally garnered some real interest.

"Do you know how to work this?" she asked, frowning at what she hoped was a shower of sorts.

The fact that Sam knew told her even more about the man. Conjured questions about the places he'd been, the experiences he'd had. Just as quickly, though, she dismissed them.

She didn't want to know. Didn't want to know details or history or any more about Sam Lang because when this was ever over, she was never going to see him again.

"You okay now?" he asked.

Never see him again.

She breathed deep. Nodded.

Watched as he left without another word and shut the door behind him.

Don't think about it.

Less than a quarter mile beyond the small hacienda, their hostess had said, was a small stream. Not so small at the moment. It was rampant and wild and full from the recent downpour. In the dark, Sam stood hip deep in the middle of it, scrubbed away the mud and the muck and the stench of death they'd encountered at Nader's Peña Blanca estancia.

He'd bathed in worse places. Like the rest of the guys, he was just grateful he didn't have to sleep in his own stink and Honduras mud.

Just as he was thankful Señorita Garcia's bathroom offered Abbie the chance to wash away the nightmare she'd endured.

"She'll probably need that dressing changed after her shower," Doc said, when they returned to the hacienda. He started digging around in his medic kit.

"Yeah, you go in there like that," Mendoza said with a grin as he stepped into a pair of clean camo pants, "and you're likely to end up needing a little first aid of your own, Holliday."

Doc grinned, looked down at himself. "I was going to put pants on," he assured the room at large.

Savage snorted as he dried himself off with a clean T-shirt.

"I'll take care of it," Sam said, zipping up his pants. He reached for the antibiotic salve and fresh dressing. "You guys go ahead and crash."

He caught the curious looks before he turned to go. Decided not to tell them all to go fuck themselves. That he was just looking out for their ticket to Nader.

But he'd never lied to these guys. He wasn't going to start now.

So he lied to himself instead. Worked like hell to convince himself that his only reason for volunteering for corpsman duty was pragmatic.

Yeah, and the world didn't go 'round on Saudi crude.

"Come in," Abbie answered when he rapped a knuckle on her door.

On a deep breath, he opened it, stepped inside.

And felt his heart react again. The same way it reacted when he thought of Tina. Like it could melt like wax in the sun.

She was wearing a T-shirt. White. Short-sleeve. Oversized. She was sitting up, scooted to the very top corner of the small, narrow cot, her back pressed into the corner against the adobe wall. Her legs were drawn up, her arms wrapped around her shins, her forehead lowered onto her knees. Her damp hair fell forward, covering her face and part of her legs.

"That, um . . . advice you gave me," she said, finally lifting her head and meeting his eyes. "Not working so great."

She looked fragile and so fucking beautiful he had to remind himself to breathe.

And, yeah. He could see that his advice wasn't working.

She tried for a smile, ended up looking away, shaking her head. "I . . . I can't get those men out of my head. Their eyes."

Sam knew all about the eyes. Lifeless. Soulless. Haunting. He'd learned early on to never look at them.

"Let's check that arm," he said, knowing there was nothing he could say to snap those images out of focus for her. Only time could do that. Time and distance.

He sat down on the bed beside her, coaxed her forward with a notch of his chin. After a slight hesitation, she slid closer.

"You might want to . . . you know . . . ," another notch of his chin toward her hips. Her very fine hips, barely covered in a very small pair of very pink panties, which were *very* visible.

"Oh." Her face turned red when she realized her T-shirt had ridden up when she'd slid down the bed.

Well, at least he'd taken her mind off dead men.

Which he wasn't. He was so not dead at the moment and his dick was totally on board with that happy fact.

Self-conscious, she tugged the shirt down. Covered her hips. And the very top of her thighs.

His dick was still on board, and he was as low as tire treads for even swerving in that direction.

Face grim, he wrapped his fingers around her upper arm to steady it, then tugged the damp dressing loose. "How does it feel?"

"It's okay," she said while he inspected Doc's handiwork.

"Hurt?"

Stoic, she shook her head.

Right. That sucker had to hurt like hell. So did the bruise on her cheek. He let her have that bit of defiance. Admired her for it.

"Couple of the butterflies came loose when you showered," he said, then went to work replacing them.

Very aware of their proximity. Of the wholesome, scrubbed look of her. Of the contrasts between them.

Her skin was soft and smooth. His hands were rough, his fingers scarred. And not nearly as steady as they should be.

He was too damn aware that he hadn't taken time to throw on a shirt and that he was commando beneath his camo pants. Acutely aware, when she shifted position, that there was nothing under that soft T-shirt of hers but bare breasts and satin skin.

Time to go.

Past time to go.

He affixed a final piece of tape.

"You're good to go," he said, hearing a husky awareness in his voice that he hoped to hell she didn't recognize for what it was.

But when her eyes met his, it was clear she understood. Just like it was clear that she was thinking the same thing he was.

It would be so easy. So easy to lay her down, slip those pink panties down her slender hips and make reality go away. For her. For him. For a precious few minutes that would ease this pulsing ache in his groin and make her forget about dead bodies with dead eyes and men who wanted to kill her.

So easy. And so wrong.

Not for him. Wrong for her.

Haul ass outta here, Lang. Now.

"Get some rest," he said, then stiffened when her hand on his arm stopped him from rising.

"Don't . . . please, don't go." Her soft hand slid around to his chest and lightly caressed him.

He damn near went up in flames, swallowed back a lump the size of a grenade. Held the line. Barely. "You don't want this, Abbie."

"And that matters?" she bit out angrily.

Jesus. He deserved that. What seemed like decades ago in Las Vegas, he'd made her think it didn't matter.

"Yeah," he said through the guilt. "It matters."

Her eyes said it all when they searched his. She didn't believe him. Didn't trust him.

But she wanted to. Yeah, he realized, sobered by that knowledge. If, after what he'd done to her, she still wanted him to be a good guy, then at the very least, he owed her an explanation.

His decision was knee-jerk and irreversible.

"Nader killed my sister," he said, opening himself up to a flood of emotions he'd done his damnedest to suppress.

Before she could react with more than shock, and before he could back out, he barreled ahead. "He was pissed at me. Pissed that I was dogging him, that I was on to him. Making it hard for him to run his dirty business down here. When he couldn't get to me, he did the next best thing. He got to Terri. He had a car bomb planted that killed her and my brother-in-law.

"I'm sorry," he said as tears rolled down her cheeks. "I'm sorry I tricked you. Sorry I blamed you. Sorry I didn't believe you.

"Most of all, I'm sorry I let you maneuver me into a position where I was convinced I needed to bring you down here."

"We . . . we do a lot of things . . . when we love," she said softly.

Yeah. She loved her brother. That's why she was here. He loved his sister. That's why he was here.

"When this is over," he said making himself stand up, "if you ask me again . . . if you invite me into your bed . . . make sure you want me there."

Then, before he could get tangled in the longing in her eyes, he left her.

Las Vegas

Johnny Reed hated stakeouts. They were exercises in combating boredom. He was parked outside Crystal Debrowski's Vegas apartment building in a cramped, rented compact in the middle of the frickin' night. About an hour ago, he'd surpassed boredom and started sliding straight toward coma.

When his cell phone vibrated, it was a welcome relief. He fished the phone out of his pocket, recognized the area code as being out of country. Sam.

"Yo," he answered.

"What's happening?"

Chatty Cathy Sam was not. "Nothing and a little more nothing. On the good-news front, I've been in constant touch with your dad." The apple hadn't fallen too far from that tree, he thought. Like Sam, Tom Lang was sharp, competent, and about as capable as they came. "All's quiet on that front."

Only Sam's brief silence told Johnny the relief he felt in that knowledge. "And the diamonds?" Sam asked.

"Your guess is as good as mine. I've been on Abbie Hughes's pixie friend like white on rice. She's not giving anything away."

He hadn't really figured she would. He was providing protection for the Debrowski chick as much as he was tailing her.

"Any uninvited company?"

"If Nader sent a tail, he's damn good. And since I'm better than good, I'd say it's a big negative. Figure it's a reach to think that Nader made Crystal Debrowski as an accomplice in Abbie's sleight of hand."

"Still better safe than sorry."

"Always. So how's sunny Honduras?"

Sam grunted. "Think monsoon."

"I was thinking more in terms of Nader. What's happening?"

Johnny listened as Sam gave him a Cliffs Notes version of the action going down.

"Holy shit," he said.

"And then some," Sam agreed. "Watch your six."

"Roger that," Johnny said. "Same goes, okay?"

"Later." Sam hung up.

Johnny dragged a hand over his face, stared into space, and wished to hell he was in Honduras, where he was pretty certain his services were needed a helluva a lot more than they were here.

"Them's the breaks," he muttered and glanced toward the third floor of the apartment building, fourth window from the right corner.

To keep himself entertained and awake, he thought about Crystal Debrowski with her short, spiky red hair and centerfold bod. And he wondered if a pixie wore anything other than fairy dust to bed.

The prospect kept him awake and alert for the next several hours.

17

Cory was sick.

Wished-he-could-die sick.

In-and-out-of-consciousness sick from the beating Smith had given him . . . when? Days ago? A week? Hell, it felt like a year.

He didn't know where he was.

He only knew that he was not where he had been. Someone had moved him. He remembered gunfire. Lots of it. And then . . . nothing.

He rolled onto his back with a groan. Filthy, stinking straw on the floor. On top of broken bricks. Inside.

Yeah. He was inside. With rats again. He couldn't see them in the dark. But he could smell them. And he could hear them.

The stalking bastards were here. In the corners. Scurrying up the walls. Waiting for him to die. Fuckers wanted to eat him.

"Fuckers!" he yelled wildly, then cried out when pain seized his body.

He convulsed into a ball, tried to protect his ribs because he was six again and his father was beating him.

"Don't," he begged, tears leaking from his eyes. "Daddy, don't . . . I'll be g-good. I . . . promise. Don't . . . don't . . . kick me. Don't . . ."

He bumped his hand. Screamed as pain exploded through it, up his arm, knifed into his head.

Abbie.

He wanted Abbie.

"No . . . no," he panted out the words through a raw and scratchy throat. "Don't come here. Don't . . . don't let 'em get you, too . . ."

A burst of light made him recoil in pain. A flood of water roused him further.

"Wake up, gringo."

Cory gasped, involuntarily battling to capture life-sustaining air. To lick his dry lips and taste the water that had been thrown in his face. Water ran into his mouth. Cooled his fevered skin. Fresh air, hot and sweet and scented of a recent rain filled his lungs.

"Eat. Drink."

He squinted up through burning eyes, saw a man set a wooden cup and bowl on the straw and shove it toward him.

"Your sister, she will be here soon, no? You will live until then."

With a slam of the door, the light was gone.

Silence.

And the smell of food. The scent of water.

The scrabbling of the rats growing closer.

Abbie.

Abbie was coming? Here?

No. No. Oh, God, no. Abbie could not come to this hell.

But he couldn't stop her.

So he had to help her.

Which meant he had to eat.

He felt around on the floor for the bowl—backhanded a rat all the way across the room.

Then he cradled the bowl under his chin, held it with his wrist, forked it into his mouth with the fingers of his good hand.

Finished it.

Drank his water.

Then he hitched his way back against the wall opposite the door.

And waited. Waited for inspiration to strike him. Waited for his stomach to expel the gruel they'd given him.

Waited for them to come back.

And prayed to God he could figure out a way to help Abbie . . . Then he cried. Because he couldn't even help himself.

La Entrada, Honduras

"You been in touch with Reed yet?"

Sam looked up from his breakfast and nodded at Savage. "Last night."

"So what's happening on the home front?"

"If Nader has men in Vegas, Reed still hasn't spotted them." That was the frustrating part. The relief came in knowing that everyone at Rancho Royale was fine.

"And the diamonds?" Mendoza asked.

"Abbie's friend is as tight-lipped as a clam. Reed hasn't been able to get anything out of her and from the sounds of it, he's tailing her like a jet trail."

They all grew quiet for a moment. Sam could sense that something was up.

"You know we've got Nader now," Savage said finally as the four of them chowed down on scrambled *huevos* and tortillas Señorita García had cooked—after they'd made a generous offering to the gods of hospitality. "We don't need Cory Hughes to get to Nader and finish him off."

Sam had been expecting this. He downed a swallow of strong, sweet Honduran coffee, knew that Savage was right. Also knew that Mendoza and Doc were on board with Savage's assessment.

They no longer needed Cory Hughes. A little while ago, Mendoza had used Smith's cell phone and his contact list to find Nader's cell phone number. Then he'd made one quick, discreet call to his contact at the local CIA/NSA and Casper the friendly spook had triangulated Nader's location. The murdering bastard was currently on his yacht, which was, as they sat here, moored off the southern coast of Isla de Roatán.

"The longer we wait," Mendoza added, tucking his St. Christopher's medal beneath the black T-shirt he'd just pulled over his head, "the more restless Nader's going to get over Smith being out of touch."

"Wouldn't be surprised if he's already sent someone out to Peña Blanca looking for him," Doc agreed around a mouthful of eggs.

Sam said nothing. Nothing he could say. No argument he could wage. They were right. The longer they delayed closing in on Nader, the greater the risk that they'd lose him.

"We need to move on this bro," Savage pressed. "We don't have time for Cory Hughes anymore. Have Mendoza drive Abbie back to San Pedro Sula and put her on a plane. He can catch up with us later."

"We had a deal."

All heads turned at the sound of Abbie's voice.

"We had a deal," she restated, her eyes accusing as she honed in on Sam.

Looking sheepish, Doc, Savage, and Mendoza each snagged a couple of tortillas and headed for the door. "We'll get loaded up," Mendoza said. "Meet you outside."

Then, like rats deserting a ship, they bailed.

So did Señorita García, who'd been puttering around in the kitchen but, sensing the tension, walked outside.

The lingering silence rang like an indictment.

"They're right," Sam said, filling a plate, then holding it out to her. "We're going to lose Nader if we delay much longer."

She ignored the plate of food. "And Cory will be dead if we don't go after him now."

Sam hadn't wanted it to come down to this. Nader was the only reason Sam was in Honduras. His entire purpose was to destroy the man who had destroyed his father. To make certain Nader could never touch him or his again.

He thought of Cory Hughes. Of Savage and Doc and Mendoza, who were all risking their lives so he could take Nader down.

Guilt crushed down like a tank as he stood there, meeting her gaze.

She shook her head, disbelieving. "You bastard. You . . . you talk about trust. You talk about mistakes. You . . . you played the honor card last night as if it was your ticket to redeeming yourself for using me. You pretend to care. You make me want to believe—"

She cut herself off, fought the tears that were welling.

"Look. I'm sorry. I'm sorry about your sister. I'm sorry that she's dead. But you can't help her now. You can only help Cory. Who's alive. Please." She choked on the words. "Please . . . be who you want me to think you are. Help me."

Sam stared at her long and hard. "I really did a number on you, didn't I, if you honestly believe I'd go back on my word now."

The relief he saw flooding her face almost made it worth going against his better judgment and the opinions of the BOIs. Almost.

"Eat," he said gruffly. "You need the fuel. Be ready to go in ten minutes."

Then he headed outside, knowing he was about to ask his brothers to go above and beyond.

Knowing that for him, they would do it. Just like he knew that if anything happened to them and if Nader got away, it would all be on his head.

Near El Nuevo Porvenir and Desmond Fox's camp

"Sonofabitch," Mendoza swore as he quick-shifted from forward to reverse and the rear wheels of the SUV sank deeper and deeper into the rutted road.

"Hold on." Savage shoved open the passenger door, stepped out into the muck. "Fuck. We're buried to the hubs. This sucker isn't going anywhere."

No one was happy. Not the BOIs, who thought Sam was out of his mind for wasting time going after Cory Hughes. Not Sam, because he knew he'd compromised not only their lives but their chances of getting Nader.

And not Abbie, who was scared to death that they'd get to Cory too late to save him.

Only Doc attempted to maintain a level of levity in the midst of chaos. "Holy mud rut, Batman. Where's the Batmobile when you need it?"

"I told you this road would be impassable," Savage grumbled.

"Yeah, well, since when are you ever right?" Sam stepped out of the SUV, slamming the door behind him. He scowled down at the wheels, which were buried in mud.

"Everybody out. Abbie, get behind the wheel. Then gun it to hell when I say go.

"Go!" Sam shouted when all the guys were in place, shoulders to the back of the SUV, determined to muscle it out of the mud.

She gunned it.

The SUV rocked, slid and, to a string of curses and grunts, finally, its belly dragging, shot out of the hole.

Abbie braked, steered the vehicle to the middle of the road, and waited for the guys to catch up with her.

It was about that time that Sam smelled gas.

Then the motor died.

"Sonofabitch," Savage swore as he got down on all fours and peered beneath the undercarriage. "Ripped a hole in the gas tank on a rock or something when we pushed her out. We're without fuel, boys and girl."

Abbie got out, her eyes desperate and wild in her poor bruised face.

Everything she felt was telegraphed in those big brown eyes. *This far? We've come this far?*

Hands on hips, Sam squinted against the glaring morning sun, scanned the countryside, acutely aware of Abbie's worried gaze.

They were in the middle of freaking nowhere. A small farm sat a quarter of a mile or so to the south. "I need the field glasses."

Mendoza reached into the back of the SUV, handed them to him.

"Give me all your cash," Sam said, after seeing what he'd hoped to see.

"I hate to tell you this, but there's not enough lempira in Honduras to buy our way out of this mess," Savage grumbled.

"I had something more like horse trading in mind," Sam said after they'd all ponied up. "Mendoza, come with me. The rest of you wait here."

They took off walking across the field.

"I do not do horses," Savage sputtered an hour later. He glowered from Sam to the shaggy brown mount munching on ditch grass in front of him. "Not in Afghanistan, not in Argentina, and not in fucking Honduras."

"Then it's time to expand your horizons," Doc said, swinging easily up into the saddle.

There might not have been enough lempira to buy them a new gas tank, but Sam had had enough to buy the use of six horses. They weren't exactly Derby material but they were stout and sturdy and they'd get them the rest of the way to El Nuevo Porvenir, where the dying mole had told them Desmond Fox was holed up with Cory Hughes.

According to the mole, Hughes was in bad shape. Sam hadn't shared that news with Abbie, who had surprised him yet again with her stoic determination to do whatever had to be done. He could tell she was a little nervous but she swung up into the saddle without a word.

Abbie didn't need any additional stress about Cory's condition. It wouldn't help anything. Just like Savage's grumbling wouldn't help—except, maybe, to provide Doc and Mendoza with a source of amusement.

"Come on, Papa Bear." Like Doc, Mendoza was getting a very large charge out of Savage's skittishness around the horses. "It's just like riding a loose woman. Oh, wait, probably been so long, you forgot how good that feels."

"Fuck you," Savage muttered, hoisting his big body awkwardly into the saddle. "I hope those nags throw you both on your pointy little heads."

Sam shot them a glare that none of them misunderstood.

"You've got to admit," Doc said, "seeing Savage bent out of shape over *anything* is a damn satisfying experience."

"I'll be satisfied when we get the job done." Sam double-checked the binding on the munitions and weapons they'd unloaded from the back of the SUV and tied onto the packhorse. "Let's ride. I want to get in, get Cory, get out, then move on to Nader."

It could have been a photo ad for tourism in Honduras. A brilliant sun dazzled from a cloudless blue sky. A tropical forest, verdant and lush and teeming with life rimmed a vast expanse of gently rolling hills thick with slender, bending grass. The air smelled of sun and flowers and the aftermath of fresh rain.

Across this endless field of green, five horsemen rode, their silhouettes juxtaposed against the crumbling ruins of what had once been sacred Mayan temples. The horsemen's pace was plodding and sure; their striped ponchos posed a muted contrast to the vibrant blues and greens of nature. They rode with lazy ease, their heads hung low, wide-brimmed hats fashioned of local straw grass shielding their eyes against the sun.

Yeah, Abbie thought, it could have been a snippet of rural life in the Copán Province—or so said the sign on the road they'd left behind—had she not been a part of it. Had she not known that beneath those ponchos, Sam, Doc, Mendoza, and Savage were concealing enough weaponry to jump-start a major coup. Had she not known that lashed beneath the blanket on the packhorse tied to her own mount was a machine gun and enough ammo to take out several buildings or bad guys.

In addition to the horses, Sam had bartered and bargained for the ponchos and hats. None would make the pages of a men's apparel catalogue. The ponchos were old, dirty, worn, and weary, the hats crushed and frayed. But, as Sam had hoped, wearing them in combination with sitting astride the horses went a long way toward camouflaging four very tall men in a country where the average height was around five foot six. Any locals they might encounter wouldn't give them a second look.

The ponchos and hats also did a decent job of camouflaging Abbie's sex—although, from her perspective, flanked by these men who closed ranks around her both figuratively and literally, she'd never been more aware of her gender.

Just as she was very much aware of the fact that Sam had gone against the advice and the wishes of his men. Men who were risking their lives for Cory—someone they didn't know, didn't care about, and frankly resented for his role as Nader's mule and as a deterrent to their primary goal: Fredrick Nader.

She couldn't thank them. Wouldn't know how. She strongly suspected they wouldn't want her thanks anyway. But there was one thing she could do. She could be a player in Cory's rescue. She didn't know how yet, but she would not cower in the bushes while they took all the heat.

"According to what the mole said, the estancia should be just over that rise," Mendoza said an hour into their trek. "I'll ride ahead and take a look."

He kneed his horse and loped away up the hill.

Cory was right over that hill. Abbie's heart raced at the prospect that she might actually be seeing him soon and getting him to safety. From what she'd gathered, the man they'd found alive at Peña Blanca last night had revealed the location before he'd died. She also understood that Fox had left that man there waiting for her, his sole job to bring Abbie to Fox's El Nuevo Porvenir hideout, where Fox had had exactly the same game plan in mind as Fredrick Nader. Fox would give up Cory when Abbie gave up the location of the diamonds. Neither Fox nor the mole, however, had planned on the mole getting shot.

"One of the things we've got going for us," Sam said, "is that Fox couldn't know exactly when Smith would arrive with you at Peña Blanca. That bought us these few hours. He has no idea that his man won't be showing up with you in tow. And he won't be looking for any resistance. Not from you."

"So if he's expecting me, why don't we just give him me?" Abbie asked Sam as they dismounted in the shade at the edge of the forest and waited for Mendoza to return with a report.

Sam cut her a look that pretty much answered her question.

"Because just like Nader, Fox plans to kill both of us," she surmised.

"Give the lady a cigar." Doc, more stoic than usual, loaded bullets into a metal clip and shoved the clip into the butt of a very lethal-looking pistol.

Battle. They were preparing for battle. Earlier, when Abbie had joined them by the SUV before leaving Señorita García's, they'd all been busy doing the same thing. The precision and the automatic way they handled the guns, double-checked ammo clips, shrugged into their heavy vests, painted a vivid, telling picture of who they were and what they were capable of doing.

"You ever fire a rifle?" Sam had asked her then.

She shook her head, feeling very naive and sheltered and dependent. None of the feelings settled well.

"Show me how."

Eyebrows rose all around, but no one had said a word.

"I'm a quick study," she said defensively. "Just show me."

"She could handle the M-4," Mendoza had suggested picking up the smaller version of the M-16 and handing it to Sam. "Just teach her to point and spray."

So Sam had shown her. With the little time they'd had, he'd taught her the basics.

"Point, aim, squeeze. And never point this sucker at anything or anyone you don't feel comfortable killing."

That had been the short and the sweet of it. Of course, she'd only been able to "dry fire," so she hadn't experienced live rounds.

So now, here she was. Disguised as a local who was disguised as a shooter, who was disguised as someone who wasn't scared half out of her mind with Sam's final piece of wisdom ringing in her head.

"Welcome to the world of bullets and bad guys."

18

Abbie stood by her horse and watched Mendoza ride back toward them. Her hands sweated as she tightened her grip on the reins.

Mendoza's gaze met hers as he dismounted, and bless him, he actually looked sympathetic. He understood how anxious she was for news. He shook his head, indicating he hadn't seen any signs of Cory, before digging a pencil and a scrap of paper out of his pocket. Using his horse's hip as a platform, he spread out the paper and started sketching.

"Okay. What we've got is a small estancia just outside of the village. I'm guessing Fox routed out whoever lives there and just took it over.

"Main house here," he continued, drawing a box in the center of the paper. A slight breeze kept lifting the corner. Abbie reached out, held it down for him. "I see one entrance but figure there's also an exit out the back. One guard stationed by the front door."

"Carrying?" Sam asked.

"An AK."

Sam frowned. "That the only guard?"

"At the house," Mendoza confirmed. "There's an outbuilding here. Could be a well house, toolshed, can't tell, but there are four men stationed here, here, here, and here," he explained, marking all four corners of the building with his pencil.

"Gotta be where they're keeping Cory," Sam surmised.

Mendoza nodded. "I agree. No reason to have all that firepower guarding the building otherwise."

"Gotta be more men around." Doc frowned at the rough map. "According to the mole, there are at least twenty."

"The barn?" Savage suggested.

Mendoza lifted a shoulder. "Could be. Could be more in the house. I spotted at least three perimeter guards patrolling the grounds. Looks like they're in place as the first line of defense."

"Who are they defending against?" Abbie asked, puzzled. "For all Fox knows, I'm coming alone. And I was supposed to arrive with one of his own men."

"The reception's not for you," Sam said. "It's for Nader. Fox fully expects Nader to come after him once he finds out about the ambush at Peña Blanca."

"So he's going to be loaded for bear," Savage said with a nod.

"But he's not planning on going up against the Papa Bear," Doc said with a grin aimed at Savage, who Abbie had heard all three men refer to as Papa Bear. "By the way, how are those saddle sores coming along?"

Savage flipped Doc the bird but since he was grinning, it was apparent he took no offense. What was also apparent to Abbie was that they were up against overwhelming odds.

"How can we possibly get Cory out of there?" she asked.

All eyes turned to Sam.

"Did I see what I thought I saw in your bag of tricks?" he asked Mendoza.

"Brought a lot of toys, Sam. Narrow it down for me."

"A few well-placed mortar rounds could create a nice diversion."

Mendoza grinned. "Thought you might like those."

"Mortars?" Abbie did a double take. "Now wait. I'm no expert on guns or whatever shoots mortars, but I've seen enough combat footage on TV and in movies to know that there's no way you have something like that tied to the back of that horse."

"Smart lady. No mortars, but what we do have are mortar simulators,"

Mendoza explained, digging under the blanket and pulling out a black metal bar. Three cylindrical tubes about eight inches long and an inch or so in diameter were welded to the bar in an upward trajectory.

"We're outmanned and outgunned, but we also have the element of surprise on our side. They're not expecting an assault. At least not yet. So right now, they're most likely full and lazy from breakfast," Sam said. "We're going to wake 'em up. Use a little pyrotechnic smoke and mirrors to convince the bad guys someone's lobbing mortars at them. Give them reason to believe Nader's arrived in force, means business, and has the superior firepower."

"More than anything else," Doc added, turning to Abbie, "mortars scare the hell out of you. You don't know where they're coming from, what they'll hit, and the odds are damn good a shell can drop in like unexpected company."

Sam nodded. "If we can get them disorganized and scared enough, some of them are going to run. That's when we clear a path to snatch your brother and go."

"Go where?" Abbie couldn't help it. "How do we get out of here? I mean, Cory may be too injured to ride. And even if he isn't, I'm assuming these guys have vehicles. Correct me if I'm wrong, but I don't see us outrunning them on horseback."

"Talk to me, Raphael." Sam turned toward Mendoza.

"Two pickups and one damn pricey Suburban are parked in front of the hacienda. I figure these came with Fox. One of them is going to leave with us. The other two are going to be profoundly disabled. If there are more vehicles with the men in the barn, it won't be a big deal to shoot out a few tires."

"What about the horses? What happens to them?"

Savage rolled his eyes. Okay. So Abbie knew it was incongruous to be worried about the horses when there was a major gun battle minutes away, but she couldn't help it.

"We slap them on the ass and head 'em toward home," Doc said, taking pity. "Don't worry. They know where the feedbag is. They'll be home long before it's time to strap it on."

"This is the way I see it going down," Sam said, keeping them on task. "Abbie, we'll position you at the top of the ridge to fire the simulators on my signal." Mendoza handed her the field glasses so she could watch for Sam's cue.

"Mendoza, Savage, and I will make up the entry team. Doc, you'll hang back on the ridge with Abbie and the M-249. The machine gun," he clarified for Abbie. "Pick off anything that gets in our way."

Doc grinned. "I just loves me a belt-fed machine gun."

"It'd be nice if we could keep the decibel level down initially when we go in after the perimeter guards. Might buy us a few minutes." He turned to Mendoza. "Any chance—"

"That I brought sound suppressors?" Mendoza cut in. "You had to even ask?" He fished around under the blanket on the packhorse again. When he turned back, his hands were full of long black cylinders. He handed them out.

"And one for me," he added, pulling out his own M-4 and affixing the suppressor to the end of the barrel.

Sam turned back to Abbie. "We're going to leave you with an M-4. You shoot only if you're under direct fire, okay?"

She took the rifle. Nodded. Understood that he was telling her he didn't want her shooting and hitting one of them.

"Okay," Sam said, with a hard look. "Once we take out the perimeter guards, we'll head straight for the shack. That's when I'll need the mortar fire, okay?"

Abbie nodded.

"That should send feet flying. I'll head for the shack, take out the four guards, and get Cory. Mendoza, you and Savage check the barn for stragglers, disable any other vehicles, then go for one of the pickups."

"What if the trucks are locked?" Abbie asked.

Mendoza just grinned. "That's what they make these metal stocks for," he said, patting the butt of his rifle.

"As soon as you see Savage and Mendoza pull around in front of the shed in the truck, beat feet down the hill. I'll spring your brother, get him on board, we'll pick up you and Doc, and we're out of here."

He made it sound so simple. If you left out the part about real bullets and real bad guys, it probably was.

"Questions?" Sam encompassed everyone with a hard look. "Okay," he said when he was met with silence. "Let's check our watches, set the charges for the simulators, and get this show on the road. Doc—"

"I know. Be ready with my medic kit."

Abbie had absorbed every word with stoic fatalism. Until then. The plan was clean and fast and complete. It was the outcome that was unknown. It was the knowledge that they called Colter Doc for a reason.

There could be blood. Any one of them could get hurt—or worse.

They knew it. Yet they didn't hesitate. They were laying everything on the line for Cory. Whom they didn't know. Didn't care about. Didn't even want to help.

It's what we do, Sam had said.

These men . . . *these men who made things happen,* these capable, accomplished, hard-edged men, were all running head-on into danger because she'd asked them to.

"Don't think about it," Sam said, seeking her out while she stood away from the activity, struggling with the weight of these men's lives.

"What have I done?" She met his eyes. "What have I asked of you?"

"The same thing I would have done if I were in your position. The same thing I would have asked."

She swallowed, tried to settle her pulse.

"Abbie." Sam touched her hand, squeezed. "It's not our first hostage rescue."

No. She didn't suppose it was. Knowing that, however, didn't make things any easier.

"Be careful," she whispered, hearing more than concern in her voice, seeing in his eyes that he heard it too.

He leaned down, kissed her. Lightly. Sweetly.

"Careful is my middle name," he promised against her mouth. "Besides, you and I have unfinished business. I plan to come back and settle it."

• • •

It was never easy. And it never felt heroic. What it felt was necessary. If a man lost sight of the reality that it was "kill or be killed," that man ended up dead. Sam had every intention of leaving here alive.

With Mendoza flanking him twenty yards to the left and Savage to his right, they worked their way slowly toward the perimeter guards, belly-crawling through the thigh-high grass, rifles cradled in the crooks of their arms, until they reached their targets. Within ten minutes, and without one round of gunfire, three corrupted souls kept long-standing dates with *el diablo*.

Three down, too many to go.

Sam dragged the dead guard behind a tree, then stripped him of his hat and bandoliers full of ammo. He crisscrossed the bandoliers over his own chest and donned the guard's hat. The attempt to disguise himself as one of Fox's men wouldn't fool anyone for very long. He didn't need long. Neither did Savage or Mendoza, who were doing the same. In this game, split seconds counted. Split seconds made for minuscule delays that allowed for maximum effect. A slow reaction by a puzzled guard gave a necessary edge. Tipped the scales in favor of the good guys, especially when there were few against many.

The short clipped chirp of a sparrow—their prearranged signal—first from the left, then from the right, told Sam the BOIs were ready to move on. He answered back then lifted his hand, thumb up, Abbie's signal to set off the charges.

"Atta girl," he said under his breath when ten seconds later she fired off the simulator. A shrill screech whistled through the air, followed by an explosion that stomped like, roared like, and looked like mortar blasts and rocked the open area near the shack where they suspected Cory was being held. Dirt and debris and enough hellfire and brimstone to wake the dead flew thirty feet in the air and just as wide and clouded the area with dust.

On cue, Sam, Mendoza, and Savage came tearing out of the tall grass. They ran toward the compound like their tails were on fire, shooting wildly behind them as if shooting at a combatant, yelling out a warning that the compound was under attack. "¡Un ataque! Socorro! Rápido! Somos atacados!"

They hoped like hell that in the chaos no one noticed they weren't part of the jackal pack.

Just as the front door to the hacienda burst open and four more bandolier-wearing bad guys joined the stunned guard already positioned on the porch, Abbie launched the second "mortar" attack.

As he sprinted low toward the shack, Sam caught sight of Mendoza and Savage belly-diving under the tailgates of the pickups. The staccato burst of automatic-weapon fire followed—unmistakably M-16 and M-4's. The five surprised guards never laid trigger finger to metal of their AK's.

Five more down. The odds were getting better.

Sam ran toward the shack, shouting wildly. *"¡Protéjense! Tomen refugio!"* *Take cover.*

The four startled guards ducked, stared, finally realized he wasn't one of them, and raised their rifles.

Four short bursts from his M-16 and the poorly prepared, poorly trained guards dropped like sandbags.

He stepped over their bodies and bolted for the door.

Wooden. Old. Padlocked.

"Stand back!" he yelled in case Cory could hear him.

Then he put his weight behind his foot and kicked like hell. The old dried wood splintered around the padlock hinge. The door swung inward, slammed against the wall.

"Fuck!" He jumped when a rat scrambled across his foot, then shouldered his way inside.

The sunlight shattered the dank darkness that stank of filth and fear and desperation.

A man lay on his back, legs splayed, head and shoulders bolstered crookedly against the far wall. He'd lifted a hand to shield his eyes from the sunlight. The other hand, wrapped in dirty, bloody bandages, lay cradled against his abdomen.

"Cory," Sam said.

No answer. Rats skittered in the corners.

"I'm a friend of your sister's."

That finally got a reaction. He lowered his hand, squinted up at Sam through feverish, bloodshot eyes. "Abbie? Abbie's here?"

"Yeah. Now come on. We've gotta move out. Can you walk?" Sam hooked his rifle sling over his shoulder, went down on one knee beside Cory, and helped him sit up.

"Get her out of here!" Cory begged. "Don't . . . don't let them get her, too."

"No one's going to get her, but we've got to get you out of here now."

Sam grabbed Cory's good hand, draped it around his neck, and hefted him to his feet. Outside, the sound of AK-47 fire and Doc on the machine gun rang like a hailstorm of bowling balls on a tin roof. If all had gone as planned, Doc and Mendoza had already taken out a few more men in the barn, disabled all the vehicles but one of the trucks, and should be about to spin around the shack and pick up Sam and Cory.

Sam heard the rattle of the M-249—closer now—and realized Doc had moved it farther toward the compound.

"Come on." Supporting Cory's weight, Sam grabbed him by the waist of his pants and walked him toward the open door. Sam glanced outside, left and right. Satisfied there was no fire coming their way, he propped Cory upright against the frame.

"Stay," he ordered and, ducking outside, peered around the corner of the shack.

Fuck. Mendoza was pinned down by a water trough. A spray of bullets *thuwnked* into the water, shooting it skyward like a progressive fountain. Sam searched the perimeter, found the shooter, sighted down the barrel through his holographic scope, and fired. A body tumbled off the barn roof and landed on the dry ground with a lifeless thud.

Mendoza shot to his feet, firing from the hip as he ran toward the closest pickup. He tried the lock, then quickly slammed the butt of his rifle through the driver's-side window when he found it locked.

He jerked open the door and lay down in the seat just as the passenger-side window shattered in a spray of gunfire. Sam searched for the new shooter. Found him in an upper window of the hacienda. One pop and the gunman tumbled forward through the glass windowpane, bounced off the porch roof and landed on the roof of the Suburban.

"Come on, Mendoza," Sam urged, knowing Raphael was working to hotwire the truck.

Through the constant spurts of gunfire, an engine roared to life.

Mission accomplished.

Sam swung his rifle around, crept past Cory, who was still on his feet, and peered around the opposite corner of the shack, where he came face-to-face with the barrel of an AK. He dropped, rolled, and fired, and another one of Fox's hired guns hit the dirt.

He rolled back toward the shack, vaguely aware of a burning sensation in his upper arm. Fuck. He'd been hit. When he reached the porch, he checked his arm. Blood seeped out of the hole in his sleeve. Nothing major.

The rapid-fire burst of Doc's machine gun had him ducking back behind the building. He quickly surveyed the real estate between the shack and the barn where Savage crouched in the open doorway, holding off gunmen Sam couldn't see.

About that time, Mendoza roared to a rolling stop in front of the barn, his M-4 firing out the passenger window, laying down cover for Savage who, running backward, sprayed rounds toward the open barn door as he sprinted for the truck. When he reached Mendoza, he launched himself, landing face-first in the pickup bed. Quickly righting himself and steadying the barrel of his M-16 on the sidewalls of the truck bed, he emptied a mag into the barn.

"Get ready," Sam told Cory, knowing Mendoza's next stop would be for them.

With a squeal of tires and laying a rooster tail of dust behind him, Mendoza sped their way, then screeched to a stop at the shed.

Sam tossed Savage his rifle, scooped up Cory in a fireman's carry, and ran the three yards to the truck. Bullets kicked up the dirt at Sam's feet as Savage caught Cory and dragged him into the pickup box.

Sam hiked himself up on the open tailgate, grabbed his M-16 from Savage, and joined him in laying down fire.

"Punch it, Martha!" Savage yelled to Mendoza, who promptly gunned the motor. With the rear of the truck fishtailing wildly, they flew toward the edge of the grounds, where Doc and Abbie would be waiting.

The truck roared across the bumpy ground, hit a rut, and sent Sam flying to the edge of the open tailgate. He scrabbled for a hold, lost it when they hit another chuckhole, and flew out the back.

He hit the ground with a thud that knocked the wind out of him. He was convulsed inward, gasping for breath when he saw a shadow loom over him.

"*Hola, gringo.*"

Still gasping, incapable of moving, Sam squinted against the blazing sun. He couldn't make out a face but the unmistakable sight of the business end of an AK-47 was crystal clear.

"*Y adiós.*"

So, this was where it ended.

Sam thought of Abbie, of the guilt she would bear, as Fox's man hiked the rifle to his shoulder, aimed —

A crack of gunfire rent the air.

And Sam was still alive.

The gunman stood above him, stared, eyes bulged in stunned horror, as a circle of crimson stained his chest.

The AK fell from his hand. He looked down at himself, looked at Sam in disbelief. In slow motion, he crumpled to his knees and fell face forward in the dirt.

Sam finally found the strength to push himself upright. He squinted against the sun that silhouetted the figure slowly walking toward him, the rifle that had saved his life still butted against a slender shoulder, dust swirling all around her.

Abbie.

Before he could yell at her to get down, the pickup barreled up beside him. He rolled to his feet, snagged Abbie's hand, and, running alongside the moving vehicle, jerked open the passenger door. He hauled Abbie up against him, lifted and stuffed her inside, piling in after her as Mendoza put pedal to metal.

Doc emerged from the deep grass not thirty yards ahead. Another rolling stop and Doc leapt into the truck bed with Savage and Cory. On his back, he quickly set up the M-249 between his spread legs and started spraying a trail of lead behind them, effectively dissuading anyone stupid enough to try to follow.

The last thing Sam saw as he looked back at the decimated estancia grounds was Desmond Fox, standing feet spread wide, a rifle hanging from his hand, helpless to do anything but watch as they sped away.

19

~~

In-out—less than fifteen minutes. Fifteen minutes that had seemed like fifteen hours. It always did when bullets were flying.

They weren't flying now. Still, Sam kept a vigilant eye on the rearview mirror for any trailers that Fox might have dispatched to follow them. So far, nothing, but no one was doing any deep breathing—yet. Considering they were all wired and revved on adrenaline, no one had much to say either. No one but Mendoza, who turned the air in the truck cab blue with a litany of Spanish curses as he fought the road, fishtailing and gunning his way back toward Señorita García's hacienda at La Entrada.

The stolen pickup scorched a path down the muddy road, cruised right on past their stranded SUV. The heat of the Honduras sun had dried the roads just enough that they managed to keep from getting stuck—barely.

Abbie kept twisting around in the seat beside Sam, casting worried looks at her brother.

"He'll be okay," Sam assured her gruffly. "He was conscious and with the program when I found him."

She whipped around. "He talked to you?"

"Yeah," Sam said. "He knows you're here. He ordered me to get you out of there."

Her eyes brightened.

"Points for the kid," Sam said, still reluctant to see him through his sister's eyes but knowing she needed that little bit of propping up. Knowing she was going to need a lot more than shoring up when it hit her that she'd killed a man.

"You're bleeding," she said in horror when she noticed his arm.

"I do that sometimes," he said, making light of it and trying to lighten the load for her. "It's a scratch. No more. We were lucky," he added pointedly. "Everyone's present and accounted for and other than a few bruises and minor wounds, we're fit and fine. Well, except maybe Mendoza. You're going to stroke out, man, if you don't take a breath."

Mendoza's response was to switch to cursing in English.

The miles passed. They didn't stop flying until they skidded into Señorita García's drive. Mendoza drove straight into the shed where they'd hidden the SUV last night. The engine hadn't even shut down when Sam jumped out of the passenger seat and, with Mendoza right behind him, started covering the truck with a tarp.

Abbie scrambled toward the back as Savage and Doc slid Cory toward the tailgate.

"He's passed out," Doc said, jumping to the ground beside her. "Let's get him into the house so I can assess his condition."

Sam watched, stoic and concerned for Abbie, as she helped Doc and Savage carry her brother into the hacienda.

"The woman has *cojones*," Mendoza said casually as he finished tucking the tarp around the truck.

"Yeah," Sam agreed quietly. The woman had balls.

The woman had killed to save his life. And when everything caught up with her, she was going to suffer because of it.

"You'd better go have Doc check that out." Mendoza nodded toward Sam's arm.

"In a minute." Doc had his hands full with Cory Hughes. Abbie also needed this time with her brother before Sam sent them both away.

He worked his jaw as he sat down beside Mendoza on an overturned bucket, reached for his M-16, and started tearing it down to clean it.

He'd kept his word. He'd rescued her brother.

Now he had another job to do.

One he couldn't afford to delay any longer. Thank God he no longer needed Abbie to do it.

He finished reassembling the rifle, went to work on the machine gun.

"When do you want to move out?" Mendoza asked as he took a quick inventory of their remaining ordnance.

"The sooner the better. Nader's gotta be damn antsy by now. I want to get to him before Fox does."

Mendoza grinned. "Yeah, gotta figure Fox tagged Nader for that little raid we just pulled off. Stands to reason he's going to be pissed."

Join the club, Sam thought, as Terri's vibrant, smiling face filled his mind.

"Can you finish up here?" he asked.

Mendoza nodded. "Got it covered."

"I'm going to go talk to Hughes. See what intel he can give us about Nader. Then we need to get him and Abbie out of here. What have you got on the ground for contacts?"

"Let me make some calls," Raphael said. "We'll get 'em out of here speedy quick."

Speedy quick.

That's what Sam wanted, to get Abbie out of here speedy quick. Out of danger. Out of the country. And, until this was over, out of his head.

"How's he doing?" Sam nodded toward Cory, then jerked when Doc started cleaning his wound. "Ouch, dammit. What are you using, steel wool? And wipe that damn grin off your face."

Doc poured more alcohol on a sterile gauze pad and swiped it over the grazed skin on Sam's upper arm. "Not often I get to make the great Sam Lang wince. Give me a sec to savor the moment."

"Savor on your own time. Just clean it up and slap some salve on it."

"Don't rush the doc," Doc warned. "If I don't get this cleaned up, your arm'll fall off, and then you'll come after me with one of your big manly guns. Almost done, so suck it up there, tough guy."

Sam let out a frustrated breath, accepting not only that Doc was a smartass, but that he wouldn't be rushed. "So how's the kid?" he asked again.

"He'll be okay. Starved. Dehydrated. Got a raging infection in that hand. Ugly bit of work, that."

Sam could see by the concern in Abbie's eyes just how ugly it was. He watched her across the room where she sat by her brother.

She looked like she'd been through a war. Which she had. Her cheek, where Smith had hit her, had transitioned from red and swollen to shades of purple and swollen. The new dressing Doc had apparently put on her arm gleamed stark white in contrast to her tanned skin. Her hair fell wild and tangled around her face. Still, she was quite possibly the most beautiful sight Sam had ever seen.

"Shot him full of antibiotics and painkillers," Doc said absently, applying antibiotic salve to Sam's wound. "Cleaned up the amputation. Started pushing fluids. Once they take hold—say another twelve hours or so—he's gonna start to feel human again. In the meantime the morphine's going to keep him pretty mellow."

"Is he coherent? Can he talk?"

"Sort of and sort of. Give it a try. You're done."

Sam frowned down at his arm where Doc had covered the grazed skin with a big-ass white dressing. "Was that really necessary?"

"Hey. I was all out of Bugs Bunny Band-Aids. Deal with it."

Sam pushed himself to his feet, walked over to the sofa where Cory Hughes was now sleeping.

"How's he doing?"

Abbie didn't look up at him. Just shook her head. "He's not a bad kid," she said thoughtfully, as if she'd been waiting for him to say otherwise. "He just—" She stopped, shook her head, never taking her eyes off Cory.

"Our father used to beat him over . . . over anything. Cory had a . . . a tough time in school, you know? Every time the school called expressing concern, or Cory brought home a bad report card, he ended up getting a beating. Never occurred to the bastard to have Cory tested to see if he had a learning disability. If he would have, he'd have known Cory was dyslexic. Not even the teachers put it together until the damage was already done."

She touched a hand to Cory's hair when he stirred. "When he was ten, Cory took a beating so bad he ended up with a broken ankle. The ankle never healed right because, according to Dexter Hughes, Cory wasn't worth the trip to the ER."

"Abbie—"

"No." She cut him off when he would have stopped her. "I want you to know who Cory is. What he came from. What he was up against. He was a beautiful, brave little boy who should have been protected and loved, but never was."

"*You* loved him," Sam said gently.

"I was a kid myself. I wasn't enough."

"Where were social services in all this?"

"Where they always are. Overworked, understaffed, and unaware. We slipped through the cracks. Cory paid the price."

Okay. Sam got it. In spades. There were no black-and-whites in life. For Cory, there appeared to have been a whole lot of gray.

"He told me . . . before he went to sleep just now, he told me that he'd screwed up. That he'd gotten sucked into Nader's organization a few months ago. By the time he figured out what he was involved in, he couldn't find a way out."

Sam could believe that. Nader was slick, sinister, and ruthless. "Did he say how he came by the diamonds?"

She nodded. "There was this other guy. Derek someone."

"Styles?"

She glanced up. "You know who he is?"

What Sam knew was that Styles was dead and Cory Hughes was damn lucky that he wasn't. "What about Styles?"

"Apparently he worked for Nader, too. Planned to double-cross him. Derek set up a deal to sell the diamonds to Desmond Fox. Something went wrong and Derek was shot in the process. He came to Cory for help and before Cory could get him to a doctor, he died."

So it was Cory who left Styles at the church. Sam could almost figure out the rest. "Cory was left holding the diamonds."

She nodded. "And stuck between a rock and the proverbial hard place.

No matter what he did he was in trouble. So, he decided since he was going to die anyway, he'd just as well make the deal Derek had set up."

"But he was smart enough to mail the diamonds back to Vegas."

"Yes. He arranged to meet Fox, but Smith intercepted him."

"And that's where you came in."

"Yeah. That's where I came in." She looked up at Sam. "What's going to happen to him?"

She was asking about criminal charges. She was asking Sam if he was going to turn Cory in to the authorities.

"Let's worry about that later. Right now, we need to get him back to the States where he can get some medical attention. Doc's good, but his resources are limited."

"What about going after Nader?"

Mendoza burst in the door right then. "We've got a problem."

He'd blown it.

Sam braced a hand on the wall beside the window and stared, unseeing, outside.

Nader was gone. Once again, Sam had missed his chance to deal with the fucker once and for all. By doing the right thing and going after Cory, he'd done the wrong thing. Now a murdering, thieving, morally bankrupt felon was out of Sam's grasp again.

Mendoza's words played back in his head like a bad movie.

"We've got a problem. I made that call we talked about. Figured I'd double-check Nader's coordinates while I was at it. He's weighed anchor, Sam. He must have gotten antsy waiting to hear from Smith. Figured something was up. Looks like he's heading out to sea."

Then as now, Sam felt like he'd been broadsided by a tank.

"How long ago?"

"Earlier this morning."

Too long ago to have any chance of catching him. Yeah, they could line up a chopper out of San Pedro Sula but it would be too late. They were talking hours before they even reached the Isla de Roatán. Nader would be well beyond the island and out of assault range long before then. Even if they could miraculously catch up with him, Sam knew for a fact that the *Seennymphe* was equipped like a fucking battleship. At sea, it was pretty much unbreachable.

He closed his eyes, lowered his head. Thought of Terri. Thought of little Tina. Of his dad.

Sorry. He was so fucking sorry.

"Can we still reach Nader with Smith's cell phone?"

Abbie. Feeling guilty. Thinking there was something she could do.

"Wouldn't matter if we could. He knows something's up."

"He *suspects* something's up," she amended coming to his side. "But he doesn't know anything."

"She's right," Doc agreed.

Sam turned away from the window, glowered at him.

"Well, she *is*," Doc said defensively. "Even if Nader sent scouts to Peña Blanca and they found his men, he'll figure it was Fox who offed them."

"Nader doesn't know you're here," Abbie pointed out, thanking Doc with a nod. "He only knows about me."

Sam met her earnest eyes. "Let it go, Abbie. It's over."

"It's not over." Conviction rang strong in her voice. "Until Nader is either behind bars or dead, it's *never* going to be over. Not for Cory. Not for me. From everything you've told me about him, it's pretty clear that there's not a place on earth where Cory will be safe from this man. When he's ready, Nader will come after Cory. He'll come after me. I don't want to live with that hanging over my head."

Weary. Sam felt so weary. And concerned. Abbie was one hundred percent right about Nader. He'd wait. Then he'd pounce. He'd come after them. Just like he'd come after Sam's family again if he ever made the connection. "There are programs we can get you into."

She made a sound of disbelief. "Witness protection programs?"

"We have connections. We can make it happen."

"I don't *want* you to make it happen. I want you to get Nader. Not just for me and Cory. For you. Sam," she touched a hand to his arm. "I think I know how you can do it."

"I've been after this bastard for two years. Lost him more times than I can count. And you think you know how to take him down? Abbie, you're way out of your element here," he bit out.

Silence.

Then, to his amazement, Mendoza and Savage joined Doc on the bandwagon.

"Let's hear her out, Sam," Mendoza said carefully. "Can't hurt to hear her out."

Sam was too stunned to speak. Didn't matter. Abbie had plenty she wanted to say and she said it fast.

"Let me call Nader on Smith's phone. I'll convince him that Cory is dead. That he was killed at Peña Blanca but that I escaped and have been hiding out, waiting for an opportunity to contact him. I'll tell him that if he wants the diamonds, he's dealing with me now and I'll set up a place for us to meet. From everything you've told me about him, he'll be too greedy to pass up the chance. And he won't see me as a threat, just a nuisance."

"What he'll see you as is bait. Which is what you'll be. It's not going to happen."

"I'm not bait," she insisted. "I'm your ace in the hole."

"Consider it, Sam," Savage added. "And consider it fast before Nader has too much time to think about what happened at Peña Blanca."

20

Bridge of the Seennymphe

Fredrick considered himself a renaissance man. He held a great appreciation for the arts, for fine wines, a robust cigar. He drew deeply, appreciatively, on his *maduro habano*, delighted that he would never have to contemplate life without them.

Fine things. Yes, he took pride in his fine things, just as he prided himself on his knowledge of his vessel and that he could gladly do without the computers that his captain so relied on to steer the *Seennymphe*.

So it was with great pleasure that he told his captain to take a break, deactivated the computer-charted course, and manually took over the helm himself. He loved the feel of the wheel in his hands, the crisp cut of the bow slicing through the rolling swells, the power of a well-maintained engine.

What he did not appreciate were interruptions when he manned the bridge himself. He'd come here to escape his anger. Anger with Rutger Smith for getting himself killed. He knew this with certainty now. He'd sent men to check. Smith's bloated remains had been found at the estancia at Peña Blanca.

He had Desmond Fox to thank for that. Fox had obliterated Smith and his contingent of guards, stolen Hughes, and may very well already have the Tupacka diamonds in his possession.

The diamonds had been his! He had coveted and schemed to obtain them for the better part of the past two years. Now they were gone. All because a lowly American mule and his deceitful sister had allowed Fox to move in.

They would all die, of course. No one beat Fredrick Nader. The woman would pay most dearly before she and her brother made the final payment with their lives.

"Excuse me, sir."

Edward. His steward.

"I know you wish not to be disturbed. But you have a call, sir. On the ship to shore. A woman. Caller ID indicates she's using Mr. Smith's cell phone, sir. She insists you will want to speak to her."

Fredrick turned, mildly intrigued. "Does this woman have a name?"

"She identified herself as an Abbie Hughes, sir."

Fredrick felt his sphincter muscle tighten with rage. He reached for the phone, dismissed the steward with a nod, then turned back to the helm.

"Miss Hughes. To what do I owe the pleasure?"

"I have something you want."

Short and to the point. Fredrick could appreciate the ruthless brevity, if not her rudeness.

"Ah, I see that you are a true businesswoman." More likely a simpleton like her brother.

"You don't see anything, you bastard."

Beyond rude. She was an impudent American bitch. Too stupid to realize exactly who she was dealing with.

"I do not see the need for vulgarity," he stated, biting back the desire to hang up on her. She claimed to have something he wanted.

"Look, do you want to talk terms or not? If not, I won't waste any more of your time or mine."

Fredrick clenched his jaw, wanting to reach through the phone line and rip her throat out for her impertinence. He forced himself to command composure.

"How do I know you still have access to the merchandise? For all I know, you could have already sold it."

"To Desmond Fox?"

He felt heat flush his face at the taunting inflection in her tone.

"What about Desmond Fox?"

"Don't play dumb, Nader. You were sloppy. Your mistakes led Fox to Peña Blanca, where your men held my brother captive like an animal. Because of you, my brother is dead. Everyone is dead except me. I was the only one who got out alive. Lucky for you because I'm the only one who can deliver that *merchandise* you're so willing to kill for."

As angry as he was, he needed to play this smart. A rush much like a climax flowed through him, just thinking about possessing the diamonds. Like it or not, he must play this greedy, manipulative woman's game to get them. First, however, she must understand there would be a price to pay.

"Smith was one of my best assets. I consider him a great loss, my dear. That falls on your brother's head."

"And my brother's death falls on yours. You cost me his life. If you want the diamonds, it's going to cost you, too."

"Truly?" He couldn't contain his anger. "You *truly* assume you can dictate terms to *me*? You had best tread carefully, Miss Hughes. And tell me this, if you will. How do I even know you still have the diamonds? You've been out of touch for some time. Where have you been? What's taken you so long to contact me? Could it be you've already been in negotiations with Fox?"

"I've been hiding out, where do you think I've been? I've been burying my brother. Now I'm ready to deal with you. Like it or not, I'm calling the shots now. I say where we meet. I say when. I say how. And I say who."

"Your insolence is intolerable."

"What's intolerable is what happened to Cory. Now do you want the diamonds or not? If not, then we're through here. And I *will* make that contact with Fox. He'll be more than happy to pay my price."

The thought of that cretin laying his hands on something as exquisite as the Tupacka diamonds made Fredrick's skin crawl. "Fine. Let's talk price, then, shall we?" he gritted out.

"Four million. American."

He would have laughed had it not tipped his hand. He'd be willing to pay twice as much. Not that she'd ever see a dime of his money. "Three point five and not a penny more."

"Good-bye, Mr. Nader."

"Wait, wait." He made a *tsk*ing sound, allowing her to think she had played him. "If you're going to dabble in international commerce, you must learn to appreciate the subtleties of a lively negotiation."

"What I appreciate is cash. You know the airstrip near La Jigua?"

La Jigua was mere miles from Peña Blanca. He knew the area intimately. "I believe so, yes."

"Meet me there tonight, sundown."

"I'm afraid that's impossible," he said, stalling for the time he would need to get a team in place on the ground. "I'm a hundred nautical miles from shore. Even after I alter course to return to the mainland, I'll have to arrange ground transportation after I dock."

"So use that pricey little chopper riding on your bow. It's sundown today or the deal is off."

He closed his eyes, struggled to keep a seething rage at bay. She would die slowly, this one. "I'll have to access the cash."

"Then access it. You have seven hours. Come alone. If I see anyone but you, this is the last you'll hear from me."

She hung up.

Dead.

The woman was dead. Disrespectful, demanding bitch.

Smarter and gutsier than her brother, he'd give her that—but just as corrupt. That, at least, was something he could appreciate about her.

Just as he appreciated that she must have something up her sleeve. Fine. He welcomed the opportunity to outsmart her, see the look on her face just before he killed her.

And he *would* kill her. He didn't need Smith for that. He didn't need anyone.

Energized on the prospect, he gave control of the ship back to the computer. Then he left the bridge in search of the captain to inform him to plot a course back toward La Ceiba where he wished to have the *Seennymphe* moored when he returned with the diamonds. While there, he would acquire more *maduro habanos* to add to his supply. A man could never possess too much of a good thing.

In the meantime, he had several calls to make. Men on the ground to mobilize and direct toward the airstrip at La Jigua.

Come alone? So sorry, my dear. That just wasn't going to happen.

La Entrada

"Hot damn. The lady plays hardball." Savage's expression was filled with reluctant admiration as Abbie hung up the phone.

Sam wasn't fooled by her tough-edged dialogue with Nader. He saw how her hand was shaking.

"*Cojones*," Mendoza agreed from the window where he watched for the transportation he'd called to take Cory to San Pedro Sula. He'd also arranged for medical attention until Cory was strong enough to fly back to the States.

"Any chance I can get you to negotiate my next loan?" Doc asked with a grin and gave Abbie's shoulders a congratulatory squeeze.

He'd been playing for a laugh from her and got it.

Sam sensed the strain ease out of her shoulders even before she exhaled a deep, pent-up breath.

His tension, however, ratcheted up several tight twists. He hated this. Hated himself for agreeing to let Abbie dangle herself as bait—and no matter what she said, that's exactly what she was.

Bait to lure a rat.

"Car's here," Mendoza said, then went out to meet the driver and give him instructions on where to take Cory once they arrived in San Pedro Sula. Mendoza had a friend, an ER doc who would let Cory crash at his place and would give him medical care.

"I'll be fine," Cory assured his misty-eyed sister as Doc and Savage flanked him and helped him off the sofa. "Just nail the bastard."

"I'll see you tomorrow. We'll fly home together." Abbie hugged him hard, clung, then finally forced herself to let go.

Sam watched quietly, until Cory's gaze locked in on him. "Don't let anything happen to her," he said.

Twenty-four hours ago, Sam would have dressed him down as a sorry little punk who didn't deserve even an ounce of the concern Abbie lavished on him.

Twenty-four hours ago.

In this hour, however, Sam gave him a nod.

A promise — man to man.

An hour later Sam watched Fox's commandeered pickup disappear down the rutted road toward La Jigua with Mendoza at the wheel and Doc and Savage crammed into the cab beside him. Piled under the tarp in the pickup bed was enough weaponry and ammo to oust Osama out of a cave.

But they weren't hunting terrorists today. They were hunting rats who aided and abetted terrorists. Rats who were sure to come crawling out of the ditches around the airstrip with big guns paid for by the head rat: Fredrick Nader. The BOIs were going to make certain they got to the airstrip before anyone else did.

Sam turned back to the hacienda, found Abbie pacing restlessly in the hot confines of the small house.

"Hey," she said, checking a full-fledged flinch when she heard the door close behind him.

He assessed her with concern. "You okay?"

She nodded. She lied. What she was, was wired and edgy.

"Where are the guys?"

"Taking care of business," Sam said.

"What business?" she asked absently, hugging her arms around herself as she restlessly prowled the small room.

"By now, Nader will have reached out and put the touch on any mercs within a hundred-mile radius of here. They'll be on their way to La Jigua to position themselves for an ambush. The guys are going to form a little welcoming committee."

She nodded — with him but not quite. "So you don't think Nader bought that I'm in this by myself."

"What I think is that Nader is in new territory without Smith to run interference for him. He'll go into overkill mode trying to cover his bases. He won't take any chances. He'll send shooters, show up thinking they're all in place, covering the perimeter. He's going to be unpleasantly surprised."

"Because his hired men will be dead."

Her statement was matter-of-fact. Impassive. Like her expression. From a woman who wore her emotions like some women wore perfume. Lavishly. It was that lack of emotion that worried him.

"Yeah," he agreed walking over to her side. "Dead, or indisposed."

She looked away. "Kill or be killed."

He reached out, touched her arm, careful of the injury from Smith's knife. "Abbie . . . this will be over soon. Then you can put it behind you."

For the first time since he'd walked in and found her this way, something other than indifference filled her eyes. Something very much like desperation.

"Is that what you do? You kill someone, then just walk away? Just forget it ever happened?"

He'd known this morning was going to catch up with her. Known she was going to crash when it did. He knew because he'd had his own crashes. And no. You never just walked away. You never forgot. But she didn't need to hear that now.

"I'd be dead now if you hadn't shot him."

She rounded on him. Eyes wide and tortured, her emotional barricades smashed to smithereens. "You think I don't know that? You think I don't know that it was him or you? It doesn't change the fact that I took a life. He . . . he was someone's son. Maybe some child's father."

"Yeah," Sam agreed. "He might have been. But he also made a bad decision. He chose to be on the wrong side."

"Like Cory chose to be on the wrong side?" Torment transitioned to accusation.

Sam understood. She was floundering. And she was lost. Trying to make sense out of something that was senseless and still keep herself together in the face of yet more danger that lay ahead of her.

"That was not a judgment," he said gently. "Look. Everyone's got a story. Everyone has reasons—sometimes compelling reasons—for choosing the paths they take. Some . . . some are luckier than others. They see the light. They get out. Or someone helps them out. Others have the choice taken away from them."

"Like I took that man's choice when I took his life."

"He put himself in that position, Abbie. Not you. You pulled the trigger, but you didn't kill him. He took care of that himself the minute he hired on with Fox."

She dragged her palms over her face. Breathed deep. Shook her head like she was trying to clear it of the memories. "So, what happens now?"

What happened now was that Sam dropped the subject. She didn't want to talk about it anymore. The important thing was, she'd let out some of what was eating at her.

"Now we eat some of those *baleadas* Señorita García made for us before she left for the market a while ago. Providing the guys left us any. They were stuffing them in their pockets like they were candy before they headed out."

"You go ahead. I'm not really hungry."

He wasn't having any of that. Sam took her elbow, steered her into the kitchen. "Doesn't matter. You need the protein."

He sat her down at a scarred wooden table. She wrinkled her nose, then sniffed, looking mildly interested. "Looks like a tortilla."

"Whatever floats your boat. Just eat. You're not leaving the table until you do."

"You like giving orders, don't you?" she said, more statement than question as she gingerly picked up the *baleada* that was loaded with beans, cheese, eggs, and guacamole.

"Yeah," he said simply. "I do."

And got the reaction he wanted.

One corner of her mouth tipped before she could think about it. "Must be why you're so good at it."

He nodded around a mouthful of tortilla. "It's a gift."

Another smile. A little wily, marginally amused even, though still guarded.

He liked it. Liked that she was finally feeling comfortable with him. And that he had her thinking about something other than this morning.

"It was from my final divorce settlement," she said after several moments of relaxed silence had passed and half of her *baleada* was gone. "New furniture. New car. The final payment arrived last week."

He said nothing, just nodded.

"And the diamond? From my engagement ring. I had it reset. Don was a lot of things, but he wasn't cheap."

"Just stupid," Sam concluded.

He shrugged when she glanced at him over her lunch, which he was glad to see she had begun to enjoy. "He let you go, didn't he? Spells stupid in my book." Then again, he hadn't exactly been Rhodes scholar material in his prejudgment of her.

He stood, then walked to the ancient refrigerator in the corner, dug around inside until he found a couple of beers. Held one up to her.

When she nodded, he found a bottle opener and joined her at the table again.

"So . . . what's the book on you?" she asked. "Ever been married?"

He downed a swallow of cold beer. "Nope."

When he didn't say any more, she gave him an expectant look. "That's a pretty short book."

He helped himself to another *baleada*. "After my stint in the military, I joined my old CO in Argentina. Private firm. It's kept me busy."

"Saving the world," she speculated with a pointed look.

He shrugged. "Little pieces of it. Didn't leave much time for . . ." he paused, thought, finally settled on, " . . . relationships. Women tend to run the other way when they understand a man in my business—former business," he amended, "has the life expectancy of a fruit fly."

"But you left it?"

He nodded. Felt the weight of that decision.

She leaned back in her chair. "You miss it?"

He looked past her, wishing he didn't know the answer so well. "Wouldn't matter if I did. I've made commitments."

Those emotions she wore so baldly were back on her face again. "I'm so sorry about your sister."

He closed his eyes. Swallowed. "Yeah. Thanks. You finished?"

He wanted to talk about Terri as much as Abbie wanted to talk about putting a hole the size of a quarter through a man's heart.

She nodded. "Full up."

"Let's get out of this house for a while. Too damn hot."

"And go where?"

He checked his watch. "We've got several hours to kill before Mendoza comes back for us. Grab a towel. Change of clothes, if you've got one. Shampoo, if you've got that."

"Um, excuse me?"

"I saw the shower, remember?" Sam headed for the door. "It's hardly more than a bucket and a nozzle."

"You stumble onto a spa or something?"

He smiled. "Or something."

21

It felt good to be out of the dark house. Out of the heat and shadows of the adobe walls. Away from the lingering scent of antiseptic and blood and fried tortillas.

The sun burned warm on her shoulders as Abbie walked alongside Sam through the tall grass behind the hacienda.

Much like the land they had ridden through this morning on horseback, here, a quarter of a mile from the house, the hills were gentle, sweeping. Up a rise, down another, and both the hacienda and the little hamlet of La Entrada were no longer visible. Just fields of green, blue skies, warm sun. Idyllic. Or it would have been if she could block the reality of last night and this morning.

Rutger Smith's head blown off.

Blood and brains matted in her hair.

Bodies in the mud.

Bodies in the dirt.

Holding a rifle.

Firing.

Watching a man fall.

Knowing she was the one who had killed him.

Killed him.

Killed.

She'd killed a man.

Yesterday, she would have felt instant, crippling nausea. Today, she felt little more than numb.

"You pulled the trigger, but you didn't kill him. He took care of that himself the minute he hired on with Fox."

Someday. Maybe she could accept that Sam's words made sense. Today, she just wanted to forget it ever happened.

And when they crested yet one more ridge and she realized that this was their destination, she realized that's why he'd brought her here. So she could forget—at least for a little while.

"Oh." She stopped. Breath caught. Stared. In wonder. In awe. In glorious, life-sustaining gratitude. "It's beautiful."

She'd needed beautiful. She'd needed a reminder of all life could be. Vital. Vibrant. Embracing.

"Yeah," Sam agreed. "It was pretty dark when we found the water last night but I could see potential. Had a feeling you'd like it."

"Better than a spa," she said with a smile and headed toward the gently meandering stream nestled in a copse of shady trees at the bottom of the rise. Flowers danced on tall stems, bees buzzed, birds sang.

Idyllic, she thought again. Perfection. A commercial for peace and tranquillity. *Calgon, take me away.*

"Bottom is sand," Sam said when they reached the edge of the bank. "Last night it was running bank full. Looks like it's only about two, two and a half feet deep today now that the runoff from the rain has made its way through."

"*Much* better than a spa," she restated with emphasis and toed off her shoes. Anxious now, she eased down the bank and stood ankle deep in the cool, clear water.

"Heads up."

She glanced up. Sam had foraged around in her pack and had come up with her shampoo. She caught the bottle when he tossed it down to her.

"Take your time. You know your way back, right?"

She shaded her eyes against a sun that burned warm and bright behind him where he stood above her on the bank. "You're leaving?"

He reached up, scratched his jaw. A heavy, dark stubble covered his lower face. Made him look imposing, dangerous . . . and darkly handsome. "Thought you might need a little alone time."

Yeah. For a little over twenty-four hours the testosterone level had been off the charts. His gesture was thoughtful and kind. And telling of the man he was. It had been a long time coming, but she knew the truth now.

"You're a good man, Sam Lang."

Something very much like relief crossed his face. "Yeah, well." He held up the blanket he'd tugged off her bed and carried out here, tossed it on the grass. "Like I said. Take your time. Take a siesta. Do you good to get some sleep."

He gave her a lingering look with those dark, penetrating eyes. It was a look she recognized. He didn't want to leave.

It didn't take any thought at all to realize she didn't want him to go.

"Stay," she said, holding his gaze. "Stay with me."

The muscles in his throat convulsed as he swallowed. Yet there he stood.

"Stay," she said again, more promise than plea this time, and reached for the hem of her T-shirt.

Sam saw the plea in her eyes. Felt the desire as Abbie tugged her T-shirt up and over her head. Her gaze never leaving his face, she tossed it on the bank.

He understood the bone-deep longing to be something more than alone, to be something more than singular. Understood it in spades. He was thirty-five years old. He'd been alone his entire life. So yeah, he understood. Just like he understood that while alone had once been a choice for him, it wasn't nearly as compelling a prospect as it once was.

"Stay," she whispered again as slender fingers reached behind her back, unhooked the clasp of her bra.

He felt his throat tighten along with his groin when she slid the straps down her arms, tossed the delicate pink satin at his feet.

There she stood—shoulders back, exquisite, proud, beautiful. It was not an attempt to tease. Tease implied playful. Tease implied pretending.

There was no pretending here. She wanted more than that from him. She needed more. Needed his strength and the physical release his body could give her. In her eyes he saw a barely veiled desperation to feel something other than terror and anxiety and the ultimate stopgap: numb.

Wise or woefully stupid, he needed it, too. Suddenly craved it as much as he craved the feel of her hands on his body.

Stone-cold fox.

Reed's words didn't even come close. She was beyond description. Sam had never wanted the way he wanted around this woman.

Her breasts were beautiful and brazenly feminine. Her movements feline and sensual as the sun danced against her hair and the wind moving through the trees shot dappled shadows over her olive skin.

She held a hand up, beckoning.

And he knew he wasn't going anywhere that didn't take him closer to her.

He dragged his shirt over his head, mesmerized by the sight of her shimmying out of her jeans, rolling pink panties down her hips and smiling with an endearing mixture of relief and anticipation when he shucked the rest of his clothes and joined her in the cool, flowing water.

She reached for him, moved quickly into him, pressed her quivering breasts and tight pink nipples against his chest. Skin against skin, heat against heat, they stood there, water lapping and gurgling around their bare legs.

"You know this is crazy," he whispered against her mouth, loving the feel of her beneath his hands as he skated them down her slender back, cupped her hips and pulled her flush against him.

"More than," she agreed and opened wide, indulging herself in the hunger she'd enticed from some primal place deep inside him.

He loved kissing her. Loved the soft sounds she made. Sounds of pleasure, sounds of surrender and impatience and restless, reckless desire. If he didn't slow things down, he was going to take her. Rough. Hard. Fast. She deserved far more than that.

"We've got time," he said, tucking her head beneath his chin and locking his arms around her. "We've got time. Come 'ere." He led her deeper into the water. "Let's get wet."

"I'm already wet." A sexy smile tipped up one corner of her mouth.

He chuckled. Kissed her hard and quick. "Good to know. We will definitely get back to that. For now, though, indulge me."

"I thought that's what I was about to do."

He didn't know when, exactly, things had changed between them. When the thrust and parry of distrust, the dodge and redirect of vulnerability had shifted to this easy, yet sensually edgy openness. This . . . trust.

"You're a good man, Sam."

Just like he hadn't known how badly he'd needed to hear those words from her until she'd said them. Or how much he'd wanted this kind of intimacy.

No. He didn't know when it had all changed. He was only glad for the transition. This woman was special. This woman, he realized with no lack of amazement, and with a clarity that left no doubt, was his.

His.

"Let me wash your hair, Abbie."

The look she gave him spoke volumes. She was surprised, mystified—and a sweet tenderness filled her eyes.

"You really want to do that?"

"Yeah. I really want to."

He sat down, cross-legged in the sandy bed of the stream and urged her down onto her back in front of him. Anchoring her shoulder blades on his crossed ankles, he guided her head onto the cove between his thighs.

Her dark hair floated over his legs. Water cascaded gently over her shoulders, streamed between her bare breasts, pooled in the indentation of her navel.

He took the shampoo bottle from her hand, squeezed some into his palm then tossed the bottle onto the bank above them.

"Umm," she closed her eyes, and he felt the lingering tension start to drift from her body as he gathered her hair and lathered it up with shampoo. "How much is this deluxe spa treatment going to cost me?"

"We'll work something out," he said around a smile, wholly mystified by the texture and weight of her hair. And by the look of her long, slim body stretched out wet and naked in front of him.

With deliberate care, he massaged her scalp, then worked his way down to her neck, kneading the aching muscles there, feeling the tension ease with each caress of his thumb.

"Very nice," she murmured. "You're going to get a good tip for this."

"Here's a tip," he said, gliding his hands over her collarbone, moving slowly toward the lovely rise of her breasts. "You are beautiful."

He covered her breasts with his big hands, molded their slick wetness in his palms, stunned anew by the silk and the weight of them and the instant response of her nipples hardening against his palms.

She lifted her arms, clutched his hands, pressed them deeper into her, arched her back in anticipation and pleasure. "Sam."

"Shhh," he leaned forward, kissed her, chuckled when his chin hit her nose and they did a little dance of redirection until they found a fit that worked.

He sucked her lower lip between his teeth as he slowly pulled away.

She stopped him with a hand around his nape, turned her head from side to side, rubbing against his erection. "I want you inside me, Sam."

"In time."

She let out a sound that was part laugh, part growl, and all frustration. "Has anyone ever suggested that you have control issues?"

"Many times," he said, carefully rinsing her hair. He loved the look and feel of it as it floated around her head, tickled his thighs. Loved the look of her as she lay there, eyes closed, sun dancing against the water and reflecting off her wet skin.

"Anyone ever tested that control?"

"Many times," he said again. "But no one more than you."

Her wet lashes fluttered against her cheeks. She smiled up at him. "Oh, I think I like knowing that."

She sat up then, faced him on her knees as the water lapped around her waist. "I think I very much like knowing that."

Then she leaned in, wrapped her arms around his neck, and kissed him. Warm lips. Questing tongue. Delicious sighs.

His control slipped away like water running downstream. He gripped her waist, lifted her, urged her legs around his hips, and settled her down on top of him. The lips of her sex opened against his cock as she rocked her hips against him.

"Inside," she demanded, nipping his lower lip, then plunging her tongue back into his mouth in a desperate plea for penetration.

Too fast, too rough, he thought, struggling to slow himself down, to proceed with finesse. She wasn't having any of it. She reached down between their bodies, encompassed his throbbing cock in her hand. Positioned him, then lowered herself hard and fast.

Penetration was instant. Amazing. Mind-shattering.

She stiffened, cried out, then took his mouth again and begin moving. Hungry. Demanding. Wild and wanton.

He claimed her mouth on a groan, gripped her hips, and rocked her up and down on him in a fast and frenzied rhythm. He swallowed her sultry sighs. Was aware of her frantic breath. The slap of water. The slap of their bodies, primal, perfect, and consuming.

She cried his name, arched her back, ground herself against him, and came on a long, exhalation of breath and a low, slow moan. He held her there, buried thick and deep and pulsing, felt his cum tighten his balls, a sweet pressure building beyond reason. He pumped one last time, gripped her hips tight, knowing he'd leave bruises, unable to do a damn thing about it, and let himself go. Pleasure, rich, electric, and beyond cataloging, ripped through him, annihilated him, transformed him.

"Abbie," he murmured, hugging her hard against him. Just, "Abbie," as she crumpled, boneless and gasping, against his chest.

They stayed that way for a long time. Knotted together like a giant pretzel in the waist-deep water, their toes turning into prunes. Her cheek on his shoulder. His chin on the top of her head. When he felt his leg start to go to sleep from their crisscrossed positions, he reluctantly roused her.

"Come on. Let's wash up and get dry."

Laughing lazily, they wobbled to their feet. Then they washed each other. It was a new experience for Sam. This tender, relaxed intimacy. He told her as much when they'd waded out of the water and lay down on their backs on the blanket to dry in the shade.

"Me too," she confided, rolling onto her side to face him.

He met her eyes, glanced down at her bandaged arm. "We'll need to get a fresh dressing on that."

"I'm fine."

"Yeah, well, you won't get any arguments from me on that count."

She smiled. Touched a finger to his lips. He opened his mouth, sucked that finger inside.

"Is this real?" she asked, a crease suddenly developing between her brows.

He could have pretended he didn't, but he knew what she meant. He breathed deep, kissed her palm. Crossing his arms beneath his head, he stared at the tree limbs overhead. "I guess we'll find out when we get back."

He was a veteran of too many conflicts—sanctioned and otherwise. Emotions ran high in the heat of battle. In the heat of the moment. What a person felt in the midst of grave danger sometimes didn't translate to the "real world."

He knew what he felt. Knew that wouldn't change. What he didn't know was how she would feel when the fog of danger had lifted.

"I want it to be, Sam. I so want this to be real."

He turned his head, felt a fresh wave of tenderness and longing at the raw emotion in her deep brown eyes. "Yeah. So do I."

So do I, he thought, pulling her against his side and urging her to get some sleep.

They had to get out of this first. They had to get Nader. If they didn't, there'd be no future for either one of them, real or otherwise.

He watched over her while she slept. Reluctantly roused her an hour later.

They dressed in silence, the easy intimacy gone.

Reality had encroached on paradise.

The black cloud cast by Fredrick Nader hovered over them once again.

"Let's go do this," she said, her emotions under wraps for the confrontation to come.

"No chances. You take no chances, you understand?"

Yeah. He could see in her eyes that she understood his equivalent of an order. What he couldn't see was if she intended to obey it.

22

Sun glinted off the hood of the black Town Car as Fredrick Nader, unaccustomed to driving himself, headed west into the setting sun. His turnoff was just ahead. There the highway ended and the dirt road began. Dust immediately attached in a thin dull film to the windshield and sucked onto the gleaming paint as he continued down the washboard-rough road toward the La Jigua airstrip.

Fredrick much preferred the German craftsmanship of a Mercedes-Benz. The vehicle was richer, cleaner, subtly striking, and superior to the American pretender. On short notice, however, he'd had to make do.

The glorious strains of Mozart's Horn Concerto no. 3 enveloped him, the rich, mellow notes resonating through eight stereo speakers. The Austrian had been brilliant. Too bad he hadn't been German.

And too bad Miss Abbie Hughes would not live to see another sunrise.

His calls had been successful. He'd worked with Caesare Fuentes and his mercenaries before. One call and Fredrick had been assured that a minimum of twelve men, fully armed, and hungry for the balance of their payment, would be in place at the airstrip far in advance of Miss Hughes's expected arrival and that of any mercenaries she may have hired to defend herself. And yes, he fully expected she would bring protection.

Fredrick had ultimate confidence in the men Fuentes would send. But, as insurance, he'd hired another dozen men, also heavily armed. They kept pace out of sight in three Jeeps half a mile behind him, ready to shoot to kill should Fredrick meet up with resistance.

Come alone? The thought was laughable.

One could never be too careful, after all. Likewise, one could never fully trust a woman. Like her brother, she was a stupid, greedy American. Before he was finished with her, she would be screaming for mercy. The thought shot blood to his groin in a rush. No more vicarious thrills. With Smith gone, Fredrick more than relished the idea of taking care of the unsuspecting Miss Hughes himself. Relished it so much, in fact, that he felt remiss for delegating the wet work to Smith in the past.

He let off the gas when the corrugated roof of the neglected airstrip hangar came into view. He cruised cautiously to the access lane, then turned into the drive and pulled to a stop.

But for carrion eaters picking at the carcass of what appeared to be a rotted wild pig at the boundary of the property, he saw no signs of life.

The hangar doors yawned open, the interior lost in shadows. A single-engine Cessna—old and out of commission—was parked on the south side of the hangar, chocks wedged against the wheels, tethers tied to the struts. A thick layer of dust coated its windshield. A sheared prop leaned against a wheel hub.

One lone helicopter sat in the middle of the tarmac. Small. Four-seater. Ridiculously antiquated when compared to his sleek little Eurocopter that had delivered him to San Pedro Sula with swift efficiency.

Fredrick sat behind the wheel of the Town Car, squinted toward the chopper, watched the slow-moving rotor blades, and detected movement in the cockpit.

While he could possibly applaud her ingenuity, he almost felt sorry for Abbie Hughes. She actually thought she could make an aerial escape? Everyone had a price in this part of the world, and he had no doubt that he could buy off the pilot.

He eased within twenty feet of the bird, turned off the motor. Then he readjusted his tie, checked his hair in the rearview mirror, and, even though he knew it was there, patted his jacket pocket for the Walther P38 tucked inside. Another brilliant piece of German craftsmanship.

Adrenaline spiked as he stepped out of the air-conditioned quiet and into the sweltering sunset heat and the whine of the chopper motor. He immediately recoiled and gagged as a wind gust kicked dust in his face and brought the putrid scent of decayed animal flesh.

"She had better be worth it," he muttered beneath his breath and waited for Miss Hughes to come to him.

"Showtime," Savage whispered into his shoulder mic. He lay belly down on the hangar roof beneath a gray tarp meant to camouflage both him and the M-249 machine gun Doc had reluctantly given over to him. "And about damn time. This fucking tin is about to burn my balls off."

"*There's* a picture that'll give me nightmares." Doc returned from inside the hangar where he'd established a defensive position behind the crisscrossed slats of a boarded-up window.

Sam had taken a position behind the wheel strut of the disabled Cessna with full view of Nader and the idling chopper with Abbie and Mendoza inside. He watched Nader's car pull to a stop. Forced a combat calm as the bastard got out from behind the wheel. "Mendoza?"

The main rotor spun slowly. Dust stirred in lazy circles from the prop wash as the turbine engine whined and rumbled.

"Good to go." Mendoza sat behind the joystick of the chopper, his M-4 locked and loaded. The bird was revved and ready to fly if the action got too hot. But for now the chopper was their version of a Trojan horse, only the plan was for Nader to come to it, not the other way around.

Inside the cockpit with Mendoza, Sam knew that Abbie sweltered beneath a Kevlar vest like the rest of them. He also knew that if she so much as set a foot out of the cabin, he'd sprint across the tarmac and haul her back inside himself. He trusted Mendoza to lift the hell out of there if the action got too hot and get her to safety.

It was almost over. The plan was straight up and clean. The boys had handled Nader's advance team of mercs. They were either dead or trussed up like slaughter chickens, piled up behind the hangar.

"Easy as taking your poker money," Doc had reported to Sam after Mendoza had returned to La Entrada, picked up Sam and Abbie, and brought them back to the airstrip.

"So let's keep things easy," Sam had said, and the four of them decided on defensive positions. While Sam hadn't wanted Abbie more than touching distance away from him, he needed to be mobile in case Nader had any other tricks up his sleeve. He also knew that as soon as Nader saw him, Sam would become more of a target than Abbie, which meant she needed to be as far away from him as possible. He didn't want to draw fire her way.

"Whatever you do, Raphael, do *not* let her out of the chopper," Sam whispered into his mic as Nader stood by the front fender of the Lincoln Town Car. Muhammad, waiting for the mountain.

He was going to have a long wait.

Sam watched the cocky sonofabitch. Nader would be shaking in his Italian loafers if he knew what had happened to his men.

"It's exceedingly warm, Miss Hughes," Nader shouted above the engine noise. "Can we get this over with, please?"

"Yeah." Sam stepped out from behind the Cessna, his M-16 butted up against his shoulder, his sites honed in the center of Nader's chest. "Let's get this over with."

"You!" Rattled Nader backed toward the driver's side door.

"Yeah. Me. And it's me you'll deal with this time, not a defenseless woman."

Nader's eyes went wild with fear. With good reason. There was nothing Sam wanted to do more than squeeze the trigger. Empty a thirty-round magazine into the hole where Nader was supposed to have a heart. He sensed Doc behind him, covering his six.

"What's the matter, Nader? Not as much fun manning the front line as it is delegating?" So much for chit-chat. It was time to cut to the chase. Time for Nader to know he was about to breathe his last breath.

"How much did it cost you to pay someone to blow up my sister?"

"That . . . that was not my doing."

A red haze filtered over Sam's vision. "Lie again, you slimy maggot. Give me a reason to kill you one bullet at a time."

Hatred sucked at his control, dragging him toward a sinkhole of rage so primal he saw himself committing acts against this man even he would label atrocities.

Every breathing cell wanted to make Nader pay in blood for stealing breath and life from his little sister. For the guilt that lashed at Sam's conscience like saber slices.

His heart slammed. His hands shook as he sighted down the barrel, his finger pressed against the side of the trigger guard, half an inch away from dropping the hammer. His breath stalled as he watched Nader inch closer to the driver's door. A round through the kneecap would be a good start. Nader would squeal like a pig, squirm in the dirt like a snake. Sam would enjoy every howl of anguish. Relish the thought of leaving him to bake and rot under the sun while vultures picked at his bones.

"Hit the dirt, asshole. Face-first," Sam ordered just as the sound of a fast-moving vehicle registered.

"Company," Doc said. "Jesus H. Christ!" he added as three pickup trucks, loaded with shooters, flew over the hill to the south and barreled down the runway toward them.

"What the fuck?" Doc added as two Jeeps, one of them firing rounds from a belt-fed machine gun kicked up dust, converged from the other direction. "What the hell's going on?"

What was going on was that in thirty more seconds they were going to be trapped.

"Get her out of there!" Sam roared into the mic.

Mendoza was already on it. He revved up the engine to full throttle as the encroaching vehicles moved in fast, sandwiching the chopper between them.

Sam turned back to Nader as he dove inside the Town Car. He pumped a burst into the car but Nader was already cranking the key.

The machine gun rattled from a distance. Savage, on the roof, answered back with the M-249. Abbie and Mendoza were about to get caught in the crossfire. The chopper lifted a couple of inches off the ground, then dropped like a stone.

"Shit," Doc swore. "They took a hit in the tail rotor."

Which meant the bird wasn't going anywhere. Nader hit the gas and Sam saw his chance at taking him down slipping away. In the end, there was only one decision to make.

He had to get to Abbie. She was more important than Nader. Mendoza could make a break for it, but she was a sitting duck.

He shot toward the chopper.

Doc caught up with him, grabbed Sam by the vest and dragged him back toward the hangar. "Are you fucking nuts?" he yelled as he shoved Sam for cover.

Yeah. He was. And Doc was right. Getting killed wasn't going to help Abbie.

From the corner of his eye he saw the Town Car cut a tight circle, gun it for the road. He turned around backward, lifted the M-16 again, sprayed the car with another round of bullets.

The two tires on the driver's side deflated like a failed soufflé. The vehicle swerved, fishtailed, but recovered as Nader floored it. Limping on two wheels and two hubs, the Lincoln shot out onto the road.

"Sonofabitch," Sam swore as Nader drove away. He ducked behind the open door of the hangar, turned his attention back to the gunman bearing down on the chopper.

"We've got to get them out of there. Savage," he yelled into the mic. "Pick your time, then take out whichever Jeep gets to the chopper first."

"Cover me," he barked at Doc. It was now or never.

"Fuck that." Doc snagged him by the vest again, jerked him back to the cover of the hangar. "You go out there now, you come back a sprinkler. And Gawddamn—look. Are you seeing what I think *I'm* seeing?"

"What are you talking about?"

"Who the hell's shooting at who?"

Sam glared from Doc to the airstrip. Assessed the action. "Sonofabitch. Are those idiots shooting at each other?"

They were, he realized, putting it together. "Fox. Has to be Fox's men in the trucks."

"And they're putting it to Nader's guns in the Jeeps."

"How the hell did Fox know this was coming down?"

They both ducked as stray rifle fire peppered a line of holes in the metal siding above their heads.

"Hell, Fox had a mole in one of Nader's camps. Wouldn't put it past him to have 'em dug in all over."

Doc was probably right. Mercs hired out for the highest dollar. It was a cutthroat and incestuous community. Loyalty was as foreign a concept as trust.

"I've got to get to Abbie." Sam sized up the chaos. Pickups with shooters firing AK's were circling the Jeeps like wolves. The wolves were barking back. The staccato rattle of Nader's machine gunner ate bites out of the dirt, the chopper, and the racing trucks.

"Savage," Sam yelled.

"Yo."

"I need one of those Jeeps."

"All you had to do was ask."

Behind Sam, Doc's M-16 fired off three burst rounds of 5.56 NATO ammo, the rifle's distinct *pop-pop-pop* discernible, even in the melee, from the heavier thuds of the AK-47 yammering away from the back of the moving truck.

Through the roar of bullets ricocheting and whizzing in the air came the sound of the M-249 rattling through a belt of cartridges as Savage took aim at the closest Jeep.

"And he scores!" Doc hooted as Savage shattered the windshield of the Jeep. Two men tumbled out of the back and ran for cover. The Jeep came to a screeching stop twenty yards from the hangar. Realizing the vehicle had become a bullet magnet, the driver unassed the Jeep and ran like hell.

Sam didn't bother to announce his plans this time. He took off running before Doc could stop him, knowing he'd lay down fire and cover him.

Hunched low, Sam zigzagged a path toward the Jeep while from the hangar roof, Savage swept the ground ahead of him with a barrage of firepower, clearing the way. Sam dove the final two yards to the vehicle, wrenched open the passenger door, and jerked the injured shooter out. He hadn't yet hit the ground when Sam piled inside, slid behind the wheel, and gunned it.

Dirt flew behind spinning tires as he arrowed toward the trapped chopper, hunching low over the steering wheel as bullets flew around him. He skidded to a stop by the cockpit door.

"Thought I was going to miss tee time," Mendoza groused as he helped Abbie out onto the skid. Sam jerked her into the front seat beside him. Mendoza bailed into the back.

"Is there anyone who *wasn't* invited to this party?" Mendoza grumbled, aiming his M-4 and firing a burst toward an approaching truck as Sam laid rubber and shot back toward the hangar.

"Can you guys handle this?" Sam braked to a screeching stop by the hangar so Mendoza could bail out.

"Can a fish fucking swim?" Mendoza joined Doc, who gave Sam a thumbs-up.

Sam hit the gas and took off after Nader.

23

⤙

Sam jammed on the gas pedal and roared down the dirt road following Nader's dust trail.

"Buckle up!"

He didn't have to tell Abbie twice. She was white-knuckling it with her grip on the dash beside him.

"And watch out for the glass," he shouted above the wind whipping through what had once been a windshield. Glass shards flew, dust swirled around inside the cab as Abbie's hair whipped around her head.

Her hands were shaking as she dutifully reached for the seat belt.

Adrenaline. Fear. Sam knew both reactions well. If he'd felt safe leaving her with the guys, he would have, but the truth was, he wanted her where he could see her.

"What happened back there?"

He squinted against the wind. "Best guess—Fox also had an agenda for Nader."

The seat belt kept her from hitting the roof when they flew over a bump. "That was Fox?"

"Looks that way."

"What about the guys?" She glanced behind them. Sam checked the side mirrors. Pickups had surrounded the remaining Jeeps. "Are they going to be okay?"

"My money's on them." His money was always on them.

Jaw set, he closed in on the dust boiling down the road like a jet trail. Punched harder on the gas.

"I see the car," Abbie said, holding her hair back from her eyes.

"Hold on."

Face grim, Sam roared up behind the Lincoln. "Hold on!" he repeated, then rammed the Lincoln's bumper.

The impact sent a bone-jarring shock through his hands, all the way to his shoulders.

He stomped down on the gas again.

Rammed the Lincoln again. The Lincoln fishtailed, righted itself, and sped on, sparks flying as the car's belly skidded against the dirt on the driver's side where the bare hubs barely kept it afloat.

Beside him, Abbie gasped but, to her credit, didn't scream, curse, or rail at him to back off.

Eyes dead ahead, Sam backed off, put more distance between the vehicles. Satisfied he had a good running start, he punched it one more time.

"Brace yourself."

"Oh, God," Abbie murmured when he pulled up alongside the Town Car, keeping pace at around forty miles per until the Jeep's front wheels were aligned with the Lincoln's rear driver's side wheel.

When they were within inches of each other, Sam steered sharply into the Town Car. The PIT maneuver worked where ramming hadn't. The Lincoln's rear wheels lost traction, started to skid. Sam abruptly braked, nosed the Jeep clear, and fought for control as the Lincoln swerved, spun out, then shot toward the ditch in a cloud of dust and exhaust and rammed, nose first, into the far side.

Where it stopped. Dead still, road dust billowing around it.

Sam tore up to the Lincoln.

"Do not get out of this vehicle," he ordered, grabbing his M-16 and sprinting toward Nader's disabled Town Car.

The driver's door of the Lincoln shot open and Nader stumbled out. Blood covered his face. His left arm hung at a grotesque angle, clearly broken. He leaned against his right side, struggling to stay on his feet.

Sam vowed he was not going to let Nader walk away alive this time. He lifted the rifle. Sighted down the barrel. Positioned his finger on the trigger—and heard the voices roar through his head.

The voice of his sister, screaming in pain, burning to death in a fiery blast. The voice of little Tina crying herself to sleep at night. The voice of his father. *"You can't not do this."*

Nader dropped to his knees. "Don't kill me. Please, I beg you. Please. I'm unarmed. Don't kill me." He was crying now. Pathetic, broken. "I have money. More money than you could ever imagine. I can pay you."

Fuck him. Do it! A new voice this time. His own voice. *Kill him! Don't make your family go through the agony of reliving Terri's death at a trial. Don't take the chance that this sick fuck will buy his way out of what he's done.*

"Please, I beg you, please. Have mercy."

Do it! Do it!

Sam's finger tightened on the trigger. He drew a bead on the spot between Nader's snake eyes.

Yet there he stood. Frozen. Wanting, gut deep, to waste this piece of human garbage and rid the world of his brutal existence.

But something made him hold his fire.

Something human, he realized, that tugged him away from the abyss. Something that delineated him from the likes of men like Nader who could kill in cold blood and sleep like a baby in spite of it.

He killed your sister in cold blood. He deserves to die that way.

He lifted the rifle again.

Watched the pathetic bastard mewl and beg like a damn baby.

Be careful in the company of monsters that you don't become one.

Words Sam had lived by. A warning from Nate Black. His CO. His former boss.

He couldn't do it.

He just couldn't do it. He could not reduce himself to cold-blooded murder. He could not become a monster like the one sniveling and broken before him.

Swearing under his breath, he eased off the trigger.

He lowered the gun. Covered his face with his hand. Realized his cheeks were wet. Didn't know whether to congratulate or hate himself for having just enough humanity left to stand down.

He lowered his head, breathed deep.

"Sam!"

Abbie's scream snapped his head up, just in time to see Nader push away from the car and lift a gun in his right hand.

Instinct. Muscle memory. The will to survive.

All three took over. Sam raised the M-16, squeezed the trigger. Heard a succession of triple pops as he fired. Kept on firing.

He felt the rifle recoil in his hands even after the gunshots echoed to silence and the brass quit spitting to the *click, click, click* of the empty the rifle. Was aware of Nader's body jump, slump, then fall over before it even registered that he'd pulled the trigger.

Dead.

The bastard was finally dead.

Abbie rushed up beside him. Threw her arms around him.

He wrapped an arm around her, held her tight, breathed deep. It was over.

Or maybe not.

His head came up.

The sound of a fast-approaching vehicle spun him around. A pickup. Full of muscle and guns.

With Desmond Fox himself riding shotgun.

Sam shoved Abbie behind him, stood his ground as the truck slowed, crawled to a stop.

Sam couldn't do a damn thing but stand there, knowing his magazine was empty.

Fox looked from Sam to Nader, where Nader lay dead in the ditch.

He smiled. Turned that sinister smile on Sam. *"Bien hecho."* Well done.

Still smiling, he ordered his driver to move on. As they rolled by, Fox made a gun with his thumb and forefinger. He pointed it at Sam's head. Pulled an imaginary trigger. "*La próxima vez*." Next time.

"Jesus." Abbie inched out from behind him as they stood there, watching the truck drive away, followed by the rest of Fox's entourage. "What just happened?"

"Fox just granted me a reprieve."

The death of Nader—Fox's blood enemy—had been the catalyst. The warning that Fox would kill Sam "next time" they met was a gesture of appreciation.

The BOIs pulled up a few minutes later.

"We going after him?" Savage was still juiced on ad-renaline from the action on the airstrip and ready to rock and roll.

Sam shook his head. He'd had enough. And the book on Fox told him the only reason Fox wanted the diamonds was because Nader wanted them. As long as the diamonds were returned to Honduras, they wouldn't be hearing from Fox anytime soon.

He pulled Abbie close, hugged her hard against him, and stared at Nader's body over the top of her head.

In that moment, he physically felt the cloud that had been casting a huge, dark shadow over his head start to dissipate.

24

"Uncle Sam!" When Tina spotted Sam across the driveway, she took off at a dead run and launched herself at him with the velocity and unerring accuracy of a guided missile.

"Whoa there, cowgirl," he laughed, scooping her into his arms and swinging her in a circle.

"I missed you so much," she declared with the uncensored emotion and innocence of a child. She clung to him, arms locked around his neck, her little legs wrapped around his waist.

"Me, too, sweetie," he murmured, savoring the sweet little-girl scent as he buried his face against her hair.

Over the top of her head, Sam saw his dad.

Tom Lang's face was expressionless, yet asked a hundred questions.

Sam met his dad's eyes, nodded. *It's done.*

His dad compressed his lips. He squared his shoulders, nodded back, his relief and thanks relayed in those minimal yet meaningful gestures.

"So what'd you bring me?" Tina asked on a giggle.

Sam held his dad's gaze for a moment longer, a world of emotions exchanged in that one prolonged look. Then he turned back to Tina, tickled her until she shrieked with laughter.

"What makes you think I brought you anything?" he teased as he set her down, then dug into his go bag for the new boots he'd picked up on a whim at the airport after they'd landed.

"'Cause you love me," she stated with a conviction that filled his chest with a love he couldn't quantify or contain.

"You got that right," he agreed, then laughed out loud when she hugged the boots to her chest.

"Just what I always wanted."

Las Vegas

"How's he doing?"

Abbie shut the guest bedroom door quietly behind her and joined Crystal in the living room. "Today? Not so good."

Abbie was doing her best not to worry about Cory. And Cory was doing his best to convince her that she had nothing to worry about. A tough trick when he'd spent most of the time since they'd come home in bed.

"They're having a hard time knocking out the infection but his temp's down a little today and his color is better."

"What do the doctors say?"

Abbie sank down on her sofa, lifted the glass of wine Crystal had poured for her, sipped. "To be patient. That he'll be fine. Thanks," she added as an afterthought, lifting the glass so Crystal would know that Abbie appreciated her being here and taking care of her.

"Thank *you*." Crystal lifted her own glass with a grin. "It's your wine. And mighty fine wine, I might add."

Abbie closed her eyes, let her head fall back on the sofa cushion. "I feel like I could sleep for a month."

"All that G.I. Jane stuff wore you down, did it?"

Abbie smiled. Yeah, it had worn her down. So much so that something was long overdue. "Crystal," she said, sobering, "I've never taken the time to thank you."

They'd talked at length since Abbie had gotten back two days ago—mostly on the phone—about what had happened in Honduras, but Crystal had been hungry for details and Abbie had felt obliged to fill her in. Thanking her for what she'd done was way past due.

"For playing hide-and-seek with the gay cop cowboy?" Crystal chuckled. "Piece of cake. I loved leading the pretty boy around by the nose."

Yesterday, Crystal had given Reed the location and the key to a locker at the bus terminal where she'd hidden the diamonds. Sam told her that the necklace was being transported back to Honduras via a special government courier, where it would again be displayed in the National Museum.

"I don't doubt that," Abbie agreed, "but I was referring to what you did for me, no questions asked." Abbie's eyes filled with gratitude. "Cory could be dead right now if you hadn't stuck your neck out for me."

Uncomfortable with genuine displays of affection, Crystal, being Crystal, shrugged it off. "That's what friends are for, babe. Oh, God. I sound just like some sappy greeting card—or an old Dionne Warwick song. Give me a minute. The melody's coming to me."

"Fine." Abbie sat forward. She reached out, covered Crystal's hand with hers. Squeezed. "Brush it off, but I can't. I owe you. Cory owes you. I'm so lucky to have you on my team."

Close to giving in to the mist brimming in her own eyes, Crystal shot off the chair. "I'll bill ya. Better yet, I'll take payment in wine. More?"

Abbie nodded, sank back into the sofa as Crystal walked into the kitchen after the open bottle of Pinot Grigio, content to let her friend step and fetch for her.

She had figured she would sleep like a log when she got back to her own bed. Instead, she'd been restless. Edgy. Plagued with nightmares.

Too many scenarios to count. None she wanted to dwell on. On top of everything else, thoughts of Sam kept her awake. Kept her wondering what was going on with him. With them.

He'd called. Three times yesterday. Twice so far today. Checking on her. Checking on Cory. Making certain she had what she needed. Alluding to their need to "talk." The "talk" they were going to have tonight when he finally came to see her. She'd been trying to stall a bad feeling about that talk. Alternately battled back the worry that he might be planning to tell her good-bye and chastising herself for her insecurity.

"So . . ." Crystal waltzed back into the living room, bottle in hand. "What was it like? Two magical, fun-filled days in sunny, sweltering Honduras dodging bullets and chasing bad guys? With four good guys as bodyguards. They *were* good guys, right?" she added, refilling both of their glasses.

"Yeah," Abbie said, admonishing herself again for looking for problems with Sam where problems didn't exist. "They were good guys."

She thought of Doc—tall, lean, all easy smiles, healing hands. Mendoza—the gorgeous Nascar-wannabe Latino who was constantly humming. And Savage—the big bear of a man who, she suspected, had been as surprised as she'd been that they'd grown to like and respect each other.

All three of them had hugged her good-bye when they'd parted ways in San Pedro Sula. And damn, if she hadn't gotten a little teary-eyed.

"I still haven't grasped who they are. What they do."

Abbie hadn't either. Not exactly. "All I know is that they're based out of Argentina. That Sam used to work with them. I think it's some private contract company—like Blackwater, you know—only what they do is a little off the grid. Kind of 'don't ask, don't tell' stuff. The only thing I know for certain is that I wouldn't want to be on their bad side. These guys know what they're doing."

"And they were after this Nader person even before Cory got involved?"

Abbie nodded. Even though it was Crystal, she chose not to tell her about Sam's connection. His loss was just that. His loss. It was private. While Crystal would sympathize and commiserate, it wasn't Abbie's place to tell the story.

"So, what happens now?" Crystal tucked her feet up under her as she settled deeper into the easy chair.

"I'm hoping that once the Honduran government gets the diamonds back, it will all go away."

"You mean Cory's involvement."

"Yeah. Look. I know he wasn't completely innocent in this, but I also know he got sucked into something, got in over his head and couldn't find a way out."

She knew everything about what had happened now. When Cory was awake, they talked. He'd told her everything over the past couple of days.

"You don't have to defend him to me, Abbie. Cory's basically a good kid. I know that."

Crystal also knew what Cory had been through growing up.

"Anyway, I just want to put it behind us."

Crystal stared at the far wall, nodded. "So. Are you ever going to tell me what happened with Sam down there?"

Abbie swirled her wine, watched the clear, champagne-colored liquid settle, wishing she could shake an uneasy feeling about that "talk" Sam wanted to have.

She thought back to those moments of idyllic paradise they'd carved out in the midst of chaos.

Is this real?

That remained the money question.

"News at ten," she said, aware that Crystal was still waiting. "Maybe I'll know the answer then."

Crystal hadn't been gone fifteen minutes when Abbie heard the guest room door open. She looked up from the sofa to see Cory walk carefully into the living room. "Hey sweetie, how you doing?"

His eyes were hollow; except for the pink the fever put in his cheeks, he was as pale as milk. And thin. Lord, she thought, her heart aching for him, he was so thin.

"I'm okay," he said and, apparently exhausted, sank down on her leather chair.

"And I'm Anne, Queen of Scots," she said with a soft smile. "Can I get you anything?"

He shook his head. "I'm okay. Thanks."

His eyes were sad and serious when he met hers.

"What?" she asked, leaning forward. "You're in pain, aren't you? Maybe it's time for more medi—"

"No." He cut her off sharply, then looked apologetic. "No, sis. I'm okay. A royal screwup, but I'm okay."

Her defense was instant and knee-jerk. "You're not a screwup."

"No? Then why did I almost get you killed because of my mess?"

"You didn't mean for any of it to happen."

"I never mean for anything to happen, but that doesn't stop me from making a mess of my life, does it? And now I've made a mess of yours."

"I'm fine, Cory. Everything is fine."

"Yeah, well, no. It's not. I've done nothing but give you grief my whole life. You don't deserve it. And I don't deserve you."

"So you're saying that if the shoe was on the other foot, you wouldn't help me out?"

"See, that's the difference between you and me. You'd never put yourself in that position. You're too stable, too solid. Too . . . good," he finished finally.

She got down on her knees in front of him, gently covered his poor, bandaged hand with hers. "He did this to you, you know. Our father. But he was wrong, Cory. You're good and you're smart and you're worth one hundred of him."

Tears filled his eyes. "Maybe it's time I start proving you right instead of always managing to prove you wrong."

She brushed the hair back from his forehead. "You don't have to prove anything."

"I do," he said, nodding slowly. "I really, really do. I'm going to make you proud of me, Abbie. I don't know how yet but it's going to happen. You're looking at a new leaf here."

She smiled at that. "New leaf, huh?"

"You know what I mean. I'm going to get my act together."

Abbie had never seen him like this. And she didn't doubt that he meant every word he said.

"I've been thinking . . . maybe I should take some classes."

She nodded, but felt the need to caution him. "Because you think that's what I want you to do or because it's what you want to do?"

"A little of both, maybe. But mostly for me. I'm not getting ahead doing things my way; maybe it's time to try it your way."

"Here's to new leaves then."

He finally smiled, then became very sober again. "I love you, Abbie."

For the first time she could remember, when she looked at him, she didn't see that wounded little boy. She saw a young man. A man who finally understood that his destiny was in his own hands. "Works out great then, because I love you, too."

"I think I might miss that five o'clock shadow," Abbie said when Sam stepped through her front door that night.

What she missed was him. He looked amazing. As always. His face was clean-shaven. His shirt was white, his jeans crisply creased.

Wrangler butts drive me nuts.

Why that little ditty was running through her head, she didn't know.

Or maybe she did.

She was scared. Scared that it *hadn't* been real and that was what Sam had come here to tell her. Scared because she wanted to fling herself into his arms and kiss him until they were both naked but the look in his eyes stopped her.

"You look tired," he said. "Not sleeping?"

"Not so much, no," she admitted, but stopped short of adding, *and you're the reason why.*

"It'll get better," he said. "How's the arm?"

Okay. They were going to do chitchat. It rang of avoidance. The scare factor inched up the charts.

"The arm is fine."

"How's Cory doing?" he asked as she motioned him to make himself comfortable.

Okay. She gave him props for being concerned and stalled the panic. "He actually had a huge turnaround tonight. I'd about given up on him but amazingly, his fever finally broke. He's in the shower right now."

That much, at least, was a relief. It had been only six hours since Crystal had left and Cory's transformation had been amazing. Abbie had even slipped out of the house for an hour or so, so she could stock the kitchen. She'd fed Cory lasagna tonight—his favorite—and he'd managed to eat and keep it down.

So yeah. That was a relief. Just like their little talk was a relief. This uneasy politeness Sam was displaying was not.

"I need some wine," she said abruptly when the silence and the awkwardness between them got the best of her. "Can I get you some?"

"Sure."

Hokay. Short. Succinct.

What was happening here? More to the point, what *wasn't* happening?

He hadn't reached for her. Hadn't drawn her against him. Hadn't kissed her.

Why wasn't *that* happening?

It was killing her.

Her hands shook as she reached for an unopened bottle of Pinot. She knew she shouldn't have any more wine today. She'd have a headache the size of a truck in the morning and it would be her own damn fault.

Or it would be Sam's fault because try as she might, at this point she couldn't fathom an end to this day that didn't involve her going to bed—alone—eyes red from crying.

"You are such a girl," she muttered and tugged the cork out of the bottle.

"Ask him. Just ask him. Get it over with."

That, of course, was the problem. She was afraid it was over between them.

"So just bite the bullet."

Bite the bullet. Dodge the bullet. Shoot the bullet.

What had once been clichés held deep meaning to her now. She'd done them all.

And she was stalling.

"Hey," she said, surprised to see Cory when she finally gathered the nerve to return to the living room with the wine. "How you doing, sweetie?"

"Sit down, Abbie," Sam said, taking the glasses from her.

That's when she noticed the looks on both men's faces.

Looks that told her she wasn't going to like what came next. Looks that told her she'd better sit down or her knees might give out on her.

"What's going on?"

Cory dropped down on the arm of the sofa beside her. "I'm going to turn myself in to the feds tomorrow."

If Sam hadn't relieved her of the wineglass, she would have dropped it. "What . . . what are you talking about?"

Cory glanced at Sam, who nodded in encouragement. "I screwed up, Abbie. I need to make it right."

"You already have," she countered, feeling panic rise like the blood that flooded her cheeks. "Sweetie, you've been punished enough."

She carefully gathered his bandaged hand into hers. "Everyone's got what they want. You got Nader," she said, turning to Sam. "You recovered the necklace. There's no point to this. There's no need."

"The point is, it's the right thing to do," Cory said soberly. "Sam and I, we talked about it."

"Sam?" She glanced from Cory to Sam, who watched them soberly. "When did you talk to Sam?"

"This afternoon," Sam answered.

"While you were out getting groceries," Cory added.

She started shaking, felt her chest tighten as her body reacted to the anger, the disappointment, the blow of yet one more Sam Lang betrayal. "How could you do this? How could you talk him into doing this?"

"I didn't talk him into anything. He's a man, not a boy, Abbie," Sam said carefully. "He's responsible for his own decisions. He's made plenty of wrong ones. Let him make the right one."

"The right one?" She felt the last vestige of hope break down between them. "You mean the one that means he'll end up in prison?"

"I know you don't have any reason to, but will you just trust me on this one? Trust that it will be okay?"

"You are so right." She couldn't keep the accusation from her voice. "I don't have a reason in hell to trust you. That's the biggest blow of all. I *wanted* to. I thought . . . God, I was so stupid. You made me want to believe in . . . in everything," she finished angrily. "And here, all you ever wanted was . . . what? What else *do* you want, Sam? Is this your idea of some kind of poetic justice? You lost your sister? Now I have to lose my brother to make it right?"

Sam's face drained of all color. The pain that filled his eyes before he could check it told her how deep she'd just cut him.

Oh, God. It was a horrible thing to say. But she was scared. Like she'd sensed she should be scared. Scared that something terrible was going to happen.

Something terrible had.

She was going to lose Cory.

As Sam rose slowly and headed for the door, she understood that, once and for all, she'd lost him, too.

The next morning, she felt the loss full bore. She watched with hollow eyes as two men who identified themselves as DEA officers arrived at the house to take Cory away.

"So, you planning on brooding for the rest of your natural life," Reed badgered as he turned into the parking lot of the Federal Building in Vegas, "or you gonna do something about it?"

Sam stared straight through the windshield, not bothering to look at Reed, who'd gone Hollywood with his designer shades and rented convertible. "You know, one of these days, you're going to cross that line."

"The one where you beat the hell outta me?"

"That would be the one."

Reed snorted and cruised the lot searching for a parking spot. "As if you could."

As if he would, Sam thought. As annoying as Reed was, Sam couldn't see himself ever getting pissed enough to take him to task.

"So are you?" Reed persisted.

"Am I what?" Sam didn't attempt to hide his annoyance—not that it stopped Reed.

"Going after Abbie Hughes."

"Got a feeling that bridge has already been burned."

Abbie might forgive him for what he'd done to her, but she'd never forgive him if Cory ended up behind bars.

That was what this morning was about. Not only was the DEA interested in what Cory Hughes had to say about Fredrick Nader's operations, a few more players had pulled on jerseys and helmets and trotted out onto the field. CIA. DIA. DHS. A handful of others. Sam expected all the alphabet agency reps to show up in force. Expected it because he'd put in the calls himself. If Interpol had had a boot on the ground or notice hadn't been so short, they'd have been here, too.

"Yo." Sam glanced up, realized Reed was already out of the car and waiting for him. "You going in or are you gonna stay out here and work on your tan?"

Sam shouldered open the passenger door and headed for the building, relieved when he saw the woman standing on the concrete steps.

"Hello, Sam." Ann Tompkins smiled, hugged him back when he embraced her. "Johnny," she added with a sparkling grin as she reached for his hand over Sam's shoulder.

"Ann. Been a long time."

"Too long," she agreed. "Robert and I have missed you."

"I can understand you missing me, Annie," Reed said with a grin, "but miss Sam? Can't figure that one."

Ann laughed and turned back to Sam. "Let's get this nasty business taken care of, okay?"

"Yeah, let's," Sam managed, not having realized how humbled he would feel by her presence. Or how much relief her calm confidence would inspire in him. "Thank you," he said, stopping her when she would have turned away.

The words were inadequate at best.

She touched a hand to his cheek. Smiled tenderly. "You're family, Sam. You don't need to thank me."

Then she put on her game face and marched into the building.

25

It was a typical government office, Abbie thought as she sat beside Cory at a long table in the front of a large, windowless room.

Industrial gray paint on the walls. Office furniture circa "several years ago," before budget crunches bit into the workings of the great bureaucracy. The suits lined up around the table were black.

Only Crystal, sitting alone at the back of the room, her wild red hair spiked and shining, her beaded earrings dangling, provided a splash of color in the otherwise black and gray environment.

Abbie wanted this over with, was impatient for it to start. While escorting Cory to a government car earlier this morning, the DEA agent had told Abbie they were waiting for someone else to arrive for "an informal interview."

"He's not being arrested?"

"No, ma'am. Not at this time."

Which implied that he would be at some point.

"I want to come with him."

"You're more than welcome to attend," the agent had said. He gave her his card with the address and told her she could follow them in her own vehicle.

She'd glanced at the card.

"Agent Larson, does my brother need a lawyer?"

"I already told you," Cory had said, ducking into the backseat of the car. "I don't want a lawyer."

Because he couldn't afford one. Abbie knew that was his reason. And because he didn't want her paying for one out of her own limited reserves.

Other than her divorce lawyer, who wasn't even with the firm anymore according to the names on the letter accompanying her settlement payment, Abbie didn't know who to call anyway. But she would find one if necessary. She glanced around the room at the hard faces, waiting in stoic silence. If this interview started smacking of inquest and even a hint of the word *criminal* came up, she was getting Cory representation whether he wanted it or not.

She nodded at Crystal, bless her, who had insisted on coming along for moral support. Then she glanced around the table again. Ordinary-looking men with extraordinary responsibilities and enough government muscle to send Cory to prison for a very long time.

It was scary as hell to be a civilian in the midst of all this federal bureaucracy. So scary that Abbie had already forgotten their names, just as in the blur of nerves and concern for Cory, she'd forget their faces when this was over. They'd all introduced themselves, along with the names of the agencies they represented. DEA: Drug Enforcement Agency. DHS: Department of Homeland Security. DIA: Defense Intelligence Agency. ATF: Alcohol, Tobacco and Firearms. FBI. CIA. Others she'd already lost in the fog of intimidation.

Beside her, Cory looked pale but steady. Steadier than she was, in fact, and not showing one bit of surprise when the door opened and a slim, middle-aged woman walked in followed by Sam Lang and Crystal's gay cop cowboy.

The room was still far from crowded but the addition of these two men suddenly filled up the space with their presence and sucked the air out of her lungs like a vacuum.

Abbie didn't know why it was such a shock, seeing Sam. The pain of it maybe, as much as the surprise.

It seemed, however, that she wasn't the only one in shock.

All around the table, the suits became inordinately still. The quiet mumblings screeched to a halt. Ties were straightened. Throats were cleared. And "what the hell?" looks were exchanged.

The woman walked straight to the head of the conference table and slapped down a briefcase. In that moment, it became very clear to Abbie that whoever she was, her presence had just invoked a major power shift. Regardless of the authority levels around the table, this woman was clearly in charge now.

"Gentlemen," the woman said by way of greeting, "let's cut to the chase, shall we? The Justice Department has declared Cory Hughes a protected witness. As such, he's been granted full immunity from any and all potential criminal charges as they relate to his association with one Fredrick Nader, now deceased. In exchange for this immunity, Mr. Hughes has agreed to provide information critical to national security regarding Nader's network."

Abbie was dumbstruck. She glanced at Cory, who remained motionless. Glanced at Sam, who relayed nothing.

"We'll need to clear the room of everyone but the witness now," the woman said, her gaze landing on Abbie with an encouraging nod. It was a nod that said, *Don't worry. Everything is going to be fine.*

When she heard the rustle of movement, Abbie realized that Sam and Reed had both stood. It finally galvanized her into action. She rose too, squeezed Cory's shoulder on her way by, and met the two men and Crystal by the door.

"What just happened?" she asked, turning to Sam for answers, instinctively knowing that he'd had a hand in this.

He took her arm, steered her down the hall. "Come on. Let's go get a cup of coffee and I'll tell you."

"Hey, wait up." Johnny sprinted to catch up with Crystal Debrowski as her sassy little hips sashayed across the Federal Building parking lot.

Not that he'd expected anything different, but she kept on walking.

He didn't care. Until Sam came back with their ride—who knew how long that little "coffee break" with Abbie Hughes was going to take—Johnny had time to kill.

"Come on. Play nice," he said, catching up with Crystal by her car.

"Getting a little tired of you dogging my tail, golden boy."

Yeah, well, Johnny wished he could say the same thing, but the truth was, that sweet little tail had intrigued him for the better part of three days. He'd gotten kind of used to seeing it, and to reacting every time he did.

Hot. The pixie made him hot. Which so did not compute. She was not his type. Not even a little bit.

"One way to stop that," he said, crossing his arms over his chest and blocking her entry by leaning against her driver's side door.

She glowered up at him—all five feet or so of her. "Do tell."

He shot her his money grin. "Quit walking away, darlin'."

She squinted, then laughed like she couldn't believe what was happening. "No. You're not really coming on to me."

Well, yeah, he was. It sort of pissed him off that she thought it was funny. "And if I was?"

She grunted. "You'd be wasting your time and mine."

He frowned when a disturbing thought occurred to him. "You're not one of those girl-on-girl types, are you?"

This time she rolled her eyes. "You are unbelievable, but if that's what it takes to salvage your fragile ego and get you off my back, then feel free to put whatever spin on it you want."

He felt more relief than insult. Would have been a shame if she played for the other team, even though he still hadn't figured out why he gave a rip.

It was a puzzle that was making him crazy.

"You're blocking my way," she pointed out unnecessarily, lifting a hand toward her car. "Do you mind?"

"Nah. I don't mind at all." He settled more comfortably against the door. "Got all the time in the world. Beautiful day. I'm in the company of a beautiful woman—"

"Okay." She held up a hand like a stop sign, cutting him off. "Just stop right there. I don't like you, Reed. You're too pretty. You're too vain. And you're beyond annoying."

He tilted his head, frowned. "No, really. Tell me how you really feel."

She heaved a long-suffering breath. "What's it going to take to get rid of you?"

"Have dinner with me."

"I'm not hungry."

"Then go to bed with me."

"I'm not *that* desperate."

"But you are desperate. Hey." He held up a hand when she glared. "It was implied."

Little silver daggers shot out of her eyes.

"Okay. I'm not interested," she amended.

He was having fun. But this approach wasn't working, so he tried another tactic. "You're a good friend. To show up for Abbie Hughes today. Not to mention going out on a limb for her like you did and hiding those diamonds. You could have gotten in a lot of trouble or that."

"And you care about this why?"

She had him there. "Damned if I know."

She tilted her head, studied him for a moment. Opened her mouth. Closed it. Finally shook her head. "I get off at eight."

He shot away from the car. "Really?"

"Just dinner," she clarified.

Oh. Well. "I knew that."

"Right," she said, sounding disgusted with herself as much as him. "Don't make me regret this."

"No, ma'am." Happy as hell, he stood aside and opened the car door for her. "See you at eight."

"You're buying," she informed him as she settled behind the wheel, cranked the key, and drove away.

"Damn," Johnny muttered, watching her go. "It might not be love, but it sure is fun."

He was still grinning when he checked his watch, then wandered back inside the Federal Building, found a seat in a row of chairs in the hall, and settled back for a little power nap while he waited for Sam to return.

"Her name is Ann Tompkins," Sam said when he and Abbie had settled into a booth across from each other in a diner a couple blocks from the Federal

Building. "Ann's with the Justice Department. Deputy Attorney General's office."

Abbie sat back. Her head was still spinning—for a number of reasons. Sam's nearness was one of them. But this thing with Cory . . . she was mystified.

"Justice Department? Attorney General's office?"

Sam nodded. "She flew in last night from D.C." He glanced up at the waitress when she arrived with menus. "Just coffee," he said. "Two."

Abbie leaned forward, elbows on the table. "Why? Why is she doing this for Cory?"

Sam met her gaze, held it. "She's doing it for me. I asked her to intervene."

Abbie blinked. Leaned back. Stared.

Who was this man?

Who was this man that he could ask one of the highest-ranking officials in the United States government to drop what she was doing and fly across the country to help someone she didn't even know?

Abbie had thought she'd known. She'd thought she'd loved him. Thought she'd hated him. Thought she couldn't trust him. With her heart. With her brother's life.

I know you don't have any reason to . . . but will you just trust me on this one? Trust that it will be okay?

He'd asked for her trust. She'd not only refused, she'd lashed out at him using his sister's death as a weapon.

She should have known. And she should have trusted him. After all they'd been through together. After all they'd shared, she should have known he was a man of his word.

"Sam." She reached across the tabletop and covered his big, scarred hands with hers. "I am so, so sorry for what I said to you yesterday. I'm sorry I didn't—"

"No." He cut her off, rubbed his thumb over the back of her hand. "It's okay. You were scared."

"It's not okay. I was horrible to you. What I said . . . it was inexcusable."

He shook his head, his dark eyes full of understanding. "You were scared," he repeated. "I'd have reacted the same way if I'd been in your shoes. Look, if I could have told you about Ann, about what was in the works, I would have. But it wasn't until the eleventh hour that I found out she'd been able to convince the AG to go for immunity. I didn't want to give you false hope if she couldn't make the threat of criminal charges go away."

"Who are you, Sam Lang?" She had to ask. She had to know as she clung to his hand like she clung to the hope that there might be a future for them after all.

"Long story." He leaned back when the waitress returned and filled their cups.

"I've got time." Time and amends to make.

"You know I was in the military," he began, reaching for her hand again.

She nodded and felt the tension of loss that had been clutched tightly in her chest since he'd walked out her door last night uncoil by slow degrees.

"Spec Ops," he went on. "Delta. That's when I was recruited to join a highly classified multibranch team. Task Force Mercy went places no one else could go. Made things happen no one else was authorized to do. We worked black—way under the radar.

"Anyway, Ann and Robert Tompkins's son, Bryan, was a team member. Helluva soldier," he added, and Abbie could see not only love and admiration in his eyes, but a burden.

"We lost Bry in Sierra Leone." He paused, breathed deep, and she understood, without asking, that Sam had been with Bryan Tompkins when he'd died.

"He was like a brother, you know? Hell, we were all brothers. And after . . . after his death, Ann and Robert invited the team to their home. Made it clear that Bry thought of us as family. Made it known that they thought of us as family, too."

He paused again, shrugged. "It was a little uncomfortable at first. I think they were trying to fill the void. Unconsciously, but, yeah, that's where they were coming from. But their sincerity, their openness . . . it resonated with all of us, you know? Doc, Mendoza, Savage, we all took it to heart. Ann and Robert and their daughter Steph, they eventually became like a second family. For some of the guys—like Reed—it became their only family."

"You've been with those guys that long?"

"Them and many others. Like I said. We were brothers. You didn't go through the things we'd gone through and walk away alone."

"So, that's when you became close with Ann Tompkins."

He nodded. "Yeah. She was a litigator in a high-profile law firm then. A few years ago she was asked to join the DOJ—Department of Justice," he clarified.

"And she can just do this? She can give Cory immunity because you asked her to?"

"Not without a compelling reason, no. Cory has information, Abbie."

"How can that be? He was—how did you put it? A low-level mule."

"Right, but still, he probably knows more about Nader's operation than he thinks. He's seen things, been places inside the organization; he can recognize faces, ID them as belonging to Nader's network.

"Look, Nader's been on the DOJ radar almost as long as bin Laden. Only with bin Laden we know he's behind the nine-eleven attacks. Nader was a sneaky bastard. He was also untouchable by legitimate government—U.S. or otherwise—because we couldn't pin him with anything, even though all fingers pointed his way."

"So that's where you came in? You and this agency you work for now?"

"Worked for," he corrected and again, Abbie detected a regret in his decision to leave the men he considered his brothers. "Yeah. The agency does a lot of contract work for Uncle. The kind of work where if they get tagged, no one in Washington will even admit to knowing the agency exists, let alone that we were on a government-sanctioned op."

Trust. There it was again. Only this time, Sam had trusted Abbie with information that was clearly confidential. The significance of his gesture was not lost on her. Neither was its importance.

"Anyway, with Nader out of the picture, DOJ and all the alphabet agencies under it figure they've got a window of time where the organization is bound to be in disarray. That window is now. There will be power struggles. A lot of jockeying for position. People trying to prove they've got the ability to take over the reins. Someone's going to get reckless. Someone's going to get careless. When they do, with Cory's help, we might be able to tie them to Nader. And then, what typically happens will be a domino effect as the big players start to topple. Once one is tagged, the rest will follow. They won't be able to rat each other out fast enough.

"That's why Cory is so important," he emphasized. "And why Ann could authorize immunity for him in exchange for his testimony."

"But he was willing to testify anyway," Abbie pointed out.

"Yeah, well, we might have fudged on that a little. Doesn't matter. Bottom line, with his help, we nail one guy, tie him to a drug deal or an arms deal, and suddenly, this becomes an on-the-books op to take the organization down. The full force of the U.S. military and half a dozen European countries can get on board, instead of a handful of guys operating black trying to do the deed."

While it all made sense, there was something he'd said that touched her to the core.

"Yeah, well, we might have fudged on that a little. Doesn't matter."

"Fudging does matter," she said, tears filling her eyes with love for this man. "You went out on a limb for him. That means you went out on a limb for me."

He met her eyes, held her gaze. "I'm about to go out on another one." He drew a deep breath, squeezed her hand so hard it hurt but in a very good way. "I love you, Abbie."

Yeah, she thought, letting the tears fall. She knew.

She finally knew.

Dinner. All Crystal had agreed to was dinner. It begged the obvious question, then: So how had she ended up buck naked and tied to her own bed with flex cuffs?

What was she thinking?

She tested the cuffs with a series of angry yanks, swore under her breath when they didn't give, and glared at the ceiling. You couldn't teach stupid. She'd proven that in spades. For her, it just came natural.

"Dessert?"

She jerked her head toward the bedroom door. When she saw him standing there, wearing nothing but that devil-made-me-do-it grin and holding a carton of Ben & Jerry's and a spoon, she almost forgave herself for succumbing to Johnny Duane Reed's line of bull. And when he sauntered back into the room, amazing man parts dangling, six-pack abs flexing, she almost forgot why dessert would be a bigger mistake than dinner.

She looked away, too embarrassed to face him. "Untie me."

He eased a hip onto the bed, leaned across her, and braced his palm on the mattress beside her shoulder, forcing her to look at him. "Now what would be the fun in that?"

Good God, he was gorgeous. Sex-tousled hair too long and too blond. Bedroom eyes too playful and too blue. Yeah, the golden boy was something. He also had the sexual proclivities of a fallen angel. And when he lowered his head and bussed his amazing lips over her swollen nipple, tickling her sensitive skin with his barely there mustache that matched his barely there beard, she forgot about flex cuffs, stupid mistakes, and the fact that she'd promised herself she'd never let this man near her or her bed.

"Umm," he murmured sucking lingeringly on her nipple before drawing away to smile lazily into her eyes. "About that dessert."

Abbie knelt above Sam in the shadows. Long, dark hair fell across her face. Slim, sleek thighs bracketed his ribs. Deep, husky sighs told him how good this was for her. How right, as she rode him fast and hard, then slow and sweet, taking him so deep inside he became a part of her.

"I love you," she whispered, leaning forward to kiss him, her swollen lips lavish and lush and desperately demanding. "I love you . . ."

He reached up, gently dragged the hair away from her face so he could see her eyes in the semidarkness of encroaching dusk. "Again."

"I love you," she murmured on a moan as she ground herself against him, enriching the contact, arousing a desire to take her to levels he'd never taken her before.

"Let me," he whispered, gripping her waist in his hands and lifting her. "Let me . . ." He settled her over his mouth, parted her sex with his tongue and indulged.

She cried out when he kissed her there, trembled and fell forward, flattening open palms on the wall above the bed when he sucked. Cried his name when he slid a finger inside her, stroked to the rhythm of his tongue, and tipped her over the edge.

"Sam . . ."

Shivering sighs, fractured breaths, he recorded it all, would always remember the honeyed taste of her release, the silken tremors as she slid boneless to the bed beside him.

He caressed her bare hip with his thumb, loving the sight of her drifting on the backside of pleasure, coming down from the high with a catlike moan of contentment.

Gently shifting her to her back, he entered her, finessed her back to arousal with a slow glide and thrust, a steady build of that amazing, sucking friction that built and swelled and shot him over the edge when her climax convulsed around him like a tight, liquid fist.

"Oh, God," she murmured minutes later, still holding him close, absorbing his weight, her ankles linked around his hips in a staunch refusal to let him leave her body.

"Tell me it's always going to be like this," she whispered fiercely.

"It's always going to be like this," he promised and rolled them to their sides so she could draw a deep breath.

They lay that way for long, lazy moments. He loved watching her face. The heavy lashes lying against her cheeks. The swollen lips that even now, when he was done in and spent, made his cock twitch and swell inside her.

One corner of her mouth drew up in a crooked smile. "Already?"

He laughed. "What can I say? I've always been an overachiever."

She touched a hand to his face; her smile slowly faded. "I'm never going to doubt you again. Know that. I need you to know that."

He knew a lot of things now. Things he'd never known before Abbie.

"I know," he assured her, tucked her face into the curve of his throat and held her.

Held her close. Held her tight. Held her the way he would hold the most precious possession known to man.

Which was exactly what she was.

EPILOGUE

Richmond, Virginia, home of Robert and
Ann Tompkins
Two months later

Boundaries, wedding bands, and babies. Those three words had once spelled confinement to Sam Lang. But as he watched Abbie mix it up at the poker table with Doc, Savage, Reed, and Gabe Jones's wife, Jenna, confinement wasn't what came to mind.

Freedom. Peace. Contentment.

Life.

"Sam, can I top that off for you?"

Sam glanced up at Robert Tompkins, the host for tonight's festivities that included celebrating Ann and Robert's daughter, Stephanie's, birthday and Sam and Abbie's big leap.

Yeah. They'd done it. Love was a drug. High on it and the hope it brought to both of their lives, Sam and Abbie had gotten married a month ago. That the baby was due in a little less than seven months was a constant source of wonder and joy for Sam—and a little slip-up that had provided Reed with fodder for more one-liners than a T-shirt shop.

Sam glanced down at his beer. "I'm good, Robert. Thanks."

"I can see that." He clapped Sam on the back and started making the rounds with the pitcher of beer he'd drawn from the keg behind the bar. Sam took a deep draw from his glass, then elbowed back against the bar and observed the men who he would always consider his brothers, gathered in the Tompkinses' game room.

He'd taken Ann's scolding to heart. It had been too long since they'd all gotten together here in the Tompkinses' Richmond home. That's why Sam had put a shout-out to the BOIs and shamed them into showing up. Not that to a man they weren't all enjoying themselves. They were.

So were Ann and Robert. Watching Robert, laughing and joking with the BOIs, you'd never know he had once been counsel to the President of the United States. Or that Ann, restocking the buffet, had the brass and the balls to pull off what she had for Cory Hughes. Just like you'd never know that they must also still mourn the man who had brought the BOIs together.

Sam glanced up at the portrait of Bryan Tompkins hanging above the fireplace mantel. He lifted his glass in silent salute. Bryan "Babyface" Tompkins had died too young, just like Terri.

Like the Tompkinses, Sam mourned but he carried on. The woman laughing and slapping a celebratory high-five with that wild redhead Gabe Jones had married was the main reason why.

"Did you see that, Gabe?" Jenna yelled across the room. "We just beat Holliday, here, at his own game."

"They cheated," Doc accused, sliding an unlit stogie from one side of his mouth to the other. "You've got to know that they cheated."

"If it makes you feel better to think so," Abbie chimed in and grinned at Sam.

"Jones. Lang. Would you two get over here and control your women?" Colter groused, knowing he'd get the response that was coming.

"Control?" Seated on either side of him, Abbie and Jenna pounced on the word together.

Laughing at the dressing-down they proceeded to heap on Doc, Ann dusted off her hands as she came to Sam's side. "So, when's the baby due?"

"Hopefully not until after it finally sinks in that I'm going to be a father," he said, still awed by the prospect.

If their calculations were accurate, that baby was going to pop out about nine months and fifteen minutes after a very memorable shampoo.

"I've heard of water *births*," Abbie had said after they'd gotten over the shock of the EPT results, "but never water *conceptions*."

"Seems we beat a lot of odds on that trip," Sam had said, holding her close.

As he'd held her close—in his head, in his heart—every day since.

"You're going to be a great daddy," Ann assured him. "I've seen you with Tina. You're wonderful with her, Sam. She adores you."

Things were coming along there. Tina would always miss her mom and dad, but she was tough. Resilient. In no small way, Abbie had played a big part in helping Tina move on. Sam loved her for that and for the effort she made with Tina.

Watching Abbie now, so easy with his friends, remembering how she'd won over not only Tina but his mom and dad, made him realize how lucky he was.

Lucky to be alive. Lucky to have her. Lucky to have these guys.

Gabe Jones joined him at the bar. "You look like the cat that ate the canary."

Ain't that the truth, Sam thought, returning Gabe's grin. He lifted his glass toward the poker table. "Ever wonder what we did to deserve those two?" he asked with a nod toward Abbie and Jenna.

"Must have been all that good, clean living," Gabe said with a grunt as he eased a hip on the bar stool beside Sam.

Sam glanced at his friend, grateful to see him looking so healthy and happy, grateful that he was alive.

"So, how long before you're back on board?"

Gabe had taken a shrapnel hit in his calf in a bombing in Buenos Aires, and a raging infection had finally claimed his leg below the knee.

"Give me another few months," Gabe said after tipping his glass for a deep draw on his beer, "and I'll be back up to speed."

That didn't exactly answer Sam's question but it told him what he needed to know about Gabe's state of mind. It would take more than the loss of a leg to slow down the Archangel. Gabe was as tough as they came, but Sam credited much of his recovery to the woman currently beating the pants off Holliday at poker.

Gabe set his empty glass on the bar. "So. A baby, huh?"

Sam grunted. "Helluva deal."

Gabe stood and clapped him on the back. "Better you than me."

Sam laughed. "Just wait. I've seen the way this works. Jenna'll get one look at the baby and she'll want one of her own."

Gabe didn't say anything but Sam got the distinct impression that the notion didn't settle all that badly on the big man's shoulders.

"Time to take pity on Holliday," Gabe said and headed for the poker table.

Sam watched him walk away, then glanced around the room, listening to the laughter, the good-natured ribbing.

Mendoza, interestingly, had Steph in a corner, talking in earnest about something that held her rapt attention. Savage and Greene cornered Gabe. Sam knew they felt the same way he did. God, it was good to see him again. Healthy, happy, back on board with the BOIs after all those months of recovery.

Even the head of BOI, Nate Black, had shown up. A little more introspective than Sam remembered, but then Nate had always been more cerebral, more subdued than the motley crew he employed.

Speaking of motley crews—Reed and Savage had moved on to the pool table. They were shooting a game of eight ball and trading insults on everything from pedigrees to sexual prowess.

"You can just feel the love, can't you?" Abbie said, grinning as she joined Sam at the bar, cuddling up against his side.

He looped an arm over her shoulders. Kissed the top of her head. "Poker game over?"

"Doc's just too easy to beat," she said, making sure Colter heard her.

"Under control," Doc suggested again with a meaningful nod as he glanced from Abbie to Sam.

"Tell you what." Sam met Doc's easy smile across the room. "You worry about controlling your own woman. Oh, wait. I forgot. You don't have one."

Sam's zinger was met with rounds of, "Whoa-ohs," from the guys who had tagged Sam's comeback as fighting words and were loving it.

"When did you get so smug, Lang?" Doc sputtered as he dealt cards around the table where Gabe and Nate had filled Savage's and Reed's empty seats.

Abbie squeezed him tight. "Yeah . . . when did you get so smug?"

"When I went to Vegas, placed my bet on a game of chance, and won me the purtiest woman in the world."

She rolled her eyes. "Okay, I'd have expected a corny line like that from Reed."

"Should I be wounded or flattered?"

"You should be tired," she said, affecting a sober look, then whispering so only Sam could hear her. "Very, very tired. So tired, I'm thinking I should take you to bed. You need your rest."

"Oh, it's rest you have in mind, is it?"

She smiled that sultry, sexy smile that had him pushing away from the bar and taking her hand. "Or something."

"Well, it *is* getting late."

"Works for me," she said with a grin. "Now convince them."

"We're going to call it a night, guys. Abbie needs her rest."

"Then you'd better let her go to bed and you stay here," Reed suggested, looking damn pleased with himself.

"At the risk of repeating myself, you outlaws worry about your own women—imaginary or otherwise. You let me worry about mine."

"So much for fooling them," Abbie said as they walked alone down the hall toward the bedroom Ann had shown them when they'd arrived this morning.

"Yeah, well, you can fool some of the people all of the time, all of the people some of the time, but you can't fool—"

"Sam." She cut him off with a kiss when they reached the bedroom door. "When *did* you get so smug?"

He backed her up against the wall. Kissed her with all the love and life she made him feel. "That would have been right about the time I got the girl."